BOOKS BY CATHERINE LABADIE

GARNER
FOR GOLD

Catherine Labadie

To my daughter—you are my beloved one.

Part I

Jubilation

I

Bettina

When the haze lifted, Bettina found herself balanced on the edge of the sunset cliffs of Ioggenica with her arms extended like wings. Her feet were bare; her toes clung to the rock as a sympathetic breeze danced around her figure. Mist from the intemperate sea separating the continent from its island capital sluiced the rest of the trance from her eyes as she reeled backwards, toward safety.

Perhaps a Saint personally anointed by Goddess would survive such a fall. Bettina didn't want to test the theory.

Dawn. Or not quite. She judged the span of daylight. The sun had already diffused the pinks and lavenders of sunrise into the clean blue of a new day. Bettina scrubbed her waking dreams from her eyes with her palms and blinked up at the passing clouds.

Her last night of liberty had passed, and her befuddled mind hadn't even had the sense to savor it.

The wind that teased locks of her unbound hair—gold without grey since the taint of age had been banished—carried the sound of voices from behind. Back from where Bettina's private villa had been tucked away from the pomp and grandeur of the world of the new Bright Age. She didn't turn toward the voices, not yet. There were some minutes left before obligation forced her to return to the realm she had rejected.

Standing still on the cliff's edge from a safer distance, Bettina raked her eyes over the far sight of Aebbenary's distant shore. When she was a child, it had been the only world that had ever mattered. She had expected to wed there, bear children, and die without ever crossing the sea to lands beyond the jewel of the false god's dominion.

Cristoval. Cosima.

She had borne her children there. Yet she would never die, nor would they.

Nor will they. Bettina seized the thought and pinned it in place in her mind. She concentrated intently on the words as she pictured the faces of her children and clenched her fists at her sides in defiance of the summons from Goddess that beat and beat like drums against her consciousness.

Goddess loathed charts, lists, and anything that could be called rules, even when She made all of them. Bettina felt the twenty odd years since Marzanna's Ascension should have mellowed Her rebellion against anything that represented Silver's order, but there was little she could do to mitigate the confusion, and less she was willing to say. All she could do was lessen the affect the disarray had on her life and the lives of those she cared about…if they allowed it.

And return when she was summoned.

Though the westerly zephyr brought the promise of cool sanctuary on Aebbenary's shores, Bettina sensed the peril lurking beneath it. It was not in her nature to test her immortality with foolish risks, though she had heard of other blessèd beings appointed by Goddess not taking to their theoretical invincibility as sensibly. Only one thing could have picked up Bettina's cognizance as easily as plucking a lily from its bed to capture its scent. Only one person could have made her rise without awareness and walk the cliffs at night, prepared to jump into the sea and swim toward Aebbenary with feverish haste…if she had survived the fall.

You took too long to answer. Bettina couldn't honestly say if she was imagining the words, dripping with amused mockery, or the conversation itself. *I sent My best ship to your quaint little beach and bid you welcome back to your home. Would you deny Me, dearest Bettina?*

Human voices grew louder, closer. Bettina winced and turned her back on the cliffs and the ocean and the last melting rays of the sunrise.

She was soaked through with sea spray and her hair was snarled with salt as if she had dove in after all, but Goddess had anticipated her needs. The mortals approaching carried drying cloths, fresh garb, and other toiletries to persuade her to board the ship that would assist her obedience.

Never, Bettina swore to the voice with the assumption that it was real. Too deep to touch—she hoped—she tucked away the thought that she would swear anything to Goddess if it meant…if only She would…

I'm coming home.

Bettina was old enough to remember when Aebbenary's busy docks had looked very different. When ships sporting the crest of Gaius Valusius—her long-dead mortal father—had sailed in and out of the port bearing news and merchandise for the betterment of the false god's rule over the continent and sprawling island capital.

Now she hardly recognized them.

I spent the entire voyage dreading my return, she wondered at her own unease, *only to see that nothing has been left unchanged. Nothing is the same.*

The docks and the city were cleaner. Prettier. Scents of a hundred or a thousand or more flowers draped with vines that subsisted on their proximity to a deity flourishing on earth wafted over the island reserved for Marzanna's favored. Bettina ached with longing even though she was already here. Dazed, she walked down the ramp of the swift carrack that had brought her home, her eyes drawn and held by the sight of the gilded tower piercing the sky near the far end of the city.

There were many streets between her and her destination, but her steps were as nothing as she left her retainers—*Marzanna's* retainers—

behind to tend the ship and journeyed to the tower where Goddess had beckoned her from across the sea. Though Bettina had steeled herself against the amazement of it all, she still looked. The cold yet vibrant city of her youth spent under Silver's authority still showcased its white stone and bustling marketplaces, though its architectural spectacles had been changed.

Plentiful fountains displaying the likenesses of conquerors and men who had influenced the past millennia of history exhibited new scenes. A beautiful woman with jasper-red hair and carnelian eyes draped across a throne in defiant repose. Lovers twined in an embrace and molded into the base of a marble tree that strained its golden boughs heavenward. A man—so handsome he might have stolen away Bettina's breath in her adolescence—carried a sword that glowed in the noon sun as he landed on one knee with four scarlet wings extended behind him.

The tremendous glory of the holy city transformed from frigid reverence into a riot of adoration for Goddess and Her Saints had comforted Bettina once. These signs and more had been signals of her freedom from the bondage of Silver's dominion and the burden of patriarchal rule. Gold had reminded her of the blessèd ichor that flowed through her transfigured veins.

Now, though…

She shut her eyes against the wonders and let instinct carry her through Aebbenary—to the soaring tower that had once been the church of a selfish, false deity. Though there were people always moving, always scurrying in the capital, they all made sure her path was clear. Bettina Valusius—Saint Bettina—was known by all. Marzanna had demanded that.

The bridge. The tower stairs. Would that she had her own wings to speed this walk of dread to where her destiny waited.

Bettina hefted the solemn weight of her skirts as she climbed, cursing her antiquated sense of propriety. Back in her day, one had always worn their best to church. Not so much to impress absent Silver, but to impress upon others the talent of their wealth and influence with the superb quality of their garments and heirloom jewelry. Though fashions had changed—or had been discarded altogether since Marzanna had little love for social constructs—Bettina wore a gown similar to the wedding dress she had worn when they'd met.

This one was red, though. Red like Saint wings and the jasper and amber Goddess smiled upon.

At the top, the unguarded doors swung inward, guided by divine, invisible will. Light poured out over Bettina; she trembled in place, quivering as luminescence both warmed and blinded her.

Who was she to be invited into the holiest of places? Who was she to stand in the throne room of Goddess?

"Bettina."

Her name was music sung by the most beautiful voice of all. Those letters had never belonged to her, not really. There had only ever been *this*. There would only ever *be…THIS.*

"Bettina."

Bettina. That was her voice. Her own, just as it had always been. She clung to it and her own sanity with desperate panic.

"Holy Goddess. I submit myself to Your Glory."

Before she could sink into the graceful curtsy she had been famous for as a mortal girl, a woman's shape appeared from the inner heart of the blinding Light. Bettina couldn't gaze on Her outright, not without agony, but features snared her awareness: blackest of black hair threaded with shining gold, red lips and cheeks flushed pink with everlasting health and youth, and eyes that had been dark like Her hair transformed into flames of living amber.

She is the same, Bettina whispered to herself in the innermost sanctuary of her thoughts, *but* you *are not.*

Marzanna ran toward her and hauled her into an embrace.

II

Bettina

Five thrones all sculpted from ivory, alabaster, and precious metals formed seats like open seashells, though only four were occupied. Bettina scanned their occupants as she lifted her leaden arms and gingerly embraced Goddess. Instantly, she remembered why even during Cosima's conception she had hesitated to do so whole-heartedly: divine beings were *hot*. Whatever stuff flowed through them to scour the wither of mortality away burned lesser beings.

Even Bettina, Goddess's third Saint.

"I'm glad to see you. How long has it been?" Marzanna allowed Bettina to extract herself from the embrace, but seized her forearms to hold her. Her eyes glowed as She looked Bettina up and down, Her gaze critical though Her expression was contented and friendly.

"A decade or so, Your Glory."

"I can tell your return has already improved your spirits. You weren't meant to stay away from Aebbenary this long. Come—greet the others."

The loss of Her touch chilled Bettina's skin; Marzanna's remaining hand firmly leading her by the wrist up toward the dais where the line of thrones stood stung like blood remembering to flow. Memories stirred where Bettina had clumsily buried them under handfuls of distraction cast like soil over a grave.

You are a swan indeed, beautiful. My heart has grown and grown. I would include you therein…

Honeyed words. Caresses that had gone to Bettina's head like wine. Marzanna had drunk up her fear, doubt, and insecurity and swallowed her whole.

Almost. Bettina forced a smile when Marzanna turned to grin at her and shoved her forward to greet the others. *She* almost *did.*

Fiammetta, Aebbenary's second Saint and Goddess's idol—the model for the fountain tribute with jasper hair. Clad in transparent violet organza with a suckling babe clutched to her bare, pale breasts, she frowned down her nose with imperious detachment at Bettina and Goddess.

Before she could halt it, an uncharitable thought broke through Bettina's tenuous control. *Another brat? When she didn't bother to raise the dozen she already spawned?*

She crushed the thought at once, strangling it where it began.

Threads and veins of gold enriched Fiammetta's skin, similar to but more magnificent than the golden freckles that adorned Bettina's own face. Her elegant hands were tipped with nails like smooth, golden talons. Sharp enough to claw out the eyes of anyone who doubted her devotion to Goddess and their children.

Däard—tame, for now. He had tucked his quartet of crimson-feathered wings close behind him. He stood from his throne to the right of Marzanna's and honored Bettina with a slight bow. She remembered when his hands had been cast in silver: when he had been only a gifted swordsman, and a potential marriage partner before her family had given up that ambition. Now his hazel eyes were as dazzling peridot, his sandy hair blond and flowing long beneath the quelling influence of a thin, complex circlet meant to contain it.

An empty scabbard hung at his side: a symbol, nothing more. The tongue of blessèd flame Goddess had granted to his keeping could not always exist in their dimension.

It will come when I call, Däard had told her once, *like I come to Hers.*

The guardian and angel of vengeance who embodied Marzanna's divine might and right to order the world according to Her wishes. The paragon of Goddess's heart and the ruling queen of Aebbenary.

That left two thrones: one draped in black veils, untouched since its creation. The last had been arranged furthest from the center, slightly apart from the others. A skeleton with gleaming bones dipped in liquid gold sat bowed slightly forward, its head down. Bettina was glad she didn't have to stare into those black, empty sockets even for a moment.

Fiammetta broke the silence and pulled Bettina's eyes away from the slumped skeleton. "Your return has been anticipated for some time. What kept you from us?"

Her looks were always melancholy, tending toward the forlorn in a way that had made Bettina wonder if this was an act Marzanna enjoyed, but an undercurrent of something else lingered around her frown. It had been twenty-five years since the Bright Age had begun: Fiammetta had learned to love being queen.

"Don't pry, Fia. She's here now." Däard said.

His intercession made Marzanna laugh. "Precisely. And oh Bett, we have so much to discuss!"

What else could we possibly say to one another? Bettina had to admit her curiosity to herself as she smiled and nodded as if nothing gave her more joy than to wait in this sanctified throne room to hear what Marzanna's next pleasure might be. Goddess unceremoniously plopped Herself down on the steps leading up to the thrones. Bettina was quick to copy Her.

"Cosima's jubilee approaches. Did you remember?"

Of course I did. Bettina choked back both the words and her uncivil tone.

"Yes. She and my son are but a few months—"

"I'm aware." Marzanna's delight soured into a blank mask that failed to conceal Her annoyance.

"Cristoval? How is the boy?" Däard caught Bettina's eye as she turned toward him. Though nothing in his expression changed, he netted her gaze long enough for her to mark the significance as he approached and sat on Marzanna's other side.

"He's—"

"We are discussing Cosima, dearest." Marzanna said. Her irritation barely faded when Däard stole an arm around Her waist and rested an elegant, long-fingered hand on the swell of Her hip. When he squeezed

She squirmed, but not from displeasure. As soon as it had come, the shadow of Her capricious mood lifted; She tipped Her head onto Däard's shoulder and sighed.

"Though I am undying, it is not fit to rule the world without a chain of order. My other children grow restless: they clamor to learn who is first among them. Who is My heir."

Oh, this was tricky, shifting sand to tread. Bettina had contended in arenas like this in her past, but never with so much at stake. Never with her children—or the progeny of Goddess.

"May I deduce that You have chosen Cosima?"

"Yes. My eldest."

"But—" Bettina caught herself; she fluffed the layers of her skirts to excuse her protest. *She's not, though. What of Sovanna?*

Sovanna. The first child born in Marzanna's Age. Conceived, she had been told, from the moment Goddess had triumphed over Silver and his High Priest.

Bettina may have imagined it, but she could have sworn she heard the clinking of metal bones against the alabaster of the last throne.

Marzanna dropped Bettina's hand and stood, rising to Her full height. She was not tall, especially compared to those who stood in the throne room, but Her eternal halo flickered in warning.

"Cosima is most fit. She is the first child of divinity and Saint—her nature is born for leadership. I will have no other."

Fiammetta interjected; at the same time, the babe at her breast began to fuss. "We have discussed it. Goddess has chosen. Do you question Her will?"

"Never. Especially not when it is my daughter who will gain such prestige." *Especially when I hear tales of the havoc the rest of your brood wreaks even in my exile,* Bettina added to herself.

The fussing infant let out a strange hiccup before their whole body shivered in and out of focus. Bettina restrained a gasp as wings that hadn't existed before unfurled from their smooth back. Their cries mellowed as the wings—scarlet like Däard's yet pink at the tips—folded neatly to cradle themself.

They're cold. Sadness mingled with longing as Bettina's heart wrenched in pity. Infants, even holy ones, didn't care about the splendor of a throne or their divine parentage. All they required was the comfort of a mother who loved them without restraint.

Fiammetta caught her staring. Before her eyes could narrow further, Bettina forced her attention back to Goddess. Standing, she inclined her neck in what she hoped was a humble enough surrender to Marzanna's plan.

"I'm glad you approve. We have already begun our schemes for her coronation, but we can discuss those after you rest and enjoy your return to Aebbenary. For now…bring Cosima in!"

She's here? The arrow struck true, though Goddess might not have fired it with that purpose.

Bettina abandoned all pretense at tranquility and sat up straight; her entire being rebelled as she held herself still. Waiting for the invisible attendants at the throne room doors to swing them open, to let her daughter in, caused her breathless pain that had her clenching her teeth and blinking back an unwelcome sting of tears.

"You called, Mother?" Cosima's halo of inherited Light coroneted her dark hair.

Bettina squeezed her hands into fists to physically prevent herself from running to yank her into her arms for a hug that would last a decade; she drank in the sight of her with eyes that didn't feel big enough.

Marzanna saw her often, or often enough to not be struck by her arrival. As Däard stroked Her back over the gauzy fabric of Her day gown, She granted Cosima only a sliver of Her attention. As if inviting her to Her seat of power was nothing.

"Yes. Your Mama has returned to Aebbenary. Greet her."

Bettina wracked her brain for answers as Cosima leveled a stare that cast cool judgment on both her mothers. *How could you be here, my pearl, when I left you in safety? When I cautioned you so thoroughly?* The betrayal of finding Cosima with her secondary mother was nothing to the spike of panic that made Bettina's head throb.

Cosima's posture was languid, but deceptively so. She had been a baby adorable enough to stop the heart, and Bettina had loved her from the instant Goddess's divine will had quickened her womb. Cosima had also been serious, stubborn, and wild. In maturity, all of that had been honed: perfected. As holiness had enhanced Goddess and uplifted Her mortal shell.

If she could take the form of a bird, Bettina had often mused, it would be a kestrel. Cosima's eyes were shaped round and sweet like Bettina's, but they had Marzanna's mortal color: brown shifting into black if she didn't stand in the sun. But the sun was her friend based on the tan shade of her skin. Where both her mothers were softened curves, she was lean muscle and strength she had painstakingly earned with her self-made tribe in the restored forests of Aebbenary.

"Hello, Mama. How is my brother?"

Cosima aimed the barb with precise talent. One of Bettina's brows arched as she absorbed it.

The last time they'd spoken months ago—after years of infrequent contact since Cosima never liked to be tied down by expectations—they had argued.

Goddess doesn't care for my mortal brother, Mama, but She likes me well enough. I will not be chased away from my home because you are afraid.

"If you spoke to him, you would know he is well."

Cosima's lips pressed into a line as she repressed a frown and a harsh reply. She deliberately turned to Marzanna, dismissing Bettina's answering shot; the long tail of her fishtail braid swung forward as she sketched a swift bow.

"I have pressing business, Mother. Please tell me why You summoned me so I can get back to it."

Marzanna smiled; Bettina saw the warmth that reached Her eyes and wondered at it, her unease rising.

Gesturing for Däard to follow, She took the hand he offered and ascended Her throne. Habit, or anticipation of Her desires, led him to sit in Hers instead of his own; She positioned Herself on his lap with casual comfort. Fiammetta reached her free hand out to Marzanna as Her head tilted back, inviting her touch and the elegant, soft fingers that began to massage Her scalp.

This time when Fiammetta smiled, it was as angelic as the sculpted likenesses Marzanna had commissioned to exalt her across the whole city.

"It's time you took on some responsibility," she said to Cosima. "Your sibling needs a mentor, and my duties will not allow me to nurse them any longer. Come, take them."

What? It had taken all her power to hold still as events she had no control of played out in front of Bettina. The second she forgot to tether herself to the ground she was moving—closing the distance between her and Cosima so they would have each other as allies in this pit of exquisite, perilous vipers.

"*What?*" Cosima's thunderous expression revealed itself in the stubborn defiance of her firm jaw; the drawing down of her intense, dark brows in a scowl that would send legions fleeing her wrath.

"Fia, we agreed to—" Once again, Däard mediated between his lovers and the rest of the world.

Though everyone ignored him, Bettina's focus lingered. *Is this your purpose now, old friend? A feeble envoy instead of your own man?*

Cosima physically recoiled from the responsibility of caring for a child—one that wasn't even hers.

"What of the babe's father? Surely he would be a willing caretaker."

Everyone glanced at Däard—including Marzanna. Under Her gaze the silence lasted but an instant.

"My duty to Goddess must come first. Always. I—"

"As does mine. Are you unwilling, Cosima?" Fiammetta said. Bettina recognized a test.

"If I may, Your Grace, I can care for—" she began. This would be a massive, unreasonable burden for her tempestuous daughter.

"Or Sovanna. Do you remember her?" Cosima said.

"*Are you unwilling, Cosima?*"

This time Goddess asked. Cosima looked back and forth between them: Marzanna, with Her glowing skin and hair beginning to stir in a breeze that only affected Her, and Queen Fiammetta. She whose doleful frowns and sobs could influence Marzanna into indulging her every whim. Her expression had cleared the moment Goddess took over on her behalf.

Cosima reluctantly climbed the stairs that led to Fiammetta's throne. Her outline of Light dimmed as she held her arms out for the baby.

"I am willing."

Liberation soaked up all the tension in Fiammetta's form. She eagerly passed her infant into Cosima's care, working to re-weave the ribbons that held her chemise and dress closed that she had kept open to nurse. When she beamed at Goddess in gratitude, it was if the babe was already forgotten. Like she didn't care if they existed at all.

Bettina couldn't help it: the disgust she felt at such a display made her stomach lurch and her cheeks heat with indignation. Ire that increased as the babe began to fret in the awkward, untried cradle Cosima made of her muscular arms.

Däard cleared his throat.

"Thank you. I am sure the child will be happy with you."

"Besides, you needn't look after them long. Soon they will express their divinity. You can explain their nature to them and send them on their way." Fiammetta exhaled what sounded like a huge breath of relief and slouched in her throne. Her legs uncrossed from their prim posture; one silken limb slipped out through a slit in her voluminous skirts, drawing Marzanna's eye to admire it.

Though she did her best to stifle it after its initial surge, Bettina couldn't entirely rein in her revulsion. Cosima huffed an incredulous snort as she shifted her weight from foot to foot to rock the restless infant.

Laughter. Both Fiammetta and Däard winced. In the moment of recognition that made Bettina risk going to her daughter's side, Cosima's eyes searched for her like they always had. Even strong, rarely daunted huntresses never forgot their need for their mother.

The gilded skeleton stirred, its own laughter waking it from its stupor. Bones clinked and creaked as—impossibly—the skeleton sat up and back against its throne. There was nothing in its mouth to facilitate its mirth, but still it chuckled.

Only Goddess wasn't perturbed. She rolled Her eyes and sat up on Däard's lap. She stood and walked down the dais to where the skeleton sat; all of them knew Her approach was an indulgence. Her will could send all of them to their knees to scrape in the dust until She was satisfied with their humiliation.

"Speak to us, Priest. Why are you amused by this charge from My queen to My heir?"

Marzanna loved to play, but Bettina had noted that Her favorite games were the ones where She had the most cards arranged to Her benefit. Bettina exchanged sideways glances with Cosima, who immediately pretended she hadn't been looking and went back to bouncing the baby with a rhythm that apparently was enough to soothe them.

The bones spoke. "Does laughter require a cause in the waking world, my love? Perhaps I dreamed. Perhaps while You safeguard my flesh I journey away from this earth and study the cosmos."

"Away from Aebbenary? Would you leave us so easily?"

The shining jaw clanked shut. "Never."

Bettina watched as Marzanna and Her Priest stared at each other. They had always circled each other this way—first one challenging with a thrown gauntlet, then one mocking the other for the attempt. She didn't know why Goddess tolerated Easoren, but she had guessed that a duel never came to fruition because the victor had already been revealed.

No one could win but Marzanna.

Still, Goddess could be generous. Light expanded from Her aureole, gentle like the dawn at first, but growing sharper as it flowed toward the bony creature sitting on the last throne. It enveloped the skeleton and shone brighter, hotter. All but Marzanna had to shut their eyes and cringe away from its brilliance until it abated.

The High Priest of Silver had become a Relic of Gold at the commencement of the Bright age. Aebbenary had watched in awe as Goddess had resurrected his body from bones and immortalized him to serve at Her side forever. Since then, he had rarely been seen outside of the Holy tower where Marzanna and Her Saints dwelled, or away from Her company. Among Her servants, where Däard played champion and Fiammetta ruled as queen, Easoren had no purpose beyond existing as an idol at Goddess's side.

His regrown eyes slid Bettina's way so quickly and away she almost missed it. Though flesh cloaked his regal form as he sat in his throne like a king born to privilege, she saw in the span of Light that the shape of his bones was still visible under the skin.

"Easoren," Goddess breathed. As if the sight of him hearty and whole and—mostly—human-shaped awed Her speechless. She opened Her arms, inviting him in; he stood, and embraced Her.

She had done so to Bettina, once upon a time. Often. So Bettina watched and understood that Easoren was powerless as he descended the dais like a man half-drunk and stumbled into Marzanna's arms. They kissed, heedless of their observers: hands weaving into each other's hair, heads slanted to kiss deeper, bodies angled in perfect parallel. A contrast of black curls and ashen, almost silver waves as an impossible breeze scented of sandalwood twined around them both.

"Mother." Cosima jostled the baby hard enough to make them fuss, though her swaying soothed them shortly after. "Was there anything else?"

Marzanna extracted Herself from Easoren's arms. "Yes."

The two of them stood together, an image of romance: his arms lingered around Goddess's waist, while Her hands rested higher, on his angular shoulders.

Bettina reached out to subtly pinch the fabric of Cosima's garments to draw her attention long enough to squint a warning. *Be careful, my pearl. Tread so, so carefully when these two are united.*

"Your majority Jubilee comes soon. On that day I will crown you My successor," Goddess decreed.

Though it was difficult to surpass, Cosima's reaction was sourer than when Fiammetta had foisted the child into her care. The throne room was silent enough to hear the flutter of wings above the rest as the bird-like constructs roosting in the ceiling stilled their ambient music.

"Me?"

"Mmm. Yes. You have the right above the rest. I'll leave it to you to inform your siblings and invite them to the—"

"No."

"No?" Fiammetta's pitch lifted in warning, like a cat flexing her claws at a rival.

"Cosima—" Däard began.

Bettina scanned the faces in the room, hunting for who presented the greatest danger. That was instinct, but she knew it was false: the foremost threat was always going to be Goddess. Her body guessed the truth sooner, and she stepped between Cosima and Goddess with a winning smile on her face and a sparkle in her eyes.

"This is so sudden, Your Glory. Our daughter must already be concerned with her new charge," Bettina said, dropping her voice to a conspiratorial murmur. "I beg a little patience. Her excitement will rouse once she has everything else sorted out."

Marzanna permitted the plea when Bettina added a spark of their old flirtation. The nostalgic playfulness the two of them had shared in the early days of the new age: giggling secrets at the theater while the world looked on, walking through the best parts of town with an arm each around their waists, pushing locks of hair behind each other's ears for the excuse to lean in for a kiss. Bettina recalled these good memories—what there were of them—by cocking her head a little left and adding a miniscule, exasperated shake of her head so the dangling dewdrop gem of her earring brushed against her neck.

Cosima started to protest again, but Bettina had caught Goddess's interest. She intended to keep it. She leaned back and crushed Cosima's toes with her heel to hush her.

Though…now Easoren's attention landed on her as well. Bettina refused to meet the lance of his gaze and waited for Marzanna to speak.

After a pregnant pause, Marzanna chuckled—all the tension that had been sucking the air out of the room diminished as if it was less than smoke. Her left hand—beringed with gifts from Her lovers bearing sapphires and rubies along with a chunky signet locked around Her thumb—traced an idle path down Easoren's chest.

"Of course. You are Saints only—adjusting to the notion of divinity takes time. And who has more of that than we do?"

Fiammetta laughed this time; neither of the men bothered. As the chirruping sound of it filled Bettina's ears it became a complete struggle to keep up the act. Black wavered at the corners of her eyes as rage made her blink it back.

Who has less time than Saints and Gods, Your Glory? My son!

"If there's nothing else...?" Bettina prompted. They couldn't leave until Goddess dismissed them.

"Go. Enjoy Aebbenary, as it's been some time since you visited. Catch up with one another. We will see each other again soon. Oh, and Bettina..."

"Yes, Your Glory?"

"Your son may attend the Jubilee. He is Cosima's brother, after all."

Hope kindled. Bettina did her best to regret the uncharitable thoughts that had soured her stomach from the moment Goddess's summons had reached her across the sea in Ioggenica. While she watched Cosima's tall figure retreat without delay through the doorway that appeared dark outside the illumination of the throne room, Bettina made a pretty obeisance to Goddess before following her out.

III

Bettina

Cosima left Bettina in the dust. Fleeing the tower like a fox running from a scene of mischief, her haste forced Bettina to move like she hadn't in years. The stairs spiraling downward faded into a dizzy blur touched with impressions of the chestnut tail of Cosima's braid; a stray feather from the babe's pink, gold-tipped wings; the heel of a worn sandal as she ran.

Call out to her, Bettina's own wishes urged. *Ask her to wait for you!*

"Wait—" She listened to them, but the word choked her into silence. *She doesn't want me. She hasn't forgiven me.*

Forgiveness was a tricky thing. Bettina would never forgive her family—aged or dead—for their mistreatment of her. She had laughed aloud with delight when the pig they had collared her to in bitter matrimony had died. Goddess had prevented him from touching her with a Miracle that had marked her face with a sprinkling of silver—now gold—forever, but that hadn't prevented her from dealing with him. *Hating* him.

Before Goddess, she had not known of love until an untalented minstrel had murmured it to her during a long winter of forbidden love-making. She had not experienced it until, after hours laboring to bring Cristoval into the world, she had met the child she had prayed for. She, Bettina—the fabled beauty of Aebbenary who had never begged for anything until then.

Oh, my pearl, I do love you. More than anything.

Outside of the tower, Cosima's already formidable speed amplified. Without the pressure of Marzanna and Her inner court, Cosima thrived on independence as if it was worth more than her life. It was as if her feet grew wings as she disappeared in the labyrinth of her home city. No one could catch her...by mortal means.

But you never needed me like Cristoval. Bettina trotted her misgivings out as the pang of loss—whetted sharp no matter how many times it pricked her heart—waned. She examined them as she gazed out past the arch separating the city from the rest of the island Goddess had reclaimed for nature's disorderly whims.

You wanted me, longed for me, but needed?

Bettina's return to Aebbenary had re-awakened the store of power proximity to Goddess's glory gave all Her Saints. She tapped into it hesitantly, like she was testing a pot of water to see if it was tolerable or boiling hot. It rose eagerly to her touch—it had missed her. A second later she was running too: a blur of halo and a rustle of her skirts in the wind as her metamorphosed form raced after Cosima.

I never wanted to stifle you. You need me now, *Cosima. That's the truth.*

She fortified her spirits, steeled herself against further rejection, and forged ahead.

The city of Aebbenary melted away as their condensed bodies travelled northward. Beyond the high towers, soaring architecture, and the people who gladly served Goddess where they had once reluctantly—but devoutly—served a false god. North of the church, the mild weather induced to storms only when commanded by Marzanna shifted from sun-soaked becalm into a greyer mood. Clouds churned and grew tall thunderheads above grassy fields.

These prairie lands had once been dedicated to agriculture and the constant feeding of a city bloated with thousands of people. Bettina slowed as Cosima began to decrease her speed, taking care to linger far enough behind to avoid discovery. She inhaled the smells of petrichor and sweet grasses dotted with innumerable flowers as they passed.

I embody Light and Life, Goddess had assured Bettina during a pleasure cruise commenced not on water, but over these same grasses in a boat that floated above the land like a ship of the seas. *Let Me use it to free the toiling from their labors and restore the land of Aebbenary to what it must have been an age ago.*

Scrolling onward for miles that would be arduous for a mortal to travel, the prairie stretched away from civilization as far as even Sainted eyes could see. The mountain jutting into Aebbenary proper was part of an extensive range, but its height and majesty was incongruous compared to the rest. Cosima turned west, toward the forests that covered the lower reach where Bettina knew she spent the majority of her days.

Under the long shadows cast by the restored trees, Cosima halted. She stood alone in the forest for no longer than a minute—as she slowed to a walk, beings streamed out of the murky gloom of the forests to greet her. Bettina eluded their notice by weaving a path between this tree and that, using them to obscure her presence.

None of them would have noticed her anyway. Five of them swarmed Cosima and Fiammetta's child; their bodies formed a commotion of earth-toned fabrics and sturdy leather around both. They blocked Bettina's view so all she could do was stare at the various thatches of hair and listen.

"You got away? What did Goddess want?"

"What *is* that, Cosima?"

"Did your mothers fight over you? Did they—"

Cosima tried to answer at least one of the questions, her voice rising to top the others, but more girls were arriving until their total numbered eleven. All of them had something to say.

"Are the rumors true? Are you the next—"

"Cosima, what are you holding?"

"Is that a baby?!"

The rest of the conversation and speculation ceased.

"Iulia. Konetta. Palmira. All of you make some space. This Saintling is *hot.*" The sea of women stunned into silence parted; Cosima awkwardly adjusted the baby until she held them facing forward. They had only just developed enough to hold up their own head, and their little legs scrunched close to their abdomen as they stared around.

The sylvan hunters ogled the child with mixed consternation and curiosity.

"Another Godling? Whose is it this time?"

Cosima had displayed the child enough. She hefted them over her shoulder like a sack of vegetables, almost dropping them. Instead of fussing, the child burbled a laugh and then burped loudly.

"No—something new. A babe conceived the normal way."

Gasps all around. Bettina would have rolled her eyes, but it occurred to her in that moment that this *was* a first. Däard and Marzanna had borne children, Marzanna and Fiammetta had conceived with Light and love the way Goddess had strayed to do with Bettina and a few others, but Däard's seed had never borne fruit with Aebbenary's queen.

Until now.

"The First Saint? Why now?"

"They've all been fucking for a quarter century. It shouldn't be a shock." Standing closest to Cosima, the tallest, broadest, and suntanned warrior with the bow strapped across her back—Iulia— harrumphed and eyed the cooing infant with a resolute gaze.

The most incredulous of the bunch—Konetta, Cosima had called her—pinched the tips of the baby's wings between two fingers and sketched the breadth of them with her other hand. "Yes, but still! Even Easoren and Goddess have *one* child."

"Now everyone has one." Annoyance was Cosima's default state, but as Bettina watched from the bower of the trees that obscured her she could tell Cosima wasn't truly irritated. Relief that softened others rendered her sharper than usual at first.

"Too many babies," observed Iulia.

Cosima grunted an affirmative. "Who wants to hold them?"

As one the rest of the women backed away. Their synchronization forced Bettina to cover her mouth with her hand to stifle a laugh.

They're so young, she thought, the tone of her thoughts turning wistful. *The ones who might end up wanting children haven't decided yet. The ones who don't have yet to discover that child-bearing isn't infectious.*

Amidst their number but set apart by her own demeanor and her relation to Goddess, Cosima clearly ruled this pack. The eleven human women who had become her family deferred to her when necessary, Bettina could tell…but Cosima didn't rule with an iron fist. None of them rushed to take the baby because they feared punishment if they failed to obey cheerfully.

Cosima sighed and cradled the baby, her posture still awkward. "Fine, leave me to it, but this is what I'm going to have to do for however long it takes for the child to express their divinity. I have to do it right."

A girl who couldn't have been older than sixteen stepped tentatively forward, her attention fixed on the infant. "Do what? Be a mother to a child that isn't yours?"

"Well…" For the first time, Cosima paled slightly—down to her lips. The shock of the responsibility thrust upon her was wearing off. Bettina risked drawing closer, gliding under the shelter of a thick sycamore tree to watch better.

"Why do *you* have their baby?" A roundish woman with bared arms that displayed her archer's muscles dared reach out to pet the shining down of reddish hair on the infant's head. "Is that why they summoned you?"

"Mother has decided to officially name me Her heir." The subject had changed enough for Cosima to calm herself down…or at least cloak her offending emotions in practical news.

Silence. Bettina didn't know what she had expected, but her heart sank at the thickening silence. Mortals understood hierarchy and bloodlines better than beings of endless life: for an heir to be needed, someone important had to die. Someone who had remade the island and the mighty continent beyond the channeling sea into Her own image.

"Why…" Konetta spoke first again. "Why, though? Goddess is eternal. What need does She have for an heir?"

"And what about Sovanna?" Iulia asked. Her question was more like a statement. Bettina mentally jotted down the observation that of these human friends, Iulia and Konetta had to be Cosima's lieutenants.

"She's still not back in Goddess's favor. Not after leaving—"

"We've gossiped about that enough."

"Well, there's *never* enough gossip—" The youngest began; Cosima cuffed her without any punishing pressure to silence the rest.

"I doubt you've all finished your chores. If you want to drink tonight I want our camp pristine," she said. "Go on ahead. I'll help when I…"

The baby made a sound in her arms. That was enough to prompt the others' departure, sending huntresses melting back into the woods as if they'd never been present.

Iulia thumped Cosima's shoulder with a sturdy hand as she left; Konetta toyed with the end of Cosima's braid as she followed. Bettina heard her mutter something, but the necessity of remaining hidden had her pressed back against the tree and shadowing her aureole in fabricated sunlight peeping through the canopy above. She didn't dare look again until all sounds of people—what few there were since Cosima's huntresses were skilled in woodcraft—had fallen silent.

Is she still there? Now they were alone Bettina debated showing herself. Cosima had fled from her. She would be angry at the idea her mother had eavesdropped, but Bettina hadn't heard anything incriminating or private…

Butterflies drifted by—violet and pink wings darkening into black. They flocked around Bettina's head to pluck at tendrils of her hair before the power that had called them dispelled. In the quiet forest the sound of their wings was audible. The surprise of it threatened to make Bettina smile and undo her caution of hiding from Cosima and her mortal friends in the first place.

I knew you were there.

A tendril of thought reached from daughter to mother. Bettina threw open her mind to welcome it; she barely restrained herself from coaxing Cosima forward like a child trying to convince a bear cub to become her pet.

I know, sweetling.

Cosima scowled at the endearment she had once begged Bettina to continue using…then stop using in public. *Stay hidden. I can't guarantee I'm the only one who noticed you. I'd rather the others not interact with you yet. Did you hear?*

Yes. Bettina nodded; her posture relaxed as she leaned her head back against the tree to look up at the swaying leaves. *Am I ever going to meet your friends?*

Mama. Focus. Cosima cocked her ear toward her friends' retreating backs. *Word spread that Mother would summon you well before She actually did. Do you know where Cristoval is?*

Of course. The answer floated to the top of her mind; she terminated the thought at its source to prevent it from revealing a secret that wasn't hers. She had promised not to tell a soul. Even his sister. *I think you should tell him to stay away from Aebbenary for good.*

How can I? Goddess summoned him.

There is something...Aebbenary isn't the same. The people have changed. Mother has been distant. Distracted.

Is that unusual? Bettina had once been one of the stars shining under Marzanna's daunting attention. Goddess's wooing had been impossible to resist. The passage of time coinciding with a decrease of her affection had been the first thing to end the dream that had consumed everything that had made Bettina herself before holy love had unspooled her.

It's different. She's...She wants something. We all feel the pressure of Her unmet desire.

Cosima shuddered; Bettina felt its echo and mirrored it subconsciously. Goddess's want could be a burden.

There's no word on what She seeks?

No. I've gone down to the Archives, but that place—

The Archives? Bettina hadn't heard of such a place, Aebbenary native though she was.

Mother made them. Made *them*. Cosima didn't need to explain that Made meant that Goddess had expelled a prodigious amount of Her Light to create something from divinity alone.

Where are they? I will try to find out what She wants.

So you can trade it for Cristoval?

They both knew the answer to that. Just as Bettina knew what Cosima was not prepared to comprehend: Bettina would pay any price but Cosima's life and happiness to save Cristoval from his own

25

mortality, though Marzanna had and might continue to refuse based on Her whims. It was not gratitude Bettina expected to earn if she beat Goddess to whatever answers She sought from the Archives.

Cosima spoke into the silence Bettina hadn't meant to let dangle. *It's where the Sallustius catacombs used to be.*

"There?" Bettina forgot her secrecy in her surprise. She sensed rather than saw Cosima's displeasure as the baby snorted in their doze and almost woke up. *Citizens and students tour that area regularly. You mean to tell me She's just loitering around—*

Lower. Past the Scholar's Grave.

Down further, nearer to the belly of the earth that made Bettina's breath come short and fast and her head throb with pressure. Even as a Saint, she still feared the dark and confined spaces. Everything felt heavy, suddenly: her skirts weighed her down like they'd drown her, her cinched bodice tightened as panic made her fear swirl like a storm…

Are…are you well, Mama? You've changed too. Cosima's mental voice trespassed through her gale of doubt.

Bettina wanted to open her arms to welcome both her daughter and the reminder that she was here—safe for the time being, powerful beyond the measure of most, and clever in the face of adversity—close to her heart.

This time it was easier to lie. To pretend. The secret she hid was for the benefit of her children, after all. For Cristoval—and to prevent fierce, independent Cosima from protecting Bettina when she didn't need protection from herself.

Just tired. Perhaps Aebbenary will restore my spirits.

Though Bettina's tone was airy, Cosima expressed her doubt with a skeptical sniff. She didn't see fit to challenge the matter though; as quickly as her mood had shifted upon return to her coterie, she turned her back on Bettina and left her hovering on the fringes of the wood.

"Don't fret," Bettina whispered after her. "I love you."

IV

Bettina

Waking up in Aebbenary—*at home,* part of her still insisted—had already changed Bettina. Though she kept to her usual routine with care that bordered on fixation, her familiar habits failed to satisfy her. She could not scrub away the verve returning to flush her cheeks with health during the bath she took in her room after servants she had not asked for set it up. The glow of her eternal youth only increased as she brushed her hair and watched it almost consciously resist any style other than a waterfall braid wrapped around her head that let the rest fall over her shoulders and down her back in a flaxen wave.

Seated before a mirror that could not lie about her escalating beauty, Bettina rolled up her sleeves and winced at the sight of the scars slashed with meticulous habit over her inner elbows. As a Saint, her healing was supernatural. Her blood had been sanctified from the hour Goddess had greeted her past mortal self when Bettina had visited Her throne room at the turn of the age to offer her gratitude and service. Though the ichor was not as pure as those who possessed unalloyed divinity like Godlings, gold still mingled with the red.

She had needed to cut herself in the same place many, *many* times before the wounds began to scar.

Draining my ichor here is too dangerous, Bettina reminded herself as she pursed her lips at the sight of her scars—wounds inflicted by her love for her son. For Cristoval…who had drank of the essence of her Sainthood in everything she had ever made him without knowing. Who used sword and bow and any other tool bathed in her ichor and sworn to protect him throughout her entire immortal life without knowing what it cost her to leach away her holiness for his benefit.

Besides—he wasn't here now. Until she extracted a vow from Goddess Herself that She would let Cristoval join her in immortality, Bettina would see to it that he never returned to Aebbenary at all. Cosima's warning had been serious, though Bettina had not needed to hear it to know the only thing protecting her family was caution and their wits pitted against divine caprice.

Bettina readied herself for her first day back in the city. Cosima had given her signs to follow to find the answers she sought: she intended to take full advantage of them as soon as possible to head off any hazards the approaching Jubilee might present. Goddess—and Fiammetta by extension, possibly even Däard—could be planning anything.

Humoring her wish in spirit if not in truth, the servants who had assisted Bettina vanished as she walked the familiar paths of her home. She passed through one silent room after another on her way out the front entrance. Every line and arch that met her view was pleasing to the eye, every dignified column and washed brick as unsullied as if the estate was only days old. Every table had been adorned with Aebbenary's plumage of flowers: vivid, fiery phloxes, hollyhocks of various shades, and aurea lilies showcasing white or yellow petals.

The flowers extended toward her as she passed, growing rapidly for the chance to brush against her fingertips, but she ignored them and hurried through the house.

The Valusius estate resembled absolutely nothing of its age or its previous structure. As a wooing gift long ago, Goddess had asked Bettina what sort of home she wanted and provided her dream with Miracles of Light and waves of Her hand. Bettina had been too troubled to take in the sight of her ancestral home yesterday; as she left for the day now she walked backwards a few steps away from the house to take it all in.

Back then, she had expected to remain here forever. With genuine humility she reserved for no one else, Bettina had rocked an infant

Cosima in her arms and requested a private solar with spotless windows and filigree for her and Goddess alone whenever She visited. The memory of Marzanna's smile preoccupied her to this day.

"A worthy place for Me, pet? Ah, but your arms are deserving enough."

Bettina shaded her eyes from the sun as she stared at the home she had abandoned. Time had degraded the memory enough by now for her to remember the rest.

Cristoval: banished frequently to a nursemaid's care until Bettina began to question his dismissal from Goddess's presence.

Cosima: welcomed more often, but still relegated to the sidelines whenever Marzanna required Bettina for an impassioned romp or entertainment.

Swans—her social namesake—would be gliding in their pond around the back of the villa. They remained there most of the time, beaks gilded with living gold and feathers tipped with red like Saint wings as yet another showing of favor Bettina had outgrown like a snake shedding skin.

They called me a swan, a beauty, a true Saint. Cynicism left Bettina stony with disapproval she couldn't inflict on a version of herself that no longer existed. *I was only another fool.*

She turned her back on the modest yet luxurious estate and started her walk to the city proper, toward where Cosima had said the Archives would be. Bettina rarely liked to recall that by serving Marzanna she had become the one thing she'd sworn she would never be: a pretty bauble as easily discarded as cherished.

The locals claimed their beloved Goddess knew everything. The report had spread across the sea to Ioggenica and beyond—further than Silver's reach had ever gone. After almost a millennium of his dominion Marzanna had claimed the right to rule the world, crowned Fiammetta as Aebbenary's queen and Herself as supreme ruler over everything else, and demanded the rest of the world bend the knee to Her will. Not in conquest, not to compel religious obeisance from every soul...not yet. Life with Her chosen people seemed to have sated Her thus far.

That had changed too, but not as much as the rest. Before Bettina's exile, Goddess had begun sharing Her dreams of victory over the world to forge *all* of it in Her design rather than endure the mere tolerance of distant lands and foreign peoples…all during their pillow talk.

Bettina hadn't resisted that idea at the time. Let the world tend to itself. She had seen Silver rule long enough; she'd seen what the will of men held for a world sickened by their greed and lust for authority. Let women have a chance to change things, she had thought. Even before Marzanna had Sainted her.

Nevertheless…where faith was sown, not all ground would bear fruit. Not everyone was devout, even in the holy city itself. Bettina knew this better than anyone. Devotion to a deity—even Goddess— could not inspire pure goodness in mortal beings bound by the necessities of survival and the shortness of the hours appointed to them by oblivion. Flawed as she was, Bettina couldn't blame them for that.

She blamed them enough for what they had made of Aebbenary. While she traversed the shining streets and watched with careful detachment as denizens went about the business of their days, she recognized the sight of beggars and orphans that had no hope of anything better no matter who sat on the thrones in Goddess's tower. Their queen, Fiammetta, had only ever cared for Marzanna—was she aware the suffering that was as plain as day to Bettina existed?

Submission to Silver brought evil enough to this island, she thought as she sidestepped a child creeping closer to a food cart laden with pears and spit-roasted chunks of mutton. A wave of her hand sent the child away with coins in his pocket and one of the spits in his hand.

Has submission to Marzanna only darkened the skies further?

Goddess as a mortal had craved freedom above all else. She had whispered secrets of Her past and Her visions for the future to Bettina in the steamy hours of their nights together. Even then, Bettina had had fewer illusions: there could not be freedom for weak human beings, not when deities existed in the world.

The halls of the University hadn't captured her interest before, and they didn't now. Like many daughters of the nobility, Bettina had been educated by governesses and private tutors. Further than most young women of the time…but she had had no desire to mingle further in the world of men who saw themselves as superior in every way but that of child-bearing. Now she hastened through the hallowed halls under the cloak of her own manipulated Saint glow and worked her way downwards level by level.

Bettina had not visited this part of Aebbenary before, but the tomb Goddess had dedicated to the lost catacombs linking the University to Silver's former cathedral was known to her. Rumor had it all the lost architecture and history buried under the city had been wiped clean from the maze of tunnels Marzanna had solved during Her last days as a mortal. Bettina had no room for inquisitiveness, but it niggled at her anyway as she approached the massive triplicate doors created from ebony agate. She chose the one in the center—knowing Marzanna had not relished the maze the catacombs used to be—and waited as a dormant Miracle swung the door open inwards as if it was weightless.

Remnants of the original church had been preserved…but only those parts Goddess had deemed worthy. Miracles had transported the friezes and reliefs from lower down to the tomb's entrance so anyone invited could see the story of how the primordial gods had fallen under the false god's siege of their lands. How they had waited almost a millennium for a savior to return them to power, and how they had lost hope until one of Silver's lowly Founts had claimed power and renewed the dying spirit of the island.

Marzanna had never told Bettina how She had gained Her power in the first place. Bettina knew part of the story, of course, but surmised the full secret was one only Goddess's upper echelon would ever know.

With her Saint's halo blanketing her form Bettina didn't require a torch. Her luminescence spread a yard or so outwards, which sparked the awakening of sconces meant to aid Saintly sight in viewing one of the newest sacred spaces of Aebbenary.

The Scholar's grave. Bettina knew who Marzanna—and Däard and Fiammetta—had lost here. Who the empty throne arrayed in weeds of grief was for. She had not known Lior Betilienus in his time, but his impact on Goddess and the destiny She had wrought for Aebbenary was one no one could deny. This tribute to the place of his passing spoke the truth even if She had contradicted the obvious.

A statue greater than even the conqueror's fountain that had once stood in prominent glory in the city towered in the center of the circular vestibule. Supposedly somehow in the last few decades a team of sculptors had built this memorial effigy without Miraculous aid. Bettina couldn't guess how; she paced around the sculpture and marveled at the skill and beauty as grudgingly as Marzanna had brought up the relics of the old church from below to honor their history. She hadn't known Lior, but his likeness could have resembled most of the men from the Betilienus bloodline as it had once been.

He looks sad, Bettina thought. *Like he knew he was going to die.*

The pose of the sculpture created from dozens of varieties of stone and precious, rare materials was meant to be uplifting: a warrior and a scholar with one hand on his sword hilt and the other holding aloft a book of learning that shone with sapphires and an accompanying aura. Even the expression had been meant to be inspiring, or thought-provoking.

All Bettina knew, down in her heart, was that if the man this icon had been built for could see what his lovers had become he would feel shame to rival her own.

Enough. She had brooded long enough. Shrugging the weight of the past off her shoulders, Bettina pulled her halo back into her immediate space and progressed past the effigy to venture into the dark.

Others would not have been able to do this. Bettina was counting on one thing: that Marzanna had underestimated both her dedication to her cause and her sheer audacity. There were many sacred spaces arranged across the entire island, either claimed by Goddess or bickered over by Her host of offspring. Aside from petty prohibitions between one sibling and another, anyone with Saintly or divine ichor or blessing had the power to waylay any barriers.

Magnificent as it was, the Scholar's Grave was only important to Marzanna and Her consorts in the end. There was nothing to steal; little to no chance for anyone slinking into these eerie depths to dare deface a mighty symbol of love. Besides—Bettina had been brought here before.

Quieting her thoughts, Bettina concentrated on her straightforward stroll down the singular path. Like an echo, Goddess's presence lingered. The imprint of Her feet formed a trail on the dusty stones leading downwards. Bettina didn't bother trying to match her feet to their stride, though the temptation was there: her gait was longer than Marzanna's, as were her legs.

Ultimately, the walk was long and dull. Bettina's calves would have ached from the exercise, but she had kept herself busy during her self-imposed exile to the continent. As it was, she felt the bellows of her lungs inhaling and exhaling more strongly than usual as she approached the unobtrusive arch at the bottom of the passage. The tunnel had been a massive part of the original cavern where the Scholar's Grave resided; without her noticing, it had narrowed down to barely taller than herself.

No door stood barred and forbidding. No embellishment decorated the simple peaked arch carved from plain white rock. Bettina moved as close as she dared to the threshold and cautiously rested her hand against the bone-white column; it was cold. Her nose twitched as she caught the odor of mildew wafting from inside. Looking in, all she could see was the idea of a room that might resemble a library. She could guess nothing else until her whole body passed under the arch.

The Archives. Bettina decided her sinister impression of the place from the moment Cosima had hinted about it had been correct.

The curtain barring one reality from another lifted as Bettina stepped into the Archives and immediately fought the impulse to walk right back out. While her assumption that the Archives would resemble the illustrious halls of the University library had been correct, she had miscalculated one thing.

The room was *full.*

Gliding between bookcases stocked with gloomy artifacts from the catacombs instead of only books, figures emerged, disappeared, and emerged again. Their transparent bodies cropped in and out of focus for Bettina as she stood stock still to avoid their notice…yet, now she looked, she noted that none of them had startled at the sound of her entrance.

Though the tunnel had narrowed down to the arch at the entrance, the Archive lobby had no ceiling. The bookcases elongated up, and up, into nothing. Knowing some of the price of fickle Miracles, Bettina averted her gaze. If there was an end to the rising black, she didn't want to see what waited there.

The ghosts couldn't help her, Bettina decided. If they saw her at all. *Are we even on the same plane of existence? Can they really not tell I'm here, or are they ignoring me to report to Goddess later?*

She strategized a plan of escape: leaving wasn't an option until she found *something* to manipulate Goddess's favor, but the sight of a door—normal oak by all appearances—around a slanting shelf and to the right of the foyer cheered her. Anything to put between her and the mysterious Archive occupants would be a comfort.

Her halo warbled in her ear. *A warning? What—*

Bettina flinched as soon as she noticed. The Archive ghosts didn't *need* to see her to notice her. In her dismay at the perturbing atmosphere of the foyer, she had neglected to notice one important detail: *the occupants were absorbing her glow.* By doing that, they were absorbing *her.*

Her fortitude collapsed. Scooping up her skirts, Bettina made a break for the door.

Nothing pursued—the *nothing* of the ghosts locked down in this unnatural collection of things Marzanna must have ordered them to investigate and catalog. Bettina dropped her skirts and slammed her hands over her ears so hard she almost boxed them as wails of alarm assaulted her senses. Her aureole coursed behind her like water as the collective entity of the ghosts sucked it in. She didn't know how she guessed, but supernatural instinct assured her that beyond the door the beings would not be able to touch her; she could regroup and think of a way to leave.

And also wrest the knowledge she needed from the bosom of this cold hall to convince Goddess to spare her son the rot of a mortal life.

It took longer than it should have to reach the door. The main aisle elongated to trap her, but Bettina sidled in and out of the shelves on the right side to evade the ghosts and get closer to her destination. Between one moment and another she hauled the door open—its hinges shrieked as she slammed it into the wall—then yanked it shut behind her.

Instantly, her spirits improved. Her halo steadied and strengthened as she leaned back against the blessed wood and caught her breath.

Bettina allowed her eyes to flutter closed; they snapped open as a wordless *impression* assaulted her senses. *What?*

"..."

The illusion of solitude cracked like glass. She blinked as her eyes watered from a sensation she couldn't name—heat, cold, dryness, she couldn't tell. She jammed the heels of her palms into her eyes and rubbed them furiously to clear the fog. By the time she finished she saw the figure that had materialized sitting at the table in the center of the private study.

The room was sparse, as was the being. A cloth shifting in various shades of yellow and gold hung over the vague shape of a human figure, but no matter how closely Bettina looked she couldn't see anything but the suggestion of a silhouette under the ripples of what appeared to be velvet.

Outside the room—the *private* room, she understood, safe or not—the ghosts were only basic curators. *This* was the Archivist. This was who she had come to find.

"Who are you?"

It wasn't speech as Bettina knew it, but she understood. Pages from the volume arranged on the edge of the table in front of the Archivist flipped back and forth. Though there were no words, symbols, or images on the parchment, it sloped over the tome as if it had something to study.

"I—" *Don't say.* Prudence stilled her tongue. "I heard tell of this place from a friend. I hear Goddess visits these Archives frequently."

Whispers assaulted Bettina's ears. Moaning at the door she had slammed behind her to escape the specters rose, then silenced with a whimper like a kicked dog. She conquered the urge to turn as the hair on the back of her neck prickled.

"Goddess. Yes, we know Her well." How could something that could not really speak imitate a wry, ironic tone? A giggle quavered in Bettina's throat, but she stifled it with an audible swallow.

"May I assume you are the Grand Archivist?"

"At your peril, Swan-of-gold. I may allow it once."

Oh, it was proud. She shivered as the book slammed shut and the being slowly "stood" up. Courage threatened to abandon her, but Bettina had already glimpsed veiled horrors as Marzanna's favorite pet. Expertise was on her side when it came to dealing with those who valued pride.

"My apologies. Would you be willing to tell me who you are?"

"I am a friend to knowledge. I am what She Made."

A friend to knowledge. Was it true? Her life here—both before her Sainthood and in the early days spent in Marzanna's arms—was a fever dream. A mirage bred not from dehydration in the desert, but from Bettina's systematic drowning in Light and Miracles. She had been first of the disciples outside of Goddess's beloved angel and paragon.

Whether that was the making of her existence or the ruination of it, she doubted she'd ever know.

"A friend? Or a keeper?" She tried to match the being's calm, but its single-minded focus on her made her itch. She smoothed her hands down her bodice to wipe away the clamminess dampening her skin.

"Does it matter to you?"

She tried to smile. "A keeper will guard. A friend might share."

Could the entity laugh? Bettina steadied herself against the sturdy column of a stuffed bookcase, then immediately jumped away from it as her hand passed through the stone.

"Friend enough, yet servant still. Knowledge is a taskmaster beings rarely wish to serve."

Thrown off by the repellent sensation of her hand sliding through dimensions, Bettina didn't have time to react as the being looked *up* at her from where it "sat" and greeted her with the sight of emptiness under the sumptuous cloak it wore.

With no eyes, it could see. See—and engulf.

It combed through her thoughts like bristles. It parted the waves of her mind like sifting hairs for louse and began to pluck memories and thoughts for itself. Bettina screamed knowing no one would hear—or care—as the pieces of herself that made up her identity began to blur and slide against each other with horrible, destructive friction that would grate her entire self down to nothing but shreds.

The being took no note of her suffering, the doom of insanity if not total bodily destruction that awaited her for trespassing, but Bettina clung to her *self* with all her might. As *it* could see into her, between pulses of unmaking, Bettina stared back with eyes that disintegrated and reformed every few seconds.

Knowledge. The Archives purpose for existence was to gather all knowledge for Goddess to sift through at Her leisure. Guided either by impatience or a lack of concern, Goddess had willed this creature into existence and left it to its own devices: it had built the Archives based on a shard of memory from Marzanna herself. Even the ghostly attendants were a product of memory.

Bettina understood. Disembodied entity or not, this being had known it was alone.

She'd seen through it. It *knew* she had seen through it. Though it scarcely paused its review of everything she had ever thought and done and said, the cruel spikes raking her consciousness for information slowed.

"Offer."

"Offer?" Bettina could speak, somehow. A second ago that wouldn't have been possible.

"Knowledge costs."

"Oh." *Is it trying to help me?*

What could she give? Bettina was saving so much of herself for her children, even the core of her very soul that had somehow survived being a plaything for a deity. It had taken many years of isolation for her to remember who she even *was* after Light had addled her brain and riddled her heart with a thousand cuts of rejection.

The entity extended...limbs of some sort. From beneath the drape of ocher cloth that hung over emptiness, the impression of something resembling hands reached for Bettina. She scurried backwards, around a table stacked with books. All of them crumbled to dust and reformed as her hip clipped through the corner of the table as if reality had absorbed it and labored it back into their dimension.

Blood leaked from a rapier-thin slice that curved around Bettina's side. Shining in the oppressive dark, drops fell onto the ground...and remained. The only solid thing beside her in the Archives.

"Life." *What am I doing? What am I offering?*

The limbs paused mid-air. Frozen—by curiosity instead of offense, she hoped.

"Life." Bettina repeated her offer. She was too terrified to charm, but part of it was second nature. "You exist in this tomb where Marzanna stashed you. What if you had the chance to experience the things you know instead of just...knowing about them?"

She was going to die. Saint or not, the Grand Archivist would suck her consciousness from its famously pretty shell for being an idiot.

"In exchange for?"

Careful. Bettina guessed that if she phrased her request poorly the Grand Archivist would hold her to it. Besides, who knew for certain how loyal it was to Marzanna? How strictly Goddess supervised the being She had summoned into isolated existence, down here with dust and empty pages?

"I want to know what Goddess wants. I want to know what an omnipotent being desires so badly She'll Create an entire other entity to seek answers for Her."

"That is not what you seek."

It had seen, Bettina reminded herself. She would have to take care not to lie.

"Not quite. But it's the next step on my road to claim what *I* want."

"How will you trade life to me, Swan-of-Gold? If you die or I take your life you have nothing to grant. Your knowledge, though..." Tendrils developed from the stretched out "arms", seeking Bettina's skull.

This was where she got stuck. She had a concept in mind for somehow trading a portion of her Saintly aura to the Archivist for power it clearly lacked, but how? And would it drain her completely at the first chance?

Bettina backed away, one foot then another as she tried not to appear like she was running away. There was nowhere to go, after all. Her back touched the closed door and felt the lock of power holding them shut. Locking her in with this…this…she couldn't perceive the energy approaching her as her doom. Her gaze dropped down…

…and she saw the beads of her blood dotting the floor.

My blood has helped Cristoval ascend past the rudimentary bonds of mortality, though only for brief days. Could it help this creature?

She had no sooner thought it before the tendrils changed course. The Archivist had no scruples over sipping the drops of her ichor up from the dusty floor. Light and its hungry opposite spread from the site, reaching again for Bettina. Just before it touched her skin, the strands hesitated. Paused—waiting for consent that would mark her pledging to this deal.

Cristoval. Cosima. Bettina cradled their names like she had once rocked their tiny infant bodies to sleep night after night. Then she extended her arms and watched as the strands wrapped around her wrists and tightened to suck blood from her like leeches.

Cosima, my pearl. Cristoval, my angel.

She didn't know how long it went on. How much the being devoured. By the time it retracted—reluctantly—her scarred arms were ribbed with cobalt welts she would struggle to hide if they didn't heal with Miraculous help. Bettina looked up from studying her new, fascinating wounds and saw the strands of the entity twisting and snapping like beheaded snakes around the cloaked emptiness of the Grand Archivist.

Blink. The shape grew somehow more solid: more *there*.

Blink. Her lashes dampened with involuntary tears as Light—a replica of her own, a Saint's—ignited to saturate the study with itself.

A last, drawn out *blink* that divided one facet of reality from the next. When Bettina opened her eyes for good the figure standing in front of her was as corporeal as she was.

All angles. All sharp. Only the same garment that had enrobed the vacuum of its presence concealed the rest of the figure from her perception. It was still better this way: though Bettina was afraid, she could hear them breathe. Sense a heartbeat, of sorts. Though their skin had bubbled as it had emerged from the seed of Bettina's blood, she saw the pieces they had used to construct a frame of humanity as they stepped closer to the aureole of her Saint glow.

He.

A sheet of black hair as straight as the edge of a page. His skin was pale gold bordering on brown; when Bettina looked closer, she saw threadlike seams of midnight blue woven across his face and chest and arms like pieces of pottery melded back together after they'd been shattered. Where his lips had parted she glimpsed the hint of teeth that looked a little too sharp and a little too gold.

"Magisend."

"What?" She'd been riveted by his eyes—empty sockets still growing an eyeball made of something entirely black—but his audible voice made her fight not to squeeze her own eyes shut and scream.

His smile cut across his face without touching the weeping dark of his eyes. "My name. You'll need it."

"G-Grand Archivist Magisend." A name and title that sounded more formal than a Made creature probably deserved; Bettina shuddered, briefly losing her restraint. "A pleasure."

"Shall we begin?" Though he appeared a decade or two older than the twenty-five years Bettina had earned as a mortal and forever halted aging to enjoy, he already owned the ageless quality inhuman beings seemed to always possess.

Let's get this over with. She rubbed her cold arms with her hands and waited for the answers her sacrifice of vitality had earned.

"First lesson, Swan-of-gold. Even deities are not omnipotent."

V

Cosima

In the bearded chrysanthemum bassinet, the infant Saintling finally, *finally* slept from the wee hours of after midnight doldrums to dawn.

Cosima reclined in a bed crafted from living moss and obliging branches swathed in her preference of cotton bedding. Iulia cradled her thighs with her brawny arms and kissed between her legs until pleasure brought a release to the tension that had wound her so tight it had taken all but one of the several hours the babe had slept to unravel it.

"Better?" Iulia smiled up at her, tilting the shaved side of her head against the pillow of Cosima's leg.

She had been satisfied. Iulia was attentive like few lovers Cosima had enjoyed in the past. But lovemaking, while soothing, would not solve the problems that plagued her and grew larger in count by the day. Eventually, the bill would come due…even for Goddess's heir.

I am satisfied, Cosima ordered herself like a general barking orders at a subordinate. Her irritation at losing sleep had been assuaged by Iulia's caresses, though other wishes had yet to be abetted.

Would *never* be fulfilled.

Cosima smiled wanly down in response to her lover while her thoughts wandered a million miles away. *I'm too much like Her now. Will I stray closer to Her image the longer I live?*

"Still thinking too much?" Prompting her again, Iulia brushed a last kiss against Cosima's sex and reverently closed her legs. Then she hauled Cosima down by her hips to blow an irreverent raspberry on her bare stomach, loud enough to wake the baby sleeping in the flower.

Thankfully, they stirred but didn't fuss. Cosima had already stifled a laugh and shoved Iulia off her to rush and check the frost white chrysanthemum. Its petals unfurled at her approach to show the slumbering child wrapped in their red and gold wings. Behind her, Iulia slipped closer and wrapped her arms around her waist; willowy like Bettina, Cosima had to lean back to allow Iulia to rest her chin on her shoulder.

"I'm so tired it feels like my face is melting off my skull."

"Should I apologize for keeping you awake?"

"No. This little brat should, though." Turning, Cosima kissed Iulia's cheek and moved away to start preparing for when the babe would inevitably wake up. *Any minute now.*

"They're loveable enough." Iulia chided her. "And they've done no harm by staying with us."

Cosima chuffed an agreement as she scooped her hair—dark as Marzanna's but shot through with Bettina's sunny blonde—on top of her head and called a strip of leather to her hand to bind it. She knew from experience that Marzanna was a lax, inattentive mother…and that that was the best anyone could expect out of Fiammetta. Laziness, self-indulgence, and neglect was the better option compared to the other methods Aebbenary's queen had used in the past.

She and Iulia were quiet as they began to parallel the familiar rhythms of preparing for another day: cleansing in a basin of gathered rainwater routinely cleansed by Cosima's power, dressing in their ordinary garb suited for life spent predominately in nature, and other tasks. Today, though, Cosima paused over a set of diaphanous garments preserved in layers of paper in an oak chest carved with ivy-like patterns.

Watching as she lifted the gauzy lilac fabric and accompanying buttery yellow ribbon meant to secure the orchid-patterned wrap around her waist, Iulia sat back down on the edge of Cosima's bed and sighed at her silence. She never expected Cosima to talk when she didn't feel like it, but some questions begged for answers.

"It wouldn't kill their father to raise one of his own children. Besides, you said he seemed fond of them. Why didn't he offer?"

Thinking back to the audience Goddess had hosted to celebrate Bettina's return and announce her Jubilee, Cosima hesitated to reply. Iulia—and the other huntresses—wouldn't understand the strain everyone in Marzanna's orbit was under the closer they strayed into Her gravity. A portion of that fault belonged to Cosima herself for dreading conversations that provoked her emotions, but there was nothing to be done about that now.

Her camp had been burdened enough by the woes which had driven Cosima to their rescue in the first place.

"Mother wants Her companions fixated on Her for the near future. It doesn't seem like any of them expected Fiammetta and Däard to conceive at all."

"But to burden you with the child..."

Burden. Cosima didn't want to blame a helpless child—especially one encumbered with divinity—for the responsibility of their care, but there was no way around it. Fiammetta had dumped the child unfortunate enough to share no bloodline with Goddess on Her second born, second most rebellious daughter both to free herself from obligation and to tame Cosima.

Which was why Cosima was considering visiting the firstborn, most rebellious daughter of Goddess in the first place.

The baby stirred. Accepting that Cosima had nothing to say, Iulia scooped up the infant and cooed at them as she inexpertly hefted them over her shoulder to pat their back. Cosima dressed as quickly as she could, daubed her temples and wrists with a mixture of oily perfume smelling of florals and faint ylang ylang, and offered her arms for the babe before she lifted the thick curtain barring her portion of the treehouse community from the common area and joining the rest of her camp.

In the few minutes since dawn had broken like a quail's egg over the horizon, most of the women Cosima sheltered had emerged from their own quarters to break their fast. The scent of frying mushrooms and peppery eggs wafted past them.

Grisel is cooking, Cosima sniffed, hungry after the last couple of hours of lovemaking. Though all of them were hunters in the camp she had built, Grisel and a couple of the others never ate meat. After all, it wasn't only deer they hunted.

Helpfully, one of them—Palmira, the youngest—had tracked down a basin of fresh milk and a clean rag for the child to suck on. Guilt at her forgetfulness and unexpected shame at her unsuitable temperament for mothering made Cosima cringe beneath the smile she offered Palmira for thinking ahead. Divine children did not require mortal food for sustenance, but it comforted them most of the time and helped them build a routine, she belatedly remembered.

"Where are you going today?" Palmira asked; her eyes were on the baby, who started to whimper as they also realized they were hungry. Cosima gratefully passed her the child.

"When will you come back?" Ricla, another huntress, piped up from where she knelt by the cooking fire arranged by a casual Miracle from Cosima in the center of the room in a pit. "We—"

"Cosima, we have—"

"Peace, all of you!" Konetta stood from the common table to offer her seat to Iulia since she had already emptied her plate. Iulia thanked her with a pat on the back and helped herself to the bowl of warm seeded bread Grisel had painted with butter. "Not all of us relish mornings. Especially those who didn't do much sleeping during the night."

Easy laughter. Love and its acts hadn't been taboo to discuss since Goddess had reordered their world; though not every woman in Cosima's camp had a lover or loved women alone or at all, none of them begrudged the relationship she and Iulia enjoyed.

"Good morning." Cosima restricted herself to the two word greeting.

"Morning." Konetta beamed; she bumped her hip against Cosima's as she passed by to carry her empty plate and cup to the basin of soiled dishes further in the cooking area.

Mortals could not help being awed by and enamored of beings touched by the divine. As ichor ran through the veins of the chosen, humans flocked to worship and revere the bearers of Goddess's blessèd will. Cosima had to remind herself often that even these rare souls she had vowed to nurture and protect were not invulnerable to the aureole she had inherited from her Mother's Light, even if they had proven themselves resistant to the slavish admiration other divine spawn took advantage of.

Admiration others had begun to suspect wasn't…natural. Wasn't a right and just part of their world.

Iulia she could be sure of: she had welcomed Cosima's influence in her life, and she had sought her help to purchase or trick her way to freedom from a foreign slave galley, but she never needed it the way the others had. There was no disproportion of power to balance like the handle of a kitchen knife on the tip of her finger, fearing at any minute it would fall and cast blame on Cosima that she could never forgive.

"She's off to the marsh witch's nest," Iulia told the others for her.

"With the *baby?*" Palmira asked, aghast. The infant spluttered as she accidentally choked them with too much milk squeezed from the cloth. "Don't you think that's risky?"

"I'm going. I'll protect the baby, don't worry." Asking for trust still made Cosima uncomfortable. She took the plate one of the other women offered and stabbed her dull fork into the spicy eggs.

"Do you want company?" asked Konetta. Iulia held up a hand with two fingers raised to volunteer as she slurped milk sweetened with honey from a mug carved from the horn of one of Aebbenary's wandering sheep herds; Palmira must have bargained for enough milk for everyone.

Already shaking her head, Cosima ducked down to pretend to focus on eating. It was comfortable here, still, though she suffered quiet moments of agony trying to communicate. Only in Marzanna's court and with her family could she succeed in wearing the mien of confidence—even arrogance, which was more useful—long term.

After she ate, once the baby was secured to her back with help from Palmira—who, young as she was, had been a mother once—Cosima condensed their forms into shapes in the Light and began her swift journey over the island to reach the marsh.

Godlings could not fully experience aches and soreness from exertion, but Cosima still felt the languor in her extremities as a result of Iulia's tenacious attentions over the night. The pleasure had silenced her noisome thoughts and her worries, but under the early morning sun they returned one and all to occupy her as she traveled over the island.

Bettina had stolen away in a banishment she hadn't really bothered to explain to Cosima…they had had plenty of things to argue about before her departure. Opposite that flight, Sovanna had made a tactical retreat, which in Cosima's opinion had paid dividends. After years of silence from Marzanna's and Easoren's only offspring, Cosima intended to use her Goddess-given excuse of informing her cornucopia of half-siblings about her new status to venture into Sovanna's lair and remind her of the duties she had forsaken in the name of independence.

We can't all do what we want, Cosima thought for the hundredth time. *Not always. And not when it harms others.*

Sovanna's marsh had been born as a small patch of swamp past the north and to the west of the mountain that graced Aebbenary's holy city. Under her decade or so of care since her retreat, she had nurtured the marshes into a domain any deity would be proud of. As a bonus she had indubitably considered, her realm was far, *far* away from the capital and even as far as the other Godlings and Saints Marzanna had blessed by whim or bargain had claimed for themselves.

Cosima's thoughts wandered back to her own fiefdom: smallest and plainest, though Goddess had seen fit to name her heir for reasons Cosima dreaded. Populated by mortal women who had been broken—sometimes again and again—by their lives and even other divine beings who had not been taught care for those who could never compete with them. Whose lives were as ephemeral as mist.

What she and Iulia had could be called love without any falsehood. Godling or not, Cosima had had to work to earn Iulia's favor over the course of a few years; aside from their enthusiasm for hunting and the seclusion of their camp of chosen company, their natures were as opposite as summer flowers twisting to follow the sun and a brooding storm sweeping down from the mountain ranges.

Iulia was mortal and always would be. Konetta too. Every single one of the humans she had hauled from ditches where families had abandoned them or coaxed off the streets as children had been born with the hourglass of time already turned over for their existence. Every day that passed was the youngest they would ever be, while Cosima had nothing but unasked for and unearned time.

She understood that was the way of things…though it pained her more than she would ever share with a living soul.

Flawed as she was, as complicated as their relationship had to be in part because of mortal Cristoval, Bettina had taught Cosima well in some aspects. Mortals were worth *more* because their lives were so transient. Moments spent with them were gifts, albeit fleeting ones. Time would pass regardless of how much of it one had: it was up to Cosima what she made of her minutes and hours.

But Iulia. But Konetta—always ailing but ever fair, she of the lissome build and brown skin. Konetta who laughed the quickest to brighten any room, who nurtured all of them but never stifled, who looked upon Cosima with unreserved affection in her oak brown eyes.

Konetta—who Cosima would never allow herself to have.

Much of the day passed, even with Cosima and her infant cargo condensed into Light. By the time she sensed the aura and glimpsed the sheen of multifaceted wards shielding Sovanna's dominion from intrusion, the afternoon was well underway. Several more minutes ground by as Cosima scanned the wetlands for a suitable place to land, offer the squirming babe more food, and walk toward her ambiguous impression of where her quarry lived.

She had missed it earlier, but the child had cut several teeth overnight. Rejecting the jug of milk Cosima unstoppered to trickle past their rosy lips, they squalled until she offered them a strip of dried, salted venison to gnaw on. Meanwhile, the drone of insects roving through the overcast wetlands in a swarm hummed outside the thin bubble Cosima had expended power to cast for their protection.

Why make something so unpleasant worse? Why live in such a humid, remote land all alone? Cosima allowed her mind to wander as she hoisted the Saintling into a better position in her arms for looking around and began walking along ground that squelched under her shoes—though she'd dressed well for Sovanna's approval she had worn her high boots, elegance be damned—toward the distant shape of a rooftop.

In the water, crocodiles peered up from their lairs with their eyes aglow with Miraculous influence. Cosima would have been disappointed not to see them, or see anything that proved Sovanna was as full of empty bravura as the rest of Goddess's progeny. Gods and their children couldn't die, not properly, but more than rumor supported that awful things could be done to them as well. Even a secluded marsh inhabited by one solitary Godling shouldn't forgo any guardianship.

"Do you suppose she's named them?" Finding herself conversing with the baby as they peered through the haze at the wildlife, reeds, and long grass swaying in a humid breeze, Cosima bit her tongue to stop herself. In her arms, the child giggled.

Don't. She wanted to pick up the child by one ankle and shake them like a doll. *Don't bond with me, sweetling. I don't have anything to offer you.*

Sweetling. Bettina's endearment came readily to her tongue.

Regardless of how long Cosima walked, the sun never moved from its position in the heavens…and the house at the end of the misty path never got closer. As a Godling, she didn't need to carry weapons on her person in the visible dimension, though she used mortal arms to share her hunting gifts with the women in her camp. Now, her right hand itched for her spear. For the brush of an arrow's fletching against her cheek as she drew back with her considerable strength to bring down a worthy trophy.

"Sister."

The voice came from behind; Cosima didn't smile. "Sister. Were you ever planning to come back?"

"No." Sovanna smiled when she turned to face her, and oh, was it a thing to behold. "Is there anything new there to tempt me? Or only more of the same from the Shining Court?"

Marzanna's dark beauty and Easoren's silvered charisma had joined to conceive a marvelous being in Sovanna. In a world ordered by Light and gold, the vestiges of conquered Silver remained in her appearance: white streaking her black hair, skin marked here and there with silver freckles, nails naturally tipped in the same. Ordinary markers of her genetics had revealed themselves as she'd aged as well: Marzanna's compelling brows, Easoren's gray, deep-set eyes, lips that so easily performed contempt from both of them.

The antler-horns—neither one nor the other—protruding from either side of her head that marked the contribution of the beast form her father had been shifting in and out of at the moment of her conception. Cosima was brave, was arrogant, but even she had never dared to ask if Sovanna—or Goddess—had ever tried to remove them.

"Only that I've been chosen as Mother's heir."

"I see. And you've come all this way to tell me I'm second best? Perhaps third, or fifth? Seventh?" Though she was vain—as the pristine use of cosmetic shadows and gloss and the moss-green dyed ends of her tousled curls proved—Sovanna revealed no dismay at her news. Like she had expected the tidings for longer than anyone could guess.

"You might have settled higher in the hierarchy if you had endured life in Aebbenary a little longer." Cosima winced as she laughed, sweet and clear like an unclouded sky contrary to the gloom that filled the swamp. In this way Sovanna was nothing like either of her parents: there was no complacent triumph in her bearing, no unwelcome edge to her smiles that cut others even in her joy.

"Enough sparring. Cosima—is that *your* baby?"

Might as well be. Cosima puffed an irritated sigh. At that moment, the child swallowed the last of the jerky she'd given them and began to squirm until she repositioned them so they could flare their wings and then blanket themselves in their own feathers. Like other babies, their favorite time to sleep was during the day.

"Fiammetta's."

Sovanna's mouth formed a *moue.* "Another one? Don't her and Mother—"

"Not Goddess. Her and Däard."

"Why do you have their baby?" Interest brought Sovanna's hands together in a steeple under her slightly pointed chin. "Did you steal it?"

The baby wriggled, kicking Cosima's ribs. She struggled for a moment with the wrap to shift it to the front of her body, gave up after her frustration built and the baby began to cry in earnest, and helplessly cradled the child in her arms to rock them. An unlooked for blessing, they settled at once and began to toy with one end of the ribbon securing her dress to her body.

"No," Sovanna thought aloud. "That's not something you'd steal. Even though we both know that court is no place for an infant."

She understands. Relief weakened Cosima's knees before she recovered her firm stance. No, not relief—it was the mucky ground beneath her feet shifting as Sovanna used her power to command it. The mud hardened into a sturdier path; a short distance away, the house appeared through the mist as the irritating bugs that had annoyed her the whole journey here flew away.

"You'd better come inside. Just for now." Sovanna gestured a curled forefinger and led the way to her front door.

The cottage was normal enough at first look, except for the fact that it was too spacious and well-maintained for what had probably once been a hermit's rundown shack. Rotting wood had been replaced with stone overtaken by kudzu vines and creeping moss tinted shades of green, brown, and sometimes indigo. Contrasting the rest, pallid lilies emerged through the greenery no matter where Cosima looked. Though the earthy stench of the marsh lingered up to the front door, the lilies and their leaves *breathed* with a faint aura of Sovanna's power that filled the air with scents of pure spring.

The three of them proceeded through the overgrown garden of vegetables and scattered herbs surrounding the cottage. Letting herself in first, Sovanna barely remembered to prop open the door for Cosima and the child before it slammed in their faces. Though there were few visible windows from the outside, several lined the walls to allow the eternal twilight of the swamp to permeate the common area and kitchen.

The world outside seemed bigger in the space of the cozy home Marzanna's eldest had made for herself. Cosima no longer wondered quite so incredulously how Sovanna hadn't gone entirely mad from the seclusion she had chosen.

Without more than a glance, one of the windows creaked open to allow a pair of lilies to grow through the gap. Something began to bubble in a pot hanging in the hearth as Sovanna approached it; the lilies twined together, twisting and curling until they formed an approximate bassinet, like what Cosima had made with the bearded chrysanthemum back at the treehouse.

Grateful—and hopeful—she laid the infant down in the hollow dip of obliging lilies and watched as the petals transformed from white into the same red that tipped the baby's wings on contact with their soft skin. Sovanna whispered a suggestion for Cosima to join her at her table to talk while the infant rested; she obliged, and took the cup slid to her from across the polished wood.

The cup was filled with blood. Revolted, Cosima tilted the liquid this way and that, watching the crimson stain the gray pottery.

"It's not what you think." If Sovanna had been testing her, she had failed. "I've cultivated an array of herbs for tea and convinced the marsh bees to bring me others to make this brew. It's a little unappealing, but you'll like it."

Since it would be rude to refuse, Cosima set her jaw and took a gulp of the tea. Though she hadn't trusted it the flavor was unforgettable and piquant the way early mead tasted. It took more resolve to get past the texture—thick like cream and oddly grainy—but her impression was pleasant.

"The fun part is that it tastes different every time I brew it. What do you taste?"

"Chocolate, strangely. And…lavender. And—" Cosima sipped again. "Malt?"

Sovanna nodded; her eyes dipped down to her own clay cup—most likely formed by her inexpert skill before she'd crafted the rest of her pottery by hand—like she wanted to brood awhile over its contents in silence.

Cosima didn't feel any sympathy over her awkwardness: she must have had plenty of time to ruminate alone since she'd left the city years ago.

"Sister—"

Cutting her off with an uplifted hand poised in elegant command, Sovanna frowned.

"I'll start. Do you think I can't guess why you've come? No one from that lion's den does anything without promise of gain. You want me to relieve you of the queen's child."

She should have been put out, but Cosima was only grateful. It was always easier for her to speak plainly rather than dance around a difficult subject. Even her huntresses didn't always remember that.

"I have no room in my life for a baby. I'm sure it won't be long before they come into their power and you can—"

"No. I'm afraid there is no "me" here. Whether it is one day or three years or three hundred before the child matures, I want no part in raising them. You'll have to make room."

Cosima had known she could be punished for disobedience by leaving the baby with Sovanna to raise. She had risked Goddess's—and Fiammetta's—ire to do it anyway; it wasn't unreasonable to bet on her Mother's goodwill in naming her as heir trumping whatever transgression she plotted. A slap on the wrist was worth the freedom she was accustomed to…and the mental well-being of her huntresses.

Somehow, she had never imagined Sovanna would deny her.

"Make room?" *I never wanted this. This is a torment for more than just me.* Cosima reminded herself that the fault for this lay with others, not Sovanna, as she tried to wipe her scowl off her face. A sour look, Bettina had often chided her, produced less results than a sweet one. "I would, but the child isn't going to thrive in a treehouse with different people coming and going and no one to remain a constant in their life."

"A camp full of women isn't good for an infant? With so many to rock and soothe and entertain them?"

How can she miss the point so badly? Cosima chugged her tea, scalding her throat as her own temper heated her halo and affected the temperature of the brew; she tried not to slam the cup down on the table. *I can ask this of you as a divine sibling, but for them to waste their time?*

"*Fiammetta's* child. The woman directly responsible for the circumstances in which most of them suffered. Can't you see why I—we—don't want this particular baby around?"

"As opposed to the other imps you commonly host in your quaint little treehouse."

"That's—you're—you left! How can you speculate on my life? You live alone, out here away from everyone, almost like you're free. Would it inconvenience you so greatly to do me this favor, since you call me "sister" like it's supposed to mean something?"

Sovanna weathered her outburst with one refined brow arched. As Cosima rambled she leaned back in her chair as gracefully as if it was the throne she hadn't been chosen to inherit from Goddess. Instantly, Cosima regretted how much she had revealed.

"*Do* I seem free? Does it seem like the solitude I have chosen—that, believe me, I have *earned*—begs obligation on my end to mitigate your woes? You've made your world, Cosima, with your mortal waifs and your greenery. I know well the reason you keep that life separate from the rest of them. Me, though…" Standing, Sovanna drifted with dreamy lack of haste to one of her overladen tables, shifting stacks of clutter that curiously lacked a layer of dust or mildew from one side to the other. "I don't think you understand why *I* had to leave."

"How could I? You never bothered to explain to anyone."

"*You* never bothered to seek me out until now. Though we are closest in age you haven't addressed me as sister our whole lives until today. Do you think it's fair to demand explanations from me now, much too late? To call me "sister" and try to manipulate me to take that bitch's child just so you can return to your mortal girl's arms and forget about the rest of the world?"

Imperious, proud Sovanna had never looked more like her sire than now. Yet they were both Marzanna's daughters, and Cosima's own ego roused at the accusations thrown her way.

"As you wish, then. Stay here and rot in your loneliness."

"Better loneliness than regret."

Frustrated, Cosima stood and moved to pick up the bundle of wings and wriggling arms from the makeshift bassinet. "I thought you had gone away for better reasons. I thought you'd want to have a hand in the future of Aebbenary. Oh well—this is not the first time I've been mistaken."

Cocking her head to the side, Sovanna's superior aura dimmed. "Better reasons? Compared to whom?" The answer occurred to her. "Bettina. You're right—you are often mistaken. I think if you had talked to your mother years ago—as you should have with me—you would know the exact reasons why we both left. Maybe I'm not here to idle, but to plan."

Guilt was no stranger for Cosima. It settled on its comfortable perch in her chest and began to sing as she avoided Sovanna's insightful gaze.

For lack of something else to do besides match glares like swords with her, Cosima fiddled with the ribbon looped around her waist to secure it and stood to approach the twin lily cradle to pick up the baby. They had woken up during the heat of the argument; with two fingers stuffed in their toothy mouth, they looked up at the mossy ceiling as more flowers began to bloom and drip their scented pollen as a gift to the child.

"You don't have to rush back. I wasn't going to evict you for bad manners. And the child—"

"—needs to go home if you'll not host them here permanently." Listening as the infant gabbled something with their eyes glowing pinkish-red, Cosima pretended to understand as she wrestled the uncooperative wings into allowing her to get a proper grip on the baby's body.

"Is it really so onerous? Motherhood?"

Cosima glanced down at the babe she held under both arms and then back up at Sovanna…then back down at the child once more. Just before either of them had been born, Goddess had done away with the rule women had to serve as only wife and mother. Opportunities—for the most part—had opened up whereas before only servitude to men had been viable options for security in life. As if the baby had known, somehow, they had yet to reveal their gender if they had one at all.

Your parents didn't trouble themselves with a name for you, Cosima thought; it occurred to her that this was the first time she had intentionally addressed the babe at all, even in her head. *How could they do that? How could they make someone innocent, who didn't ask to be born, and then abandon you?*

"It's…" She had no words to explain—as often happened when she suffered the unpleasant liability of her own emotions—but Cosima tried. "It's work. I still think another surrogate mother would be better for everyone. But I'm getting used to it."

Both of them were silent as she prepared to leave. Sovanna had given her the perfect opening to ask why she'd left, why she'd built this marsh and guarded it well, but Cosima was too proud to take it. Yet, from the corners of her eyes she watched as Sovanna fidgeted at her table and slapped away a trespassing liana dangling over her antler-horns; would she be too proud to share anyway?

They were sisters, after all. Ones who could have been as close as the lilies that had surrendered their independence of one another to make a bed for the Saintling. Even if they both preferred to forsake the bond of sharing the same Mother most of the time.

"I won't promise to come back. Lonely or not, it's been…better here, for me. Mother can't harass me. Father can't use me. And the others…"

"Goddess ordered me to report Her choice of me as successor to everyone. I started with you." Cosima didn't have to add that she understood. Though the holy court was perilous, in some ways it failed to compete with the petty brood of vipers all the offspring of Goddess and the array of Saints She had appointed over the years since Her Ascension.

Groaning in sympathy, Sovanna decided the bitterness between them had been resolved for the moment.

"I won't take the child—and you were wrong to ask me to—but I never said I wouldn't help. I know the journey takes time, but I…

maybe I would like to visit the little one again. Soon, perhaps. If my studies allow."

Judging by the ominous state of the marsh she'd grown by hand, Cosima stifled a wince and decided she didn't want to ask what Sovanna was studying.

She offered the information freely. "I'm on the verge of something important, Cosima. Silver erased much of the history before his era, so we as divine beings are basically new. I have asked myself...what could help us discover what we are? What few things can harm us, if anything exists in this world that can bleed life and power from gods and Saints? And...what effect does our presence have on mortal things?"

Cristoval had spoken of similar questions a long time ago. Cosima, the younger of their pair, had dangled on his every word like he'd been the one to hang the stars in the sky. His interest in the world had outstripped her own even then...and while she had listened, she hadn't understood. Not until she was older.

An answer Cosima had been hunting for began to dawn in her mind. As she held the child and rocked them on her hip while they tangled their chubby fingers in the ends of her hair, she fought the awful realization for fear she would never be able to face it.

No. That can't be why they all worship...

Before she walked out, Cosima hesitated as she faced it and counted the nails binding the planks together.

"Lilias."

"Hm?" Sovanna had already turned away; Cosima's drained cup dangled by its handle around one of her fingers.

"The Saintling. Fiammetta forgot to name them."

A hint of a singular dimple on her left cheek brightened Sovanna's melancholy looks. "Oh. My lilies inspired you?"

Cosima shrugged; the baby—Lilias—cooed and unexpectedly flared their wings out to their full span on her back. They'd grown bigger, too, as if the choice of a name had brought them one step closer to expressing their divinity. This time she caught herself halfway into a smile before she smothered it.

"Lilias. I like it." Sovanna had no reservations: her smile, when she offered it, was genuine.

VI

Bettina

Bettina's parents hadn't raised her to be brave. They had prepared her to be beautiful and charming; by their indifference and erratic punishments they had instilled in her only surface virtues. It had been completely up to Bettina after her Ascent to Sainthood to decide what kind of person she wanted to be.

It had been four days since she had made her bargain with Magisend. She had yet to return to the Archives.

The thought of forcing herself to cross the city to the University, descend past the Scholar's Grave, and endure the creeping dread watching the specters cataloguing the Archives again made her pace the confines of her tranquil estate. For the first time since Marzanna had chosen her, Bettina felt undertones of pain and suffering rippling through her blessed body. Staring obsessively in the mirror of her vanity showed nothing had changed on the outside, but she could feel the decay the Grand Archivist had wrought by sucking ichor from her veins with his insubstantial body.

So, though she recovered after resting for two days, Bettina dawdled in her forsaken home and fretted over what she should do.

I'm no good to anyone maimed or as dead as a Saint can manage. Cristoval needs me…and Cosima would miss me, I think, after a century or so, she thought as she paced the hedge maze Däard had once chased her, Fiammetta, and Marzanna through.

The energy of the city was still in the process of embracing her return according to Goddess's will. Whenever she treaded upon earth instead of stone, tiny white flowers followed in her wake. When she trailed her indolent fingertips against the fuzzy leaves of the maze hedges, lilies with yellow pollen in their throats blossomed and sang a few pure notes before they retreated back into the bushes to wither without her continued attention.

Bettina had expected this. She had *counted* on it, even as long ago as when she had left Aebbenary.

You may think you are ready for me, Goddess, but I'd wager You're not. I think as high as You sit on Your peerless throne You have forgotten what it means to be desperate.

What could soften a heart—even a divine one—better than absence? What else could whet an appetite into passion but careful, studied denial administered with the refined lure of temptation?

I will give all of myself, Marzanna—to You or the Archivist. Whoever will spare my son first.

Troubled by the persistent torpor of sun-drowned indulgence that wrapped the city, Bettina made the journey through the streets to the Holy Tower as essence compressed into Light. She couldn't help but see the things she wished she didn't as she travelled from her estate to Goddess's home.

Everything is the same, Bettina thought, *yet nothing is. I shouldn't be able to liken Goddess's rule to Silver's. She promised things would be different.*

Things *were* different. Just not necessarily for the better—not when Marzanna had carved a place from the old cathedral for Herself and Her darlings, set Her eternal progeny loose on the mortal realm, and absolved Herself of all responsibility for the power She had, somehow, earned.

You've come to visit, Bettina?

Goddess's voice in her mind startled her, though she had expected it. Bettina stood at the round base of the tower and looked up to where Marzanna's Light had vaulted it so high into the heavens its crown was out of even a Saint's sight.

Yes, Your Glory. Will You see me?

Of course.

The doors swung inward with a *whoosh* of air losing pressure. Cool air flowed from down the stairs into Bettina's face, as soothing as the sea breeze she already missed. The moment her foot ascended the first stair, she realized she was not alone. Something—someone—had been waiting for her arrival for a very, *very* long time. Not only that: it shielded its presence from Goddess with power she didn't recognize as a product of golden Light.

Now who are you? Curiosity enticed Bettina to wander. There was nothing to follow, nary a shadow, but the magic playing on the edges of her awareness—beyond the scope of all her senses—might lead her somewhere if she deigned to follow.

Instead, she ignored it. Obeying the whisper of wind caressing the strands of her hair, she followed Goddess's welcome all the way to the top of the tower on legs that didn't tire and a heart that pumped true and constant up more stairs than a mortal could bear.

Whatever it was, it followed only so far as the forest green and rose quartz tiles of the portico instead of venturing into the throne room through the single door barring the tower stairs from Goddess's domain. Bettina gave nothing but her peripheral attention to the watcher as she lifted her skirts, which were still from her own era and heavy with brocade compared to the barely-there fabrics preferred by the Shining Court and its clingers. She had a suspicion who the being might be…but whoever it was, or whoever had sent it, it could chance nothing in Goddess's presence.

Sheltered by obedient clouds that floated in place of a ceiling, the sacred pleasure garden that had replaced the High Priest's sanctuary from the false god's time appeared much the same as when Bettina had last visited. Its size matched whatever mood Goddess felt each day. It could sprawl farther whenever the clouds conformed to Her desire.

Today, the green lawn where Godlings and Saints amused each other and the dipping pond were empty and diminished. The portico dappled by sun allowed in by the clouds was the only place to go.

Alone, Goddess studied bejeweled pieces on a game board She had invented, playing against Herself as She waited for Bettina's arrival. She didn't look up as She lifted one elegant hand sporting nails painted exotic indigo in greeting. Though She was a picture of luxury untouched by even a nightmare of earthly toil, with Her feet slippered in silk and her dressing gown voluminous around Her slight body, Her shoulders were stiff with tension Bettina knew she was responsible for.

Guilt set in. Rejecting it, she shook her head slightly to make her pearl drop earrings dance.

"Where are the others?"

"Around. Däard has gone flying. Fiammetta is sailing with a favorite."

It was known by all that no others could sink deeper roots within Goddess's heart than those two. When Bettina had been courted and chosen by Marzanna as a lover almost but not quite on par with Fiammetta and Däard, even she—jealous as she could be—had not minded their preferred status. They had welcomed her with open arms and fervent kisses, after all, which could addle anyone's brain.

They had all been eager to please Goddess then. Years later, after dozens of paramours had come and gone, she wondered if either of them minded Marzanna's voracious taste for range and novelty. Bettina had been different to a degree…but how much?

How much generosity can I expect? That was the question that mattered most as she approached the couch Marzanna had waved her toward without lifting Her eyes from the gaming table. Beyond Her, Bettina glimpsed the flash of a bare ankle and heard the din of several attendants departing to leave the two of them alone as long as Goddess required. This encouraged her, though she stifled her satisfaction in favor of her contrived appearance of feminine delicacy and hesitation. As if nothing made her more afraid than disturbing Marzanna's relaxation.

You still can't abide solitude. That's good.

"Thank You for seeing me, Your Glory." Bettina infused her voice with a perfect balance of mischief to invite banter. *Come, play with me. I will remind You what it was like to frolic with me.*

"I've been waiting for you." Marzanna watched Bettina curtsy and sink into the chaise lounge across the polished table balanced on seven thin legs intertwined with yet more flowers. "The only game I enjoy at present is this one, Bett. Won't you tell me why you left Aebbenary?"

How can You not know? Bettina squeezed her heart with a mental hand and lounged with her elbow propped on the cushion beside her; a flick of her eyes up at Marzanna, then back down at the crystal figures on the board completed the impression she wanted to make. Risking impertinence, she called one of the pieces to her hand and weighed it in her palm. The nature of the game was complex, but ultimately it involved sacrificing pieces to claim territory. Not too many, though, and not without balancing the talents of the beast each piece resembled.

The one Bettina held was a coral horse. At her touch its mane and tail began to flow like living stone, but a drop of power from her banished its uncanny movement.

"Even Saints grow bored, Goddess."

"Marzanna. Goddess from you sounds too impartial."

Setting the horse back in its place on the board, Bettina inclined her head in acknowledgment. "I confess I've saved a little room for shame for the way we parted."

A gleam exposed Her notice even in Her aureole; Marzanna mirrored Bettina's posture, a favorite trick Bettina had paradoxically taught and learned from Her during their first courtship.

"Why is that?" Goddess slid an aventurine dragon around the left sphere of the board about three squares, circling her yellow jade leopard.

"I wasn't entirely honest with You." Bettina shied away from the dragon with her leopard and dropped two pearls from the fingerbowl next to the board into the chalice in the middle as a sacrifice for the move.

"You and your secrets. I thought you'd told Me all those."

I did. While waiting for Marzanna's next play, Bettina swiped one of the pieces whatever Saint playing before her had lost into her hand. Beady, black onyx eyes winked back at her from their setting in the longhorn bull's face carved from polished rhodonite webbed with pink.

Remembering the way the Grand Archivist had grown his eyes, she felt her stomach turn; she set the piece back down.

"Our lives are long, Your Glory. Maybe I wanted to find new secrets to keep from You—like a dragon hoarding treasure. Maybe I wanted to find dragons for myself."

"Did you?"

Bettina laughed. "Unless you Made dragons for me to find, then no, Your Glory. I had to return to Your side to find wonder again."

Though She had protested the title of "Goddess" from her, Marzanna didn't dispute the dutiful "Your Glory"ies Bettina spent like coin to buy frivolous trinkets. Considering both the placement of the leopard and a selenite dog on Her curve of the board, She summoned three sacrificial stones from Her bowl and let them drop one by one as She claimed the leopard with Her dragon, evaded a forthcoming attack She anticipated from an ebony goat on Bettina's front line, and brought down the coral horse she had been counting on to unseat Marzanna's most threatening pieces.

After that the dragon would be out of play, but the game was won. Goddess had spent too many hours on this game to lose it easily, and the Saint playing before Bettina had been cowardly enough to throw the game before her arrival.

"Then why leave? Why make Me all but force you to return?" Goddess said once She had won.

"I was ashamed. How could I face You again after how I left? You had been merciful enough to allow my sulking to last longer than a heartbeat. It took time to ready myself to beg for Your lenience in enduring my presence once more, if only to apologize for my sins."

"You feared Me?" Marzanna said it like the concept was unfathomable. Like it had never, ever occurred to Her that Bettina could doubt Her steadfastness after the way She had first refused her plea to save Cristoval.

Ducking her head to conceal her trepidation, Bettina nodded. "Only when I came back did I remember the depth and breadth of Your regard for me. It's taken me this long still to brave approaching You...for I have missed You, Your Glory. With all my soul."

Divinity had uplifted Marzanna's compelling features into blinding splendor. When she looked up, Bettina caught her breath at the engulfing pools of gilded amber that were Goddess's eyes. Enhanced by scarlet liner, Her pale skin looked as smooth as glass.

"I have missed you too. Would you like the chance to atone for making Me wait to embrace you again?"

"*Yes*. Please tell me how to regain Your esteem." Sliding from the chair to her knees, she gripped the edge of the gaming table with both hands and rested her chin on the corner as she looked up at Marzanna with tears beginning to flow down her flushed cheeks. Lowering a hand to gently, dotingly cup her chin, Goddess tilted it up to the threshold of pain to gaze down at Bettina.

"Our daughter's Jubilee will be a celebration for the ages—I have seen to it. Disinclined or not, Cosima will be as honored as she deserves as the chosen one among My children. I did this for *you*, My contrary Swan. Would you like to know why?"

Bettina had forgotten—Marzanna loved to hear her say "please."

"Yes, Your Glory. Please tell me."

"In twelve days, when I grant Cosima her position by scepter and crown, I will formally welcome you into My court. Given your absence, you have until midnight on that propitious day to convince Me you are worthy of a place at My side for eternity along with Fiammetta and Däard. Do you accept?"

One dozen days. Not even a fortnight to accomplish her conquest of Marzanna's changeable heart and bend it to her will.

Bettina smiled as if this was the best tidings she had received since those of her arranged husband's death. "As You wish. By Cosima's Jubilee You will see what I am willing to do to earn Your love again."

Though she wasn't willing to heed its allure, anticipation electrified Bettina from heel to heart as Marzanna leaned in to sweep Her warm lips over her forehead in a chaste kiss. The gilded freckles She had marked Bettina with burned with Light—only for a moment, but one that sent the same heat spiraling down to her core. Desire pulsed there, in tune with Goddess's heartbeat rather than Bettina's own.

Not long after, Marzanna allowed her to take her leave. Though she was distracted, Bettina sensed the presence that had followed her return the moment the door shut behind her and she began to descend the tower stairs. It didn't linger, but the cold brilliance of its aura made frost accumulate at the corners of her mouth and on her lashes.

The message was enough: Bettina would have to confront this being, and soon. The price of delay would be steep—more than she, already compromised by this bargain and that, could afford.

When she left the tower, she allowed her qualms and reserves to reconcile and disperse under Aebbenary's frolicsome sunlight. Marzanna had snapped at her bait, at least in part. If She wanted Bettina badly enough to let anticipation between them build rather than simply taking her, if She was offering a way for her to keep her pride by earning her way back into Marzanna's good graces rather than accepting charity...perhaps there was hope.

Before she could make her way home or wherever she would go, the aventurine dragon materialized in Bettina's hands as she cupped them together, sensing the approach of the gift. It lived, briefly, twining its lithe body between her fingertips and up her left arm before it settled into a forearm band and stopped moving. The rain that had threatened outside Marzanna's portico of sun above Aebbenary transformed in a sphere around Bettina as she looked up at the sky to watch petals the same blue as her eyes fall down.

I look forward to unlocking your secrets again, dearest. One by one.

Goddess was wooing her all over again. It was so easy—too easy—for Bettina to melt back into Her favor. She wanted to scoop the raining petals into her arms and kneel on the muddy streets to weep her gratitude to the empty heavens.

She had been mistaken—*this* was the more dangerous path. Compared to withstanding Goddess's goodwill, only the Archives held the key to help her buy Cristoval's immortality. Only Magisend could help her save her son before she paid for rapture in Marzanna's arms with his life.

VII

Cosima

Returning to the treehouse by nightfall with her spirits slightly improved if not entirely lifted, the sight that greeted Cosima after climbing the ladder leading inside almost made her drop Lilias. Before the infant could knock their head on the mossy carpet of the treehouse floor, they flared their wings by instinct to soften their fall. Their eyes had transformed to hazel by now—like Däard's.

"What are you doing here?" Without looking up, Cosima knelt by the baby to sit them up. Over the journey home they had grown larger, developed another stage.

Maybe Fiammetta was right about the child expressing their divinity soon, she thought.

Laughing, Cristoval sidestepped Lilias—who cooed as he passed and flung a hand out to snatch the corner of his cloak—and lugged Cosima up into an embrace. His scent enveloped Cosima: mortal sweat, but also something rich like myrrh and the leather fastenings of his brown gambeson vest and the linen of his shirt beneath it.

"I knew you wouldn't be in the city if you could help it. Da and I claimed horses and braved the plains to find your camp so I could introduce you. Your ladies were kind enough to—"

"Not ladies." One of the women loitering in the common area interrupted to insist. "Huntresses."

"And the best ones I've ever seen. Damn near peppered us with arrows before we even strayed into the torchlight!"

Cosima rolled her eyes and extricated herself from Cristoval's wiry arms in time to see him do the same. Perched on a footstool in the corner of the room—as much as a round treehouse could boast any corners—Cristoval's father kicked a booted heel against one of the rungs and nursed a cup of licorice wine they could all smell was not much watered down.

"They're not torches. They're Miracles made by—"

"You shouldn't be here. Either of you, but *especially* you." Indicating Cristoval's father with a jerk of her head, Cosima waved her other hand at the nearest huntress—Grisel—to lead him and the huntress who couldn't resist correcting him off somewhere so she and Cristoval could talk.

They were similar, father and son. Brown hair that curled, though now the minstrel who had wooed Bettina was in his early fifties the hairline had receded somewhat and there were more grey strands than brown. Strong, handsome features that were more delicate in Cristoval but promised the same rugged bearing as age collected his years. Both were tall, but Cristoval had the Valusius height that put him just above level with Cosima.

Once they were alone, Cosima glanced down at Lilias and watched them cautiously roll onto their stomach to begin crawling for the first time. The sight might have been tear-inducing for a real mother, but all she felt was a disconcerting insistence that something was wrong with the baby that she couldn't yet parse.

"Mama didn't want to tell me you were searching for him, but I guessed. If you care about him, why bring him here? Did you come here for my protection? Not that I—" Cosima had idolized Cristoval, her older brother, once upon a time. Mellow by nature, he had always tolerated—even encouraged—the chatter she rarely indulged in around others.

Now, though, she caught herself doing it and snipped the words short to give him a chance to talk.

"This is just a visit. Once we beg a night's stay with you, we'll return to Aebbenary to take lodgings with mother. She sent word of her return, but she didn't say why. Do you know?"

"Goddess summoned."

"She summoned me too—a mandate on the winds of Ioggenica just before I left the continent with Da."

Displeasure soured any joy Cosima felt over seeing her brother again. Disappointment in herself nipped at its heels: before he'd left Aebbenary, she had wrested all of her Miraculous power into both hands and attempted to cast a protection spell over Cristoval that would prevent anyone, even Goddess, from finding him. From using him as Cosima was already being used.

It hadn't done any good. On his own, willingly, Cristoval had returned. Whether it was destiny or Goddess's far-reaching will that had drawn him back, he was here now. Cosima would simply have to try more diligently to protect him.

"From what she told me the rift between her and Goddess could never be mended. I wonder if she's decided to give Her another chance." This he said as if he was thinking aloud; puzzling through the mystery that was Bettina and Marzanna in a way Cosima had already given up on years ago.

Cosima loved her brother. She revered him and envied his good nature and stout heart. She had been covetous of the protective affection Bettina had bestowed on him throughout their childhoods. But the source of the rift in their families had been and always would be Cristoval's mortality.

"Goddess doesn't care about you. She might not have done anything if you'd stayed away. And why in oblivion would you bring *him* here? Don't you know how jealous Marzanna can be?"

Cristoval shrugged. "He's getting old. He was born here, so he wanted to visit Aebbenary at least once more before we leave—and I wanted to see you and mother again. I couldn't dissuade him when it was my heart's wish as well."

"Leave." A leaden, awful word. Swallowing her undesirable sentiments, Cosima turned and clenched her fingers around a scratchy woven blanket one of the huntresses had already knitted for Lilias hanging from a wooden rack. But Cristoval had always been sensitive to her tempers; his arms slid around her shoulders from behind, embracing without stifling.

"I never had a place here. I never will…and it's been some time since I thought I wanted one. Now I've found my father, I have someone like me to care for. It's no bad thing to make do with what you have and build a life from that," he said.

The dilemma that was Cristoval was this, according to both Bettina and Cosima: they loved him enough to never want to lose him for the entirety of their eternal lives, but they didn't accept him enough to let him enjoy the life he had been granted—like every other mortal—in peace.

Well, Bettina didn't: Cosima knew Goddess well by now. If there was anything they could do to convince Her to raise Cristoval from mortality into the Shining Court, they would not be able to think of it in his lifetime. He was a walking reminder of Silver's era and Her precious Bett's former life. While Marzanna was free with Her own heart, She could not fool Cosima when it came to Her possessive nature.

None of that had affected Cosima until now…when she felt, with foreboding that smacked uncomfortably of prophecy, it would be a problem sooner rather than later.

Cristoval let her go and moved away to sit on the floor with Lilias. Rather than crawl to his open arms, the baby sat up again and examined their fingers and toes with intense concentration.

"I heard Goddess appointed you as Her successor. Did you think I would miss your Jubilee? I think you could do wonders for Aebbenary—for the world."

"I'll never have the chance, Cristoval. Mother is immortal."

How easily mortals—even her brother, raised by Saints and Godlings—forgot the infinite time belonging to those decay would never touch.

"Right." His concession was soft, almost muted; then Cristoval recovered and smiled so his blue eyes crinkled. Cosima hunted anxiously for lines and wrinkles even though he was only twenty-seven or so—the years blurred—and none should yet be apparent. "I still wouldn't miss it. Not for the world I'm going to see."

Though the most apparent feature on him was his handsome looks and his youth, Cosima sensed his growing discomfort with these dire topics. She stepped easily back into the role of comforter and protector, almost puffing out a withheld breath in relief at the routine of it.

"What's Crespin like? Is he what you imagined?" Bending at the waist, Cosima called Lilias's body to her with power and caught them from behind. They fussed at first, squirming and flailing all their limbs out to batter her when she turned them around, but when she propped the baby on her hip they settled down.

"I can see how he charmed mother, but he's no paragon of fatherhood. He likes to drink; he likes to amuse himself in poor company. But his heart is good, and he's kind." Laughing again, Cristoval offered once again to take Lilias; this time they took him up on his offer and leaned into his arms. Satisfied, Cosima went to fetch water from a nearby pitcher for herself and the child as she listened to Cristoval's answer. "She was right about him not being able to sing, though. If he offers to sing poems for your huntresses see that they gracefully decline if they want to protect their ears."

He went on about his journeys through the extensive continent of Ioggenica following word of his father with prompting from her as she passed around cups of water from the Miracle-blessed pitcher and scrounged their storage closet for victuals no one would be obligated to cook. Her huntresses would be able to fend for themselves for an evening, since it had been a few years since Cosima had seen her brother at all.

Though worries and her conversation with Sovanna eddied in her mind, Cosima did her best to enjoy both the reprieve from Lilias—who had suddenly learned to drink from a cup and accept solid food—and her brother's companionship. When morning came, he and his father would be off to Bettina's…and she would be forced to return to Aebbenary to stake her claim on the scepter no one wanted less than her.

With or without Cristoval, Cosima had a job to do. Her world—as wide and unrestrained as she had been able to make it on this island without leaving the women who depended on her behind—had shrunk down to two directives: raise Lilias, somehow, and inform her perfidious half-siblings of Goddess's decision to overturn their ambitions to succeed Her as heir.

They would know by now. It wasn't really a matter of letting them know by formal announcement. This was yet another test of resolve from Goddess for Cosima: make her siblings fall in line, crush their rebellions in advance, and earn the scepter Marzanna would pass to her for a symbolic role she had never fucking asked for.

Cosima was tempted to refuse out of unadulterated spite. It would feel incredible to disavow the treacherous Shining Court and leave the Bright Age to those who cared about it. All she needed to vanish into the horizon was a way to keep her huntresses safe for the length of their lives. She had taught them woodcraft, weaponry, and survival skills, and they had taken the name of the hunt because she had hunted down those who had hurt them with her presence as security to avenge themselves however they wanted...but none of that was enough.

They had no protection from other divine beings and their whims but her.

For as long as they lived—from strong Iulia to sweet Konetta down to young Palmira, who had already lived through worse days than most inhabitants of Marzanna's Aebbenary—Cosima could not shrug off her responsibilities and leave.

Lilias mattered too, now. And Cristoval's life would be as short as the huntresses if Bettina didn't scheme her way into thieving him of his mortality. And Sovanna. All these weights threatened to break

Cosima's back as she steeled herself against the whispers of rebellion stirring in her own breast.

It was Konetta's idea—encouraged strongly by Iulia, who loved strategizing—to send invitations to all the concerned siblings to gather in the park for Cosima's announcement. Many if not all of them would already be there: idlers to a man, even if they had claimed territory throughout the island and Ioggenica and squabbled over it incessantly, none of them had ever tried living outside Goddess's realm for longer than a quarter year.

Their meddlesome, quarrelsome spirits would tempt them to the park, but by doing so they would be stooping to answer what could only be a summons from Cosima. That instantly gave her the high ground, though what she said and did once she had their attention could convince them either to accept her or throw her down from a precipice at the soonest opportunity.

Goddess could be fickle, after all. Her favor was far from a permanent gift…as Cosima knew well, based on how Bettina and other former favorites had been treated.

"Rest, for now." Cosima told her huntresses as her body hung half-in and half-out of the treehouse entryway on the rope ladder descending to the forest floor. Part of her was on edge with the anxiety of leaving Lilias behind, but she didn't want to risk bringing them for the others to gawk at. "I don't plan for this to take long."

"When should we expect you back?" Crouching with her bracer-covered arms balanced on her knees, Iulia tapped a finger against Cosima's nose in farewell. The implication that she would rescue her if the Godlings made mischief didn't need to be spoken aloud for Cosima to know it.

Affection prompted a rare, shaky smile from Cosima. "Tell Ricla I want boar and roasted sprouts for supper. And ask Grisel to dig up the plum wine too—I'm going to need a full cask after this."

Impulsive, she stretched up to kiss her. Iulia chuckled against her mouth as she captured the back of her neck with her dry, calloused hand and held her there for a longer caress.

"You can do this. You're the best of them, you know." The

encouragement should have gladdened Cosima's heart, but Iulia had misread a crucial facet that spoiled the rest of the gem.

I don't want to be one of them. I never asked for any of this.

She couldn't say that. Cosima only smiled at her again and began to climb down the ladder. As soon as her feet—in dancing slippers this time rather than the boots she had insisted on to visit Sovanna—touched the ground she was off, winging her way as Light back to Aebbenary.

Though the city was as large or larger than it had been a quarter century ago, a lifetime of activity had mostly adapted her to its pathways. North—the Holy Tower and the seat of Goddess's dominion, topped by the mountains over which gloomed Sovanna's marsh. East—the edge of the island that faced the continent. South of the city lay farming land and rural villages blessed but not unduly so by Marzanna's will. West was where Cosima travelled in from: a land of plains rolling into forests either tropical or boreal depending on which direction someone wanted to go.

Aside from where Goddess resided, only one place had a greater signature of sacred presence: the blessèd Arboretum where all beings not mortal loved best to assemble and play.

Cosima had not spent much time here in the past, but the landscape was familiar. A wall of trees tended by gigantic constructed beings beholden to their existence by Marzanna's power—and, rumor claimed, the former High Priest's experimentation—were still dwarfed by what they tended. Vines latticed with gleaming thorns slithered unending paths through the mile-high trees, ready to capture any trespasser and drag them in for nature to devour. Only those who could fly on wings or travel as a beam of Light could pass through the insular greenery and enter the park.

A circular path wide enough for several people and equestrians to walk and ride abreast wound around the central green…which was white and beige, really, since every plant in the park had been plated with gold-tinged majesty. Wildlife meandered with the people, though they were not like any that existed off the island or out of the city. Sleek wildcats with prismatic fur purred and sought attention like domestic pets; other predators wandered while bejeweled fowl either sang or preened and gifted feathers of all shades to whatever divinity they fancied that day.

Tables animated by Miraculous will and laden with shimmering fruit that never rotted or ran out crawled around on barely visible legs. One passed close enough to Cosima to catch on the hem of her vermillion chiton, forcing her to pick up a cup of sugared pecans before it let her be. Sighing, Cosima scattered the pecans on the ground in front of a sleeping bear with sable fur and ruby claws; lazy but watchful, it refused to eat until she turned her back. The crunching that followed sounded like bones splintering as teeth crushed them.

Garish though it was, the park's purpose was clear: it was a shrine of self-worship built solely for the deific beings linked to Goddess's will. Every being, from the first in Her regard to the least, had contributed in a myriad of ways to the park.

Cosima could fault their imagination all she liked. Her vanity had led her to find people who appreciated her for herself and not her power; her stubbornness had made her learn how to exist in the wild alone as close to a mortal as possible just so she knew she could. These conceited beasts would be better served by attempting the same.

Occupied though they were with the diversions in the park, their eyes tracked Cosima's progress into their midst with assessing, disapproving frowns.

Giric—the first Godling conceived by Marzanna and Däard.

Barone—a Saint, not a sibling, but one who had once been Fiammetta's platonic lapdog and had since ingratiated himself with Cosima's various brothers. A permanent fixture, though not a welcome one.

Agnese—the fourth progeny of Fiammetta and Marzanna. Her birth—and resultant neglect—were when both Bettina and teenage Cosima had begun to realize the Shining Court was not a haven of perfect, sacred will as Goddess demanded everyone believe. Agnese had been an adorable infant, not too different from Lilias, but child-rearing from indifferent nursemaids and the cruelties of her older siblings had whetted her into as poisoned a blade as the rest.

Druda, Evrard, Ormanno, others. Related not just by parental ties or divine favor, but by the ichor that surged in place of blood through their holy veins. Only the Godlings could have counted themselves as contenders for Goddess's nomination of Her successor, but Saints were not immune to covetousness. Whether this host of beings had been conceived naturally between Goddess and Däard or various men, born of divine Light from Marzanna's dalliances with women or Her most loved Fiammetta, or chosen as paramours to reward and uplift other servile beneficiaries, they all tallied Cosima among their number.

Agnese looked away first, feigning boredom as she returned to combing the mane of a unicorn someone had gifted her for her birthday the year before. Ormanno stared long enough to make her feel his glare. Once she could no longer pretend she hadn't spotted him, he stood from where he had lounged with his head on the lap of a pretty Saint and crossed his arms.

"What a blessing, Sister!" He sketched a formal yet insolent bow; all his retainers with him rose and mimicked his jape, stifling their cutting hilarity. "Do you bring good tidings?"

Cosima's discomfort had no place here. To survive the snakes, she had to persuade them she was one of them. One of them, but *better*.

"Dear ones." Cosima pictured Bettina's face in her mind and imitated her most charming, razor-sharp smile. "You came. I can hardly believe it."

"Could we do otherwise, with such sweet messengers to flatter us?" Ormanno smiled back and allowed Cosima to kiss the air on either side of his handsome, hollow cheeks; with the mixed heritage of a mortal traveller from another distant isle across the world from Aebbenary, his skin was reddish brown and his frame broad and powerful. He had Her favor because his father had taught Marzanna new tricks of pleasure and built her a boat She sailed on Aebbenary's western seas whenever ennui drove Her offshore.

"So you liked my hawks? I'm glad." Bubbling with laughter, Cosima squeezed his bicep before she drifted with airy disregard to where striving Barone promenaded with a pink-winged Godling. All of them were lucky she hadn't instructed the birds to pluck out their eyes or rend their perfect skin with their talons.

"Tell us, Cosima: did you instruct the hawks to mark who you would have accompany you in your court?" The Godling beside Barone held up one of his bare arms wrapped in a garland of white leaves and winced theatrically as the leaves retracted to display several sets of brownish ichor scabs caused by sharp talons. "Should I thank you for your partiality or berate you for your pettiness?"

"Neither. My hawks react negatively to people with two faces. Perhaps you should stick to one to avoid their ire in the future."

Titters filled the Arboretum, some of them shifting into outright cackles. None of them had ever been fond of Cosima, though some of them had faked affection well enough. That didn't mean they loved each other with any greater diligence.

Ormanno sallied again. "You might be familiar with all our faces if you joined our company more often than your temporal friends, Sister."

"Brother, dearest, your twittering wearies me already. Wouldn't you like to listen to my news instead of the drone of your own voice?" Cosima observed without seeming to observe as everyone in the Arboretum gradually meandered over to hear what she had to say.

Regardless of whether or not word had spread, her visitation was enough of an anomaly to rouse their indolent natures with novelty. She progressed with a thread of Miraculous power outflowing from her pores that wordlessly spoke to her position as Marzanna's chosen: flowers bloomed where her steps left indentations in the grass, and the animals in the park lifted their noses to scent her unique Light on the breeze. The sun itself slanted an ear down to listen with a ray transforming into a convenient highlight.

"Mother wanted me to assemble you make the announcement. I imagine it amuses Her to picture us all together like a happy family." *With Her as the matriarch.*

Giric addressed her this time from where they had been balanced on a lounge to twiddle with a lyre; their hazel eyes glinted with spite.

"A happy family? Ah, you would know best about that. With news that your mortal brother has returned with the human who bred him."

Don't fucking talk about him. Muscling down her violent burst of rage, Cosima brought her hands together and then slowly spread them apart as a Miracle emerged between them. Small butterflies rotated around and around the garland of pansies she Made.

"My brother does not concern you. Or me, for that matter. What Goddess has chosen does not concern the trivial lives of mankind. Will you really not share my joy?" Cosima asked. She brought the fragrant garland to Ormanno first, slighting Giric on purpose. "Would you deny Her wishes rather than exalt Her wisdom?"

Their eyes locked in a silent battle as Cosima lifted the garland in offer to adorn his neck with it. A trickle of sweat slithered down her back as she held her ground. He wanted to refuse—badly, maybe more than he'd desired anything in months—but did he dare?

Slowly, Ormanno ducked his head in submission to accept her gift. Cosima suppressed a breath of relief as she slipped the wreath around his elegant throat and stepped back to continue the plan she'd come up with on the wing.

Bringing her hands together again, she spread them out and crafted another identical garland of pansies orbited by diminutive butterflies. And another, and another as the wreath in her hands propagated itself until another push of her power sent a garland to hover in front of every Godling and Saint in the Arboretum.

"As Mother's heir, I act in Her name. I don't know why She chose to honor me, but that's not for me to question. Now—will you exalt Her alongside me?" Clasping her hands a final time to feign veneration, Cosima bowed her head as if she was avoiding witnessing who donned the garlands and who refused. She guessed none of them would since she had tied the acceptance to honoring—or rejecting—Goddess so neatly.

When she looked up, she saw everyone staring at her with pansies faintly aglow around their necks, as if to ask *What now?* Bracing herself for the self-loathing she would endure later, Cosima smiled as beatifically as she could manage.

"My Jubilation gift to you, beloveds. So you will *never* forget our favor."

That *"never"* made them pause. Barone tried to remove the flowers first, then Ormanno. Then the others.

Disgust at her prank spread. Dismay followed as they realized the more they fought to remove the garlands, the more they tightened until half the beings present struggled for breath the wreaths cut off at Cosima's will. Only those who had accepted her gifts—none too willingly, but at least without undue averseness—without attempting to discard them stood tall instead of falling to their knees to rip at the unblemished flowers cutting off their air.

"Why do you fear? Gods and Saints cannot die by my hands. At least. Not. Yet." Enunciating the last, Cosima laughed and spun with her arms outstretched to accept the rays of dying Light streaming from the siblings and sycophants she had trapped. For a moment, though she didn't consume their power, the savor of their individual essences made her drunker than she'd been able to get in years.

When the park had fallen silent as beings one by one succumbed to strangulation, Cosima waited two of her own, easy breaths to singe the wreaths into fragments, then cinders with a blast of Light from her hands. Though they were hurt and she had felt the various signatures of power battling to unweave the pansy flowers, all the Godlings and Saints were still conscious.

"My Jubilee approaches. I expect I will see every one of you there to kneel before Goddess…and me."

Agnese's accusing eyes followed her the longest as Cosima turned to walk away, just like they had lingered upon her arrival. She had fallen with the rest of those who had tried to reject their wreaths. Though— for a moment—the indulgence in superior power and authority had intoxicated Cosima, the guilt that followed was worse than anything she had felt before.

She should have saved Agnese as a child, somehow: she had seen the abuse and turned her back on it, which put her in the same rank as those who had perpetuated the cruelty.

I'm more like Her every day.

Nauseous, Cosima covered her mouth with the back of her hand and lurched into her traveling Light to go home.

VIII

Bettina

Cristoval's appearance at her gates brought Bettina more joy than she could stand. Even the sight of Crespin, his mortal father, and the awkwardness their reunion brought—a little over their son's lifetime in length—couldn't dim her gladness.

The danger that would haunt his steps the moment Marzanna realized he was here—if She didn't already—stiffened her smiles and hollowed her laughter at his clever banter.

After ages of drowsy quietude, the Valusius manor threw its gates wide in welcome according to Bettina's wish. She had not been lazy when it came to learning the bounds of her power all these years: leading her guests through the house as windows flew open to allow the evening breeze in to cleanse the house of torpid air, she directed them to her kitchen and began to cook a delicious meal while they watched.

All the joy in the world brought by the sight of her glorious son and even the fond memories of her first tryst as a maiden with the dashing yet tone-deaf minstrel could not banish what news Cristoval brought. Goddess had summoned him to Aebbenary.

The manner of the summons was similar: a gale-blown decree bridging the sea between the island and Ioggenica to find them and call them back.

They ate and talked; Bettina urged Cristoval to stay close to the estate and not wander—most likely to no purpose since he had been willful since birth though his nature still tended to goodness. While the setting sun bathed the solar she had reclaimed in amber hues, Crespin's expression caught her notice.

He had been a fool even when she'd chosen him as her first lover. Benign, but imprudent without specific instructions from her. She didn't doubt his following Cristoval's return to Aebbenary had been an impulsive lark he would learn to regret the more he heard about Goddess and Her court. Yet when he met Bettina's gaze over their cups of blackberry wine, she saw he had garnered *some* wisdom over the course of the life he had lived that marked lines on his still handsome face.

Though he put on a jovial act for their son—convincing due to his profession as an entertainer—Crespin had gleaned enough to be concerned for Cristoval's welfare in Aebbenary. While a breeze from the open window teased the graying hair he still possessed back, Bettina tilted her cup in a subtle toast of acknowledgment while she smiled at one of her son's stories of his travels in Ioggenica.

The lines around Crespin's eyes creased in an answering smile.

Still handsome…and still a sweet, kindly fool, Bettina thought as she sank back into the padded chair to get comfortable. *What could a man do against Goddess?*

She wondered if Crespin would come to her room that night. If she had aged naturally, Bettina already knew she'd still be a beauty in her fifth decade of life, but she was a Saint immortalized in the flush of youthful womanhood. If he thought he had a chance, what man wouldn't pursue a night of satisfaction with her? If she considered it— and the man himself—it wouldn't be a stretch to admit her amicable fondness for him could be kindled into attraction without much wooing on his part.

Instead, she re-devoted herself to Cristoval's conversation and tried to amuse him with her own stories of her cottage by the seaside and the travels she'd taken before settling there. He tiptoed around the subject of why she'd left Aebbenary in the first place: Bettina evaded each charge with a noncommittal reply and turned matters elsewhere.

When the stars had emerged from the clouds and the moon had long since risen, Bettina's mortal guests sent their yawning selves to bed in rooms she had instructed the invisible servants to prepare with a wish.

Maybe it was his own pride that kept Crespin away; he had wooed her in their early days with songs sung in hushed tones outside the windows of her quarters to avoid her father and the servants. Bold he had been, but not unduly so since he had scampered away into the hedgerows to avoid discovery and to make her laugh time and again.

Bettina exhaled a wistful sigh as she rolled onto her back in her own bed and pulled the lilac-scented sheets under her arms to sleep. *Loneliness aches…but maybe it's better to be wise than flattered.*

Morning dawned without seeing her sleep more than an hour or two. Hastening to finish a toilette even Saints couldn't completely ignore, she readied herself for the busy day ahead of her and walked over to Cristoval's room—next to hers—when she was done.

He had been a beautiful child. Not as easy as Cosima as an infant, since a baby conceived by Light from Goddess's love was born in a similar fashion rather than through natural means. As he'd grown he'd become her calmest child while Cosima had veered toward being stubborn and independent. Thanks to Bettina's small measure of influence over Marzanna at the time—and the fact that Goddess had not had much experience conceiving holy children before—she had matured normally over the years rather than accelerating in growth when her divinity expressed itself.

While Cosima resembled Marzanna, Cristoval looked like Bettina. His features had a masculine cast to them, but the refined tilt of his eyes, his slender nose, the clear-cut jawline, the dusting of freckles…they were all hers. As he belonged to her and would forever be her baby.

Overcome with tenderness, Bettina sat on the side of his bed and leaned down to kiss his smooth forehead. Saints could not drag the passage of time back to the years they missed. In theory, Bettina would be able to bear children forever…but they were not replaceable, or interchangeable. Each baby she bore would be as unique as a snowflake in a drift or a star in the heavens. The loss of one could never be assuaged by a new birth, love the baby though she inevitably would.

"Whrr goin?" Cristoval's voice—no longer a boy's—was gravelly as he started to drag himself from slumber.

"I have a few errands, angel. I wanted to see you before I left for the day." Bettina traced the bridge of his freckled nose with a knuckle, as she used to do when he was a boy.

"Oh." Granting her the precious gift of a sleepy smile, he dropped his head back on his pillow; seconds barely had time to pass before he was asleep again.

I will not lose you, angel. Not ever. Bettina recited this familiar vow to herself as she watched Cristoval a while longer before she reluctantly left the room to make the journey to the Archives.

Word had begun to spread among the commons of Cosima's Jubilee. Try though she did to master her apprehension, Bettina perceived the zealous happiness bordering on fixation that bid the city folk try in their own ways to bedeck the city in more finery than it already bragged, clean streets that were already maintained, and otherwise expend themselves esteeming a Goddess who rarely thought of them and an heir who didn't want the job.

Others might accuse Bettina—as they had in the past—of ambition. Of a ruthlessness implied in the delicate influence she cultivated over time with people she decided were powerful enough to help her. It had never been about power, though, not truly. In a world ordered by divine beings and people willing to worship them to the detriment of those around them, it was necessary to find power to use to her advantage.

If something happened to Goddess and Cosima had the misfortune of replacing Her, this world could not be fixed by her Ascendance. The streets were clean, but people still starved and fought over scraps. The powerful took advantage of the weak—now with Goddess's tacit sanction and Fiammetta's amused encouragement rather than Silver's decree. The monarchy still drained Aebbenary's coffers and yoked the laborers in invisible chains to their service.

Still, everyone worshipped. They all paid homage to divinity and the hollow gratitude she saw in the average person's eyes had begun to erase the fringes of their souls like a plague.

Bettina believed in her heart—strangle it, crush it, bury it though she did every single day so no one heard the secret truth she harbored—that no one person, not even a court of Saints deserved the power they had been granted to rule over mortalkind.

The Scholar's Grave waited as she had left it: imperious, lonely, and sorrowful. Striding through it as swiftly as she could without running, Bettina hastened to the Archives before she lost her nerve. The plan she had begun to construct was still in its embryonic stage, but there was potential in it that she might survive and keep her sanity outside of Marzanna's enthralling courtship.

With the Scholar's citrine eyes at her back, Bettina followed the path down to the white arches of the entrance to the Archives. As she laid her hand on the column to pause, to persuade herself to continue, she realized two things. One, power that was *not* Miraculous barred the way.

Two—she wasn't alone.

Without turning her back to the archway, Bettina spoke into the chasm behind her and let her Saint's glow spread to illuminate a wider circle around her body.

"Is it you who has barred the way?"

"Why should that concern you? Marzanna Made you Her plaything—a pretty bauble to dance at Her command. What does a bauble need from the Archives?"

Easoren moved from one shadow to another, this one closer. Bettina backed away until she felt the hum of power from the Scholar's statue on her heels, warmer than the rest of the chasm. Would he hurt her? Would he risk Marzanna's fury if he took the toy She had taken interest in again away for good?

"I see Goddess did not trouble to make this place secret. Bauble or not, I have no interest in explaining my activities to a sack of bones."

"It is not your explanation I desire. It is well known what favor you want to demand."

What could he possibly want from me? Easoren had never once bothered with her before.

Scrambling for a position to negotiate from, Bettina reached out and trailed her cold fingertips through the presence of power—not Light, it could never be Light—blocking her way through.

"Let me pass."

"Not yet. Do you think Goddess is the only worthy bargainer in Aebbenary?"

The gloom blocking the door thickened, but Bettina had already lowered her hand. Despite her caution, she was intrigued. Only Marzanna could anoint Cristoval to Sainthood and eternal life. Bettina had one last chance to persuade Her; it had occurred to her before to ally with others in her quest, but the list of possible supporters of her cause didn't name anyone useful. Däard's spirit had been gelded the moment Marzanna had chosen him as one of Her primary consorts, and Fiammetta's heart was stony and riddled with decay so nothing like empathy could ever penetrate it.

Easoren, though…could she trust someone who had never—*could never*—truly betray Goddess?

"You fell out of Her grace ages ago. You have naught to offer me," she said. A starting proposal: a standing offer to convince her he wanted something attainable that she could trade for what she required. She turned and crossed her arms as if in serious thought. All she could see were the moving shades shifting this way and that through the Grave's cavern, but she knew Easoren was present.

"Nor you to offer me. And still, we might help each other."

"Is that why you whisper lies so sweetly in my ear? What could you want that—" She guessed. Bettina's laugh was breathless as she realized. "Oh, Priest. Surely not."

Frigid hands lunged out of the shadows and closed around her throat. Her amusement vanished as he squeezed the laughter into silent choking.

"Fetch me my skin, woman."

As soon as he had begun, it was over. Bettina coughed and pawed at her throat to erase the cold touch of metal bones bruising her skin.

Instinctive terror made her want to shrink back and scream as she compelled herself to look at Easoren. The High Priest of Silver fallen low—the gilded framework of a man stripped quite literally of everything that had made him who he was.

"Goddess remade you. Re-*makes* you. Over and over." Bettina had known this—had heard others joking about it—but witnessing as the flesh rapidly rotted and then melted off Easoren's bones was a horror Marzanna had spared her from back when they were together.

Fell Light kindled in the black pits of the skull's eye sockets as Easoren cocked his head; under his feet his flesh liquefied and sank into the ground as punishment for whatever transgression he had committed to annoy Marzanna. "It is the unmaking that matters, bauble. You will fetch me my permanent cloak of flesh...and I will share with you the keys to do more than save your wretched son."

"I have my own plans."

"Plans and plots again. None will avail you without my help."

"That's what you want me to believe, but you forget. I know you to be the chief among liars."

Amusement brought a grin to the skull's already exposed teeth. "Not I, trinket. Not I."

Chuckling with an eerie, hollow sound that echoed in the chasm of the Grave, Easoren walked backwards into the shadows. As quickly as he had appeared he was gone.

"You will come to me before long. When all your tactics fail I will wait for you to crawl on your belly to beg for the keys to the garden."

He said nothing more. Bettina was alone.

Garden? A strange choice of word. If there was a message or parting barb there, she could not deconstruct it. With his departure, the blockage hung between the columns in front of her guttered like a last ember and vanished. All she could do was file the phrase away for later and go about her business for now.

Bettina entered the Archives prepared to sprint to the Grand Archivist's room ahead of the malevolent specters. What she saw instead made her pause; caution screamed something was wrong, but she tried to ignore it. She had to stay.

No more books. No more scrolls or artifacts curated by specters puppeteered by the Grand Archivist's consciousness. She could see the silhouettes of the vacant shelves soaring upwards toward a ceiling she had doubts existed at all amidst the gloom, but little else.

Perturbed, Bettina crept through the empty shelves in silence so total each of her steps and each breath she took sounded as loud as waves crashing against the shore. Instinct led her on a swerving path to the door at the end of the cataloguing room no matter that all the specters who had harassed her the first time she'd come here were gone. When she skimmed the knob on the door at the end where the Grand Archivist had to be waiting for her, it swung open without a creak.

An invitation if ever she'd seen one. Bettina wanted badly to refuse…but she entered and listened for the sound of the door closing behind her. Distraction made her neglect it.

She saw a stone platform smooth of everything but engravings that reminded her of a compass rose that filled the center of the room. Grand Archivist Magisend stood in the center like a figurine carved from gemstone. Like the aventurine dragon arm band that Bettina had removed as soon as she was home. When she entered the haze of cobalt and night sky atmosphere of the room he was already looking at the door.

Waiting for her.

"I…" The courtesies she had been raised to utter abandoned her. Unworthy—she could not speak them into this realm.

"You kept the Archives waiting." His voice was a glide of oil down her spine; a spoonful of honey coating his throat without any sweetness. "Why?"

"I didn't want to return."

The Grand Archivist lifted a hand and splayed it over his blurred face. When he pulled it away a moment later, the water-like mask covering it was gone and she could see him clearly. Confronted with a mostly human face, part of Bettina relaxed.

"You came to an accord with me, Swan-of-gold. I will honor it."

The non-being environment of the room—larger than the

approximation of a library that had been here the first time she'd visited—could never provide relief, but Bettina dared hope as she clasped her hands in front of her and walked forward. Interested despite herself, she circled the platform where Magisend stood centered and examined the sigils.

"I don't wish to trouble you in your…contemplations, sir."

"Magisend. Names matter."

She resisted the impulse to roll her eyes or wrinkle her nose. "As you wish. I have some questions—will you answer them?"

He was silent. Insectile eyes—all black, jewel-like facets rimmed in gold—watched her and promised nothing. If it weren't for the lack of humanity there, the face could be handsome: imperial features enhanced by the fashionable gauntness to his face, and a body that looked lithe and strong beneath the golden robe draped around his figure.

Bettina nervously bit her lower lip instead of returning to the bad habit of nibbling on one of her glossy, lacquered thumbnails.

"Goddess Made you. What for?"

The silence *streeetched*, pliant as soft wax. Magisend's features blurred and reformed as the presence of ether in the room converged. "Ask something else."

Her frustration was instant: she kicked the raised lip of the platform to test what would happen if she stepped on it. When nothing changed, she did so.

"Why?"

Magisend studied her. When she walked, so did he, moving too fluidly on legs and feet so threaded with cobalt she couldn't see any skin under the glimmers.

"The order of questions matters as much as the asking. Even knowledge can be bound by divine decree…to an extent." Enunciating the last three words a little too distinctly, his lips warped in a smile that revealed metal-capped teeth.

If I don't ask him anything, he might take the questions from me… Bettina stuttered over the next nearest thing on her mind.

"What do you know about Easoren?"

"I know all."

Bettina threw her hands up in the air, omniscient being who might extinguish her Light on the spot or not. "Then tell me what Marzanna wants so I can trade it for what *I* want."

"I don't know that."

"How is that possible?"

Magisend's eyes shuttered, all expression in them flattening to a blank. "It should not be. Your Goddess has been very careful in Her use of my skills. No direct questions. Ever evading the range of my awareness, treating knowledge as a compass rather than an immediate resource."

"How long has it been since She's come down here? Has She noticed..." She gestured vaguely to Magisend's room. Blinking once, he rotated his head quickly to the left, then slowly to the right...then an inch or two too far for a human neck to stand.

"I do not allow Her to see the traces of your presence. She does not ask."

"You can...conceal me from Her?" *How is that possible?* Bettina thought it again. *This* answer had promise, if Magisend could be persuaded to help her further.

"If I so desire." *And I so. Desire.* His disjointed voice rebounded in her mind, bouncing off the walls of her skull like a child's ball. Another distorted smile preceded a step forward.

Fine. I'll play. Bettina thought; treating it as a game, she dared herself forward and lifted her chin to indicate the fear he seemed to want her to feel didn't control her. "Can you conceal others?"

Silence. He wouldn't answer or acknowledge the question.

Not relevant. Was that her thought or his? Regardless, Bettina learned another rule: the Grand Archivist's powers were not up for discussion. She had a bushel of other queries to tempt him with.

"The Priest, Magisend. Tell me what you know of him," she said. *If I have to shepherd his attention back to my questions every time I ask one a hundred years will pass before I get the answers I need.*

"...No."

Bettina's fingers dug into the surface of the table. *Table?* Briefly, the ordinary room she'd first discovered Magisend in had materialized. She'd forgotten nothing was real except for the two of them: the impression of her nails biting into varnished wood skated across her senses before it evaporated, leaving her stumbling and cursing while the Archivist watched with impassive attentiveness.

"Why?"

"It was life you offered me. What life is there down here but what illusions I generate?"

She scoffed, shaking her head. "Is that all?"

Cristoval was not the only one who was reckless. Crossing the "room" in a few strides, Bettina sliced one of her pointed nails across her forearm and used her other hand to smear through the streaks of ichor. Before she could rationalize herself out of it she grabbed Magisend's arm and held it in determined offering.

It took but a millisecond for the cracks in his skin to accept her sacrifice. She remembered too late to fear the grip of otherworldly tendrils, but his form had been altered once already by her gift of blood.

She felt needles in her hand, hundreds of them: none of them pierced deep, but more drops of blood welled to satisfy their hunger. In an instant they were gone, and she had never lifted her hand to glimpse them.

The blue midnight coalesced in front of her like a mask. It settled over her face and eyes like one and rendered her blind. Bettina fought the panic making her pant and kept her hand locked around Magisend's arm. She could feel that it was warm, his skin similar to her own temperature, but it was…missing something. It almost felt glossy, like glazed pottery.

"What have you done?" Not angry; inquisitive. His words in her head still made her flinch. Bettina tried to gather her consciousness in a bubble and lay her hands on its spherical walls to stabilize her shield from the howling, awful void.

"You wanted more than illusions. I will help you build something more…in exchange for more knowledge. Fair enough?" Bettina couldn't speak, but her

thoughts were too loud and too soft in the tempest of All-knowledge too vast for any but the greatest of the Archivists to tend.

An image shifted to the forefront of her mind. When she'd been a young girl, she had loved playing with a glass apple pilfered from one of the centerpieces of a cousin's wedding table. She had tossed it up into the air to watch it refract the light through its smooth, pale blue surface. Until she had dropped it and it shattered into an astounding number of pieces.

Her consciousness was like that apple. If it slipped from her control into Magisend's hands it would fragment into a million shards. What would happen to her Saintly body then?

My children are braver than I am. Though she was a loving mother, she was not too much of one to imagine even heroic Cosima wouldn't quake before the terrible weight of All-knowledge. But Bettina had entered this bargain willingly. Sacrifices were necessary to lift Cristoval into immortality and protect Cosima from Marzanna's clutches. *I will do this.*

"What will you do, Bettina?"

Her name emerged from the churn of Knowing. The letters of it formed and shattered in her mind and were built back up by the authority in Magisend's voice. He, a conduit for knowledge, hadn't expected this. He could not predict everything.

"I'm going to help you make something real." Bettina's own voice grounded her, though she could scarcely hear herself think let alone speak. Linked by touch and blood to his peculiar form, she began to transform the nighttime ether into something corporeal.

A garden. Inspired, unfortunately, by one word from the former High Priest. Its presence expanded the room into a fair replica of her estate's flower beds and fruit trees and the hedge maze. The All-knowledge receded sluggishly from Bettina's mind along with her mask as if relieved she had unburdened it of this reproduction and all its details, but she squinted her eyes closed to maintain her tether to it.

"Wait. I need something in return."

"In time. Look at what you have wrought." Magisend used his audible voice instead of the Grand Archivist's authority in her mind.

Midnight bled from her vision in a river of tears; Bettina blinked in the unexpected brightness that greeted her. While she looked around she staggered off the circular platform that had remained despite her transformation of the room into a green haven.

She and Magisend had transformed too, embarrassed as she was to admit it. Her lusty urges from the night before had colored her interpretation of the garden where, long ago, a minstrel had flattered a spoiled daughter of the nobility into a passionate tryst.

Her mind had tamed the riverfall flow of hair drifting around his head into a brushed sweep of black hanging over his left shoulder, with some strands pulled back to keep it from falling over his eyes without the uncanny gravity of the Archives. Instead of a goldenrod robe, he wore something she would have curated for Cristoval: leggings patterned along the side with embroidery in stars or flowers, a loose linen shirt partially covered by a dark plum vest, and the fine leather gloves covering Magisend's unworldly, void-tipped fingers and gold-threaded palms.

"What would you know?" Satisfied by their bargain, it seemed, the Grand Archivist asked for her requirements without further haggling. His attention didn't stray down her body—clothed in the diaphanous layers of a rose pink stola with ivory ribbons to secure it and enhance the frame of her shape—but she *felt* his look. It made her shiver, though she would have denied it.

"Three things. If you cannot tell me what Marzanna wants, I want to know if I can trust Easoren as an ally…so I need to know exactly what he wants from me. And…" She paused. A plan had begun to unfold during her exile, eroding her pride and challenging her commitment to earning the greatest of favors from Marzanna; Her offer to let Bettina earn Her love once more had strengthened it. "The knowledge of the best dancers in the world. I need that."

Bettina shook her head as she picked up and discarded final requests as they occurred to her. Too many things were necessary, yet now it had come to this it was difficult to think after the tax of knowledge had been extracted from her.

"The third question?"

*Ask for the questions Marzanna asks. Ask for the reason Aebbenary is so altered from before. Ask for...*Bettina clapped her hands over ears at the volume of her inner voice. When it quieted and she pulled them away, she shook fistfuls of flower petals off her ichor-slick palms with a shudder.

"This isn't my question, but...I can come back here and trade with you again, yes?"

Magisend must have appreciated the garden she had helped him Create, but he had yet to look at anything besides her or move to explore it. "Would you dare?"

"If I must."

"Ask."

"I want to know how to protect Cristoval from Goddess. How to hide him from Her sight." Bettina sighed into the wind as a breeze began to stir. The garden smelled like petrichor, suddenly, as if a storm was blowing in. When she looked up she saw clouds rolling on a tableau sky she had pulled from her mind for Magisend's enjoyment.

Looking back down, she glimpsed a flash of movement before the Grand Archivist stood directly in front of her, reaching out his gloved hands to cradle her head. Bettina flinched with her entire body at his touch, even through the leather; when her knees crumpled beneath her he knelt alongside where she fell, still connected. All the while knowledge swirled like a thunderstorm in the false sky and in her mind.

"You might use the Priest, but you cannot trust him." The first of her answers. *"The knowledge you ask for I bestow now."*

As choreography and skill and everything that meant *"to dance"* poured into Bettina's mind without the reprieve of a filter she screamed, piercing and shallow. The pain didn't last long, though—when it was done, she began to laugh, because with this her plan to woo Marzanna would work beyond the shadow of a doubt. If it didn't...

"Do not let arrogance tempt you, Swan-of-gold." Magisend's thumbs—bare now the gloves had melted into the ether—scraped against her cheekbones as his eyes bored down into hers. Light linked them by the

windows to their souls, and darkness followed. *"All ends cannot be glimpsed by finite minds."*

"A-advice? For free?" She couldn't stop laughing. Bettina thought she'd suffocate before her giggling would cease.

Saints can't die, she reminded herself. *But we can suffer.*

Something prompted Magisend to intervene. He opened his gilded mouth—only a slight parting of his lips, but enough of one to let more shadows trickle out and down his chin as the flow of them slowed. He breathed in her Light…and leaned in to touch his dripping mouth to hers, letting the Knowledge seep through her pores at his touch.

Bettina gasped, her arms flying up to clutch his shoulders, to shove him away. He wasn't kissing her: while her laughter had stopped, this too she could drown from if she didn't find the strength to push him away. When she tried to voice some—*any*—protest her tongue brushed against his and a smattering of sensations made her groan into his mouth.

Then it was over. She was alone in the room—in the garden she had built for the Archives to use. Knowledge had become her sword and shield: a sword to make Goddess surrender, a shield to protect her son, and an ally. A Priest, perhaps…and the Grand Archivist himself.

Go, someone whispered to her. *Go, and see what your works will bring about.*

Bettina obeyed.

IX

Cosima

Running across Aebbenary's night-washed streets, Cosima felt in her element. Not because Aebbenary was her home, but because she and her huntresses were like a fleet of nimble deer as they drove their prey toward the snare where he would meet his doom.

Justice may have turned a blind eye to Goddess's island, but they had not. Cosima had sworn to her huntresses she never would.

Flanked by Iulia and Konetta, she ran through the quiet streets with her lungs pumping from delicious effort. *This* was what her power was best used for: it quickened their speed and muffled their footfalls on the cobbles while the joy of the hunt made all of them glow with the flush of health, youth, and her shared aureole.

It had been several months since they had all hunted together—since their prey had been worthy of all of them gathering to run it down. Their pursuit had lasted most of the night when one of the girls had enticed the Saint out of his estate with promises of dark amusements and forbidden pleasures even a divine being had not tasted before. It would have been easy—too easy—to take him then, but Cosima and the others wanted to chase. To bay and bark like hounds and scream like hawks in their hearts as the night sheltered their sin in silence and covered their sacrilege with its curtain of darkness.

If sin it was to avenge true evil, Cosima would accept the title of worst offender and wear it as a better crown than the one Goddess would grant her at her Jubilee.

This Saint thought himself cunning, the best in his generation of anointed ones, yet he was indolent like the rest. A body blessed by Marzanna's Light to never wither or tire still required frequent use to strengthen it, if not to beautify it; he had never bothered. He was no match for nearly a dozen human women in the prime of their days and strength, let alone Cosima herself. When his strength flagged, he tried to hide himself from them in the dim retreat of an abandoned storehouse littered with wooden crates, glass shards, and other debris.

As others before him had done. The huntresses had herded him here to handle him privately. Discreetly—hidden from the watching eyes and ears of the city that had not marked their passage thanks to Cosima's power. Cornered and panicked, he tried to grab Iulia—*Iulia*, who could crush him under her thumb—to use as a hostage, but to no purpose. After Iulia knocked him down, the others as one raised their bows and staggered their shots to poke him so full of arrows he resembled a pincushion.

Then the fool had the audacity to pass out from the pain. He fell into a graceless heap of hair and silk and shining skin. Never once had he cried out for help: Cosima's power would have stifled it, but pride had sealed his tongue to the last.

"Feel better?" Ricla patted her on the shoulder as she passed.

"Maybe." Cosima grinned. "This one has been a long time coming."

"Think how much more you can do once you're officially part of Goddess's court!"

Cosima said nothing. She had concealed next to nothing from her friends. With eleven women living together there were bound to be disagreements and heated disputes...which the matter of her coronation as successor had become. At least three-quarters of the other women were optimistic that she would be able to change some things when Goddess granted her more authority over the divine beings on the island.

The rest—including Konetta—had what Cosima thought was a more realistic idea of what might happen: the title would be an empty one. Soon they'd learn the unpleasant secret behind why an immortal Goddess felt the urge to appoint an heir at all.

For now, flushed with the high of the hunt, Cosima let the remark pass and approached the unconscious Saint with a dagger she had personally blessed with Light clenched in her fist. The huntress in whose name they had pursued this scoundrel followed with her, and they joined hands as they stared down at the body.

Sovanna had not yet come to discover this in her infamous love of experimentation—or if she had, the knowledge was too blasphemous to risk whispering in the wrong ears. At the start of their lives, her past and Cosima's had followed a similar trajectory: they had been born in Light and divinity and raised amidst decadence and neglect.

Then again, Sovanna hadn't had anyone in her corner...and even with Bettina and Cristoval mostly attuned to her wellbeing, Cosima had endured enough viciousness from her siblings and new Saints to necessitate a method of removing them from her orbit.

Saints could never die...but if another immortal cut mortal wounds into their body, drained as much ichor as they could, and left them alone somewhere the consequences on the physique and mental state were catastrophic. The merest trace of Goddess's Light within them would revive them, but without their blood, their memories and all that made them who they were would be gone when they awakened.

And the horrors they would suffer in the meantime, walking between the conscious world and the terrors of watching their sanity and spirit melt into the void...justice would have decreed death was better for the crimes their prey committed, but this was at least *some* punishment. Cosima was content with their suffering if she could not grant the victims fair vengeance.

She passed Palmira the dagger by the hilt and felt her hand tremble as she took it.

"Where...you'll leave him where?" Transfixed by the fallen Saint, Palmira slowly knelt at his side to grab his head by its shining mahogany hair and yank it back. She had confirmed to Cosima that this was the one who had laughed when the child he had forced on her, that she had loved, had died from sickness he had refused to heal and sold Palmira to a brute for the coin her comely face would fetch him.

"I think I'll throw this one over the docks. He'll emerge bloated and sick when he wakes up, but that'll heal as soon as his ichor rejuvenates. Then he'll be like an infant—no memories, barely conscious, and with all his evil cleansed to start anew."

Glowering into the slack face of their prey, Palmira's shoulders began to shake as she choked back sobs of grief and catharsis. The words took a moment to come, and Cosima had to strive to hear them, but she said them.

"More than my baby ever got."

"I know. I'm sorry." *I know, I'm sorry* were paltry offerings for the kind, generous women Cosima could only protect after the worst days of their lives had broken them. Her own inadequacy disgusted her, but she reached out a tentative hand to rest on Palmira's shoulder to offer support. "I can't replace what you lost. This meager vengeance is all I can offer you, Palmira—but I will promise with everything I've ever had or will have that you will have a better life. I promise you there is more goodness in store for you than the wickedness you've endured."

The dagger gleamed under the moon as Palmira let out a ragged cry and slashed the captured Saint across the throat. Ichorus blood fountained from his throat as she cut deep…and slashed again, and again, as Cosima had instructed before the hunt. She cut and stabbed all across his body as she wept and shouted her child's name in a singular invective of condemnation she clearly wished the villain was awake to hear.

Cosima thought many Saints and Godlings needed this treatment to wash them clean of their sins against regular mortals—and often each other—they should have enjoyed harmonious coexistence with. Yet unless she rescued someone or someone came to her to report a heinous deed worth such a torturous rebirth, she didn't have it in her to cleanse their entire race. The secret as to why so many of her kindred lunged in the direction of evil with eyes wide open had evaded her for decades.

They all waited—Cosima supervising Palmira while the others held respectful vigil in silence—until it was over. Then Iulia intervened, kneeling to embrace Palmira before she led her away from their group to mourn in peace. As she passed Cosima, Palmira looked up at her with blood and tears smeared on her heart-shaped face and murmured her thanks as she squeezed her hand in gratitude. Her hands were calloused from all the work she did to make herself feel worthy of her place in the treehouse—among the other, older huntresses—but her touch was as soft and affectionate as what she used to care for her new obsession: Lilias.

Though she was skilled at withholding emotion, even Cosima had to blink back tears at the sight of the anguish that could now, one day, possibly heal in Palmira's sage-colored eyes. All of their hunts had moved her: she couldn't say such a terrible necessity brought her joy, but the trickle of peace that filled her as she brought resolution to each wonderful woman she had rescued—that her own kind had hurt— could not be undervalued.

If Goddess knew what they did, She never made it known or attempted to stop them. Struck by the notion that occurred to her, Cosima paused as the others left to meander through the city in pairs and trios to purchase necessities or briefly entertain themselves in ways that didn't require violence. She trusted that they knew enough to not be recognized as huntresses, or as anything more than citizens going about their business. As far as anyone knew, the only thing Cosima's women hunted were plains deer.

Maybe it was *because* of her vigilantism that Marzanna had chosen her as heir. When Sovanna—absent though she had made herself these past years—was Her firstborn and heir, when there were plenty of other flatterers to persuade Her, what distinction had set sullen, disrespectful Cosima apart from the rest?

*Could She be…*Cosima crushed the words, but the rubble reformed as the drained Saint's consciousness eventually would. *Could She be proud of me? For cleaning Her messes and taking care of Her people?*

It didn't matter. Cosima had to continue as if what she and her huntresses did would be treated as gross sacrilege and a capital offence. Which meant the grim task of lugging the Saint's body to the docks, scrubbing away blood and any tracks they had left from their hunt, and arranging all the other details of how she would handle the Saint eventually waking up with a blank consciousness were left solely to her.

"Cosima?"

One of the huntresses had stayed behind. Lost in thought and on edge, Cosima startled as she turned to face the door. The shining moon obscured the figure and blinded her for a moment, but then Konetta moved toward her and revealed herself. The ramshackle door swung shut behind her, enclosing them again in the storehouse lit only by Cosima's aureole.

"You stayed?" *Konetta.* Yearning made Cosima careless—reckless—like control over herself was slipping out of her grasp. There was something meek in Konetta that contrasted her unyielding strength of spirit. It showed in her woods-brown eyes, the crooked flash of a smile she showed often to those she loved, the self-conscious little shrug she'd do when one of the other women complimented her archery or speed.

"I have a question." Breaking Cosima's reverie, Konetta moved deeper into the capacious room, toward the drained Saint. The *draining* Saint, since the only reason Cosima hadn't done anything yet was because she had to wait for the rest of the ichor to ooze out before she could cleanse the area.

"Ask." She loved Iulia. She always would. Cosima reminded herself of this often; the more she stayed around her, the less often she had to remind herself of this.

But there was a frightening possibility that she *needed* Konetta—to have and call Konetta her own—that she had to work to reject every single day lest she imitate her fellow divine beings to an unforgiveable result.

Konetta knelt a little ways away from the body; carefully, so she wouldn't have gold-tinged blood on her leggings. "How has Goddess—or Her consorts—not noticed members of Her court vanishing for a while before they reappear without any trace of who they were or a shred of memory left? The others don't want to ask, but

I know enough of us have wondered what happens to these gulls once they wake up."

Cosima sighed. Buying time with an exaggerated focus on turning her head to crack her neck, she cast Konetta a sideways glance to see if she was likely to give up at this sign of her reluctance. Konetta only lifted her brows in challenge that was friendly but unconvinced.

"I see that they're taken care of. I have various people in the city I bargain with to teach them the basics of life and divinity and persuade them that it's normal for them to have gaps in their memory. They think they're brand new…and that Goddess gave them a mandate to leave the city and make lives for themselves elsewhere on the island or in Ioggenica. If it ever occurs to them to question any of that, there's nothing left for them to find. No trails for them to follow to the truth."

"What about the people who introduce them to the world again? Wouldn't they become the first steps on the path that leads back to us?" Konetta asked.

"They know how to contact me at the first sign of anyone sniffing around, or a Saint or Godling pursuing them for information. No one ever has…but if that happened, I have plans to get them out of Aebbenary for good."

Konetta processed this information well; without more than a short delay, she surprised Cosima again. "I want to help."

"Why? It's a tedious business." Cosima tried to dissuade her with nonchalance. "Besides, it's better if none of you know anything. Your denials, if ever necessary, will be plausible."

Konetta's story was as tragic as the rest, but not quite as heartrending as Palmira's. She'd been born to a wealthier family, but she'd been sickly as a child and for various other reasons they had fallen on hard times. One thing led to another when a Godling had taken interest in Konetta for reasons that turned out to be undiluted spite against another Godling who had used her family's business to thwart a scheme of some kind.

Petty beings or not, Konetta had paid the price with her family's ruin, the Godling who had feigned care for her had used his power to pass her sickness to her family—who were all gone now—and poverty had driven her to the oldest trade in the world before she'd come to Cosima.

With Cosima's help a few years past, they had hunted that pair of Godlings down. Their numbers had been smaller, then, and Konetta had been sick at the time. Cosima had risked corralling two of her divine half-siblings (born of Fiammetta and Marzanna's Light) into a small neighborhood so her mortal friends could hunt them safely. Though she had hardly been able to lift the dagger, Konetta had managed to avenge her lost innocence, her parents, and her sisters by her own hand.

It was because of this that Cosima jerked her head in an allowance for Konetta to accompany her. She wasn't sick at the moment—her cheeks were flushed with health—and while she could act as delicate and ladylike as she pleased, she was rarely squeamish when it came to skinning the prey they caught to eat rather than what fed their souls.

Smiling in acknowledgment, Konetta followed Cosima's lead as she crouched to inspect the fallen Saint. Their arms brushed together at the elbows as they waited for the last drops to seep from the wounds Palmira had sliced into his flesh. To avoid considering that, Cosima began to rip out the arrows her huntresses had downed him with and dissolve them into ash with a puff of Light.

"Are you ever going to tell us how you discovered a way to subdue blessèd beings?" Joining her, Konetta pulled out the arrows on her side with little grunts of effort accompanied by the squelching sound of tearing meat.

The flashback was so instantaneous Cosima couldn't hide her flinch. Her ladies had asked her before why she had not only taken pity on them, but to this day sheltered and cared for them. Even Iulia only knew part of her story.

They had hunted her. Would-be Saints and younger Godlings grown to rapid maturity from the milk of Goddess's will had pursued her, hounded her, driven her far and away out of the city in jealousy of the favor shown to Bettina. Cosima had pleaded and cried as they beat her, since she was only a girl and had no grip on the raw power that coursed through her, and accepted the promise that they would do worse if she dared return to Aebbenary or tell anyone what they'd done.

Petulant in her fury, Cosima had obliged only so she could wait for Marzanna to find her and punish those who had tried to bring her low. She had waited, and waited…and waited…

Bettina had found her eventually. To her credit, she had been searching almost since the hour Cosima had gone missing from the Holy Tower…but it had still taken too long. The scars on Cosima's heart deepened the more she had carved into them to keep her angry rather than lost and afraid.

The memories hurt every time someone asked. Cosima could never bear to wound her ladies with the full tale; nor could she bear even a measure of the pity she had offered them. But right now, it was just her and Konetta…and she found herself opening the door to the discussion.

"I was a child once. A foolish, weak little thing. We…we all become as we are now through the same suffering." This explanation, vague as it was, took effort enough to make her sweat as hunting had not. Her chest tightened; she burned the last arrow Konetta passed her with too much vigor and sent stray sparks skittering over the decaying rushes on the floor.

"Did you give yourself vengeance?" Konetta asked.

More memories. *The Saints-to-be hadn't bothered her again, since they were cowards, but the younger Godlings had been another story. One had attempted to kill Cristoval…so Cosima had all but obliterated them to the best of her burgeoning abilities. Only Bettina's guile had kept Goddess from intervening against her then.*

Ugliness had compounded on ugliness after that. Cosima loathed reflecting on what exactly she had done to the Saints she tracked down, alone, to test exactly how far their immortality protected them.

Cosima tried to answer without letting any of the details creep out of the mental prison she stored them in. "I didn't need to. Mama protected me…and Cristoval. At great personal cost."

"I thought…"

Silence wound between them as Cosima gestured for Konetta to stand with her and back away. Beckoning her power, she let her eyes fall half-lidded as she twisted the will she'd used to turn eyes and ears away from the storehouse to absorb the ichor into itself. If another Godling—or a snooping Saint—ever came looking they'd see nothing, even if their senses were on alert to the ominous remnant of danger the blood would mark forevermore. Only if Marzanna Herself—or Her consorts—came here would the ichor rise to betray Cosima and her huntresses.

Cosima had little fear of that. Goddess did not tend to meddle in mortal affairs in person or wonder where any of Her progeny had gone astray.

Just a body was left—drained, dry, and ready to be heaved into the waters off Aebbenary's docks. Cosima lowered her hands as their glow faded along with the ichor stains and her energy for the tasks at hand. Revenge was a gift she granted her followers with a glad heart, but the pressure of Konetta's perceptive questions and Cosima's overwhelming awareness of her frayed her resistance to the thinnest threads.

She *wanted* to tell her story to Konetta. She wanted, she *wanted*...

Cosima voluntarily resumed their conversation. "Thought what?"

"I've heard things about your mother. You stayed in Aebbenary rather than follow her, and...word has it you fought bitterly before she left." Konetta observed while she waited for instruction. Cosima tried to look at her without being noticed from the corner of her eyes as she walked to one of the back corners of the room to fetch some supplies she'd hidden days earlier.

"Our relationship is complicated. I don't like to think about its nuances—for me, it's enough to know Bettina loves me and my brother with everything she has."

It wasn't enough. It never had been. Cosima had hungered for the position of Bettina's favorite, her cherished daughter, for her entire life. She had craved the same care given to Cristoval: tender as a kiss on her forehead before sleep, sweet as the melodies Bettina used to sing for them on their daily excursions into the city or the wilds.

Guilt twinged as Cosima swung her long braid over her shoulder and picked up the moldering roll of oilcloth with one arm. She gestured to a pile of rope with her free hand, and Konetta scurried to get it.

Mama loves both of us. She never denied me any part of her heart. It's my jealousy and greed that ruined it all, Cosima reminded herself.

Whether she had inherited it from Marzanna's covetousness or her lonely upbringing as a divine child during Bettina's period of adoration for Goddess, the desire to be someone's ultimate object of love had plagued her adolescence and adulthood. It had led her down paths shadowed by monsters riddled with Light, a tempestuous youth that left her feeling ancient by her twenty-fifth year, and littered with regret over the relationships she'd ruined.

Iulia treasured her as no one ever had. It still wasn't enough for Cosima—the evidence of her failure to be better than the other divine beings and their foibles was right in front of her.

As she began to wrap up the body for transport, Konetta anticipated her wish to knot the rope around the oilcloth parcel and got to work. Though she was dressed as simply as the rest of the huntresses, her leathers—handmade since each huntress had crafted their own with Cosima's guidance—were a lighter brown dotted with white from the piebald deer sacrificed to make them; Cosima wanted to trail her fingertips down the ridges of her spine to see if she'd laugh.

Say something. The silence was too heavy. When Konetta turned to smile at her—maybe encouraging her to divulge more about her past— Cosima blurted anything to distract herself.

"You don't have to worry. There are more divine beings here than you know if you include the Saints, and no one pays enough attention to them to miss them. I've even spread the word, with great subtlety, that these rebirths are a test from Goddess. So the others don't question any strange disappearance and reappearances at all."

"And our hunts are spaced far apart. I gathered."

Once they were done, Cosima rolled the drained Saint behind some crates and left him there. Leading the way, she dusted any debris from her clothing and left the building after assuring herself they were still alone.

"What next?" asked Konetta.

"I'm going to contact one of my…hm." *How to explain?* Cosima told her women almost everything, but not all of them cared for politics or the machinations of court; most of them didn't listen. "I could take the body to the docks myself under the cloak of my Light. But sometimes Godlings and Saints can see through it, under the right circumstances. With my star on the rise people will be looking for me. *At* me—to see what I'm capable of doing."

Konetta nodded; with instincts taught by Cosima and the others, she kept her gait silent and her reflexes on alert as they left the storehouse and journeyed closer to the city proper. Their conversation paused by necessity, but she spoke up once they picked their way through side streets and alleys without allowing any eyes to trespass on their doings.

"Not everyone is a devotee of Aebbenary's regime. I'm not surprised you have people to help you." It wasn't like Konetta to disapprove, but Cosima heard the underlying tone beneath her cautious wording.

"They're well-compensated for the risk. I bargain for their help as infrequently as I can." Though Cosima explained, Konetta didn't seem at ease. She scratched her arm with her other hand, as if she could pick away the scab of a bad memory.

"Is there enough compensation in the world for what would happen if Goddess discovers what we've done?"

Oh. She's not disapproving, she's just scared. Embarrassed she'd misread her, Cosima tapped her shoulder into Konetta's. Konetta was a lot shorter, so stooping was awkward, but Cosima reminded herself it didn't matter. Other people didn't always notice the excruciating time she had trying to fit in amongst people she actually cared for.

"You're right—there isn't. What we've done is a sin that would not be punished lightly. But like I did with you and our huntresses, I left the choice up to you. Many who live in the shadow of the Holy Tower dream of a life…" Cosima stopped. Konetta didn't finish her sentence for her, but her nod was as good as a verbal agreement to her sentiments.

"A *life*." She grasped Cosima's free swinging hand on her side in one of her own for reassurance. Her palm was hot against her skin; Cosima let go, practically throwing Konetta's hand away in her haste to quell the dismayed longing that made her gasp.

"Iulia has taken to Lilias, don't you think?" Cosima blurted—anything to distract from what she'd done. If anyone—especially Konetta herself—knew the twisted roots of her wishes, desires she'd told herself were the insatiable product of her half-feral upbringing, she'd probably try to drain herself to start her life anew the way she did with the divine beings her huntresses punished.

Going back to scratching her arm, Konetta ignored the haste with which Cosima had rejected her touch. "All of us have...except for Grisel, but she's contrary about everything. Like Iulia is agreeable about everything."

Iulia, Iulia. Cosima loved her with all her heart—didn't she? Was it love to have someone you were fond of, someone who rested forever on your mind?

Who you almost forgot about whenever another person you couldn't stop thinking about was present? When their touch ignited you beyond all possible belief? She and Iulia had become friends first when Cosima had begun to crave companions in her independence; comrades in arms became casual bedmates became true lovers. Konetta had been around for a long time...and Cosima had wanted her for most of it.

Iulia's love *hurt.* It reminded Cosima every day that someday she would lose it, because her penchant for mistakes or her immortality would sever their ties forever. With the surging of her contemptible hunger for Konetta, the possibility that it was better to lose her connection to Iulia *now*, before she grew older or Cosima grew more monstrous, had already started to haunt every waking hour...

A few more twists and turns down dilapidated streets populated by laborers who kept the rest of the city running according to the Shining Court's standards and thus were too exhausted to make much mischief at night led them to their destination. With Konetta quiet at her side, Cosima made quick work of their business: entering the shop through the unlocked back door, she grabbed a nearby broom with the handle polished by frequent use and tapped a peculiar pattern on the ceiling. A few seconds later, she tapped again, then set the broom back where she'd found it.

Next, she removed a leather pouch filled with an exact count of the (stolen) coins she needed and hid it away in a floorboard. In a whisper, she explained to Konetta what she'd done: the broomstick pattern alerted the shopkeeper in residence to check her various haunts for the results of their hunt, and the coins with a coded message in the note tucked inside the pouch would assure the matter would be taken care of. Thus they rarely needed to meet face-to-face, and had less likelihood of being identified as associates.

Then they left. Cosima wanted to get much deeper into the sleepless entertainment districts of Aebbenary before she sent a signal to her other huntresses that it was time to go home. They would be content to do so; to avoid any kernel of suspicion, they didn't only come to the city during their hunts.

After they'd left the shop and walked some ways away, Konetta turned to look back to see if anyone had followed, stopped in her tracks, and yanked on Cosima's sleeve.

"Is that…" Konetta trailed off, gesturing toward the way they'd come.

Cosima didn't bother finishing her sentence. They could both see Cristoval—with Crespin trundling cheerfully behind him—enter the derelict shop they'd just left. It was almost Miraculous he hadn't spotted them.

Brother of mine, what have you stumbled into now?

She didn't pause. Cosima grabbed Konetta's wrist and pulled her along, back toward the shop. By the time they entered, whatever deal Cristoval had planned was done. She arrived in time to see a small black bag disappear into an inner pocket of Cristoval's cloak.

There was still no sign of the reclusive shopkeeper: Cristoval would have had to know someone important to even hear the name of this dark business partner, and they would have had to meet a few times before he had the trust to enact trades the way Cosima did.

"Cosima?" His expressive brows lifted; he'd been careful, Cosima had been able to read from his posture, but he hadn't been alert against her.

"What are you doing here?"

"Hello, Cristoval. Crespin." Konetta greeted both of them in place of Cosima. With the easy, open affection of the treehouse residents that newcomers would have to labor years to earn, she snaked an arm around Cosima's waist and tipped her head onto her shoulder. Her deliberate touch electrified Cosima—even her aureole sang brighter, warmer.

Exasperated, Cristoval granted Konetta a half-bow that was both gallant and impolite only because he had been thrown completely out of sorts by their unexpected arrival. Crespin waved with the hand that wasn't holding another parcel wrapped in plain sackcloth.

"Konetta. Where's Lilias?"

"Asleep for the night in their chrysanthemum. If they wake up Cosima arranged a Miracle to let her know."

"Tell me what you're up to." Cosima said. "Now. You shouldn't even know about this place."

"Are you going to tell me what *you* are doing here? Why should I share my business while you keep yours to yourself?"

I can take care of myself. You can't! Old words to an old series of arguments that had fractured their relationship as siblings. What elder brother didn't expect to care for his little sister? What older sibling would accept care from a younger one they had known since infancy?

Furious, Cosima glared at him and tried to resist the impulse to rip the pouch he'd hidden away in his cloak to beat him over the head with it.

"Should we stay here?" Konetta asked; as was her habit, she broke the tension between Cristoval and Cosima like she broke up arguments at the treehouse. "If we keep moving—"

Cosima grunted an acknowledgement. With the others following her lead she steered them out of the seemingly abandoned shop and kept them moving toward the wide-awake districts of the city rather than the forlorn jurisdiction of the laborers too poor to afford the upkeep they provided to Aebbenary proper.

"Do you really want to know?" Cristoval asked, relenting after half a mile.

"*Yes.*"

"Fine. I'm—"

"Lower your voice!" Crespin admonished as they ducked under the valance of another closed shop. Rolling her eyes, Cosima risked a measure of power to fan out her halo with one smooth roll to reveal any souls loitering nearby to eavesdrop. Cristoval had seen this trick before: he waited for the Light to return before he continued.

"Aebbenary isn't thriving. Not compared to the rest of the world. All the tribute sent from other lands to placate Goddess goes directly to Her—with none left for Her people. Poverty is rife beneath the surface…as is sickness. A plague concerning more than mortals."

"Divine beings can't sicken. They can't die."

"Can't they?" Cristoval asked. Two discreet words, yet they chilled Cosima.

He can't know. He couldn't possibly…

Fear—that hated companion thrust on her by Bettina's perpetual anxiety and validated by Goddess's inconstant esteem—for her brother left her sick to her stomach with dread.

"*Someone* needs to care about the people here." Mistaking her freezing for disapproval, Cristoval continued. Taller, he looked down at her as if he was resisting the urge to scold her.

"You. A mortal Goddess is already annoyed with." Her incredulity aside, Cosima forced the muscles of her mouth to form an approximation of a smile. She had always felt different from Cristoval, especially in Bettina's eyes. He was sweet where she was sullen; he was patient and smart while she was bullheaded, and so on. "And your aged father to boot."

"Not so elderly I can't help a good cause."

"With what? A tuneless lyre? Your angelic singing voice?"

Crespin laughed at Cosima's jibe, but Cristoval frowned—imperious in his disapproval. Konetta elbowed her in the ribs.

"Don't trouble yourself to assist us if you'd rather not—there's another Godling willing to help us if you aren't," said Cristoval.

Cosima's smugness faded. *Another Godling?* "Who?"

"It would not be honorable for me to tell you. It's not safe for either of us, but especially for her."

"Her?"

Crespin barked another laugh. "You're my son, surely enough. And you're Bett's daughter." Though they didn't know each other at all, his smile was fond as he gazed on Cosima, who fought the impulse to cross her arms and look away in petulant temper. "You got more out of him about this mysterious partner than I have since he told me about his plan."

"At least he *told* you." Resentment didn't become Cosima: she felt the angry, mottled flush rising to her cheeks. Her halo crackled with static, making some of her hair stand on end before she jerkily smoothed it down. "When will you meet her?"

Cristoval scraped his neck under his mop of hair, uncomfortable with her disapproval. "Your Jubilee. Don't—*don't* start yelling. It will be in passing, no more than a second or two. I've left her a letter—indirectly—with what I have observed since my return to Aebbenary, and she's going to impart some information about her studies of the sickness so far again. It's all arranged."

The lightning in her aureole spread its shoots into Cosima's eyes as she stared at him, aghast. Even Konetta took a few steps away from her, making room for the storm that could spear every mortal near Cosima if she lost her grip on her temper.

"You *wrote down* damning information and left it for someone to find? Did you sign your name with a jaunty little flourish too?"

You're only this angry because you're afraid. This is fear. Her emotions always felt like a battleground where she suffered loss after loss without reprieve. Mastering herself had never been so difficult: why did no one endlessly think things through the way she did? Why was she the only one who agonized over every decision or felt the weight of tangible responsibility for the people she cared about?

Cristoval—and Crespin, she supposed—had a distant dream of a better world, but how much would it cost to get there? And who would pay?

Her brother waited her out, refusing to speak until the lightning died down and Cosima took several deep breaths, his frustration with her softened into concern. Taking one of her clenched, shaking fists in his hands, he didn't talk until she looked up at him.

"I've been working on this for a long time; my associate has as well. We're not inexperienced, and we've been incredibly careful. All I know is she's a Godling interested in…positive change for this island. There are always going to be risks, though, and we have to be the ones to take them sometimes. I won't let haste or my ego ruin the work we've done."

"Is that why you really went away? Besides what Mama wanted." Cosima felt Konetta's steadying hand on her back, offering the comfort of a sister Cosima should have considered her to be. Everything was awful—her wonderful, brave, fragile brother, his jolly father who seemed to really care about him even though they'd just found each other, and Cosima herself. They were all bright springs of hope while she was a shadow person burgeoning into Marzanna's heir in every sense of the word.

Maybe that's why She chose me—I'm as selfish as She is.

"In part. I had my studies abroad, and I wanted to travel like Mother wanted." Mother for him was Bettina, not Goddess.

Crespin interjected; he'd turned away from their group to grant the siblings a chance to talk, and used keeping a look-out as an excuse. "I don't think he expected to find me at all, let alone find me willing to help."

"Why are you helping? Just because of Cristoval?" Cosima gave Konetta a grateful look, glad someone else had asked that question besides her.

"I'm an Aebbenary native. Cristoval is my only son, and Bettina…" Sighing, Crespin faced them fully and scratched at the peppery stubble on his jaw. "I'm fond of her still. She made the only child I'm likely to have."

"That you know of." Cristoval nudged his father, making Crespin chuckle and hold up his hands in a shrug.

"Aye. Either way—I've travelled. I've seen most of the continent and a fair glimpse into lands beyond the comprehension of folk stuck on this island. Beautiful though it is, warm though I feel toward my homeland, the rest of the world thrives compared to this city and this island."

"Aebbenary is the last bastion of divine rule in the world. We are fortunate Goddess has not seen the need to conquer all other lands the way Her predecessor did. *The world* is lucky."

Beginning to understand—and stirred by the valiant picture the two of them painted—Cosima did her best to let go of her fear, or make it let go of her.

If Marzanna ever set Her sights on conquest, the toll She and Her court would inflict on this teeming earth...

She loved her family. Though they could resent her for it, even hate her, Cosima wouldn't risk losing them. Even if they parted for the rest of their lives—for the eternity promised to her and Bettina—as long as they were safe she would be content. But was her security worth the price of letting the rest of the world pay for her comfort?

"Fine. Go. The less anyone knows about this the better. Have you told Mama?"

"Of course not." With unintentional concurrency the two of them rolled their eyes. Bettina could be canny when it came to plots and scheming, but when either Cosima or Cristoval was involved, she dissolved into a sentimental puddle. Neither of them could fault her for that, not really. That was the lot of mothers, after all. *True* mothers.

There was no such thing as hope—not in Aebbenary, not for mortal beings. If Cristoval was right, their lot might be worse than Cosima had expected. Confusion frustrated her, and when she was frustrated her first response was anger.

It took everything in her—everything *left* after the cathartic evening she'd spent draining a Saint and resisting her longing for Konetta—to stifle her worst instincts as she let Cristoval and his father go and rendezvoused with her huntresses.

She used her Light to carry them home one by one. Iulia was first, and in high spirits from her successful evening out. She'd remembered to fetch a parcel of spiced walnuts mixed with honey for Cosima, who kissed her in thanks and tried to be fully present in her arms as she brought her back to the treehouse.

Palmira was second to last, so when she made it home she would have friendly arms to collapse into to continue grieving after Iulia and the others had done their best to help her celebrate her successful hunt.

Last of all—Konetta. Who grabbed Cosima with steady arms and held tight so she could gaze into her face to read it.

"I think you're capable of greater things than you allow yourself to dream. I think it's a shame, how much you doubt yourself."

Shame. A funny word when it came to Cosima. It kept closer company to her than condensation on glass, or mist to breath in winter. As she met Konetta's tranquil gaze and tried to let it keep her she couldn't help glancing at her soft, inviting mouth.

"What if I'm capable of harm instead of good? What if all I can ever do is make things worse?" Cosima asked her. Her voice was deeper than she'd intended, husky with want she'd forgotten to disguise.

"Not possible. Even if you were…" Unexpectedly releasing her from her spell, Konetta withdrew with a self-conscious little laugh. "I'm not going anywhere. I'll wait around until you come to your senses."

You're going to have to wait for me forever. Cosima thought, rooted to the spot until she shook the energy sparking her power off like a dog shook rain off its coat. *I don't think I have much good sense at all.*

X

Bettina

Every other day for the dozen days leading up to Cosima's Jubilee, Marzanna summoned Bettina to the Holy Tower for company. There was not—and might never again be—an option to refuse Her. Not if Bettina wanted to provide proof she wanted to exalt Goddess with her entire body and soul again.

In those days, as she feigned love and devotion with all her might and all the charm she had ever possessed, Bettina pretended even to herself that she didn't dream of denying Goddess anything.

They danced around each other as casual entertainment filled their days as it once had: riding through the countryside untainted by human occupation, sailing along the coast and fleeing a rainstorm in gusts of laughter as they huddled under the edge of one of the cliffs to avoid the worst of the tempest, lounging under trees and fans wielded by ambitious Saints while they fed each other delicacies.

When it came to Marzanna, there was no such thing as armor. There was no shield that could withstand the crack of Her hammer against its edge—Her joy. No chainmail that would prevent the arrows of Her regard from penetrating down to the nadir of Bettina's heart.

Though she had no defenses, Bettina had one weapon to retaliate against the onslaught of courtship from Goddess: the knowledge granted to her by Magisend. A plan to awe her with the performance of all lifetimes; a way to protect her children from her failure if that was her destiny; and a dubious ally in the former High Priest of Silver.

If she ever found him. He'd made himself scarce since his skin had been ripped from him again. Marzanna hadn't seemed interested in summoning Her favorite whipping boy to intrude on their courtship.

Mortal members of Fiammetta's court—Marzanna's court in truth—had been invited, surprising Bettina. It would have been difficult to tell them apart from the other divine beings aside from their lack of Light based on their style and regality alone. Like Silver before the Bright Age, Fiammetta had populated her court with only the beautiful and talented.

Yet years had still passed since the dawn of the age. Even if the chosen mortals had been selected quite young, they and their offspring were showing signs of time's relentless grind and the price of decadence beneath Goddess's halo. Bettina didn't recognize many of the mortals, but part of her doubted she'd be able to. Once she started noticing the bloodshot, drink-addled eyes and the bloated necks and swollen features of the mortals, she couldn't un-see it. Under the noon sun they appeared miserable as they sweated and smiled—but they'd endure it. They'd endure much suffering for the chance at eternal life if they revered Fiammetta and she recommended Marzanna anoint them to join Her ranks of Saints.

To greet the visiting and returning dignitaries, Fiammetta had arranged for everyone to gather in her palace—the former seat of the Betilienus family, where Goddess's revered Scholar had come from.

Bettina looked around with interest she disguised with a cool, bored expression and a lazy flick of her wrist as she batted away a gnat. Before the Bright Age the palace had been furnished handsomely but left to squalor as the mortals in power surrendered to their lesser urges; pennants of their house had hung in tatters of proud flags once humbled by neglect. After the palace had been reduced to mostly rubble and rebuilt from the ground up, the circular throne room built with love and care for Marzanna's favorite consort was a place of repose mingled with a display of power none but Goddess could rival.

An aisle demarcated with ornate tiles depicting the likeness of the old god for disrespectful feet to trod on—the only silver in the building—for guests to promenade or dance around based on

Fiammetta's wishes. The columns supporting the other walls of the huge room were wound around and around with vines perennially supporting lemons that were as sweet as candy. The ones that draped from the ceiling bore no fruit, but they had been Made sturdier to support hanging swings and the cushions the leaves curled themselves into when others were permitted to sit.

Only lucky friends like Bettina or the other consorts were granted lounges that twisted themselves off their base vines and crept by Miraculous power to wherever they wanted to position themselves in the room.

"Has Marzanna announced where She will host the Jubilee?" Bettina asked Fiammetta as she settled onto the chaise the room had provided as a sign of her increasing status as one of Goddess's current favorites. This was who she had to guard her thoughts from the most lest any of her abhorrence show in the slightest word or deed.

It was Fiammetta, after all, who had used her influence with Marzanna to dash Bettina's hopes for her children to pieces. When she had demanded Cristoval be given to her as a nursery playmate for her first son with Goddess—like a plaything that could be picked up and thrown away when a child grew bored—Bettina had uneasily allowed it…until the Godling had lost his temper and nearly killed Cristoval. Cosima had been there to protect him—ferociously, vindictively. She had almost been the only one left alive that ill-starred afternoon.

In Her way, Goddess had been merciful. She had spared Cosima any punishment other than inflicting on her the same wounds she had wreaked on Fiammetta's son…and banished Cristoval to a family of human nobility as soon as She healed his injuries. It hadn't been long after that that Bettina had made her final entreaty to Marzanna to anoint him as a Saint…and Goddess had commanded her never to ask Her that again.

"He is the last of your mortal life before Me, My swan. I will let him live the life he has been granted—a fine enough life for a human boy. You have Cosima, Me, and other children if you so desire," Marzanna had said to her, smiling indulgently; Bettina recalled they had been laying on the grass together after a vigorous spell of love-making that still made her legs shake at

the sensational memory. *"I will give you everything you need, dearest, but do not ask Me to anoint your son again. I have not chosen him."*

With a sour taste in her mouth very different from the saccharinity of those old memories, Bettina returned to the present and resumed trying to charm her way into success.

"Goddess left the arrangements to me. I've decided to host it on the water: our leisure ship could use an outing. Marzanna's Light on the sea is a splendid sight." Fiammetta sighed, dreamy as she always was except when she surrendered to the wisps of insanity everyone could see but Goddess Herself.

Appropriate. A lark for Fiammetta and inconvenience for everyone else. Bettina reminded herself it didn't matter.

"How grand! Cosima will be pleased," she said.

"Will she?" Sniffing with disdain, Fiammetta's dreaminess evaporated. "Marzanna had to force her to agree to the Jubilee in the first place. That girl's raising has been *your* responsibility, as you insisted. Was the ingratitude you entrenched in her intentional?"

Bettina's temper flared along with her nostrils. *Bitch.*

"Children will do as they will despite their nurturing." No, that made it sound like she was absolving herself of guilt when neither she nor Cosima had done anything worthy of blame.

Fiammetta didn't give her time to correct herself. "Then those children should be punished. Defiance is not something Goddess will tolerate for long."

Shifting her position, Bettina waved a servant bearing a tray of drinks over to claim two goblets for her and Fiammetta. She passed one into Fiammetta's hand when she held it out in expectation of service. Even if the wine had been aged to perfection, it still would have tasted sour as Bettina silently toasted and sipped from her own cup, buying time for an answer.

"You are right, Goddess be praised. It is a very good thing there's no one left in Aebbenary who intends to challenge Her." Honeying her words like she wished she could sweeten her wine, Bettina ducked her head in a performance of chagrin and made herself reach for

Fiammetta's other hand as she drummed her fingertips against her thigh in a rhythmless beat.

I can't believe I ever fucked you or took pleasure in it. I have sinned my own sins—with more to come—but you are rancid to the core. Smiling, Bettina kissed the row of glittering diamonds arranged over three of Fiammetta's fingers. Frowning down her nose at her, Fiammetta patted her cheek the way she'd pat a stray dog and waved her away as she settled into her lounge to drink her wine.

Submission or not, they had nothing else to say to one another. Fiammetta became occupied with her court of mortal flatterers—including a troupe of jesters who paraded amongst the guests to belittle or uplift them based on where they stood in the convoluted hierarchy—and Bettina resigned herself to boredom as they waited for Marzanna's arrival.

Something interesting enough to peak her curiosity happened first: Däard arrived.

He landed outside the open doors with trumpets announcing his descent so the milling crowd would make way. Fanning his wings to rearrange their feathers, he folded them neatly away as he entered the palace vestibule and approached Fiammetta and Bettina. Before he sat in the chair built especially for him and his wings, he uncurled one of his fists to pass Fiammetta a small scroll wrapped in a string of violets.

She took it, tipping her head sideways for Däard to kiss her cheek as she unraveled the message. While she grumbled over the contents, he touched his lips to the edge of her cheekbone in formal acknowledgment, then seated himself to watch the proceedings alongside Bettina. She granted him a sideways smile, but it was difficult: his mood was off, and she could tell the way she'd always been able to.

"What have you been up to?" She kept her tone playful, but she really wanted to know.

"Overseeing the Jubilee preparations. Marzanna's plans require a firm hand to see them through," he answered. Punctuating his reply, Fiammetta hissed an indelicate curse and tossed the message aside. One of the violets clung to her thumb and she pinched its petals to crush them before she flung it aside in disgust.

"This is *ridiculous.*" Bettina recognized Fiammetta's infamous pout when she saw it. Pretty enough, but with enough venom to send the mortals dancing for her entertainment and performing tricks on command nearby scattering. "Must I do everything myself? Bring me the decorators. They need motivation."

Catching Bettina's eye again, Däard rolled his eyes as he explained. "Goddess will be late. She's been mesmerized by Her studies again."

The Archives. Magisend. Bettina laughed to cover the stab of alarm that made her freeze. "Her studies? What could She not already know?"

"We all have to pass our time somehow. She has always been inquisitive about the world. The only one who begrudges Her this is Fia…she doesn't like when Marzanna is distracted."

"Has She been distracted much lately?" Bettina asked. *If I asked, would he tell me what Goddess hopes to find? Why She won't ask Magisend direct questions?*

"Distracted enough to create discord between Her and Fia. She's promised to make it up to her soon, but who knows when that will be?" Unconcerned, Däard called the violets Fiammetta had cast aside to his hands and coaxed life back into their crushed petals with a Miraculous breath.

A server with a trembling grasp on his tray returned with another goblet for Däard, this one full of an ale imported from Ioggenica that he'd discovered decades ago and brought to the island to be replicated. Teasing him, Bettina grabbed the cup before his fingertips could touch it and swigged a hearty third of it before she handed it over.

He traded the violets he had revived for the goblet. Bettina cupped them in her palms as they unfurled with more and more petals while their stems sent new lianas to curl around her wrists.

"Have you visited much with Cosima since your return? I know Goddess claims much of your time, but…" He laughed, self-conscious. "I've never been good at skirting a subject. I want to know how the baby is."

Bettina's smile was genuine this time. *At least someone cares about them.*

"Do you worry about the quality of Cosima's maternal care? You shouldn't. Cristoval visited her recently: the baby is growing well. She named them Lilias."

"Lilias." Däard repeated. "A gentle name for a Saintling. Better than what I would have come up with."

"You have other progeny. Didn't you name any of those?"

"Marzanna loves choosing names. It's..." To speak negatively about Goddess could be considered blasphemy. Bettina indulged in her private thoughts, and Marzanna couldn't be reading everyone everywhere all the time...but for a consort to speak ill of Her would also be a betrayal. Would he risk it?

"My other children grew too swiftly for me to mark. When I'd begun to care for them they were already too old to need a father. I had hopes this time..." Däard was all hesitation. All reluctance to choose bold words and stick to them regardless of Goddess's disapproval. "Lilias. Perhaps when I see them again they'll remember me."

Bettina gestured to yet another servant carrying cups; instead of taking one of the goblets they presented with a rote flourish, she whispered a word into their ear to bring water instead of wine. Däard heard, but didn't mark; he sank into his chair with regal discontent she had commiserated with when they had both been mortals tossed about by the whims of their world.

In another life, they would have been long wed by now, with children of their own all raised. She could have loved him: her heart had been painfully open to the idea back then. Now, while he drowned in his impotency as Goddess's superfluous sword, all she could do was pity him.

And gently, prudently rebuke him for standing by while Aebbenary decayed all around them thanks to Goddess's indulgence of Fiammetta and humanity's baser impulses.

When the servant returned with their clean, mint-enhanced water she dropped the violets—after disentangling them from around her dominant wrist and forearm—into the cup to further flavor the beverage. "Refresh yourself with me, Ranieri. It's been so long since we bonded."

"I assume we'll have an eternity to do so once Marzanna decides to forgive you and claim you as Her own again." His words were a light jab, but he took the cup she offered and drank from it until a trickle of the faintly glittering water drained out of the corner of his mouth and caught in the shadow of his stubble.

"Can I persuade you to tell me what transpired while I've been away? I didn't want to trouble Her Glory with trivialities when I'm supposed to be earning my way back into Her grace."

"Everything is much the same. Goddess reigns, the numbers of divine beings increase each year, and the island seems to prosper. The conquest of other lands still crops up in idle conversation, but Marzanna has lost interest in its prospects. She lost interest in most things lately aside from Her studies…and you."

The island prospers. Bettina wondered how Däard—who flew over the city every day and kept watch over its people—could have missed the sweep of sickness and the return of poverty that had yoked Aebbenary more surely to the beneficence of divinities. The holy children who behaved as such since maturity had been thrust upon them by Miraculous will rather than earned by time and experience.

"Bettina?" A picture of ennui, Däard propped his chin on his hand and surveyed her with interest he couldn't quite conceal. "You have your own impression of our realm now, I'm sure. Will you share it?"

"Will you forgive any foolishness I utter as an outsider? I've been a recluse during my absence, you see, and my manners aren't as honed as they used to be." An artful pause…though not as contrived as Bettina willed herself to believe. "Aebbenary—I *have* missed it. What I missed, though, seems to have vanished. Though we will live in blessèd Light forever, time's passage cannot be lost on living beings. The world I loved is gone forever, replaced by—"

When he passed the cup of water back to her she scooped the violets out of it and cast them onto the ground. Instantly they took on life again, putting down roots and letting their sprouts roam to mingle with the lemon vines perfuming the air with the scent of citrus that mostly concealed the stink of the sweating guests who danced to Fiammetta's minstrels.

"Fia is accustomed to having her own way." Däard gestured to Fiammetta with a head tilt; his volume dropped lest she overhear them through the ongoing tantrum she was inflicting on the servants and mortal guests. "Goddess humors her in all matters."

Do I finally hear some discontent? Though she was pleased, Bettina chose to isolate the sympathy his words kindled in her and express only that.

"From what I have heard, Her Glory is not the only one who gives way before her whims. Do you not also obey?"

"If it is obedience to listen to the one who commands your heart, then yes. I obey. It is what I am meant for."

You're not! Futile insistence if Bettina dared utter it. *No one is meant to simply obey. No one exists only to serve.*

All she could see was Däard's profile as his attention drifted toward Fiammetta. Bettina had never seen her in the role of a Fount, so she couldn't reference any seed of beauty in her appearance…but as Marzanna's queen she was radiant. An idol with glowing pale gold skin and a river of red hair, round eyes with liquor brown irises rippled with amber, and a skill for pretending to have a sweet, virtuous disposition that had captivated Goddess so thoroughly.

"Do you…love…?" The question had to be put delicately, so delicately. Bettina lost her nerve to speak what might condemn her aloud. She gestured with a subtle lift of her finger toward Fiammetta's throne.

Years had passed since her spell—Marzanna's spell—had broken for Bettina. All she saw now was a horror whose quirks of conceit and lunacy controlled every mortal and divine being in Aebbenary. In the world, if Goddess ever decided to conquer other lands in earnest. Bettina had learned the truth the hard way…had Däard?

"It's not a question of love. I have spent a lifetime at their sides already. The question is…" Däard halted; Bettina laid the hand she had gestured with over his own, leaning in to reassure him the secrets they murmured would be safe with her. "Is it enough? Is there enough of it to excuse…the rest?"

Well? Impatient, she prompted him. "Is it?"

A Saint carved from stone, he sat perfectly still with his ichor-filled veins strained to sharp relief in his forearms where they rested on the arms of his chair. "I have known *transcendent* joy. I have been privileged above all others on this earth. Even...even Lior would not deny me that. That's why he..."

Grief was as eternal as the rest of the divine beings. Bettina had wondered what it would feel like to grieve someone she loved, dreading all the while that the fatal axe she feared would land on her son. She had learned well enough that grief could only be passed through, not diverted or inevitably delayed. Whatever you cocooned yourself in to avoid it would disintegrate before long; any bubble of protection you constructed to spare yourself pain and madness would have to pop at some point.

"He denied me nothing except himself. And I am still...I will always be..." He refused to shed the diamond tears that glazed his eyes. Bettina wondered if Marzanna had—accidentally or by choice—taken the ability away from him.

"Bereft," she finished for his sake.

Pity moved her: she could have cried for both of them if it would do any good. What could she say? They were not allies and they never could be: Däard's love for Goddess was faithful, pure goodness—it was how he had loved their Scholar, she imagined. Bettina's ambition could not sway that.

It was time to turn the subject. She had inflicted enough pain...but her questions demanded answering, and she couldn't afford to spare him.

"The Priest."

"What?"

She swallowed, wishing the perfumed reek of violets wasn't so strong in the air. "I know you're watching him. Is he trustworthy?"

All Däard's melancholy vanished as steel returned to his expression and spine; he straightened, the picture of a soldier about to embark on the voyage that would transform him into a hero. "What have you heard? Or seen?"

*I'm sorry. But I have to know...*Bettina set aside her shame and pressed on.

"He was not always Marzanna's. I see him more rarely than I used to. Is everything well in this court? *Our* court?"

Däard drummed his fingertips against his leg as he studied her, assessing how much she knew that led her to ask that question. "Retaining the Priest has always been like keeping a snake as a pet. It might pretend to sleep, it might curl up beside Her pillow and keep Her company when She chooses, but it will always be a serpent."

"Goddess does dote on Her pets." As soon as she said it Bettina noticed how close those words struck. Though her sins were not as great as what the ex-High Priest had committed, was she not also a pet? A snake, even—one who hissed flattering deceit in Marzanna's ears in hope of reward.

"She was not treasured in Her youth. Cosseting Her darlings is a pastime that brightens Her days. Do you begrudge Her that joy?"

Before she could answer, a resonance made the palace foundations shake. Not the foundations, Bettina noted: it was the leaves on the ivy and the sulking vines that marked Goddess's arrival in a beam of Light to the occupants of the reception. As Marzanna materialized from the rays like She stepped through the roaring cascade of a waterfall, everyone rose and bowed to Her.

Ignoring them all, Goddess smiled at Bettina and rushed toward her.

"Oh, Bett. I have longed to see you." With a diverting, dramatic performance, Marzanna threw Her arms around Bettina's neck and stood on Her toes to bring their mouths together in their first kiss since her return to Aebbenary. The taste of Her was achingly sweet, rich, and cold: like cream poured over ice and sprinkled with sugar to drink down to the crystals that wouldn't dissolve at the bottom.

"Y-you saw me only yesterday, Your Glory. Has it felt so long?" Bettina's heart raced. Her hands shook as she rested them on Marzanna's hips, fighting the urge to drag Her closer as well as shove Her away.

"Say that again."

"What?"

Goddess's halo began to scintillate; luscious, silken warmth enveloped both of them as She cupped Bettina's chin and scraped the tip of her thumbnail on her bottom lip.

"Call Me Your Glory. I love how you sound when you're worshipping Me."

Heat that wasn't just hers suffused Bettina's cheeks. If Marzanna didn't let her go she was going to burn to cinders. She was already smoldering into ash, consumed with the return of her old obsession: Goddess.

Goddess, who still wanted and favored her and might…this time, if Bettina was patient…

"Your Glory. You, Your Glory, Goddess." Bettina steeled herself against the loss of dignity that had never bothered her in those initial days and pitched herself into the present moment with all abandon. She flung herself onto her knees in front of Marzanna and embraced Her, burying her face in Her stomach. Her hands still rested on Goddess's hips. It would be so easy to kiss Her through the gossamer fabric that left most of Her sacred body exposed to the eyes of the court.

"Again." Marzanna's inviting half-smile played around Her mulberry lips as She wove Her fingers into Bettina's crown of braids. She began yanking out the pins that bound it all together as Bettina spoke.

"Your Glory, how could I dare worship You? Your servant is not worthy—I never have been. I chance only to kneel at Your feet, dream of the love we once shared, kiss…" She brushed her lips against the translucent satin of Goddess's gown. "Kiss anywhere You will allow my mouth to profane Your body."

"Soon, My swan. The restoration of your faith has cheered Me to no end." Stooping slightly, Marzanna used the fingers She had woven tightly through Bettina's locks of hair to tip her head back to look up at Her. "Are you happy here?"

"Yes." Goddess would suffer no hesitation from Bettina. "Yes, yes, I am *so happy…*"

"Hm. I wonder if that is enough?"

No. How did she see? I'm on my knees, dissolving into the sweet nothing of sugar in water—

Bettina's panic increased as Marzanna guided her upright and skated Her hands down from her head, past her shoulders, to grip her by the wrists and stretch out her arms like wings. Her mouth went dry as she began to shake, unable to control herself as Light from Goddess began to circle her body and anchor in her flesh.

"You here, side by side with My consorts, has brought Me joy I haven't felt in years. Would you like a reward, beloved?"

Beloved, beloved, beloved. Bettina heard singing in her head and heart—though not in her soul—and nothing else. Her answering nod was vigorous. She had to blink back tears of delight to even see Marzanna through them.

Goddess's eyes began to swallow her. They grew and grew in Bettina's perception as it distorted—as *reality* distorted to reflect Her wishes. Whorls of black and gold formed a dizzying illusion that devoured her head to heel like a cosmic void feasting on a lone planet, aureole and all.

My will alone. The voice: Marzanna's. It shook Bettina apart and remade her at the same time.

Ichor sprang from slits the Light carved into her back, spraying the guests and the walls with scarlet and gold drops. Rather than falling to her knees, Bettina went rigid as she felt the crawling caress of feathers growing from her vertebrae and bones. It would have been *agony,* she guessed, if Goddess hadn't transformed her pain into euphoria. As it was, she laughed, and laughed, giggling uncontrollably at the unbearable tickling sensation of the Miracle that gave her wings.

Wings. Blue as a peacock's with gold rachides and tips, arching high and proud as if she had been born a Saint rather than Made. Even the color was a gift: no other divine being had wings this shade.

Bettina teetered under their shocking weight, but caught herself with Däard's help as he dove forward out of chair to assist her. One of her knees hit the ground hard, though, and she felt her meniscus tear before the energy coursing through her body healed it.

"What favor you have shown this unworthy Saint, Your Glory."

Fiammetta said from where she sat again on the throne Marzanna had gifted to her. When her eyes slid Bettina's way they were poisonous, the brown reminiscent of a spider hidden in amber.

"Do not the unworthy appreciate My gifts more for their own lack of merit?" Goddess's mood could not be dampened. Her Light flashed as She materialized at Fiammetta's side to kiss her before She flashed again beside Bettina and Däard and grabbed an arm each. "Come now, My own. The weather is beautiful today, and we are skyward bound!"

She didn't wait for either of them to ready themselves. With sacred strength, Marzanna launched the three of them upward, further and further, until the ceiling and sky opened at Her unspoken will and Bettina's gorgeous wings carried her into the sunlight to fly.

XI

Cosima

Goddess was not one for hymns and songs of praise, but She had made an exception for the day of Cosima's Jubilee. The morning of the destined day had dawned with the sounds of innumerable throats—feathered and human—intoning praise for Marzanna, Her Godlings and Saints, and Aebbenary's beauty all across the island.

In the forest, through the walls of the huntresses' treehouse, the songs resounded with majestic formality that had reduced Palmira to tears already. All the huntresses—even the ones who had hope Cosima's appointment as heir would mean better things for mortalkind and the island citizens—had been unsettled into brittle endurance that pained Cosima to witness. Only Lilias was soothed by the hymns, mostly because in the serene woods the predominant singers were songbirds.

There was still time before Cosima would be expected to appear at the celebration. Delay though she might, fight the compulsion to obey that was no doubt the work of Goddess's Miraculous will, she knew she battled the inevitable the longer she stayed out foraging dinner for the treehouse residents.

At least they'll have a nice evening. Contemplating the fullness of the dirt-stained satchel hanging over her shoulder, Cosima poked around the patchy lichen for more mushrooms before she headed home. *No dressing up to suffer, no speeches to practice, no tedious niceties to exchange with people who'd rather see me dead...*

Grousing didn't make her feel better, but Cosima carried on in an attempt to stoke her self-importance to such a peak that no barbs or disappointments of the night would touch her. *I can't believe I still care what Mother thinks. Mama, yes…Cristoval…but Marzanna?*

The unanswerable question—why had Goddess chosen Cosima over any of her siblings? She had never been gifted with the ability to drift easily into sleep, but more than usual her musings had kept her awake from dusk to dawn without more than an hour or two's reprieve. The responsibility of caring for Lilias had only added to her insomnia regardless of how enthusiastic the huntresses were to help her tend the baby.

The only choice she had—besides fleeing the island like a coward and hoping Goddess would be too lazy to search for her—was playing along with the events of the Jubilee and accepting the heir's scepter.

Cosima thought of it all in a series of steps to prevent herself from panicking as she climbed the ladder up to the treehouse: *clean up, dress, go to the city, find Mama and Cristoval…*

The huntresses had made themselves scarce so she could get ready in peace. Cosima listened for their chatter and other noises coming from the rooms various duos and trios shared, but all she heard was Lilias burbling something in baby talk and some jingling bells as one of the women played with them. They'd be coming with her, of course: it wasn't unlikely that Fiammetta would want to see her child from a distance at least.

Someone had sent a paper-and-twine wrapped parcel to the treehouse; one of her ladies had left it in the room she shared with Iulia and Lilias. Prepared to hate whatever she found, Cosima tore off the packaging and stared at the mask and dress that waited for her. She'd never know if Marzanna or Fiammetta—or a random assistant—had chosen this for her, but whoever it was had taken her taste into account.

A volto mask adorned with tinted gold, seed pearls, and a crown of living orchids and ivory feather plumes. The scent of lavender emerged from the fabric as she set the mask aside and lifted the dress out of its nest of paper to examine it. The filmy cloth was tinted the same heliotrope as the orchids, but as she turned it this way and that, she saw the shimmering layers that would reveal the beauty and strength of her divine body without unveiling all the charms of her figure.

If Bettina was Goddess's prodigal swan, Cosima was the violet-backed starling they had made together. That Goddess had joined their Light to let Bettina conceive. That had to be what her Mother thought.

Unwilling to consider the princely apparel further, Cosima cleansed herself in a basin of fresh water, combed through her wavy hair to let it fall, and donned her costume as if girding herself in the shroud she'd be buried in. She knew she was beautiful: she knew the city would be in awe of her, as Goddess intended. It was why She had chosen everything, arranged everything, ordered each and every item on whatever list She kept so nothing would fall outside Her bidding—including Her chosen daughter.

Daylight shone through the common room windows as Cosima left her room and shut the door behind her. Marzanna wouldn't anoint her until after twilight. There were hours between the time she'd been instructed to arrive and the coronation, and hours after that before she could return home.

When she faced the room again, she saw all her huntresses emerge from their rooms to stand together. There was no judgment in their faces, or naked concern that would have put Cosima more on edge. Only affection and determination for whatever they had gathered to tell her.

"Did you think we were going to let you go alone?" Grisel asked her, reproving.

"I *know* so." Touched though she was, Cosima refused to give in to the emotion. "These so-called revels will be no place for mortals."

"That's for us to decide." Iulia said. "You love us, and we all love you. How could we honor you at your Jubilee by our absence?"

"If all is well, we will rejoice with you. If anything goes amiss—"

My kin will eat you up and spit out your bones. The likes of Ormanno and Giric would relish destroying who she loved with the attitude of overindulged brats stomping on wooden soldiers to prevent other children from playing with them. Deep down Cosima wondered how

133

many more women wandered lost in Aebbenary like her huntresses had before she'd rescued them.

"What could go wrong? I am being uplifted, like you said. I don't need your protection." *Don't waste your care on me.* A lump formed in Cosima's throat. *You deserve better than service under me, a useless Godling.* "Give me Lilias. I should be off—"

Konetta interrupted. "It's our choice. *You* gave us choices, and we have all chosen to accompany you." She gestured to herself, the others, the plain but pretty raiment they had clothed themselves in to avoid shaming her at her Jubilee. "If you take that away, what do we have left?"

Cosima's arms hung loosely at her sides except for the hand that clutched her mask by the curve of its cheek tight enough to crack the plaster if she wasn't careful. Shame plucked her strings again. Konetta was right—all of them were. Danger or not, how could she reject their company when *she* was the one who had encouraged their fearlessness and love of freedom?

"Well—let me—" Cosima struggled. It would be easier to *give* instead of announce her gift...so she did.

Summoning her Miraculous power, she lifted her hands and approached her ladies one by one to grant them the smallest of favors. The ordinary, affordable fabrics they had chosen for their Jubilee dresses—though Cosima granted them an allowance from the wealth Goddess granted to all Her children they loathed spending her money on extravagances—transformed into mimicries of Cosima's dress in shades of the forest instead of purple. Sweetgrass green, daffodil yellow, pumpkin and russet and cardinal red. As she passed her hands over each of their faces, her Light materialized masks for them that look lately carved from raw wood and painted with swirls of walnut ink.

One by one they thanked her. As if they were supplicants, and she a mighty queen who had promised to grant their wildest dreams. Cosima gulped her sentiment down and smiled in acknowledgement. What else could she do? If she shouted at them for their ignorance, for fault that wasn't theirs because it was in their nature to worship holy beings, what would that make her?

Cristoval's passion for change—even if he had to enact it with his own fragile hands or build a new world brick by brick—returned to her with the memory of his passion-lit face.

What could it be like, Cosima began to wonder, *to live in a world without gods to rule it? Where mortal beings decide their brief destinies without fear of arbitrary, divine retribution?*

Finally, they were ready. Twittering in excitement—a party was a party, and most of them were young women who had lived hard lives—they didn't wait for Cosima's cue to leave. Lilias fussed in Palmira's arms until she bounced them in play as she climbed down.

"Wait. My sash. Can you…" Konetta trailed off as she gestured to the stays that had loosened inexplicably after Cosima had transformed her garments last. Her dark eyes flickered up, a gesture of their own filled with meaning.

Cosima acknowledged the pretense with a nod to the others to climb down without her. The two of them waited for the others to go down before Cosima approached.

Coughing into a handkerchief, Konetta turned and lifted her arms to allow her to gather the plain green ribbons at her sides to bind the dress tighter around her body. Because of this, Cosima felt the way the effort made her sway with exhaustion that meant her sickness had flared up again. She heard the rattle in her lungs and bit back the worried scolding she wanted to unleash to persuade her to take better care of herself.

"Are you sure you're well enough to come with us?" she asked; that was a question instead of an order and it pertained only to her welfare, so it was safe. It wasn't an acknowledgement of the tension thickening the air in the common room abandoned by everyone else except the two of them. Konetta, who smelled of cedarwood and the geraniums she'd tucked into her rows and rows of braids interweaved into her own style of crown—and Cosima, who wanted her.

"I'm sure. Don't worry about me."

A picture emerged in Cosima's mind—a fantasy she both longed for and dreaded. The crown of orchids and feathers of the mask she would wear only during the Jubilee and not a second more became a *real* crown: the crown of a Goddess. The one who would replace Marzanna should death befall a being with all power. With Iulia at her right hand, Konetta at her left, and her ladies arrayed in a choir around her throne, Cosima would rule with scepter in hand and remake Aebbenary into whatever shape she desired.

A *better* shape.

Ignorant of Cosima's imaginings, Konetta lowered her arms when she felt Cosima's hold on the ribbon ends slacken after she tightened them.

"What do you dream of? When you go away from us in that land inside your head." Her tone was wistful. "You never leave us for long, but…I miss you. I always miss you when you're not here."

Cosima stood still behind her, unable to move closer or away. *I didn't think anyone noticed. I was so careful to never let anyone see…*

"I don't think I could carry on if something happened to you. And the others." A blurted confession that embarrassed her immediately. Konetta was kind, but not above laughter: if she teased Cosima now she'd never let herself utter another word to anyone ever again.

"Nothing will happen. This is a celebration—will you try to enjoy it?" Konetta held very still as Cosima's hands settled as light as clouds on her waist.

"I'll enjoy anything if you're with me." *What are you doing? The others are right down the ladder!* Though Cosima screamed at herself internally, her conscience rattled only the cage she locked it in as she watched herself from afar yield to the longings that had tormented her.

Konetta's breathing thinned as Cosima slid her hands down from her waist to her hips and pulled her back so their bodies aligned. The perpetual halo she kept dim so she wouldn't blind her huntresses flickered like a lantern as Cosima slanted her nose down to trace Konetta's neckline with it…then the faintest graze of her lips.

"Tell me where you go when your eyes fill with shadows. I want to know…everything," Konetta said; the two of them were all hesitation, all secrets breathed out like steam over tea and delicious gossip. "Paint a picture for me so I can imagine myself there with you."

"I couldn't inflict that on you—on anyone. More than shadows fill my mind. But…" Seduction came naturally to Cosima. She had never attempted it, not fully, but words began to pour from her lips like the endearments Goddess must whisper to Her consorts and lovers to lure them to bed. "My dreams. Though I dread them, though they fill me with complete loathing…you occupy them. I cannot rest for thoughts of you. I dream of kissing you day and night while the shreds of my integrity cover our wrongs."

"Are you this afraid?"

"Of myself?" *Yes. And I've never been so alive.* Cosima had already sinned enough to condemn herself. Maybe that was why she couldn't stop, or why Konetta failed to stop her.

She kissed a path along Konetta's throat as her left hand slid higher, grazing a firm breast at its lower curve while her other hand stroked lower. *I'm no better than the others. Not at all.*

"I am a Godling: I am Marzanna's daughter. And I'm so *tired* of fighting my inevitable disgrace, Konetta."

The arc of her spine a bow tuned to Cosima's touch, Konetta clenched her teeth to stifle a moan of pleasure. Her hand fumbled at Cosima's right hand, squeezing it to make her stop. Instant chagrin made Cosima try to yank away, to withdraw and recover her better judgment, but Konetta refused to let her go.

"Everything will be fine as long as we're together. I promise." A laugh as Konetta humored herself; slowly, *agonizingly,* she put Cosima's hands back on her waist. "Look at me. A mortal, a feeble one at that, promising safety to a Godling."

"I like your promises." *Promise me more, Konetta. Promise me yourself.* "But I made promises of my own. Promises to someone else I I—"

"Cosima, are you—"

They had been unforgivably distracted. Lost in their forbidden world, neither Cosima nor Konetta had noticed Iulia clamber up the ladder to see what was keeping them.

Iulia's smile slid from her face as speculation formed a mask more complete than the one she would don for the celebration. Her gaze passed between Konetta and Cosima with calculation that only revealed itself in the manner of how she crossed her arms and the coolness with which her olive green eyes met theirs.

Cosima didn't bother leaping away from Konetta. Haste would only solidify her fault and deepen the mortification she already felt. *Chose* to feel—anything was better than another fatal bite from the jaws of guilt she danced over every single time she looked at either of the women she was in love with.

"I'm going down now. Excuse me, Iulia." With an idle pat on Cosima's cheek, Konetta chose obliviousness as she departed. Wondering if Iulia would let that stand, Cosima watched in frozen alarm as Konetta passed her to reach the ladder…but her fears were groundless. Iulia didn't even look at her.

Now they were alone.

"Iulia—"

"No. Not tonight." Someone so warm could never perform coldness, but Iulia's features settled one by one into neutrality with what looked like heroic effort as she interrupted whatever explanation Cosima tried to utter.

"I want you to know I—"

"Save it. I know your heart." Leaving her, Iulia began to descend the ladder again. "I know it already, Cosima."

Disgraced, Cosima had no choice but to follow. The next several minutes would be spent transporting her ladies one by one from the treehouse into Aebbenary. Grateful for the reprieve though she was, she still had to bear those moments alone with both Konetta and Iulia. The last thing she wanted was to touch or be touched by anyone, but necessity had no regard for her wishes.

I know your heart.

What? What can you know that I cannot stand? Like Iulia could never be cold, Cosima could never be angry with her. .Too much had passed between them and the respect they shared trumped everything else. Her mortification increased the more she thought about how Iulia must have witnessed her leaning into Konetta, her weakness as she had allowed her hands to tremulously trace the narrow shape of Konetta's waist and hips.

The Jubilee—and placating whatever ire her fickle Mother felt toward her—was what Cosima needed to focus on. To the exclusion of all else, this was her responsibility.

I know it already, Cosima.

If she couldn't stop thinking of those damning words she wondered if they had all already lost.

Everyone was here. They were together before they marched as a unit through the gates of paradise that could slam behind them and trap them for good. Even Cosima could not save them if Goddess decided their lives were forfeit for one slight or another.

Breathe, Cosima reminded herself as she noticed she wasn't. *This is your celebration. All will be well…won't it?*

She wished she could ask Iulia, but the others blocked her way, and Lilias half-lunged out of Palmira's arms for Cosima to carry them instead. Hefting the winged child on her hip, she led the way through the Light-constructed arch brimming with prisms that cast rainbows over those who passed beneath its bow.

Though Goddess loved revels, it had been many years since Aebbenary had been this transformed by Her will to this degree. Sunrays—deprived of heat that would trouble the guests—had been filtered through Miraculous glass or crystal structures to form patterns on the shining, gilded streets. Where afternoon had dipped its fingers into evening, the rays and reflections took on a dreamy purple sheen like blushing moonlight.

One and all, the denizens of Aebbenary and the invited guests had been instructed to march through the main thoroughfare until they reached the docks, where every ship but the one where Cosima's Jubilee would take place had been banished to farther seas. Though everyone saw and made room for her, Cosima didn't press the issue of her seniority over the excited mortals and walked along with her huntresses and the crowds with her eyes roving their numbers for signs of trouble.

Damn these costumes. What are they for? If there was going to be trouble even Cosima would not be able to predict it. In a fit of unprecedented generosity, Goddess—through Fiammetta—had granted each citizen a white robe or dress so clean it hurt to look at and a paper mask each. In true Aebbenarian fashion, many had decorated the white canvas of their clothes and mask with paints and flowers and other ornaments if they could afford them.

The consequence of this mingled sameness and personalization befuddled her sharp mind and cultivated instincts. Cosima was as lost as everyone else as they proceeded like lemmings toward the docks where the pleasure boat would soon embark on a trip around the island.

Beautified or not, the crowds reduced their progress to a creep. The Cosima who had lived earlier that morning, who had never touched Konetta or heard her throaty laugh when she touched her, would have been grateful for the delay so she could dither hopelessly over her lack of preparation for this event. Now she was impatient; she couldn't avoid the awareness that Iulia stood at her side, masked and most likely unwilling to escort her as the heir's consort. Cosima realized she had forgotten—or subconsciously neglected—to ask her about that.

"Cosima!"

She didn't have to turn to guess that voice; Sovanna didn't make her wait and see. From a bubble of clear space—her curling horns made mortals uneasy—she appeared and glided unhindered to where Cosima's group halted to wait for her.

"You came." *Stupid—of course she did. Goddess summoned her,* Cosima thought.

Sovanna might have raised an eyebrow in mockery, but her mask concealed her expression. She had dressed for the occasion in her own eccentric fashion: fabric the same shade and texture as lamb's ear wrapped tightly around and around her figure up to right above her breasts. Parts of the copious leaves formed sleeves that draped with gossamer spiderweb imitations down to the wrists, where they clung so her hands would not be encumbered. She had piled her silver-streaked hair in artful disarray on her head, and aside from her lower lip and her grey eyes her face was entirely obscured by a wooden mask painted to resemble a badger. She wore no jewels other than a cinnabar medallion carved with the likeness of her reptilian marsh guardians.

"I will be the first to admit my own curiosity. I am Mother's firstborn in all respects. Maybe I will ask Her why She passed over me," Sovanna said.

While everyone stared at the interaction that unfolded, she stood unmoved while Cosima wanted to squirm where her piercing focus speared through her disguise as a worthy successor to Goddess.

"Cosima has been here the past several years while you were…where?" Iulia answered when she couldn't. Humiliation heated Cosima's cheeks at her defense.

Unaware, Sovanna laughed. "You misunderstand. I really am just curious. I have no intentions whatsoever to compete with your…" A pause as she scanned the masked faces of the huntresses and their body language to guess their relationship. "Companion."

"That's good. We hear all sorts of things here at home about what curiosities you get up to in your bog."

"Iulia!" One of the more cautious huntresses tugged on her sleeve. Iulia ignored that along with Cosima's quelling glance her way. She only crossed her arms—still clad in her standard greaves to hide the scars of that which had led her to join the huntresses—and frowned at Sovanna: an impressive look on a face always ready to smile.

"Would you like to come with us?" The offer surprised Cosima as soon as the words left her mouth, but she discovered she wasn't sorry she'd presented it. Eternally cool and collected Sovanna probably had no use for her charity, but they were sisters, after all. After their conversation in the swamp Cosima couldn't forget...and maybe, in this one case with this one half-sister, she didn't want to.

It must be caring for Lilias that was making her soft. The babe had been comforted by her presence in a way even Palmira's generous affection sometimes couldn't manage. Cosima let them lean their head on her shoulder to watch the proceedings with their hazel eyes wide.

The badger mask hid everything that would have given Sovanna's mood away. She hadn't bothered to remove it to greet them; now she still only nodded and gestured for Cosima and her ladies to follow. With her in the lead the crowds parted to allow them passage from the eastern streets leading to the docks.

This should be her Jubilee, Cosima thought again as Sovanna straightened her posture—which had already been perfect—and led them on. *If anyone is suited for leadership it's her. Not me.*

From a distance the ship looked more like a barge than an armed vessel ready for ocean travel. It had been one of Goddess's lavish gifts to Fiammetta some years ago, crafted by the best shipbuilders and artisans on the island and continent, but apparently neither of them had hesitated in breaking it down to craft something unique for the Jubilee.

A canopy of rich cloth supported dangling vines and flowers populated by singing birds instead of proper rigging for the ship. The entire deck had been converted into a floating platform for Godlings, Saints, and mortal dignitaries thanking their lucky stars for an invitation from Fiammetta to amble and dance upon. Just for this trip, the ship would not technically be seaworthy.

What need did anyone have for a sturdy mast or furling sails when Light guided the ship? When Goddess could influence the weather over Aebbenary, what need was there to fear a tempest blown in from distant climes to ruin their fun?

Two people waited at the bottom of the faceted glass gangplank that led up to the ship. Cosima saw them clearly from a distance since, after a certain point, a foggy barrier had been set up by one divine being or another to bar the rest of the city from storming the ship to glimpse the wonders of the Jubilee without permission. Sovanna paused when she saw them—perhaps she was uncertain who they were since she would have recognized most of her numerous half-siblings or any of the appointed Saints.

Cosima moved closer, leaning in on her right to explain. "That's my brother and his father. Goddess summoned Cristoval to Aebbenary along with the rest of us."

"Does that concern you?" A loaded question. Cosima knocked her shoulder against Sovanna's as she took over shepherding the group. One look at Iulia—their differences set aside in the face of whatever chaos waited for all of them as soon as they boarded Fiammetta's ship—passed the torch of protecting the mortal huntresses to her. Thumping her fist over her heart with a thud of finality, Iulia led their procession up the ramp to give Cosima and her family a moment alone.

"You shouldn't have brought him." Cosima didn't need to say who: Crespin waved at her with an amiable grin from under the white mask painted with rudimentary outlines of lutes, harps, and other instruments.

"Why not? You brought the entire treehouse out for the occasion. And this is…?"

Acting first, Cristoval lifted his mask to reveal his face: his eyes landed on Sovanna and remained there. After a pause, Sovanna did the same by passing her haloed hand over her face to temporarily banish the badger mask obscuring her features.

All Cosima could do was watch it happen. Watch the stars align and the earth halt its spinning in the cosmos as Sovanna, child of the current Goddess and the false god, and warm, human Cristoval met. With strangely mirrored expressions, they perceived each other: eyes that had been filled with calculation going round with surprise, softening with whatever emotion zinged over their heartstrings. Sovanna didn't flinch, but she resisted the pull of profound connection that was already binding them like chords of music linking motif to melody by stepping back, as if to flee.

Cristoval's mask—his entire costume—was a bold flair of scarlet and black with pearl accents; in contrast, a wreath of grapevines boasting his Valusius heritage adorned his curly hair. Without his mask he might resemble a god of the natural world who had preceded both Goddess and Silver, to eyes other than Cosima's. All she saw was her brother, starstruck and humbled by one soul's recognition of its destined pair.

"You, at last." Sovanna said first; the "at last" got her the way their initial contact hadn't. Bashful, she started to duck her head, but caught herself and instead lifted her chin and arched a brow in challenge for him to mock her. With her antler-horns and odd nature, Cosima guessed she'd grown used to ridicule in the Shining Court. That was why she'd sharpened her tongue so skillfully after reaching maturity.

"And you. At last." Cristoval fought his smile, but failed to prevent the silly but charming grin that warmed his expression from taking over. Foregoing Sovanna's hesitation, he claimed her hand in his own and bowed over it, brushing his lips against her knuckles in a kiss Cosima already knew Sovanna would never forget.

It hurt to watch.

She wouldn't dream of diverting her attention to anything else.

"We're not supposed to meet each other." Sovanna blurted.

"But I'm glad we have. Putting a face to the intelligence of the letters I received has been a gift all the sweeter for its unexpected arrival."

Oblivion. He's trying to be gallant. Cosima rolled her eyes, tempted to shoulder through the pair standing transfixed on the street leading to the docks where the boat would soon embark to initiate the Jubilee.

Then the import of their words struck her: *"we're not supposed to meet"*... *"letters"*...

"Cristoval. This is your—"

Sovanna flapped a hand to hush her. "Not here! Not ever. We never saw each other. I've never met your brother, Cosima, and I never mean to."

"Wait! Please, wait!" A humble plea from Cristoval, though he had been bold enough to kiss her hand upon meeting her for the first time. Could Sovanna resist?

Seems not. Crespin caught Cosima's eye and shook his head, almost mournful. He had been a minstrel all his life: she supposed it was in his wheelhouse to recognize soon-to-be lovers when he saw them.

"How could it be *you?* You…I knew you were mortal, but…wait. I don't care." Sovanna's cool cheeks flushed with color Cosima had never seen on her; it was becoming but unsettling. "I can't care. Don't speak to me again."

Picking up her skirts, she waved her hand over her face to restore her mask before she turned and ascended the ramp leading up to the ship. Her halo—silvery-white compared to every other Saint and Godling in Marzanna's order—shimmered like a mirage around her svelte figure as Cosima watched her go. Cristoval wouldn't know what that meant, but she did.

Sovanna was an expert at detachment. At remaining aloof and above all worldly complications. She could be as ruthless and reptilian as her swamp guardians if pushed: Cosima had seen her climb the ladder to the top of the Godling hierarchy before she had thrown it all away and went into exile. Surely she was wondering herself how one mortal man could begin to melt that polar core that kept her standing when Goddess's regime demanded every soul fall to their knees in worship?

"I'd like to know how she knew it was you," said Crespin, interjecting on the moment with all the grace of a stampeding herd. "She had you before you said a single word."

Cristoval was mortal, and a young man—his eyes were still on Sovanna's retreating figure, then on the place he saw her last before she disappeared through the crystal arch at the top of the gangplank. Cosima whacked his arm with her free hand; Lilias had fallen asleep on her shoulder somehow despite the noise surrounding them.

"Sovanna…" He didn't even flinch. When he glanced down at Cosima, dreamy, she wanted to grab his ear and pull to wipe that dazed look off his face.

So she did. This time he hissed a curse and tried to shove her away, but Cosima held on.

"When we board this ship I am going to leave you and the jester in a corner somewhere *where you will stay* so I can keep an eye on you the entire time. Understand? Don't worry about anyone but yourselves.

There are a lot of Godlings and Saints here—you know the sort of deranged "fun" they like to have," she said.

Wincing as she yanked him forcibly into the material world, Cristoval glared at her from his peripheral as he batted at her pinching fingers to make her let go.

"I'm not completely incapable of taking care of—"

"Don't. Don't even try that." Just before their interaction broke down into pointless bickering a solution came to her. "This is *my* night. Can you try not to ruin it?"

She had him with that one; with the sweet yet peevish countenance of a younger sibling who was used to her older brother's affection. He crumbled with a tolerant huff of frustration as he fingered the red mark she'd left on his ear and straightened his vest.

"It's your night."

"That's right. You're going to do what I say so I don't have to worry about you."

"We promise. I'll watch him for you." Crespin sealed their agreement with a barely-contained laugh as Cristoval offered his arm to Cosima to escort her up the ramp.

Cristoval and his father behaved with meek compliance as Cosima shoved them toward a small table near the stern and under one of the gilded columns propping up the canopy. Once onboard, Cosima wondered why her Mother had chosen a masquerade theme for the Jubilee. Sure, the spectacle everyone presented was compelling and unforgettable, but the anonymity was an illusion since most of the divine beings had brought masks with handles so they hardly had to use them at all. Right away she spotted Barone, Druda, Agnese, and a gaggle of others laughing around the figurehead of a captain lounging on a helm as pointless as he was.

Her huntresses buzzed around her again, some of them with drinks while others kept a judging eye on their welfare along with the gathering of divine beings and mortal honoraries.

"What should we do?" Palmira asked. Her eyes were on Lilias; she reached for the baby without conscious intent. Cosima passed them over gladly.

"Stay together. Be on your guard...but make merry, my friends."
Trying to smile, Cosima leaned away from Lilias so they wouldn't rip
off her mask right after she put it on. "You are attendants to Goddess's
heir. No one in the world can hurt you without consequences."

"Where are you going?" Konetta asked. Cosima tried not to wince
as she recalled how recently they had touched in the treehouse. If she
tried, she could catch the whiff of geraniums no matter how many
scents and perfumes mingled in the rarified ambiance of the ship.

Her eyes drifted to Iulia. Who met her gaze with disinterest that
cut...even though she owed Cosima nothing. Nothing at all—not after
what she must have seen and heard.

"Mother is waiting."

XII

Bettina

Alone in the kitchen of her empty estate, Bettina prepared herself for the Jubilee. On the table in front of her lay three objects: a dagger with a smooth abalone handle, a deep bowl filled with crawling, buzzing beetles as green as emeralds, another bowl empty aside from the embers of incense she had only just blown out.

One misstep and I lose it all. Picking up one of the poisoned beetles and allowing it to bite her with its barbed pincers, Bettina let her blood run over its jewel-like wings before she crushed it on the table with the hilt of the dagger.

If I fail to please Her, it is over. There will not be another chance. She dropped the shards of the body coated with her blood into the smoking incense and let her misgivings and the bare bones of her hope send the sacrifice to whoever would listen besides Goddess and Her kin.

Then she repeated the process with each of the dozen beetles in the bowl. By the time she was done her right hand was riddled with deep punctures starting to turn black from the beetles' venom. Even for a Saint these repetitive wounds would be slow to heal. Searching for anything to give her an advantage, Bettina had remembered the rarity of these otherwise friendly beetles whose pollination had made the vineyards of the Valusius lands further away on the island so irresistible and unique. Their value was matched only by their rarity, though, and sacrificing even a dozen of these was a gift many divine beings would envy had the offering been laid at their feet.

Closing her eyes, Bettina pointed her attention inward, as deep as she could feel. Tears tainted with burning ichor pooled under her lashes, but she refused to let them fall as she clutched the pain searing her nerves close before it was gone. Before her holy body healed the damage and ended the nuances of her sacrifice.

Everything. She would have to use every spark of her Light, down to the dregs of what separated her from mortality, to beguile Goddess. All knowledge had a cost besides what Bettina had given to Magisend in the form of a garden. Though it ceded information, it took pain and energy to use it.

She understood sacrifice, though. It was why she had killed the vineyard beetles: to delay the symptoms that would come for her once she finished enticing Marzanna's word that Cristoval would live forever at his mother's side.

Exhaling all hurt and worry, Bettina rose from the kitchen table and moved outside to unfurl her splendid new wings. There had been more gifts Goddess had bestowed on her—crystal earrings plucked from Her own Light and attached to her earlobes with a word, sapphires and other gems that fell from her tongue to clink on the ground whenever she praised Marzanna, birds and beasts in the menagerie they had visited to allow Bettina's blessèd hands to stroke their feathers, fur, or scales—but none compared to these wings.

For a brief set of days she had allowed herself to enjoy them. To learn to fly with Däard's thoughtful tutelage and Marzanna's blithe companionship. Regardless of where they flew—high enough that the island looked like a pinprick in the sea, low enough that they could reach down and pluck the tall grasses of the plains or sing to the birds that populated the woodlands—they didn't leave Aebbenary. Bettina was grateful the notion hadn't struck Goddess's whimsy: her children were here, unprotected as change impended with the Jubilee, and she couldn't leave them again.

Bettina fortified herself with one last look at her home. She rested a hand with nails painted like lapis lazuli on a pillar and leaned against it.

It had been so long since she'd been able to rest in another's arms. Even when Goddess had been her world, she had always needed to please. Always needed to amuse and court and worship.

It's time. She shoved everything else in her heart and in the world away as she walked, then ran through the yard and launched into the air with a powerful jump. She barely wobbled: day and night, she had been practicing. For her plan to work she had to be able to control every muscle and feather she had to perfection.

Her concentration left her feverish. Bettina embraced the sickness and let it transform her as the miles of the city blurred beneath her route as she flew to the docks and the ship waiting there. The Jubilee would have already started; the masquerade that was one of Fiammetta's silly pretensions, the wining and dining and gluttony and excess, and whatever ceremony Goddess had reserved as a surprise from all but Her primary consorts.

All of it to the queen's taste rather than Cosima's. All of it another feather in Marzanna's cap rather than something meant to show a Mother's esteem for a precious daughter. Bettina had once expected such an attitude to be a relic of the austere past when Silver had—almost—ruled the world, not a so-called enlightened present presided over by Goddess.

It was better to banish all expectations, she supposed as she flew. She would keep faith, hold onto hope with both hands until her tendons tore from the strain, but it was foolish to expect anyone possessing divinity to obey any rules. Those who had power would invariably use it to the fullest extent for their good and others' loss.

Bettina reached the ship and circled above it, gliding and swooping to draw all the attention she could. She laughed gaily as her hair—grown long and heavy by Miraculous design—whipped around her face without tangling, as the ocean air ruffled her feathers. Her raiment captured shades of blue, of yellow and gold and purple, with red beneath all of that. Translucent and gossamer, the fabric molded itself to Bettina's curves with each movement, dazzling every eye that saw her and capturing the desires of those who wanted but could never have her.

Soon she would shed everything that cloaked her beauty from Goddess's eye.

Hailing a greeting to the masked attendees, Bettina whispered a command to her Light and pulled a weapon from her own aureole with effort that made her bicep shake from exertion. The spear was a relic of her mortal heritage she had repurposed into a blessed weapon: she had altered every atom of its original material into solidified Light with her power. Another gift from and now for Goddess she hoped would be appreciated.

"Your Glory!" Bettina called down in salute as she aimed for the exact center of the deck and waited for Goddess to acknowledge her from where She sat away from the masked guests on a balcony with petal-strewn stairs leading up to Her throne. Däard and Fiammetta were with Her—one standing at Her back with his hands kneading Her shoulders, the other rushing to sit down after she extricated herself from a dancing partner who didn't look like she mourned losing her.

No Priest. Interesting. Bettina didn't want to speculate whether the lack of Easoren's attendance was ominous or not. She banished the thought and moored herself in the present by hurling the spear down to sink several feet into the wooden deck. Following it by flicking her wings further back, she landed with one bare foot on the round tip of the haft and balanced for a moment before she fluttered down to the deck.

Love filled her, painful as a cramp as she watched Cosima turn away from her huntresses and see her. Before Bettina's landing she had looked tense, uncomfortable. After her feet touched the polished deck Cosima's expression changed into dismay.

"Mama?" Cosima said; her voice carried in the abrupt silence. When Bettina had hurled down the javelin of Light the crowd had dispersed to the edges of the ship, leaving most of the space clear—as she had planned. All eyes were on her. The world had taken a breath as delicate as a robin's egg to hold their silence.

Cosima—this was supposed to be her night. Bettina intended not only to ruin it by absorbing all interest, but she would shame her with what she had to do to bewitch Goddess for good. This was not the first time Bettina had set her daughter's care aside for her more fragile son's.

I'm sorry, Bettina started to send her before she stopped herself: Goddess might overhear. *After this I won't need to protect him so much—we will be a family forever. Maybe someday you will forgive me for this humiliation.*

"Goddess. I have prepared a gift for You in honor of this sacred Jubilee." In the middle of the deck the spear of luminescence began to grow taller, stabbing the heavens as if signaling the stars to fall as soon as Bettina gave the word. "Will you receive it, Your Glory?"

Fiammetta answered first. Marzanna allowed the imposition as She always did.

"It is your daughter whom Goddess honors. Shouldn't you have a gift for her?"

Bettina smiled, radiant—so wide she felt like her cheeks would crack.

"Dearest Cosima has been a gift to me all her life. Such joy has she brought me that this gift for Her Glory has been an age in coming. Goddess, will you let me praise You with my gift?"

A pause. Marzanna waited long enough to make the silly girl Bettina had been squirm as She leisurely propped Her chin on Her hand on the throne's padded arm and snared Bettina in Her eyes.

She was always beautiful—the most glorious, unmatched in heaven and earth—but She had put effort in for the Jubilee. A red-gold crown resembling brambles ornamented the dark hair She rarely tamed. Rather than a dress of any style, a purple robe embroidered with cerulean songbirds loosely tied at Her waist slipped off one shoulder. Cosmetics tinted the same shade as Her crown and the bluebirds shadowed the lids of Her eyes, added color to Her fair cheeks, and drew the eye to the unyielding yet alluring lips that had yet to utter the permission Bettina needed.

"Proceed." Her smile was slow to come, but Marzanna offered an appearance of one…though the expression didn't quite touch Her eyes.

That lone word should not have weighed Bettina's heart down with stones to sink as low as the pleasure ship's anchor. Though it did, though it made her sick with regret and shame, she kept smiling and curtsied once before Goddess, Fiammetta, and Däard before she returned to the place she'd come onboard.

The sun had yet to sink into the ocean like a sliced orange plummeting into a pitcher of refreshment. Thanks to Bettina's precise timing, it bathed the ship in its setting hues as she sashayed back to the spear buried in the deck and got in position. A delectable sideways lounge against the spear, with one hand poised against the metal within the Light and her body loose for her dance.

She began.

Whirling around to embrace the spear like a lover before she threw herself away from it as if scorned, Bettina called music from captive instruments—the troupe of minstrels permanently attached to Fiammetta's court didn't try to hold them. She plucked threads of Light in the air to keep time with the sultry tune that would guide her.

First one way, then that, all surrounding the spear that served as the focal point of her performance. Gliding, grasping the spear to spin herself around and around the haft in a controlled rise and fall, swaying her hips in tempo. Bettina leaned back with her right heel propped on the spear, gazing upside down toward the thrones with her wings splayed.

The music paused. Watching Goddess, she tore the first layer of fabric off her torso and let the breeze she coaxed on time carry it away. Beneath the rest, the Light Bettina had spent hours painting on her skin began to glimmer. If the mortals in attendance were not careful they might go blind for a time after the dance from exposure to so many Miracles.

When the music resumed a beat later, she saw Goddess lean forward slightly with Her hands gripping the armrests of Her throne. The distance between them should not have offered Bettina such clarity, but she saw the way Marzanna's eyes devoured her body as she continued her dance. They'd almost swallowed her—heart and soul as well as her body—a long time ago. For what she wanted—*needed*—she'd let them consume her again.

During her time as Marzanna's pet, Bettina had learned to dance in many styles. Sensuality had been restricted in Silver's era if it was not to his glory. She and many others had developed an interest in their own bodies and how they moved in delicious vengeance for the knowledge denied to them for an age. Dancing was the first skill she had garnered on her own merit and by her own talents. Aside from her children and Goddess, it was the first thing she had ever loved: the strain it put on her form, the perfection it demanded without punishing personal style, the focus it took to execute each move successfully.

Calling on the All-knowledge granted to her from the Archives was an abominable form of cheating. Another fault Bettina would loathe herself for when she had the luxury of reflection.

For now, no one would shine brighter for Goddess. No one would sacrifice more. All her existence had been and would forever be *for* someone—Marzanna, Her Glory, Her love.

A thought came to her from someone she had not expected. A whisper of a thought.

"..."

Bettina nearly faltered as she wrapped her legs around the spear and flung herself into the next movement. The music was approaching another crescendo; her Light flaked off her in wisps she transfigured into unadulterated power that bent the heavens to her desires long enough to lure some of the cosmos down to join her dance.

Magisend.

Under the glittering stars she had scattered under the canopy, betwixt the nebula wheedled down to their earthly atmosphere to increase the potency of her hypnotic dance, the Grand Archivist watched Bettina from his place in the assembly. No one around him appeared to be able to see him or sense his presence, but they must have felt something to leave him room to walk among them with his eyes on Bettina. She felt him the way she had before her blood had granted him a body: nettles and splinters in her consciousness, friction meant to rend sanity from soul and life from her body.

Here? How could he be here? He's never left the Archives... Her mind stuttered at the thrill of what she realized. *That I know of.*

She glanced again where he stood with a flutter of her lashes meant to disguise that anything had taken her attention off Marzanna, hoping

155

he had gone or had never been there at all. For nothing: as Bettina's dance carried her to and fro over the ship, as she shed layers of Light like silks and cast pearls from her fingertips like a maid of the sea, he paced behind the front line of the encircled, staring, practically drooling crowd mesmerized by her show.

He knew what she was doing—he had helped her, had persuaded the All to grant her an enhancement to her natural talents in exchange for a garden of life. Magisend could not be enthralled by the sensual swaying of her hips, the bending and turning of her limbs like she was a creature of water rather than of once-mortal flesh, the clever footfalls of the pattern she had chosen for this, the dance of all dances meant to stoke a Goddess's lust for beauty as well as power to a tumult.

…could he?

The sensation of the appalling, needle-like touch of his skin against hers visited her mind again before she could banish it. Like a breath had blown out her candle during the wee hours, Bettina's power flickered out for half a heartbeat. Ebon eyes her ichor had grown from scratch bored through her skull to make room for themselves as she endured a waking dream of Magisend when all her thought and energy should have been bent on Goddess.

"Swan-of-gold," he would croon to her as she lay back beneath him and stared up into the glistening maw of his teeth. When he opened his mouth she saw the All-knowledge swirling over his tongue like smoke wreathed around a dragon's mouth. He exhaled, choking her, smothering her with that and his weight as his shifting, crack-lined skin drew blood from her pores.

Holding her breath, Bettina sat up on her elbows and arched her body up to meet his, her own tongue lolling as he and the knowledge moved inside her along with the terrible burden of his unmasked presence. She sucked in the knowledge orbiting him like a drug as their lips met in a debauched kiss unlike anything anyone had ever—

Yes. Magisend wanted her. Her spell had worked too well. That, or the blood she had traded to him had bound his attention more than she had ever planned.

Take care, dancer. There is more peril here than you can see.

Magisend's voice. She ignored it. Any price he wished to demand from her for his secrecy would have to wait.

Using her wings, Bettina wrapped her right one around her upper body and the other around her hips and legs. As if the moment of fatal distraction had never happened, or had been planned from the start. Goddess's eyes still lay on her, heavy as the anchor that kept the ship they were on in port.

When she flared them out along with her arms, Bettina tipped her head back as far as it would go as she unleashed all the love she had ever had—had once had, ages ago—for Marzanna in a piercing song. They had met at the reception of her doomed marriage, had shared a glass of wine that had solidified their communion forever…had made a child together, a daughter so wonderful it was she whom Goddess had chosen as Her heir in Her eternal, Light-filled realm of bliss in Aebbenary.

That she could grab. *That* she could use. By the time her dance finished, evening threatened to swallow twilight's dusky aura in darkness.

It was over. She had given it all. Bettina slumped on the ground, her flesh and bones an unbearable encumbrance as her Saint's glow guttered in and out of reality. Her filigreed wings covered her sweat-slick body in a subconscious act of preservation as she wheezed from her efforts and tried to kneel before Goddess instead of collapsing beneath her shining spear.

Masked faces surrounded her as far as she could tell from where she waited, on her knees, panting for air that wouldn't come as the bellows of her lungs barely functioned. The only face she could make out was Cristoval's: Cosima was nowhere to be found.

Cristoval stared at her, distress plain on his youthful features. No aversion, no judgment—it would not matter to him that his mother had played the dancing whore for Goddess. They had argued about her desperation in the past, but he wouldn't condemn her now. It probably hadn't occurred to him that there was a possibility Goddess had lured Bettina back into Her eternal service again.

If I did nothing else right, he knows I love him. That I will never, ever betray him again.

Bettina had one last task before their destinies were sealed. Feigned weakness had bought her a last look at his face—she could remember every version of it, from infancy to adolescence to boyish manhood—but it was done.

Nude except for the markings of Light still draining her power when all she had left was sediment and her jewelry, Bettina lifted her eyes to Goddess where she knelt.

"I love You, Your Glory. Have I pleased You?"

Because Marzanna was Goddess, She could not always be contained in Her shell. No one possessed power like Hers, but Bettina's dance had been potent in its own right—Marzanna could not claim She was unaffected. Her aureole had grown as large as the ship.

Bettina should have looked away. Instead she forced herself to look into the Light as tears began to streak down her cheeks and drip on the deck from her chin. *Blind me then, Goddess.*

"What would you have of Me, beloved? I sense your desire." Some of the punishing Light dimmed so she could see. Goddess sat with Her knees spread wide and Her body almost stooped, as if She intended to reach out and lift Bettina up with Her own blessed strength. Her pupils had dilated from desire; from attraction stoked into lust. Their black centers consumed much of the gold irises that had hypnotized Bettina long ago. That still could.

No one could *know* Goddess, not truly. Not even Her consorts. But Bettina knew beyond the shadow of a doubt that Marzanna was considering claiming her right there. Her legs were splayed already, waiting to guide Bettina's head between them once the flimsy robe parted easily, so easily…

She was supposed to utter Marzanna's name in total worship. This was the test—Bettina would intentionally fail it. But she had to fail it *right.*

"You will give me anything?" Petals and pearls were crushed and scattered under her hands and knees as Bettina crawled up the deck toward Goddess; she let her wings drag on the ground, catching debris that dirtied her beautiful feathers. "Do you promise, Your Glory?"

"Ask anything of Me, My swan. Speak your heart."

Her smile, Her radiance. Bettina began to weep: tender, ragged tears of plain saltwater. With her head too heavy to hold, she dropped onto her belly to rest her forehead on the stair before Goddess's throne.

"M-my son. Grant my son everlasting life at my side, I beg You." Her nails dug into the wooden stair as she pulled herself up; one of them cracked down to the quick from the strain of draining herself. Bettina ignored the pain—what was a trickle compared to the tempest making her beg for rest that would last a thousand years, and what was that compared to Cristoval's immortality hanging just beyond her reach? When the answer to her hope could fall from Marzanna's lips at any moment to banish sorrow forever?

Spent of all pride, hope, and weary to the bone, Bettina crumpled. She felt a hand brush the top of her head, stroking the riot of sunshine curls with fingers so warm she could feel them down to her scalp. She sobbed again as she watched her halo wink in and out of existence through eyes closed to slits. Each flare stabbed her with agony the way the tip of her Light spear had punctured the deck.

Above her, half-bent out of Her throne, Marzanna crooned in a comforting voice.

"You were not made for this game, I fear. Can you even comprehend the gravity of how you have failed Me?"

No…NO.

Bettina felt her world crack. The instant it did, her attention shot back to the crowd. To where her children were, to where they were exposed and in danger and *it was all her fault.*

Goddess tilted her head back with unparalleled tenderness, though the tips of Her shining nails dug into Bettina's scalp.

What have I done? Oh God—

A prayer of her childhood to a false god so indifferent Bettina might as well have shouted her fear into the wind. *What have I done?*

XIII

Cosima

The moments it took to reach Bettina dragged too long. Cosima elbowed and shoved her way through the crowd she had done the same to minutes ago in an effort to leave. She hadn't wanted to watch Bettina debase herself to worship a selfish Goddess who only appreciated her flattery, or her physical beauty—anything but what made her herself.

Terror had overcome Cosima in a premonition she feared down to her soul would come true. Cristoval found her; he and Crespin stuck close as they pushed through the masked, muttering crowd. Her huntresses joined her along with one addition—silent, watchful Sovanna. They formed a coterie of outcasts and exiles that struggled as one—goaded by Cosima's unintentional projection of her premonition thanks to her fickle power—to reach Bettina. To stop her from saying the one thing that would damn her.

Don't, Mama, please. Choose Her—I will find a way to save Cristoval, I promise. Just don't—

Cosima surfaced on the front line of the assembly to Bettina's right, but there was nothing she could say or do to prevent what was about to unfold.

"M-my son. Grant my son everlasting life at my side, I beg You."

I know you love me too. But you knew this would happen. Even Cristoval knew She'd never, ever anoint him. Was eternity with your daughter not enough?

Am I not enough?

"All of you—listen well. Your Goddess speaks." With authority in Her voice like a herald tapping his staff against the floor to resound through a royal hall, Marzanna released Bettina's scalp and leaned back in Her throne. For an instant the haze of the aureole blurring Her figure took on a silver cast to Cosima's trained eye...but it passed.

Whatever punishment Goddess proclaimed on Bettina's head would not pass that easily.

"While this one's dance pleased Me, her motives are impure. I am a lenient divinity—I allow most their pleasures and let their own hearts decide the meaning of sin. Though I am tolerant, though I don't meddle in the affairs of you people Myself, I am not without My pride. It is wicked, wicked and badly done, to deceive Me and break My heart." Stretching out Her slender leg, Marzanna nudged Bettina with Her foot; with a grunt of pain, she collapsed and rolled down the small set of stairs to land on her back on the deck.

Cosima saw she had already managed to stop crying, but the sight of Bettina's blank face, the wings crumpled profanely beneath her exposed body, and the raised goosebumps on her skin made her want to weep. Deep down, like a spark in a forge, something kindled in Cosima. Cinders in an old, tired bed awakened by a breath of heat—a susurrus of hate that stole her serenity forever at the sight of weak, spent Bettina cringing before the Goddess who had loved and lusted after her mere moments ago.

"Mother." Donning her mask to signal her submission—which was just as much of a pretense—Cosima dared enter the scene before Goddess could damn Bettina with Her decree. "This is supposed to be a celebration. You have honored me with this Jubilee, haven't You? And You *did* enjoy Mama's pretty dance. As a gift to me, couldn't You settle for a scolding to remind her of her duties and let us get on with the party?"

This disguise chafed. Cosima endured the abrading from the yoke she stuck her own head through and bowed formally before Goddess...and Fiammetta, who hadn't bothered to hide her smile. She leaned forward on her seat in anticipation of whatever penalty Marzanna had in mind.

Goddess's eyes formed whorls of hypnotic yellow gold in inky black as She turned them on Cosima. Her heir: Cosima supposed she was about to learn how much weight that title really carried after weeks of wondering what all the fuss for the Jubilee had been about.

"As My successor, do you think it is fitting to interrupt Me to beg for imprudent mercy?"

If it hadn't been for Bettina, Cosima might have shrunk from that rebuke. Her girlhood self would have scrambled for whatever way pleased both mothers at once. In the present, though, she had learned to tamp down those fears that would render her as helpless as an abandoned fawn. As helpless as she had been, once upon a time, when she'd chosen to defend Cristoval from a volatile Godling and nearly gotten all of them destroyed by Goddess.

"It is as Your heir that I speak. You have uplifted me greatly with Your choice—I wish to practice the influence You've granted me so Your regard won't go to waste."

Cristoval's hand lifted to rest on Cosima's back as they looked down where their mother lay. Bettina didn't look at either of them, but she *was* staring at something. When Cosima followed her gaze to see who or what it was, all she saw was a sea of faces hidden behind plaster, paint, and other ornamentations.

Bettina's wings rippled under the shadows cast by her children's auras as she tried to flatten them beneath her. Though the flame of Sainthood smoldered in her soul, she had depleted her Light so thoroughly her body could not endure the simplest movements without agony. Cosima heard the creaking and cracking of her wingbones and had to choke her sympathy with all her spare concentration.

"Our daughter is like You, Goddess," Bettina said, attempting to intervene as she rolled her head to the side to plead with Goddess again. "V-Valiant and—"

"Quiet, *viper.*" The sting of betrayal brought out an ugly side of Marzanna—jarring for a being who could never, ever be anything but beautiful to every eye in existence.

Above them, lanterns carved like flowers swung into existence when the Miraculous will that had timed their arrival with the falling of evening darkness ordained. Between the fluting calls of invigorating songbirds descending on the ship to serenade the guests, Cosima watched as Goddess's true form peeked through Her immortal flesh.

Ghastly. A knot of features both human and animal locked in a wheel of Light—all barely contained in the shell Marzanna had Made for Herself after defeating ancient Silver. A single second had not passed before the vision vanished as if it had never been and never would be.

Monstrous. Cosima thought in her secret heart as she watched Goddess restore Her sun-kissed flesh, Her sylphlike shape, Her commanding features. All lovely once again. *I've dealt justice to divine beings on my own. I will not fear You the way You want, Mother.*

"If I may suggest—" she began only to be interrupted.

"I will beg if You require it, Your Glory."

Shut up! She lunged for the cuff of Cristoval's scarlet-slashed sleeve and caught it, hissing unintelligible warnings through her teeth, but he shook her off. A shriek in Cosima's mind reminiscent of the scuffles most siblings fought throughout their childhoods slowed her down. *You fucking fool!*

"You." A simple word. In Goddess's mouth it spat loathing like venom to corrode steel or wither any backbone sturdy enough to withstand Her. "The cause of her offense. How could *you* placate Me?"

"Forgive my brother, Goddess! He's been ill—"

"Cosima." Light rooted Cosima in place, unable to move or speak. On her face the mask heated to near-burning in threat of punishment if she tried to subvert the lock around her body and tongue. From what suddenly seemed like a great distance, Marzanna watched. "Your excuses shame you. By all means, let your bastard brother speak."

Cristoval bowed, low, then lower still. As if he would not risk a single glance toward Goddess to affront Her twice.

"My mother has offended You, Goddess, for which I apologize from the bottom of my mortal heart. But—here I covet Your tolerance—I believe You love her well despite her... thoughtlessness. She believes she acts for the best as my mother, and grieves the thought of losing me one day. I understand in her desperation she has offended You most cruelly in her shortsighted folly…"

Cosima watched as Cristoval sank to one knee.

"…so I beg you, Goddess. I beg you to bestow any punishment You feel is necessary on me and me alone." He sank to the other knee as he finished.

The waves cradling the ship began to rock it gently, to and fro. Marzanna's power had instructed the heavens to provide a night unmatched in tranquility and wonder for the Jubilee. Cosima guessed that with the absence of Her good temper the weather was about to take a turn for the worse. She wrenched at the Light binding her, or to rip off the mask that symbolized her helplessness as a figurehead, but failed to do anything but twitch her fingers where she stood.

Goddess frowned down at Cristoval where he debased himself in supplication. She watched as his head tipped down on his humble neck so he could touch his forehead to the ground.

On either side of the throne Her two consorts observed as well. Fiammetta with barely suppressed glee as she fanned herself with a living array of citrus leaves; Däard with his head partially turned to the side, as if he was bored. Or as if he couldn't stand to witness what Goddess was about to do.

"Punishment is warranted for both mother and son. There is enough for both of you, bastard."

For what? You called Cristoval, and he came. Unless…

Could Marzanna know what he'd done with—*no.* Cosima dared not imagine it. Even thinking as much as she had might condemn all of them to oblivion.

Cosima risked the next idea that came to her. Though it was a taboo, she sought the sparks of Goddess's mind and flung her thoughts against the indifferent sphere with all her concentration. She was out of practice with this method, and the power took its toll. Sweat beaded on her top lip and along her spine despite the mild evening.

Please, Your Glory. You offered Mama a reward for her dance. Let Your mercy be the prize if You don't wish to grant her request.

All for nothing. Goddess ignored her. Hiding his reaction, Cristoval had yet to look up from where he had prostrated himself next to Bettina's barely conscious form.

"May I ask what my crime is, Your Glory? I have obeyed Your word from my youth and onward," he said with his head bowed.

"You speak to Me as a supplicant, but I sense your pride. Your arrogance that led you by the nose back to Aebbenary to argue over your mortal destiny."

"It is not my destiny I argue for, Goddess—"

"It is often the case with men, I have seen, to assume they can feel a divine hand guiding their way. More's the pity for you and your conceit. Yet, *dear* ones...I am willing to show mercy." As Marzanna raised Her voice to drown out Cristoval, She waited after Her last statement had finished ringing over the gathering for him to look up. When he did, once he sensed Her will, the thunderclouds in Her visage gathered in the skies above the ship to accompany the sentence She would utter.

Cosima's gut churned.

"Your banishment was informal, but the manner of your return has been cumbersome and disrespectful. You brought your mortal father to profane this Jubilee and distract Bettina from her duty. And Bettina..." Goddess sighed in sadness. "I fear you will not learn your lesson without what I must do next. For your sin—I take one of your wings. For your son's crimes I claim his sire's life as forfeit."

The result of the last was instantaneous: in this one thing Goddess showed a ration of kindness. Horror-stricken, Cosima watched as Cristoval rose, turning, already running toward where Crespin stood in the crowd observing the proceedings with a forlorn expression.

One moment he lived; the next he was dead. Gone before his body struck the floor. The mask painted with the instruments he had loved instead of mourning his lack of vocal talent fell with him. Where his arm landed, stretched out toward his son, it clattered onto the deck. His body rocked softly with the ship while his empty eyes stared at Cristoval.

Cosima fought the Light root even harder. Surely Mother would let her go to Cristoval where he knelt beside Crespin, mute with shock while grief marshaled its forces to overwhelm him. Surely She would understand, on some level, what She had just taken from the human boy who had never demanded the immortality Bettina had risked all defiance to earn for him...

Clad in fanciful dancing slippers, Cosima's feet lagged as she stooped as if leaning headfirst into a hurricane would grant her the momentum to overcome Goddess's divine will.

Oh Cristoval, I'm sorry—

Bettina didn't move. Fresh tears streamed from her red-rimmed eyes as the lanterns and surrounding haloes of all the divinities reflected off the gradients of blue in her wings. Her wingtips vibrated with the force of her struggle as she managed to roll onto her side and attempt to creep toward where Cristoval knelt, cradling his father's body in his arms.

Mother, please! Cosima screamed at Marzanna. Over again. And over, and over. She wanted to tear out her hair, beat her breast in shared suffering with two people she had always loved but never shown enough of it. For all the good her useless, impractical feelings ever gave them.

"For your reward...oh, clever swan, you should have made Me promise something specific before you played your hand. I may have toasted your wit with lenience." Still holding an impromptu court of ostensible justice, Goddess took the hand Fiammetta offered from the throne on Her right and squeezed it in comfort or twisted solidarity. As if She was the one wronged, and not the one wreaking havoc on the lives of people She should have loved.

Marzanna continued. "I will grant your son life at your side...but not for much longer. I have seen your struggle to accept the boy's mortality—it provokes My sympathy along with My jealousy. The sooner you come to terms with his departure the sooner I can welcome you back into My heart. For a time I will not disclose I will allow you to enjoy his company. Now, though, I give him sickness. As he weakens, you will know his time draws near. If you hurry back to Me, Bettina, I will grant him a resting place in the Scholar's Grave among one of the greatest men in existence."

The world held its breath. Cristoval had not risen from where he knelt by Crespin's body. Had he heard his sentence? Cosima wondered if the sickness had already been planted in him by Goddess's command. If more than mortal decay already leeched through his strong body until he withered.

It did not matter if he heard, she realized. Marzanna did not care about him. This had always been about Bettina.

"No. N-no, Your Glory—"

"Mother!" One word was all Cosima's searing rebellion could buy her. An admonishment Goddess refused to heed—as She refused to look at Cosima where she stood alone watching the end of her family—while She studied Bettina's reaction to her "reward".

Bettina did not care that she would lose one of her wings and the coveted ability to soar through the heavens on the strength of her sacred limbs. Though she had been fond of Crespin long ago, Cosima doubted his untimely death meant as much to her as her son's suffering. Misery that would only increase by the day—hour by hour until Goddess decided to banish Cristoval from life the way she had banished Silver from existence.

Godlings and Saints observed as Bettina worked with all her might to crawl back toward Goddess. Back up the steps to the throne where Marzanna and Fiammetta frowned down at her with imperious, genteel repugnance.

Cosima imagined she could hear them: *"Poor thing. She doesn't know any better. It's only instinct, and a mortal one at that. As soon as the boy dies…"*

A glittering array of divine beings gathered to glorify Goddess. Marzanna was neither satisfied with their number and the slavering quality of their worship nor were they brave enough to speak on behalf of their own. Late in the day Cosima saw how foolish she had been to ignore her responsibility of cultivating amity with any of these sycophants. Would they have cared to vouch for the heir apparent if they thought her friendship carried any faithfulness or worth?

Would any of this have happened if Cosima hadn't resented Cristoval's place in Bettina's priorities? *If I had tried to save him too instead of letting him stay mortal, would all of us be safe now?*

"Goddess. I have not greeted You since my return."

Sovanna. It could only have taken Goddess's most wayward offspring to draw her attention from pathetic, weeping Bettina.

Of all the Godlings and Saints present, she was one of the last Cosima had expected to intervene. Her neck creaked as she turned to watch Sovanna emerge from the host with smoky remnants of her vanished mask lingering around her eyes. Like Marzanna, her voice had a husky quality that caught the ears of others and held their attention like an enchantment.

Marzanna did not greet her in return as she approached the bottom of the stairs and performed a complicated, exotic bow learned from distant lands in deference. Brash and fearless—especially compared to the other Godlings—Sovanna climbed the steps to kneel delicately in front of Goddess's feet.

"So. Has your adolescent rebellion run its course?" Fiammetta leaned back and away from her even at the cost of letting Marzanna's hand go; disgust marred her features.

"I think of my separation as a plunge into independence, not as a revolt." Taking her impudence in stride, Sovanna rested her forearms on Goddess's knees and gazed up at Her with bravery that would fascinate if not particularly endear her. "Mother. You called me. Are You glad I answered, or would You rather I had stayed away?"

When Marzanna gazed down on Sovanna, there was only a whisper of love there that Cosima could see from where she stood. Confusion angered her more than she already was—what was another stab of envy in a heart wounded unto death by everything else Goddess had done to her and now her loved ones?

That's more regard than I've seen Her show for any of us. What was Her game in choosing me over Her firstborn?

Sovanna propped her hands and her chin atop them on one of Marzanna's knees and looked up at her Mother. They were cold-blooded, the two of them. Cosima had seen the thread of the relationship of natural-born daughter and divine Mother linking them and still understood that the emotions they felt could not possibly be likened to those felt by other human beings.

"Yes, daughter. I am *so* glad you came back to us. What reward would you like for your belated obedience?" Marzanna laid a hand on Sovanna's head—on one of her horns—and smiled.

Unlike Bettina, Sovanna knew better than to answer truthfully. "I don't need a reward. It's enough to see You again and know we understand one another."

"What do you think I understand?" The hand that had been gentle curled around the horn and began to squeeze; Cosima could see Her knuckles turning white around it.

Embracing the discomfort—though Cosima could only see her profile—Sovanna leaned into the abuse with a wry smile on her dark-painted lips.

"This is a Jubilee, Mother. Though it is in Cosima's honor, we all know our own successes have their source in You like a tributary. All should be according to Your preference, but…divine beings remember eternally. Would You have us think back to this event with joyous, wistful sighs of nostalgia, or recall with shuddering horror the punishments You enacted on some of Your first servants?"

By the time she finished her speech Marzanna had dragged her head down to her shoulder. Still, Sovanna didn't act.

"How bold you are to try to school Me on decorum. Is it that you've forgotten your place, or that you don't care if you incur My wrath?" Goddess said.

"Neither. Your choice of Cosima made Your design perfectly clear, Your Glory. And yet—" An artless yet strained chuckle from Sovanna. "You raised me on tales of Your Ascent and Your former life. I know You admire audacity and courage. For the sake of the servants I know You love in Your heart, how could I not speak on their behalf with any influence that has been left to me as Your firstborn, if not Your heir?"

Together, Marzanna and Fiammetta considered her as everything went silent except for the shushing of the waves against the ship's hull. Cosima admired Sovanna's efforts. Never had Cosima been so helpless since the hour she had been chosen as an irrelevant puppet for Goddess's regime. *I can only stand, and watch, and seethe…*

In a way, perhaps she had been spared. Fiammetta clapped in

delight when Marzanna dropped Sovanna's horn and instead seized her exposed neck to lift her into the air with blessèd strength to choke her.

A test. One *last* test, if Cosima knew Sovanna any better than she had before she'd carried Lilias into her swamp to trade them away for her freedom. Goddess could not fail, not ever—yet She had failed in this.

"You were not like this before." With Marzanna's hand around her throat Sovanna could barely utter a word, but Cosima heard her well enough. Beneath her outward fear there was a practiced hand twisting her strings around its fingers. A squirreling away of evidence behind a façade of distress that concealed the cunning with which Sovanna dared approach already irate Goddess.

Partially for her own ends...but also for Cosima. For Cristoval's sister, and his mother. Without glancing her way, Sovanna's consciousness brushed against Cosima's in acknowledgement of her silent torment. A benediction she had no right to grant, but all the audacity as the heir Goddess should have chosen led her to do.

"Since you love Aebbenary and these sinners you speak for so well I will reward you with their company. Look—" With a wave of Goddess's hand a window slicing through one reality and the next appeared before their eyes. Sovanna peered into it as Marzanna let her go, allowing her breath her Godling lungs didn't need but would suffer without.

"You are too much like your father. There is little you understand besides punishment and penance in a cycle that never seems to end. Since you love Me, daughter of Easoren, I will let you dwell in My city forever. Forever, and ever, and..."

"*No!*"

Abandoning both performance and any satisfaction she felt at being right about whatever hypothesis she had been considering, Sovanna lunged toward the window with a hand flung out to pass through it. Her white aureole formed rings like those that marked a tree's age, passing through the portal with shuddering speed that baffled the eye.

While malicious satisfaction brightened Her visage, Marzanna sent Her own Light through the window to scorch the marsh from afar. In moments, all of it was gone. With nothing to gaze upon but blackened earth and smoke that curled toward the heavens, the portal shrank by inches until it was nothing but smoke lingering on the air like a rumor of war.

Sovanna did not weep. She refused to shed a tear or vent her fury to a divinity who wasn't capable of caring. She met Marzanna's gaze and held it—painfully. Even for a mature Godling, she was nothing compared to Goddess and the Light that eclipsed Her figure in the aftermath of the destruction.

"As You have ordained, Goddess." A veiled oath like a dagger concealed under a cloak. Sovanna promised Marzanna something more than obedience as ichor trickled down her cheeks from her bloodshot eyes. With a refined sweep of her pale fingers, she painted her cheek with a smear that shone moonlight pale in the lantern light—almost like silver.

Then she was gone. A flash in the air as she left the ship and her divine star flew back toward the city to find sanctuary where she could lick her wounds…and plan her own retribution. Once again, Goddess did not care.

"Now—My sword thirsts to punish those who have sinned against Me. Däard."

When they used to converse easily during tranquil nights in the Valusius estate, with Cristoval whittling by hearth light and Cosima resting her head in Bettina's lap, she had told them Däard Ranieri had been a valiant firebrand back in his mortal days. Cosima saw nothing of that now as Däard—Goddess's peacekeeper and executioner—left his place next to Marzanna and approached Bettina where she lay. There had not been much justice in Silver's era; neither had the false god preached leniency during his rule.

What else can we call this, Cosima thought, surrendering to the vicious side of her nature she blamed Marzanna for, *but resentful retribution for an empty slight? Not justice.*

Cristoval had lingered by Crespin's body all this time in a trance of grief that had blinded him to the punishment Goddess inflicted on Sovanna. When Däard advanced, pulling his sword of Light from thin air, the haze seemed to break. Scrambling and desperate, Cristoval left his father where he'd fallen and went to cover Bettina with his own body to prevent the shining sword from falling on her.

"I beg you, Saint, take from me instead. An arm, a leg, what have you…spare my mother. I am to bla—"

With his wings unfolded in showy magnificence, Däard battered Cristoval with two beats that rippled through the air like a wave that threw him back. The crowd scattered to let him crash onto the deck several feet away from Bettina. Hundreds or thousands of miniscule wounds had been sliced into his skin, resembling tiny fish gills more than anything else. Blood and the curious tinge of lingering ichor leaked from the cuts.

Cosima caught its scent because of how familiar it was: gardenia and neroli, the ichor of the womb and her home. Bettina must have fortified Cristoval with blood from her own veins time and time again, she could see it now…but to no good.

Groaning from nausea and strain, Cosima *pushed* herself as hard as she could to go to him…but the root on her suddenly increased in strength. She collapsed like her ankles had been kicked out from under her; her forehead bashed onto the deck, making stars dance behind her eyes.

His face stony, Däard lifted Bettina onto her knees and extended her wings with another flash of power. No hero had ever looked so empty to Cosima's eyes. Devoid of all but resignation for the onerous task Goddess had commanded him to accomplish as yet one more thing to prove his love for Her.

Don't look. Two words from Bettina. She stared up at the flaming sword with her head lolling back on her neck in submission to the atrocity that was about to be done to her. Cosima bit her tongue nearly through as she tried not to scream, flinch, or react in any way that would cause Goddess to punish her loved ones further—

Däard carved. Even for the best warrior in the world, with the most powerful weapon in Creation, it took work to maim a Saint. One blow did not cleave Bettina's right wing from her body; two also failed. It took three to cut through the sinews and bones while ichor splattered the crowd and flowed over the deck. He still had to tear the bottom portion off with a heave of effort that made him grunt.

Bettina didn't scream; Cosima couldn't. Goddess must not have wished to hear the results of Her reprimand after all. Since Bettina had asked her not to look, Cosima tried to tear her horrified gaze away…only to have her eyes drawn to Marzanna. Who watched as Däard heaved the sundered wing over the side of the ship like yesterday's catch and sheathed his sword in the air he'd drawn it from.

She wasn't sad as a lover—or even as a parent scolding a child to prevent them from doing themselves harm with their own folly—should have been. She wasn't exultant the way Fiammetta was over witnessing the fall of a rival; detached the way Däard was as he released the power holding Bettina up and let her slump to the deck with a muffled cry of torment.

Her look was…resigned. As if mutilating Bettina was a chore to be done with to achieve another, more desirable end. As soon as the name of that face occurred to Cosima, Goddess's eyes slid her way as if She'd overheard it in her thoughts.

The mask, Cosima realized, had borne meaning after all. The Jubilee had been an excuse to lure every revolutionary—directly and indirectly—back to Aebbenary for Marzanna to discipline. Bettina for loving her son more than Goddess; Cristoval for being that son and deadweight on Bettina's heart. Sovanna for choosing solitude in her swamp over the wealth of power and influence in Aebbenary…and Cosima herself, for elevating her huntresses over every Godling and Saint she should have treated as her brethren instead.

"You and your son may leave us for now, Bettina." Fiammetta dismissed them while Goddess's attention lingered on Cosima. "What? You can't walk? Perhaps you could fly—oh! Not that either, I see."

The silent crowd knew better than to remain so at that tone. The laughing and jeering began as if on cue. Cosima's hands curled into fists at her sides. Outside of her control, her aureole flickered dangerously like the shadow of raptor wings passing high over a rabbit den.

Disinterested now the spectacle was over, Marzanna gestured with a single finger for some of the redundant crew members manning Fiammetta's ship to approach.

"Throw her over the side. She'll find her way back home on her own…eventually."

"The boy?" Däard called; whether his matching apathy was feigned or not, Cosima refused to care. "His body won't withstand the same."

"Does that matter?" Fiammetta encouraged the gathered beings to mockery again, but a cutting frown from Däard wiped the smile from her face.

"Stow him below until we make port. I care not." Goddess washed Her hands of the situation.

More of a ceremony than the Jubilee had been, the crew hauled unconscious Bettina portside and dumped her over. Divine beings conscripted for Fiammetta's pleasure or no, none of them looked like they relished the task. As soon as Bettina's remaining wing dipped over the side they turned their backs on her. Slowly, music began to disperse from the minstrel crowd to liven the solemn pause back into a celebratory atmosphere to ensure Goddess wouldn't be forced to wreak Her dissatisfaction on anybody else.

The world had ended. Dawn would not bring anything but sorrow…and Cosima couldn't do anything but wait for Goddess to set her free.

"Oh! My baby." Clapping her hands like a child, Fiammetta sat up from her languid lounging—a studied copy of Goddess—and perched on its edge. At once, the last of the Light root evaporated from Cosima's limbs; she staggered as the responsibility to keep her own balance and breathe on her own folded her into its rhythm again.

"What?" Cosima had forgotten. Everything else—her troubles with Iulia and Konetta, her huntresses, Lilias and their parentage, the stars aligned or misaligned to prick Sovanna's and Cristoval's hearts with love—had fallen away at the sight of Bettina's punishment. Fiammetta's interruption barely scraped her raw nerves, but when Cosima heard her voice a frenzy of bloodlust almost provoked her into an even less forgivable sin.

"You brought them. I can sense their aura." Gesturing Däard to her side like he was her servant, Fiammetta scanned the crowd for where Palmira held Lilias. "Well. You've let one of your mortal urchins hold them. Amusing—I entrust my precious offspring to your care and you dump them on your underlings. You there—bring me my child."

The crowd parted again to let Palmira and the squirming bundle that was Lilias through. Empty of any maternal affection, Fiammetta's gaze tracked Palmira's approach with vulturine concentration. Cosima saw Palmira's arms shake with her impulse to clutch Lilias to her breast and run away, even to dive off the side of the ship and let the waves bear them away from the island into the deep ocean.

"Stop. You dare approach this throne?" Fiammetta clucked like a matron appalled at a lack of decorum in an ingénue. "Give them to Cosima."

A better solution for everyone. Cosima didn't want Palmira anywhere near Fiammetta, and Palmira was relieved enough to pass Lilias into the care of a strong Godling who could protect them better that she almost tripped over her own feet.

"Cosima—" she tried to whisper as they came close.

"I know." Neither of them could say anything that wouldn't be overheard by many divine ears. Giving Cosima a tremulous smile, Palmira squeezed Lilias's chubby thigh one last time and let Konetta and Iulia fold her back into the huntress' ranks.

Resigned like Däard had been, Cosima carried them to Fiammetta's throne. Her shark-blank eyes fixed on the squirming bundle with interest, but not that of a mother who had missed her infant. When she held out her arms and accepted Lilias she pried their wings away from their small body like tearing off the wrappings of a present only to discover the gift hadn't been what she'd anticipated.

"The child is…" Gagging, Fiammetta shoved Lilias to the side; Däard caught them before they fell. "It *reeks.* The stench is ghastly. What have you done to it?"

Stench? Cosima sniffed the air as she watched Däard clumsily form a cradle with his arms to hold wriggling, squirming Lilias. "We bathed them this morning. It might be soil—"

The sea breeze wafted it toward her at last. Her senses no longer dulled by the Light root, she inhaled and tried to name the scents that came to her. *Asphodel. Wild boar roasting over a fire. And—*

Brimstone.

"Get back!" Däard shouted suddenly as the baby in his arms began to shine with Light, gleaming brighter and brighter…

Red.

True red. Crimson and scarlet that swallowed Däard's golden aureole and cast deeper shadows over the entire ship.

Goddess observed. While Fiammetta shrieked like a scalded cat and Däard staggered back with burns still smoking on his chest and arms from the oozing bundle of feathers rolling down the stairs and across the deck, Marzanna hadn't moved.

Cosima lunged to catch Lilias. It didn't occur to her to worry about burns and chaos inflicted on her if she dared catch the Saintling in the midst of their divine expression. They had fallen; she could hear their cries lowing in a rasping call that shook the timbers of the ship. That was something she couldn't endure.

The baby rolled to a stop in front of her in a heap of wet feathers and sinews shining with clear ooze. At the touch of her hands— warmed by the heat exuding from this form—the feathers molted and fell as new, dry ones grew in shades of black and red like Cristoval's masquerade apparel.

The child Lilias lay blinking their quartet of eyes up at Cosima on a bed of four wings. Their hues paralleled each other: two inky black, two the color of ripe raspberries. Innocent, babyish curls remained: Fiammetta's ginger mixed with streaks of white.

Nubs of something else poked through the thatch of hair more mane than anything else: *horns.* Coiling like a ram's with a sheen that defied identification.

"L—" Cosima coughed as the baby *breathed* that burnt offering and brimstone smell right into her face. "Lilias."

"You named them?!" The shriek cracked the Miraculous glass of the hanging lanterns as Fiammetta lost herself to rage. "That right did not belong to you—"

"Your child has expressed their divinity, as you hoped for." Cosima interrupted. "Do you want them back now they have? They're still young enough to answer to whatever name you choose. Or their father can choose—if he still remembers how." She took vindictive enjoyment in carrying Lilias closer, offering them to their biological mother with a hasty shove that sent Fiammetta throwing herself backwards with a hiss, while insulting Däard for his impotence.

"Your Glory, Your heir is insolent, boorish, and neglectful. She's done *something* to my baby and twisted them into an abomination! How can we let that stand? If they cannot be fixed, who will pay the price for this crime? Oh Marzanna, I can't stand it if—if—"

"Hush, dearest. All will be well." Goddess comforted Fiammetta by sliding Her slender arm around her shoulders. "This is a curiosity, that's all. It is likely the child will remain harmless. If they do not, My Light will repair their nature."

Well now, Cosima thought toward Lilias as she cautiously adjusted her hold on them. *They want to fix you. What do you think of that?*

Expressing divinity should have left the baby—now a toddler in size—silently astonished or wailing from the jolt of rapid transformation. Instead, one set of eyes glinted up at her while a discrete marker of maturing intelligence skimmed against Cosima's mind. No words yet…but she had no doubt they would come soon enough.

While Fiammetta crumpled in dramatic, false grief in Goddess's arms, Cosima attended to her own business with renewed dedication. Gesturing her huntresses closer, she passed Lilias into their care knowing they would take care of them. The differences that frightened others—even Godlings and Saints—would be no obstacle to her ladies in the face of the danger they faced now.

Then she returned all her attention to Goddess. A speech had coalesced in her mind along with a whisper of a plan on how to prevent one more helpless individual coming to harm at the hands of this court. Yet before Cosima could embark, Fiammetta recovered from her bout of hysteria…and her glistening eyes fixed on the huntresses retreating with her child in their arms.

"Cosima's ladies strike me now as a docile group. Like domesticated cats. It would amuse me to appoint them as retainers in my palace, my Love. Won't You give them to me?"

All plans flew out of her mind in wisps of dread. The cinders in Cosima's chest flared hotter as Fiammetta leaned in conspiratorially to make her request. As she asked, her eyes slid Cosima's way: strategy guided in no small part by lunacy that was stronger even than what a being twisted by divinity should have suffered.

Draining that creature would not be enough. Pictures of brash violence bloomed in Cosima's head: she could command the spear of Light Bettina had danced around to her hand. Her aim would be true as she cast it with sure strength through Fiammetta's heart, pinning her to the throne. She might squeal and thrash as the Light ignited her pale flesh to smoke and burn...

"They're not property. They're not cattle to be traded so."

Fiammetta laughed. "They are not yours to give—all things and all people belong to Her Glory. *She* will choose whether to honor my request." The "or not" was not implied: they both knew Goddess would never refuse.

Marzanna almost rolled Her eyes; almost, because She cared enough about Fiammetta to not let her see it. That same patience didn't extend beyond their pairing to Cosima.

"You corrupted the child. *You* will be responsible for them."

At last, a command I'm happy to obey. The irony struck Cosima as funny; she almost laughed. Not a month had passed when she would have gladly surrendered Lilias back to the ambiguous care of their parents just so she could huddle with her huntresses in their treehouse and pretend the pressures of her world would never threaten everyone she loved.

How many can I save from this trap? From drudgery if not outright danger?

An idea occurred. "Let me keep some of my ladies for assistance. I've grown accustomed to their service."

Fiammetta scowled. "Then you will accustom yourself to—"

"You may keep two. As a gift for your Jubilee." Marzanna interrupted their haggling.

With an idle talent for degradation, She pulled strings of Light in the air to line the huntresses up in a martial row. As if Cosima was the honored general She had named to the high position, She indicated with a subtle nod for her to choose her companions.

Iulia shook her head in subtle refusal. Her eyes darted toward Palmira, pointing to the first name Cosima should call. That was the right thing to do, after all. Gentle Palmira would suffer in Fiammetta's domain, and she loved Lilias so...

I can't. Cosima thought. No matter her turmoil, no matter who she loved or didn't love enough, Lilias in Palmira's arms kept drawing her attention. *I can't do this without you.*

"Iulia. Konetta." Which of them she couldn't do without she didn't know. Like Goddess had failed, Cosima had too.

She saw Iulia contemplate mutiny. She could be wise, but she had lived through too much to fear death at a Godling's or Saint's hand. Cosima entertained brief hope that she'd obey for once. Even if she hated Cosima for her betrayal, even if she had already plotted all sorts of retribution, she *needed* Iulia to come with her.

Konetta's little smile was the only warning she gave Cosima for the rebellion she'd forgotten to expect. When their eyes locked, she shoved Palmira behind Iulia, drawing the attention of the crowd.

"Go on, *Konetta.*" Konetta said loud enough for everyone to hear.

Brave Palmira might have hesitated before this night; she may have refused the opportunity Konetta granted to save herself from whatever horrors waited for the rest of them under Fiammetta's eye. As it was, Palmira's focus locked on Lilias—brimstone-stench, horns, and the rest—and she marched to Cosima without a backward glance.

I can't do anything. Again. Cosima ached with disappointment in herself. *By all rights I should be the one torn into pieces for my selfishness.*

As Iulia and Palmira joined her, Goddess yawned dramatically and rose from where She'd held court.

"This has been a trial upon My patience. Are we not all assembled to admire My chosen heir? Is My wisdom and mercy not worth celebrating? Come, come!" She clapped in a signal. "Approach Me, Cosima. I will crown you before all these witnesses so no one may gainsay your will as My successor. You answer only to Me and My consorts now, beloved daughter."

Wisdom. Mercy. Two pillars taught to all Godlings in their nurseries for however long it had taken for each to express their divinity. Cosima didn't wonder why none of it had stuck: what was a greater abomination than something that looked human, looked *mortal,* that would never age or die?

Even she was the same as the rest. The same terrible, gaping void of venal self-interest ruled her more than Goddess ever could.

"You were not like this before." Cosima repeated the accusation Sovanna had flung at Goddess. They assessed one another, eye to eye because Marzanna stood on the higher stair. That look reminded her distinctly of the absent former High Priest. Cosima had avoided him all her childhood and adolescence, but she had seen enough of him and heard of his trials under Goddess's caprice.

When Marzanna settled the crown on her head, thousands upon thousands of tiny butterflies emerged from Her arms as she raised them up like wings—whole, healthy, wings—behind Cosima. The leaves of her crown began to twine into her hair and bloom a new breed of flower the world had never seen.

"Look at them, Cosima. Face your kindred and honor them with your first greeting as My heir." Goddess spoke in a hushed, fervent voice as She laid Her hands on Cosima's head and turned it here and there. "Look at your huntresses. See them—how they already wither on the vine of their mortal destinies. Can you see the difference? Can't you feel the taint of their decay every moment you spend with them?"

Cosima wanted to squeeze her eyes shut out of spite. She didn't want to face anyone, let alone the two people she had let down the most: Iulia, who loved her. Palmira, who trusted her. Crespin's death-flattened eyes with their crinkles of a fairly joyous life smoothed into slack skin. Yet she did as she was bid, for what else could she do besides submit?

"Their lives are short, yes. Why begrudge them to me? I am young yet, Mother. I might have grown closer to my own kind if You had chosen to be patient with me."

"Action assures results. Not patience. You will see what I mean before long."

Goddess claimed the last word. Turning Cosima around, she laid Her hands on her shoulders and brushed a fond kiss against each of her cheeks in sanction for the revitalizing surge of power She bestowed on Her heir.

"I am gracious to those who prove themselves. If your brother's end is hastened by necessity your huntresses may not be away from you long."

"I see what You mean already." Cosima whispered in answer to Her initial comment as the crowd began to cheer, throwing their masks into the air where, one by one, they exploded into bursting stars and littered the other attendants and ship with glittering shards of Light.

INTERLUDE

Absolution

XIV

Sovanna

The bells of Aebbenary might comfort others with their tolling of the hours and solemn assurance that no matter what happened during the day, the time would still pass, but Sovanna did not love them. Everything that reminded her she was trapped in a densely-populated—albeit mostly well-cared for—city made her skin crawl with claustrophobia. The first days had been the worst, but as the bells thrummed their inexorable remembrance that time would always march forward even for those not bound by it, the panic had eased.

Her hatred had not. Her abhorrence for the calamity of the Jubilee fed the flames; the seeds of darkness her childhood had sown in her heart bloomed like nightshade.

Though Aebbenary was crowded, Sovanna carved herself a place among the soaring buildings and gleaming streets of Goddess's holy city within days. All it had taken was a thorough tour under cover of darkness—with her presence shielded completely from every other divine being who could possibly sense her besides her Mother—and clearing out a nest of thieves and cutthroats she had observed were motivated by greed rather than desperation. With ice guarding her heart from the awfulness of losing her home, she had built another with the essence she had managed to siphon from her swamp before. Marzanna destroyed it.

Streets turned to stodgy mud and prickly grass. Water with a source in the Miracle-cleansed river that separated the Holy Tower from the

the city as Silver's cathedral had been set apart from the populace had churned from the deep, building wetlands according to her instruction. With every guidance of Sovanna's words, hands, and will, a miniature of the marsh she'd lost emerged from the wreckage with a translucent barrier of Light protecting the domain from trespassers. A makeshift house bare of furnishings and her store of herbs and poisons. Rats and lizards transformed into otters and badgers and her favorites: crocodiles who would guard the area more securely than her power.

She had Made more than she intended. An entire borough of the city had to flee the encroachment of her marshland without much notice as Miraculous growth ate up several miles of the mighty city.

"Take it up with Goddess," Sovanna had called to them from behind the barrier. Lost in her wrath, sick with it and worry over those she had been obligated to leave behind on the pleasure ship, the mortal faces had blurred into a mass of humanity she wished she didn't care about.

Couldn't care about—like the other divine beings who suffered from a sickness more insidious than what their presence did to mortalkind.

The Jubilee hadn't been completely worthless after all. Unable to force her meticulous mind quiet even for a moment, Sovanna had witnessed all the evidence she needed to learn that the divinity sickness that beset the mortals of Aebbenary worked two ways. Mortalkind served with more and more compelled reverence…and the divine beings transformed into darker versions of themselves while basking in unmerited worship.

Homelessness banished, Sovanna had entered the replica of her cozy hut and collapsed in the shelter and solitude on the bare wooden floor.

I removed myself from court and influence for my work, she reminded herself as she pressed her palms over aching eyes still scorched by Marzanna's halo. *I removed myself from care for any individual so I could remember the needs of the many at all times.*

As she'd told Cosima an eon ago, her exile had been voluntary. Goddess hadn't liked it, but Sovanna had had yet to earn any of Her respect regardless. Since she hadn't left the island at that time,

Marzanna had allowed her distance with tacit disapproval that loomed over Sovanna wherever she was like a thunderhead.

Frown all You like. A thought Sovanna had indulged in like a child crowing over stolen treasures or freedom from hated lessons. *One day, one day soon, You will not be able to hurt others like You can now.*

Rolling onto her back on the floor of her new home—her *prison*—Sovanna had blinked up at the ceiling and focused on breathing through the anguish. Nature had refrained from granting her a human heart, it seemed, much like both of her parents…but Sovanna no longer wished to surrender to the hollow urges that filled the cavity left in her soul.

Others had called her cold. She *was* calculating by nature, a trait she could have inherited from either of her parents. But the problem, she knew, was that she felt *too much*. Raised by the Shining Court as the first among dozens of progeny, Sovanna had somehow never learned the ability to separate herself from the events she saw unfold before her impressionable eyes.

Several things she had perceived very quickly, as soon as a child's mind could grasp concepts: Marzanna despised as well as loved her. Marzanna loved and loathed Easoren too, but in greater measure than their daughter. Consort Fiammetta hated all children who were not hers and Marzanna's on principle, but especially Sovanna because she'd been first. Däard was different from them, but also indifferent—as useful as a square peg in a round hole.

Days passed. Sovanna foraged in the replica of her swamp for all the herbs she'd lost and furnished her house with whatever she felt like stealing from the rest of the city during the day. She compiled what she recalled of her research and evidence at night.

A week. She was used to solitude, but she couldn't forget the sting of it here, where no matter what power she used she couldn't drown out the raucous sounds of Aebbenary's people entirely. Memories beset her whenever she paused to rest; she found herself arguing with the crocodiles who visited at her window for breakfast, chatting with the furry trundlers who found their way to her door bearing gifts they'd found from the wreckage of the buildings Sovanna had leveled to Make her new home.

A trauma had taken place. Sovanna was acquainted with her subconscious enough to determine that as the source of her unsettling emotions and flashbacks. As always, she could account for everything with neat strokes from her mind and a fair bit of scribbling in a personal ledger to analyze her troubles and the ambition that drove her whether she denied its existence or not.

Everything but one ruinous variable: Cristoval Valusius.

Her work kept her busy. Observing sufferers of divinity sickness during the day wherever she could find them, furnishing her experiments with blood taken from a random sample of citizens during the nights she spent wandering outside her swamp, and generally trying to prove this plague existed. That it could be cured—that *she* could remedy it. Sovanna was sure something had changed the nature of mortalkind and divine beings on every infinitesimal layer…and she wasn't the only one.

It hadn't taken long for Cristoval to find her. The alignment that had happened as soon as they'd met in person had folded them together like two ends of the same cloth. As she opened the door already knowing who waited on the other side, she idly wondered if it had started earlier than that: when a noble son driven by compassion she felt only in theory had contacted her as the sole existing expert on what was happening to everyone in Aebbenary.

Her crocodiles understood more than she did. They allowed Cristoval to reach her house without a fuss.

"They told me…" Cristoval didn't finish. He couldn't, not while that cough racked his lungs with hollow yet wet reverberation. She could barely help wincing as she lingered in the doorway still debating whether or not to let him in.

"They?"

"The huntresses. Cosima's friends." Blessedly, the coughing eased. Cristoval swayed before he righted himself as the fit that had brought him to Sovanna's door visibly passed. She watched, fascinated despite herself as color returned to his pallid cheeks and light to his eyes.

An interesting malady. Could Mother have been motivated enough to conjure something new to sicken him rather than an existing disease?

Though it wasn't wise to welcome him, she did so by throwing the creaking door wide and turning away to start assembling her tools. A beat of silence passed before she heard his boot-shod feet cross her threshold behind her. Her home wasn't much to look at, but his manners left him waiting while she hunted down her oilcloth bag of instruments. When she told him to sit at her table—not cluttered, but covered with the detritus of an alchemical test that filled the room with fading smoke—he obeyed.

Sovanna considered Cristoval as she stood above him, her bag clutched in both hands until she remembered to set it on her second and last chair and busy herself cleaning up the remains of her experiment. How was she to begin? He had come to her for help, as she'd predicted. Should she just start and expect his compliance, or...?

"I'm sorry about your father. And your mother." *And mine. I'm sorry, sorry, so sorry...*

Apologies were worthless in the face of the real, valid work she could be doing to atone for the harm she and her kindred wrought on the world.

"Thank you. You shouldn't be, though. You tried to speak for us," he replied. "I won't forget that."

Sovanna got to work. His face screwed up in a grimace as she sliced an opening into his wrist and caught the trickle of blood in a clean vial. Not from the pain of her knife, but from her sympathy. She wasn't certain how she could know that with any confidence when she hadn't been acquainted with him in person for longer than a fortnight.

"You should. Meaningless things should be discarded to make room for the pertinent." That was how *she* lived, anyway. In Sovanna's book, few matters of the heart held any relevance. She wanted things to stay that way.

The sooner I fix him, the sooner he can leave.

Awkwardness pursed her lips as both of them silently watched Cristoval's blood slither into the vial. This close, she could feel how all of their senses were alert to the details of the other. His posture sloped toward her from mingled exhaustion and attraction, while he kept looking with glances that slid to and fro from her regal features, the slope of her shoulders where she stooped to catch his blood, anything she was doing that included simple breathing.

Breaths she had to remind herself to steady when he watched her so intently.

"Tell me what you've been feeling." There, she'd distracted them both. Sovanna hoped she'd laugh at herself later for her desperation to get away from him...or move closer.

"Weakness in the night that passes during the day, for now. There's this ache in my bones when I do anything strenuous," he said.

"Like what?"

A slash of a smile in his face as he glanced up at her. "Cosima and her huntresses run a tight ship. Though their numbers are thin, they stick to a regimen of activity I could barely have kept up with before..." The smile faded; something in Sovanna's chest twanged, like a string snapping on a prized instrument mid-note. "I try to make myself useful in other ways. I've been spying on the palace and—"

"The palace! What for? What could you..." *That was unkind.* Catching herself before she insulted him, Sovanna chose not to remind him yet again that he was a mortal—she'd wager a very sick mortal— on an island where Godlings and Saints walked.

This time when his eyes landed on her face they stayed there, as if by looking he could read her mind. After a lifetime of being reminded he was less than his mother and sister and everyone of note he'd ever met, he could probably guess what she'd been about to say.

"Stop going there. I can help you be useful without endangering yourself." Her awareness of him—his body angled toward her, his thoughts bent on reading the blank slate of her face—made her hurry to pull the vial away along with herself when she moved to another table to find a stopper.

"I have to go back there. The other huntresses are there, and...no one's been able to find my mother. Not even Cosima."

I'm sorry. You are good and kind, and no divine being can be the same. Especially not me. Sovanna swallowed physically as if that would banish the words she knew would serve no purpose to utter. Necessity made her return to him, since the cork she needed was right next to him on the main table, but sympathy persuaded her to touch a fingertip to his cut wrist and heal the slice with her Light.

The tiny slices from Däard's buffeting wings had mostly healed, but she could still see the marks they had left. Did Cristoval have enough life left for those scars to vanish?

"Take heart. She can't die. Even if she could—" Would that be any comfort? Knowing Goddess coveted his mother so much She wouldn't grant Bettina a good death even if she wanted one? "Cosima will find her soon."

When it came to supporting others, Sovanna was and always would be a clumsy novice. Especially when she truly cared.

"Can you help me, Sovanna?" He had no need to say her name since they were alone, but he sounded like he wanted to speak it into existence between them. Cristoval wanted to acknowledge the connection that had sprung to life like the source of Aebbenary's sacred, sustaining river.

Touching his skin compelled her acceptance further still. She heard and felt him take in a breath and hold it as she lingered by him, her finger pressed against his healed wrist with the thin stream of his blood drying into the whorls of its print. One more time she denied it, promising to hold her resolve in being sucked into an affair that could only be an unending nightmare.

In her heart, a private version of herself—horns and divine arrogance and all—whispered what she couldn't say. *I don't know if I can save you. I don't know if I'd survive not trying. I want to understand you, I want you to understand me. I—*

Sovanna channeled the self she had always seen as her worst to silence that insipid girl. She'd spent years in her swamp with her reptilian guardians and her research: time had sharpened her into a woman willing to cut away anything that didn't earn its keep in her mind and heart. What was one more sacrifice when the world had so much to gain from her dedication?

It hurt to move away from him—still a few beats too late—but the pain soothed her and reminded her who she was. It honed her resolve and assured her she had made the right choice. All she had to do was continue making it.

Sovanna tested a few drops of Cristoval's blood on an unblemished golden scale. In response to whatever was in it, the side with the blood dipped as the pure gold reacted to the influence of the taint. Frowning, she offset the change with a measure of blood twice the size of Cristoval's sample that she'd taken from a random Aebbenarian; then a full separate vial.

His blood was heavier.

What has She done to him? Even those stricken badly by the divine plague maintain normal blood volume, she puzzled as she re-corked the precious bottle and clutched it in her fist like a talisman. Like the key to a chest filled with either treasure or a deathtrap.

Cristoval waited patiently where she'd left him. Though he watched her work with interest, she observed how he slumped in his chair until the second she looked at him again. As if the weariness he felt thanks to his strange malady was only worth fighting if he didn't want her to see it.

"Your blood is mortal but...*more.* I don't know what Goddess inflicted on you, but it changed your essence on its primitive levels." She pretended she didn't notice, explaining her findings instead, but her resolve crystallized into dogged denial that this world would lose Cristoval before his allotted mortal time had come.

"Like ichor?" Cristoval frowned as she shook her head and, taking a risk, handed him the stoppered vial to inspect. He held it up to the murky light filtering through her round window and agitated the sluggish liquid with a shake. "It's darker now. Must be cursed."

"There's something in it. A pollution that's slowly consuming your real blood."

"Have you seen anything like it before?"

"Yes. But the circumstances are...different."

Her thoughts racing ahead, Sovanna reclaimed the bottle when he passed it back to her and hunted down another vial of blood she'd claimed days earlier from a far less willing subject. This time Cristoval followed her to the scales, which she cleaned with a fresh rag snatched from a stack of cloths reserved for that purpose before duplicating her experiment with the new vial.

Cristoval's blood remained on the right side of the scale. As the new blood, darker than Cristoval's but of similar viscosity, dripped onto the left plate she heard a faint sizzling sound as the material corroded the sacred gold. Yet the balance held, indicating equal parts. Only when the new blood corroded a few more layers did the scale dip…then crack as the plate suddenly crumbled away beneath the sample.

Looking over her shoulder—standing too close in his eagerness—Cristoval huffed in surprise.

"Where is that blood from?" he asked.

Sovanna grimaced and didn't try to hide it. "Fiammetta's spawn. Lilias."

"Lilias?" His eyebrows rose in disbelief. "Cosima let you—"

"I didn't ask. If she's going to demand I babysit, then I'm going to do whatever I damn please while I care for them." When Cristoval's eyebrows rose in amused disbelief, Sovanna jutted her thumb toward the back of her cottage to indicate her meaning. "The child is nocturnal. Thank Oblivion divinities don't require sleep."

He laughed, as if he couldn't help it. She did too. Her only regret in this moment was that her laugh covered some of his when she wanted to listen to it again and again at her prompting. Both of them had forgotten the experiment, the crumbled scale, his sickness—all of it. In her cottage in her conjured swamp all that existed was their longing for each other, so tangible Sovanna could taste it like air sweetened by fragrant spices.

Picturing her yearning like a physical door she could slam shut, she stepped back. She didn't have far to go, since a table perched precariously on four cracked legs blocked her retreat, but her body language was clear.

"You should go for now. I'll send word if I make a discovery or require more blood."

"And what if I need you?" His smile revealed a set of fine teeth that were only a little crooked, a little stained; like his father's, Sovanna remembered. She had barely observed Crespin before the Jubilee, but she had always been good with recalling details.

"You won't." She couldn't surrender to that endearing, teasing grin. The familiarity and lack of fright or repulsion she'd chased for much of her life until it dawned on her she didn't need it to survive. Sovanna hardened her heart against his charm and set herself in opposition to the Created feebleness in him that had earned her attention more than any destined love tragedy ever could.

"You are young—*we* are young. Your expectations for what can happen here should be adjusted. All I can do is try to make right what happened to you and your family and…and everyone else in Aebbenary under my Mother's reign. This thing you feel that connects us isn't something we should have. It's a mistake."

"Isn't that part of being young?" Cristoval didn't attempt to touch her, not overtly, but his longing to hold her was one she knew because her desire to feel his arms around her was an equal match. "Making mistakes?"

"Errors belong to those who can afford them. I can't—*you* can't."

I cannot think *when you are here.* Speaking that into existence, admitting she felt it itching and scraping in her bones where the marrow should have been, would only hurt both of them.

In Goddess's domain, bloodlines were of less value than they had ever been. Her favor was the predominant currency of Aebbenary. Sovanna had grown up without any consciousness of what birthrights or inheritances meant along with the lack of anyone she could honestly name as her family. Cristoval was opposite in this way too, enough to make her wonder what it was like to grow up with his mother and sister. Tetchy, intrepid Cosima, charming, affectionate Bettina—all members of a family named Valusius.

If names still meant anything, he would do credit to his. He would be a force in the world if only it still belonged to mortalkind, she thought as he took slow, careful steps to cross the short distance that parted them.

"I am not a man who cherishes faith in divine beings or the will that orders the world," he began, looking into her eyes without flinching at the sight of her obvious differences. "All I can do is whatever I am able. I don't believe in waste, Sovanna. And I'd be wasting these last days of my life by not telling you that I have faith in *you*. Whether I survive to see it, I know you can and will accomplish what we set out to do."

He did the one thing that made her freeze in abject terror: he slowly took her hand and brought it to his lips, where he pressed a kiss against her cold fingers that she would feel burning there for the rest of her life.

I can barely breathe without you. You, Cristoval, who I hardly know, yet feel as if I've spent lifetimes with you at my side already.

Sovanna forced herself to admit the rest of the truth. To pry her inner eyes open to stare at the ugly reality that was the only one that mattered. *The only way to save him is to let him go. To save everyone else, he might be the cost.*

She had to be strong enough to do it if he was not.

Pulling away from him, shutting her eyes to the hurt her rejection brought to his unguarded face, she shuffled objects around yet another small table until she found the protruding stem she was looking for and viciously plucked it from its pot.

"A parting gift," she said, facing him after a pause brief enough to convey their moment hadn't meant a thing to her. *The only one I'll ever give you besides your life, if I can spare it.* "I cultivated it from a seedling to increase energy and promote healing. I don't know if it will help you, but on the off chance it might…"

Proffering the marsh lily with ribbons of underbelly pink fluid dripping from its torn stem, Sovanna angled her hand so Cristoval couldn't accidentally touch her as he took it. Her most useful invention in flora was macabre as well as functional. As the lily wept liquid onto the floor she realized with a flare of embarrassment that he might be revolted by her gift rather than grateful.

"Thank—"

"Don't thank me. This is payment for you not returning to Fiammetta's palace."

His face fell, but he claimed the marsh lily anyway; it fell to his side with his arm, dripping on his boot. "I must—"

"You *mustn't*. Your mother would forbid it if she was here. Besides, you can do more good helping me than endangering yourself on a fool's errand."

"How?" Though he looked dubious, he gave her a chance to make her offer.

"We can continue the work we started with our letters in person."

What are you doing?! Her caution shrieked at her as words poured from her stupid mouth to protect even stupider Cristoval from getting himself killed at the palace and giving Goddess the satisfaction Sovanna intended to deny Her for eternity. *How could you push him away before drawing him in? What's the matter with you?*

It was a sickness she understood. Just one she doubted she'd ever be able to cure.

"What do you mean?"

"With Lilias here too, I can continue testing with both of you as my subjects. Well, you and the rest of this city. Even if I work every hour of every day, I feel our time to halt the progression of this condition affecting everyone in Aebbenary won't be enough. Goddess…"

Memories flashed quick as lightning behind Sovanna's eyelids as she blinked: Marzanna choking her, Däard committing the atrocities he had been made for by obeying the order to hack off Bettina's wing, and everyone else standing in silent, awful reverence as Goddess wrought Her will on them without resistance or consequence.

Cristoval kept up with her so she didn't have to explain the rest. "Even the lesser Godlings and Saints aren't immune. Is the Jubilee when you realized?"

Swallowing, Sovanna nodded. Before she knew it, they'd moved closer again, drawn to each other by the shared ordeal of that event. Unwelcome confessions crowded like seed husks in her mouth, behind her teeth, stuck until she relented and spit them out.

"How could they all stand there? How could…how could She do that to Bettina? To Cosima, to *you*? I've known Her to be cruel, but…" Again, with her body moving before her better judgment could make her stop, she moved toward him. As her voice dropped with the weight of desolation Sovanna felt his hands slide up from where they'd clasped her hands—her gift tucked into his sleeve for safe-keeping—to rub her upper arms in an offer of comfort.

Though her thoughts screamed resistance, the rest of her longed to sink into his touch like surrendering to blissful, dreamless sleep. Dreamless, because he'd be beside her, and they would be safe. What need would they have for dreams when they had each other?

"I can't pretend to fathom the doings of eternal beings, not even with my arrogance." His hand brushed against her cheek as he tried to answer; she barely refrained from leaning into it as she blinked loathsome tears back to gaze up at him. "I know you better than you think, thanks to our letters. I can promise you have nothing to fear from me. We can do this together."

"Go, Cristoval. I can't stand kindness any more than I can stand malice." She let him see her. Once only—the merest of looks into the empty, sucking void of desire and spite that drove her like a ship's rudder whenever thoughts of faltering struck would surely urge him away.

Everything was a mistake from the beginning. Answering his letters, wondering who the writer was, meeting him, this...where will it end? How else could it end but in pain?

She had no clue how he had heard of her or managed to send her a letter. Though she was devoted to pursuing her cause alone, she had spread tentative feelers throughout the city to try to ascertain the nature of the divine decay blooming in Aebbenary. Sovanna cut ties with anyone she contacted before a whisper of the word "ally" could be hissed in the wrong ears, but Cristoval had refused to be discarded.

My home has changed, he had written to her in one dispatch, *but I will not mourn. I believe it can be saved if we do the work to heal what has been sickened. With diligence and faith in one another, dubious though your trust in me may be, I know nothing is beyond our grasp. Not when it comes to the land we wish to save.*

Sovanna had memorized that last letter, though she hadn't known who exactly had sent it since it was better neither of them knew too much about the other. That was difficult to remember now she had met Cristoval.

Now destiny had crammed him into her hollow heart to roost for good.

"I'm going." The two words speared through her heart, but they barely had time to puncture it before he leaned in, eyes open as if in curiosity, to gift a delicate kiss to her lips in assurance she hadn't known she'd needed. "I'll be back, though. Soon."

Then he left, bowing with a smile at her shock that made her lift her hand, trembling, to the stain of warmth on her mouth that would keep her thinking of him for hours.

In a world where destined matches were rarer than hen's teeth, what entity had seen fit to connect the two of them so profoundly? A human son bereft of parents—Sovanna had no faith Bettina would be anything close to her usual self after what she'd endured. And her—the elder child of a reborn Goddess and a dead false god conceived through his mad High Priest.

It had been many years since Sovanna had considered her one-of-a-kind looks. She and Lilias had more in common than anyone else in Goddess's realm—perhaps the entire world. Their physical differences set them apart and warned others away similar to how vivid flowers dripping poison from their petals made predators flee the threat of their proximity.

There's work to be done, she reminded herself as she shut her door against the world.

XV

Cosima

Cosima sighted the towers of Fiammetta's palace and let herself hover as close as she dared in her Light form.

That spiteful bitch knew I'd be here. The realization stoked the rage consuming everything in Cosima's chest that had ever been kind and true. In the wake of the Jubilee she'd wondered if it was worth it to fight her nature as she always had. If it was folly to honor Bettina's upbringing and the mortal instincts that led her to reject her fellow Godlings. Childish rather than admirable.

A shield against divine influence—all but Goddess's—shimmered around the palace. Within it, the color-stained windows complex with designs depicting the romance of Marzanna and Her consorts—even the late Scholar—gleamed under the scythe of the moon covering Cosima's presence. Jewel-encrusted towers topped with gilded domes that mimicked the design of the Holy Tower would stun passersby and petitioners during the day, but not Cosima. The shield blinded her eyes and her senses with power she spat at and cursed as she winged her way frantically to and fro around the shield.

Konetta's in there, her thoughts cried and cried. *Konetta, Grisel, Ricla, the others. They trusted me—I failed them like I failed everyone else.*

Hours passed. Drudgery was bad enough for a proud huntress, accustomed to freedom under Cosima's guarding wings, but what else could they be suffering under Fiammetta and her insanity? Why had she, disdaining humans and preferring lower Saints or royalty to wait on her hand and foot, demanded the huntresses as tribute for Cosima's failures?

Eventually, as dawn drew nigh with blushes and sighs across the sky, Cosima surrendered to the call for home. Without her ladies the treehouse felt like a tomb, more than ever since…

Skittering away from the events of the past week, Cosima's mind rejected all else but what it meant to be alive and Light as she travelled back across Aebbenary's plains outside the city into her stately forest. Face and limbs and every rangy parcel of flesh that made her up reformed from the Light.

Fleetingly, Cosima hated each portion with revulsion that made her want to drain her blood and cast her current self into oblivion like she had with the divine beings who had wronged her huntresses. Though this time was the worst, it wasn't the first she had pondered if it would be better to erase herself and start anew somewhere else in the world away from the corruption and cloying decadence of Marzanna's Aebbenary.

How could you think of that when your huntresses need you? Her thoughts taunted as she dallied at the base of the treehouse ladder, staring up at the Miraculous structure and the canopy of trees. They danced in a morning breeze and did not care who ruled the world as long as disease or fire never touched them. *You have failed, but that doesn't absolve you of the responsibility to keep trying.*

Cosima scaled the ladder and pushed past the drapery of thick leaves to unlock the door with her touch. When she entered, the space was quiet. As long as at least one huntress remained in residence the treehouse would stay lit by the Miraculous glass insects one of them had persuaded Cosima to make to adorn the ceiling and walls, but the figures had reduced their potency with the prolonged absence of the rest of the household. Even with that, Cosima could sense Palmira resting in her room, while Iulia was absent.

Palmira missed her honorary sisters. Though she had been lucky enough to keep her freedom thanks to Konetta's cleverness and sacrifice, Lilias had been the one thing she couldn't keep. Cosima had taken one look at the livid burns that had patterned her mortal arms and chest after she had carried them back, and tracked down Sovanna to make her take the child. This time she hadn't protested: the anomaly that was Lilias merited close study from a divine being who could withstand a little fire.

Cosima tried not to blame Sovanna for that. Not out of any kinship, but because she didn't have any condemnation to spare with all of her impotent wrath directed at Goddess. At Däard for tolerating Her. At Fiammetta for preying on the huntresses. At Bettina for falling into Marzanna's trap.

For herself, because she was the most selfish one of all.

After the Jubilee, their quartet had returned to the treehouse to recuperate from their losses. Cosima had been a quivering wreck crowned in Goddess's ultimate favor, Iulia had been silent with rage, and Lilias had dozed in a befuddling orb of wings and horns while Palmira gingerly carried them home to settle them to bed. Unsure what to do or say, Cosima had stood in the middle of the room and watched as she comforted the babe and Iulia comforted her.

What would Iulia say once Palmira went to bed, most likely to cry herself to sleep over Lilias's flower cradle? Would she shout at Cosima, fight with her, vent the rage she of all people deserved to feel regarding the extent of Cosima's failure and betrayal? They'd have to leave the treehouse again to not wake Palmira or—

While Cosima had dithered, adorned in laurels and afraid, Iulia had left her in the common area and gone to bed in one of the now vacant bedrooms rather than theirs. Cosima had waited for her for a long time before she heard the faint sounds of Iulia's steady breathing indicating that she refused to lose precious, restorative sleep over anything that had taken place.

Standing alone in the common room now, Cosima revisited the past few days. Palmira tended to her own needs, but barely, and only at Iulia's urging; after Lilias, she had expressed no desire to leave the treehouse again. While Cosima spent her days traversing the city by sky searching desperately for any sign of Bettina or Cristoval—while also avoiding the beam of Goddess's attention in case She was on the hunt as well. Iulia had left after dawn each morning and did not return until past nightfall.

Defeated after seeing the strengthened shield Fiammetta had arranged over her palace to prevent any spying, Cosima languished in an abandoned bedchamber—probably Grisel's based on the trove of carved stone and pottery beads in all shapes and shades shoved in the corner. A bowl of dried mushrooms hung precariously over the bed to promote safe dreams. Listless, exhausted, but all too aware that divinities didn't require rest to survive the way mortals did, she stared up at the unglazed bottom of the bowl and only breathed.

"Everything will be fine as long as we're together. I promise." Konetta's assurances had been forbidden and sweeter than the figs Cosima knew were her favorite. *"Look at me. A mortal, a feeble one at that, promising safety to a Godling."*

"I like your promises," Cosima had replied. That had been true—she had always been a fine mark for those who liked vowing love and loyalty but never following through. Now she was one of those: an oathbreaker, because she had done nothing—had stood powerless—when her loved ones had needed her.

Someone cleared their throat as they nudged the door open to poke their head in. Even in this state Cosima didn't startle properly: her instincts were too honed, since hunting was one of the few skills she possessed that surpassed others. Cosima sat up as Iulia stepped inside and shut the door behind her.

I know your heart. I know it already. Every time Cosima saw Iulia the words resounded through her head like bells tolling the hour. So much had happened during and since the Jubilee, all amounting to more importance than one romantic relationship, but she still couldn't forget.

Could she say she had ever known Iulia's heart? If she had missed something that important due to her fixation with Konetta, would she ever have the chance again?

"I have a report." Iulia's formality galled like clothing soaked in seawater and dried without rinsing. Cosima couldn't answer aloud, but she shrugged one shoulder in acknowledgement.

"No one's seen them. Fiammetta's household functions as usual, but without their help. The other servants might not know our girls are in there even if they felt like talking."

"Felt?" It had been days since Cosima had spoken. Her voice croaked as she responded.

"Our liege values her privacy. It seems some of her worst punishments are reserved for eavesdroppers."

"Then you can't go there anymore. I won't risk you being recognized."

"That's not your decision."

The rebuke was harsh enough to suppress Cosima's pride. "Yet I can ask you not to go."

"Can you now?" Though divine beings loved their vindictive barbs and repartee, Iulia had never been like that. Her question was genuine, which pushed the dagger point deeper through Cosima's heart. She heard the rest: *is that something you can ask of me after what you've done?*

Changing the subject was safer.

"How did you get in? Without getting caught."

Shrugging, Iulia pulled up the hem of her tunic—a curious article of clothing now Cosima noticed it—and removed the extra layer. Other details revealed themselves as soon as Cosima was able to actually *look* at her after days of hardly daring to lift her eyes for fear of the judgment that Iulia might pass her with a glance.

A thin trail of hair leading down her stomach as the tunic lifted was darker than the straw-colored hair dangling in a braided arrangement on the unshaven side of her head; scrapes and bruises as if from crawling made a pattern along her arms, some of which sported fading tattoos Cosima couldn't remember the significance of. Haggard signs of weariness revealed themselves in the blunt lines around her eyes and the shadows beneath those, along with the faint creaking of her joints as she stretched to release stiffness that only rest could repair.

"I'm sure I'll find them soon. Goddess decreed they had to serve Fiammetta, but She never said how long. Once we steal them back and hide them, or stowaway, then—"

Cosima forgot to listen. With a lurch she realized she'd made another mistake: not thinking far enough ahead. Where could they go that Goddess couldn't find them? Where Her piercing gaze could not root them out from the earth or dredge their bodies, given to the sea rather than surrendered to Her, out of the waves?

"If your brother's end is hastened by necessity, your huntresses may not be away from you long," Mother had whispered in her ear at the end of the Jubilee. Her mind balked against the idea of paying that price. Against paying for her chosen family with her brother's life and her mother's freedom.

The only choice then, is to...

Cosima clenched her fingers in the lavender-fragrant quilts of Grisel's bed so tightly her knuckles popped. The wrath inside her shouted approval, rattling the bars of its cage. Wracked with indecision—she always, eternally made the wrong choices, perhaps like her mother before her—she wondered if she could unlock the gate and let that beast free without losing herself.

Cosima returned her attention to Iulia in time to see her kick off her boots and lean back against the wall opposite the small bed with her arms crossed.

"I can't stay here. Not while they're..." Her gaze was on the ceiling, tracking the vines Cosima's power had grown for the huntresses to hang trinkets and herbs on the roof according to their preferences to the bowl of mushrooms above the bed.

You're better than this—show her you're better! "I'll go."

"Goddess has guarded the palace against you. You can't do anything: I can. You should trust me as you always have."

Cosima started to relent, sinking back down onto Grisel's bed, but caught on. "Tell me how you're getting in there first."

Huffing in frustration, Iulia gestured to the tunic she'd stripped out of. "I steal uniforms from the laundry and change disguises throughout the day as I search. I had to be good at this to escape my old life, remember?"

"I remember. Iulia, I want you to know—"

"Don't. I wouldn't have come in here if I wasn't ready to talk to you, but if you go on you'll ruin the speech I planned."

After numerous galley brawls and the necessity of scrapping to survive, Iulia's smile had a battered look thanks to a few chipped teeth. She hadn't had time to be self-conscious in her old life, and none of the huntresses who valued her candid friendliness would have ever dreamed of mocking her looks. Cosima had learned how to care less what others thought from her example as well as Iulia's outright admiration of the beauty she had inherited from Bettina and Marzanna.

"There is no shame in loving," Iulia leaned forward on her knees as she spoke without looking at Cosima. "But you *did* betray me, Cosima. I can't pretend that wound has healed. We promised to share everything with each other, but you lied to me."

"I didn't mean—"

"You kept your heart from me. First a piece, then more. I guessed someone else had caught your eye—I waited for you to come to me and confess. You didn't. How could love do that? If your heart wanted to embrace more you should have trusted me enough to tell me. Not let me find out when…" Her jaw clicked as she shut it; she sat up straight and faced Cosima, who leaned back as if to escape the visible consequences of her betrayal. "I can always learn to love more. Thought I could, anyway. This side you've brought out in me is ugly. I won't honor it."

Iulia cradled Cosima's face in one hand and leaned in to kiss her. No one ever expected someone who looked like her—all thick muscle and undeniable presence—to be capable of the tenderness she had shown during their time together. Being wooed by her had been a dream: it still was. Someone who would pursue, rather than forcing Cosima to chase behind, grabbing at the tail end of the intimacy she craved but was terrified to request. Someone with honor who would make her laugh and talk for both of them whenever she didn't feel like it.

I'm sorry. Two hated words that hollowed Cosima out like pottery. When she tried to end their kiss to speak them, Iulia refused to let her go and clung tighter. They fell back into the bed easily, like a habit but more. How long they lay on their sides, kissing and holding onto each other like a storm could separate them any minute, Cosima couldn't tell.

"You were never a Godling to me. I never knelt at this altar," Iulia said as she gripped Cosima's waist in both of her callused hands and stared into her eyes to forbid her to look away, "for anything but love. I never worshipped you as anything but yourself."

The question was there: *how could you want something else badly enough to risk what you already had?*

Cosima couldn't answer it. With Iulia speaking to her this way, holding her with the same confidence and command as always yet darkened by the pending gale of permanent heartbreak, she could barely think.

"I'm mortal, Cosima. There's only so much time I have in this one life. You may want Konetta. You may even think you need her. I think part of you will always want more than what a single person can offer. But you *need* me. You called my name rather than making the smart decision of leaving your strongest huntress with the others to protect them."

She's right. Another thing Cosima should have done that bootless emotion and stupid panic had clouded her against.

"You will remember that need eventually. I may wait for you—I may not. But you cannot make me jealous or threaten me with that little wisp. Any heartache I feel will be because of a choice I made, not one you make for me. Once we bring our huntresses home, I think I'll set out on my own for a while."

Don't leave. A command, not a request. No matter which version it was, Cosima refused to utter it.

"Not forever. I'll miss everyone too much for that. But if you want to find out on your own if Konetta—"

"I have to leave." Cosima's voice cracked.

"What?" Announcing the decision she'd made before Iulia had come back had deviated from the speech Iulia had been set on making. Judging by the look on her face and the slackening of her embrace, the damage she had done was considerable. "Cosima—"

Their dream of togetherness faded as she sat up, Iulia with her. Cold water dumped on their heads would have been less of a shock than what she had confessed.

"I'm going into the city and I'm not leaving until I find Bettina and Cristoval. I won't come back here without our huntresses either. I…if I'm going to act like a Godling in some ways, I should in all of them. After that…none of you need me anymore. Not like you used to. I will find you a place somewhere too remote for any divine being to touch you and give you your lives back."

"Do you think that's what we want? What I want?" Iulia asked. "Me leaving for a while is not the same as you leaving for good!"

"I love you, Iulia. I don't know if it's enough to mean anything. If you call me, no matter where I am in the world, I will hear you."

"You're not listening now! How the fuck are you going to hear me if you don't fucking *listen to me*—"

She *would* hear her. But if Cosima meant to make Goddess pay for the lives She had capriciously wrecked, she had no earthly idea if she would be able to answer Iulia's summons.

That was what made her turn back—the thought of never seeing her again. Of failing worse than she had already.

"I'm sorry. I'm so, so sorry for how I've let you down. How often I've taken you for granted." She interrupted as the Light that would carry her into Aebbenary proper began to envelop her form. With divine hands she roughly pulled Iulia into an embrace and clutched her as close as their two frames could fit together.

Cosima often struggled with words; Iulia knew this. She had coddled her often, even with the other huntresses. If Cosima didn't speak now, though, would she ever have the chance to do so again? Iulia had frozen—trapped by burgeoning shock the way Cosima often was—and she hesitated to return her embrace.

"Remember. Call me if you need me."

Forcing herself to let go, Cosima vanished into her Light and left Iulia to the treehouse that had once been filled with laughter and love.

XVI

Bettina

Saints couldn't drown. But they *could* bleed out to the grim dregs of their existence and be bidden by blackened destiny to dawdle on the cusp of annihilation for eternity. Bettina discovered this as her mutilated body sank into the sea around Aebbenary.

She floated for a while. The cold water hadn't taken long to numb her injuries; shock and blood loss had done the rest. Her limbs and head coasted on the surface of the sea, barely breaking the tensile pressure of the water, but not through her own effort. Existence wasn't worth this, she had realized sometime between when Goddess's retainers had thrown her over the side of Fiammetta's ship and the ceaseless present of torment only a loss of consciousness would dull.

She didn't turn her head to look, but she felt the farewell kiss of the wingtips she had lost as her severed wing floated past her and out toward the greater ocean.

How strange, Bettina thought as she stared up at the night sky with grit-dry eyes, *to mourn the loss of something I barely had a chance to enjoy.*

Pre-Jubilee Bettina would have berated herself for her apathy. The woman she had been, flushed with health and influence, would have despised her for forgetting the most important things of all: Cristoval and Cosima, back on the ship with Goddess.

Shame was bitter regret and iron. Remorse and sorrow paired like an anchor crafted to sink her into the silt on the seafloor until nothing of witless, worthless Bettina remained. As the orb of the moon filled vision and obliterated all but the darkness that cushioned her hurts, she examined her heart of hearts as her consciousness eroded with the current.

I made things worse. I ruined it all. My son will mourn his father alone and die young, alone. My daughter will be Goddess's captive. And I...I...

What happened to her didn't matter. She came to believe, as centuries wheeled in a loop above and beneath her in this stasis of miserable failure and deterioration, that her time was done. In a world where Goddess had·exiled all sin but what She chose to deem as such, Bettina had transgressed enough to deserve not blessèd death, but permanent corrosion of her sanity and self with other once-prized treasures that had been lost beneath the waves.

I don't want to watch. I cannot bear another second of this existence if it is at Her behest.

To properly sink, everything else had to be jettisoned along with her wings. *Wing*—bizarre annoyance brought a chapped grimace of a smile to Bettina's lips as she decided she was too weak to hack off her other wing to drift away with its twin. Resentment that could scorch earth was the first to go, though its misshapen branches lunged back toward her as she cut it loose. The anxiety over the future that had clung to her was next; Bettina spread her arms to the sides like manacles had fallen from her wrists, though the absence of the weight made her sink rather than stay buoyant.

Love. Could she cast it off like the rest?

If it serves them better, then yes.

But did she *want* to? Did her wants matter anymore—here, with saltwater drying on whatever skin the water hadn't covered, at the end of everything?

Relief saturated her as she realized she didn't have to answer. What she had cast off was enough: Bettina opened her mouth and breathed in as her head sank with the rest of her so she could finally accept the just sentence her failure had brought her.

*At last...*maybe her agony would stop sooner rather than later.

Oil spread in a spill beneath her. The rising sun of morning gave it a prismatic sheen as it clung in plump droplets to the feathers of her remaining wing. Bettina watched with vague interest as it pooled around her pale figure and elevated her slowly up through the water, back to the surface. Almost like soothing arms carrying her because she could no longer move for herself.

Maybe it can kill me. Perhaps it would even be merciful.

The oil moved…like it had a mind of its own. It pooled and pushed and arranged her like a doll as it covered her without letting her sink below the sea's surface again. It crept over her face in bands, sending rivers up her nose and into her mouth and down into her filled lungs to soak up the water she had inhaled in an attempt to erase herself in penance.

"Swan-of-gold."

Who…? A voice as well-oiled as the slick coating on the water that bore her back into the world of life.

"You have been tested and found sufficient." Bettina knew she should recognize it, but she didn't yet. The reflection of the sun on the oil dazzled her. Tears of it leaked from her eyes as it withdrew from where it had invaded her willing body to coalesce on the water once more.

"The All is willing to work with you to right the axis of the world…" Something—someone—began to emerge from the pool surrounding her.

Should this mean something to me…? She wondered.

"But there will still be a price to pay."

Needles punctured the stump of her amputated wing as the being passed a gold-threaded hand over it. When Bettina screamed, oil poured into her mouth and down her throat in a flood that choked all sound.

Magisend! She remembered. *No, please—*

What felt like centuries later, power pried her eyes open. She could see nothing but the Grand Archivist's mostly human form slanted over hers, pinning her down. Pinning her, because as soon as those faceted eyes met hers instinctual horror made her struggle and flap her arms to try to fend off whatever he was about to do.

"Ask." A verbal demand, whispered directly into her ear. Magisend's hair brushed over her cheek as he leaned in. "You must ask."

Where was she? Not in the sea, not on land. Something firm lay underneath her—smooth stone with a chill like marble.

I want...

He was hurting her. He had saved her, and was saving her still. Bettina thrashed weakly against him as the cobalt threads stitching him together slithered through his Made form.

I want my children safe. Happy. I want...

"Bettina."

He sounded...human. His tone caught her so off-guard she blinked back into whole consciousness with a gasp as pain wracked her body and made her flail in his hold. Wrestling with her battering limbs, Magisend bound her to the table with power that stung like nettles around her wrists and seized her face in his right hand to force her to look at him.

Into his eyes, where the planes reflected her white face and maddened blue eyes. His was not a face that inspired confession, but the blasphemy tore from her hoarse throat anyway.

"I want Her to pay for what She's done! I want Her to feel what She has taken from me and then *die!* I want—"

"What will you give?"

I don't have anything left. Despair dispelled her last struggles as she tried to jerk her arms out of their invisible bindings. Magisend stared down at her, expressionless. He was icy to touch; she had been freezing for time unmeasured. The craving for warmth and comfort that struck her was so potent it made her shake with hunger for it.

"There's nothing..." *I would surrender my Light down to the last spark if Marzanna would let any of us die. Or if I could make Her suffer in my place, or my children's. But only She can rip that spark out of me.* "I have nothing. She took it all."

"She did, didn't She?" He spoke so softly she wasn't sure she'd heard him. "You grant life freely, and you grant love without reserve, yet these are squandered prizes before the feet of sacred beings. *One* sacred being—She who has been granted favor upon favor by destiny and still gnashes Her teeth for more."

Magisend breathed above her, in and out. Bettina realized that he was breathing because *she* needed to. He had already yoked their survival together—for now—between his physical form and her once-mortal body. She stared up at him through a film of involuntary tears as unease tangled within her like the strings of black and gold extending with an audible, high-pitched resonance from his body to hers.

"Do not fear. *I* will give you all of it."

Midnight swallowed them in a lustrous swathe that was comforting precisely because it was constructed of nothing. As one of only two tangible beings in the void that filled the Archives—that *was* the Archives, and the Grand Archivist himself—Bettina felt Magisend's weight hovering above her as he pulled something from the nothing that she couldn't see.

Then a flash, as if of gilded feathers.

Sensation returned to Bettina's hands first. Her fingers clutched the sturdy bars of a cage, or...*a gate?* Dying—almost—was a disorienting experience she couldn't make heads or tails of as her consciousness returned.

She didn't hurt. Her wings hadn't been cut from her body, but they weren't there. Tears of relief caught in her lashes as she blinked in the light of a new morning.

With sight and awareness the rest returned, overwhelming in each turn: bees buzzing, citrus and grapes casting an aroma of cleansing freshness on a timeless breeze, dishes clattering as hands set them around a table bedecked with too many flowers in too many shades for the eye to comprehend.

The gate she had passed through at some point during her delirium clanged shut behind her, but Bettina didn't acknowledge it as she looked up at the thousands of trees casting dappled shade over the clearing in a garden she recognized as one her family had husbanded for generations.

"Mama!" A boy's voice—one she'd known before it had cracked and deepened to a man's pitch. A figure tumbled into her, almost knocking her down before he caught her in an embrace and lugged her back up. When he laughed, she did too, winded but delighted.

"Cristoval! What are you doing here?"

Where is here?

The world as it might have been. *Should* have been. As the final brush strokes of a painted dream dried before her eyes, Bettina watched as a scene that had existed only in the depths of her secret heart unfurled before her eyes.

Perhaps it was shallow, in its way. Or profound the way no one who was not a parent could comprehend. Bettina didn't know or care as Cristoval—all gangly elbows and knees at this age—tugged on her hand to lead her to the table where her family waited for her. She might have recognized more faces from old friends who had succumbed to mortal destinies if her focus wasn't pinned on searching for one person in particular: she glimpsed an old nursemaid who had mothered her more than her birth mother, a childhood companion who had heard her first confessions and secrets and been her first kiss, more still.

"Where is—"

"You came, Mama!" Someone cannoned into her legs, toppling both of them onto the swaying, summer-sweet grass in the clearing. Cristoval fell beside them, beaming and laughing as the child Cosima sat with her legs around Bettina's waist and giggled.

A friendly breeze tossed her dark hair around her face. In this garden she was carefree rather than solemn, though the rest of her was as sun-tanned and leggy as she had been in her real past. Walnut brown eyes smiled down at Bettina completely free of any of the troubles that had furrowed her brow in the real world.

A dream, then, Bettina comprehended with reluctance. As soon as she thought it, the sheen of perfection over everyone present and the garden itself took on a false hue. *One I would remain in forever. Can I stay?*

"I will always come for you, my pearl. Promise me you'll never forget it," she told Cosima as she reached up to brush her hair back behind her shoulders so she could see her much-loved features better.

Another toothy grin. "You won't need to come back for me if you never leave."

"Very well," Bettina laughed as Cristoval playfully wrestled Cosima off her and helped both of them up. "I won't."

With the table set and all the guests waiting for her, Bettina tried to muster up enough hunger to join them as her children led her to the high seat of honor. Yet someone already waited there who had not existed in this dream a moment ago. A shining woman who gazed tenderly at Bettina as if she was the only person who had ever existed or mattered in the history of the world.

"My swan. Come here, dearest."

A beckoning from Marzanna had never been so sweet, so welcome. When She opened Her arms to catch Bettina, who ran to Her, Her smile was radiant enough to blind the surrounding guests. As she felt the pain Bettina embraced it…then slowed a few steps away from Goddess. Her children breezed past her until they realized she'd stopped.

Caught between, they looked back and forth between Marzanna and Bettina as their easy smiles faded at the sight of the latter's face.

"Is something wrong?" As Goddess asked, every eye turned Her way and every action stilled. Even the leaves stopped swaying.

I should be happy. Before she thought of the right thing to say, Bettina chose not to answer as she wrung the water-smooth fabric of her skirts between her hands. They were sweatier than usual…no, that wasn't sweat. It was water: she had drowned, been left for dead, torn apart.

"Mama?" Cosima came up to take her hand; Cristoval claimed the other. Both of them were warm and dry, and Bettina was too. Goddess's sun shone on her family and her garden, and all was right in the world because She had made it so.

Hadn't She?

"I should not always be afraid to say the wrong thing to someone I love." The realization wasn't new, but it was the first time Bettina took it to heart in the way that mattered.

Marzanna twiddled Her fingers mischievously, as if She'd tickle Bettina without mercy as soon as she approached. "You have nothing to fear from Me. You know your little rebellions make Me want you more."

As soon as Bettina took one step back, then another, the skies darkened. Along with the stillness in the garden, something faltered on Goddess's face. The arms She had opened to enfold Bettina lowered with peculiar grace.

"Why do you look as though you'll run from Me, Bettina? I've missed you. Don't keep Me waiting when I long to hold you." She approached; Her footsteps didn't rustle the grass beneath them as She came.

Someone was missing from the throng of people Bettina loved or had once loved. As her eyes darted hither and thither looking for an escape from Marzanna's hands that could work Miracles or horrors, she realized with a sinking dread that the someone she waited for couldn't save her from this.

Bettina had to save herself.

"Cosima and Cristoval are both my children. I live for them. I am willing to die for them. I debased myself to earn Your favor for their welfare, but also because part of me thought You were still worthy of my worship. But that was not something You should have demanded of me, Marzanna."

"I did not demand that of you. All I commanded was your loyalty and your—"

"Me. You wanted to command all of me while neglecting the parts that inconvenienced You." Interrupting Her as she hadn't often dared outside of this twilight realm, Bettina held up her children's hands as evidence. "I *was* loyal. I *was* overcome with love for You. None of it was enough unless You could erase everyone else I had ever cared about—even Cosima. Especially Cristoval."

"No, no, that isn't true."

Goddess wasn't present in this dream. Bettina had already guessed the vision she saw was just another ghost haunting her mind after the trauma that had nearly killed her fought to erase her sanity. But, as Marzanna protested, an inkling of divine presence made Bettina's ears ring from the changing pressure. Crystal vases filled with flowers and fruit shattered on the feast table. The other guests, including Cristoval and Cosima, shouted and covered their ears or their eyes as they began to bleed.

"You hurt me." The phantom wreck of Bettina's wing stump burned like fire; tears began to rain down her cheeks, hotter thanks to the rage and pain she could no longer deny. "You hurt them to wound me further. Then You called it love and expected my utter, unfaltering devotion like none of it ever happened. I cannot do it, Your Glory. *I will not.*"

These were not really her children, but Bettina could not bear to see these echoes of Cristoval and Cosima in pain. As they wept she joined them, collapsing to hold them as she wordlessly bid them farewell for good.

I'm coming home soon, she thought toward them while the memorial of Goddess stood frozen to absorb the paradox of love that Bettina had presented to Her. Their small forms melted away, disintegrating into blackened ash blown away by the wind that rose to tear apart the garden Bettina rejected every second she didn't surrender to Goddess's wishes. Though she knew they weren't real she screamed in agony as the greying dreams perished without the sustaining power of her belief.

"Our union. Our feelings." Marzanna pressed Bettina's hand over Her heart. When had She awoken from Her stupor? When had She approached Bettina to touch her, grasping again in ownership that made her want to bite and rip and tear? "What does it mean to you? Anything?"

"It meant something," Bettina agreed. As if from a distance, she heard the sound of the waves where Goddess had ordered her thrown after her disgrace.

After carving her up first.

"It doesn't anymore."

Turning from Marzanna, Bettina shouted the name of the only being missing from her blissful painting.

Magisend.

The clouds began to turn above them. Churn and grow until the skies darkened to evening. He did not answer.

Magisend! Bettina called him again.

Because of Goddess, she could not embrace her family and hope to hold onto them forever. Cosima would grieve her huntresses if anything happened to them; grief and guilt would ravage her strong but tender-hearted daughter the way nothing ever had. Cristoval was sick, dying by Goddess's hand as surely as everyone who had ever perished under Fiammetta's reign of chaos had been killed by Her indulgence. Crespin was gone too—snatched like his life had meant nothing, because to divine beings it was indeed worthless.

Midnight descended in drips and then a flood of blue-black oblivion that Bettina threw up her open hands and opened her eyes and mouth wide to welcome.

Yes, drown this memorial of everything I've lost. Her dream children had clutched at her skirts, and she could still feel where their hands had been warm before they disintegrated, but they were gone now. She knew by letting them go her real son and daughter would benefit. *Come to me, Magisend, and we will make it all right. I'll make you all right.*

Knowledge could not feel. It could neither hope, nor fear, nor desire. Its existence was a fact that could not be contested by any being, conscious or unconscious. Bettina was the one who could do all those things, though, and as she screamed for the Grand Archivist she grasped her own power and hurled it toward the rising storm of his approach.

MAGISEND!

The thunder broke; lighting struck. A whirlwind made of blue-white fire funneled down from the heavens to bear her up into its eye. A name reached her—recognition reminded her who she was as the storm tore her apart and forged her anew from the flames.

Bettina.

Magisend knew her. Aided by her willingness or the dream of the garden itself, he *knew* her as the whirlwind ripped them apart and put them back together by the parts of them that matched. A thirst for retribution enflamed her as she felt, stitch by stitch, Magisend sewing her wing back onto her body with threads from his own strange body.

Love—for herself and the versions of her children she knew actually existed with all their features and foibles—sustained her.

When I wake, Goddess, Bettina thought before everything ebbed into darkness as the flames of her rebirth cooled to cinders, *You will not recognize me when I come for You.*

Part II

Devotion

XVII

Bettina

When she awakened, everything was peaceful.

Bettina sat up too quickly. A wince made her bite her lip to stifle a whimper as her ribs twanged like she'd been relentlessly kicked. She cradled her own torso as she looked around, waiting for the hurt to pass. The pieces of her body returned to her in cascading sensations bearing more than just the pain of what she had endured. Rekindled by the spark of her Sainthood that had flickered, almost extinguished by suffering, her fingers, toes, and all the individual pores on her body tingled.

As she looked, the horrors of her dream dissolved in the glow of a garden. Not the trance-like perfection of the reality that had been her heart's desire, but the one she had made for Magisend in the Archives. While she peered around at the orderly paths and dignified flowers her mood transformed her surroundings. Bettina no longer longed for the past that was done and gone: the garden where she had raised her children and made her mistakes, some of them so often the scars of them would remain burned into the paths of her brain forever. She craved something wilder, less predictable, yet the lure of the familiar wasn't something she could completely deny.

A vineyard materialized between the shadows left by the looming energy of the All and her own steady blinks. Rows of trees—larger than they should have been—and vines spotted with corpulent indigo grapes almost bursting with their own juice populated her vision.

She was still sitting on the table where Magisend had laid her like a corpse waiting for its funeral rites. When she swung her legs over the side to hop down from it, no sooner had her bare feet brushed the grass than she toppled forward, unbalanced by something on her back that she had assumed she would never feel again.

Wings. *Plural.*

Flexing one, then the other, Bettina caught the difference between them. Her left wing glittered and shifted without effort as she flapped it. The right one had changed in both color and weight: where the filigree of gold on each feather had been, the edges shone black like they had been dipped in oil. The threads Magisend had used to sew the cleaved appendage back onto its stump pulled, but the pain was minimal compared to what it had been before. It would tire her more than before and make her sore, but if she wanted to Bettina could fly.

Instead of tears this time, her dry eyes burned along with her throat as she swallowed her relief. Goddess had given something for the purpose of having another thing to take away from Bettina whenever she misbehaved. For a price she couldn't name or guess the Grand Archivist had used the power of the Archives to give it back to her.

Bettina.

He called her from somewhere in the Archival Vineyard. Though fear of what she didn't know made her hesitate to follow, she remembered the inexplicable favor Magisend had shown her and her even less fathomable relationship with the All itself and obeyed.

Flowers littered the paths as the vineyard expanded without end into a horizon curiously blank of all but a cloud-dappled blue sky. Though flowers had ceased growing and dying in her wake, Bettina preferred the indifferent petals of overgrown grapevine blossoms in their ivory and indigo shades. Goddess's favor hadn't brought her anything but pain—with the exception of the few moments she had been able to enjoy her wings before She had ruined them—and living without it wasn't as daunting a prospect as she had once feared.

She was in danger, yes. So were Cristoval and Cosima. So was anyone under the golden eyes of Goddess and Her consorts. Bettina wouldn't deny that any longer.

Where are you? She thought toward Magisend after a few minutes of wandering. Worse than the insipid hedge maze she had once been fond of because of its simplicity, this vineyard without beginning or end could never be navigated by mortal means. *I don't want to spend the next century searching for you even if you* did *help me, Magisend.*

Fly and you will see. His answer was immediate. The sound of his voice in her mind brought a chill to her bare skin though the day in this dimension was moderate.

A memory stirred. Magisend had watched her dance with artful desperation on Fiammetta's pleasure ship. She had had another waking dream at the sight of him, or a prophecy yet to unfold bestowed by the madness that came part and parcel with the touch of the All.

The threads that linked her severed wing to its stump jerked as she launched into a run to leap skyward, but they held. Bettina almost forgot them as she climbed higher, seeking an altitude great enough to survey as much of the vineyard as she could to find Magisend.

In the aftermath of her rejection of Marzanna's so-called love at last, the liberation she felt from flying alone felt like heresy. Her lingering frailty reminded her of her purpose, though, and she scanned the vivid landscape on the ground until, not far from where she hovered, she glimpsed the rune-carved platform that was the entrance to the Archives.

She soared toward it. When she landed, Bettina struggled to fold her wings behind her. Even with one not-quite-perfect wing—whereas Goddess's design had been flawless—she hadn't had time to learn how to take off or land without her clumsiness showing. She straightened from where she'd stumbled, banging her knee against the edge of the circular platform hard enough to bruise, and walked off her discomfiture.

Magisend appeared like a vision, or like he had always been there and always would be. He stood at the other end of the stone circle, several yards away, but he didn't need to raise his voice for her to hear him.

"Parts of you required intensive repair. In a way, you're as piecemeal a Creation as I am." He looked exactly like he had last time:

all sharp edges in a body that demanded attention—even admiration—but barely fit, in clothes her mind had conjured, and unruffled by the horrors that Goddess had inflicted on Bettina and her family.

"Why…" Questions had a price. Bettina abandoned this one with regret, as if leaving a flower on its stem rather than plucking it because she knew the moment she did would be the moment its potential was done. *He's not human. He cannot feel like one.*

Magisend stood still—eerily so—as she slowly walked toward him across the platform. Something significant had happened between them: he had saved her, yes, but also returned the wing she had lost when it wasn't necessary for her survival.

Why would he do that?

"You brought a great store of fresh knowledge to the All. Until I tell you our grace has run dry, you may ask your questions freely. I will pay the cost."

A bargain. Bettina understood at last. *Foolish swan.*

Maybe everyone had been right about her. Decades after her momentous introduction to Marzanna when She had only been one of the false god's Founts, her idiotic sentiment still left her vulnerable to manipulation.

In response to the conflicting feelings coursing through her as she contemplated, the vineyard *grew.* Grapevines, flower-strewn paths, and stippled sun converged on the bare stone etched with remnants of All-knowledge, guided by the fervor of Bettina's thankfulness. Though she tried to fight it, her heart wasn't in it. The Archives were another dream, another vision, another refuge from Goddess's chaotic world. Outside the doors Bettina could see through a blur of fog far across the disappearing platform.

"What would you ask?" With an impassive voice and mien, Magisend waited for her to begin their interactions the way she usually had for every other bargain. As if nothing whatsoever had changed.

She had imagined it all. Obsessed with flaunting her own desirability, she had projected the appetites she had wanted to ignite onto the coldest being in the audience besides Goddess. Magisend was a mouthpiece for the Archives and a useful tool for her to enact the vengeance she needed against Marzanna and save her children from further harm.

Nothing else. Nothing more.

The Archival vineyard expanded with her conscious help this time: Bettina grasped the threads linking it to her mind and tied the connections she thought of as they occurred to her. Logical, seamless order arranged the vineyard by her design. New breeds of grapes grew from seedling to full, well-ripened bursting while trellises materialized to support their weight. To break the sinister silence of the scene, Bettina called birds and other beasts to the forefront of her mind to populate this vision: chattering squirrels, preening blackbirds, and others still.

Then, since she was tired, she sat down on the grass and let it climb her body to weave a simple peasant's dress around her exposed figure. She could still feel the chilly stone beneath her bottom that no machination of hers could entirely banish, but the illusionary sun kept her warm as she leaned back on her hands and tipped her chin up to the sky to welcome the rays.

"Why help me, Archivist? What knowledge was worth enough to save my life and give me back this frivolous wing?"

The sound of footfalls on the grass reached her ears. He cast a long shadow over her for a moment before he followed her lead and sat beside her. From the corner of her eyes she saw the filaments that knit the portions of his body together twisting in his skin like they were trying to escape; one snapped free, angling toward her. Magisend passed a hand over the errant tendril to push it back in.

"You have been sorely tested by suffering. Suffering that will go further should you fail to save your offspring."

A pang of agony—both new and recalled—furrowed Bettina's brows. "I won't fail. I cannot."

"Perhaps. The All has taken interest in your destiny. An alliance might buy you a better end."

With what ally? Who must I bind myself to now for protection and favor? The thought stung.

"Little bargains." A soft laugh on her part. Wincing as the ribs on her damaged side stung, Bettina allowed herself to collapse on the flower-bedecked platform. "I don't have much left to give."

"You do not." Magisend followed her lead. Lanky yet agile, he reclined beside her as they looked up through the bubble of imagined sky protecting her version of the Archives.

"It seems I can't do much of anything except make everything worse." With him next to her—quiet and unassuming if she didn't look directly at him—Bettina's mind wandered.

It was not in her power to dismiss the stress her body had undergone—the same for her mind. Though she had been healed, her vigor and Light set on the mend, her mind required restoration the same way her physical shape did. Before Magisend spoke again, she closed her eyes and let herself feel each and every one of the fifty-odd years that belonged to her no matter what youthfulness her flesh had been blessed with.

"Your dream. I don't understand it." His voice rasped when he broke the silence. Bettina opened her eyes and realized she'd flopped her arms wide like her luxurious wings as she'd dozed, unbound by the proper passage of time the Archives denied.

"No? I thought it painfully obvious." When Magisend turned to stare at her, demanding an explanation by his silence, Bettina puffed out a breath and rolled her head his way. "It was a dream of what I thought I wanted. What I thought a little time and sacrifice would obtain if only I desired it enough. But I'm not as young as I look—wisdom has trickled down to me over the years. It took the Jubilee and that dream to make me see it."

"See what?" Contrary to her picture of him as a vicious storm, Magisend seemed placid and practically languorous as he turned on his side where they lay together. He blinked with reptilian second eyelids that made her skin shiver with instinctual aversion, fixated on her with concentration that should have felt threatening but wasn't.

"My children are who they are in *this* life—*this* world. I never want them to suffer, but if I truly love them I need to accept them for who they are. Not what they might have been, or what they could yet be if I controlled their futures. I…" Bettina let the sentence dangle as longing

228

to see Cosima and Cristoval brimmed within. "I need to tell them that soon."

"It's possible Goddess is looking for you."

"Goddess." *Bah.* When Marzanna's sedate face flashed in her mind—as she'd seen it before Däard had hacked off her wing—Bettina savored the hostility that ripped through her soul. "I would let Her see I've wrenched my heart back from Her claws. If it wouldn't endanger my children I'd rip it from my chest and peel it apart to show Her no part of my love survived what She did to me. To my family."

Bettina choked on her next question as Magisend rolled on top of her, balancing on hands and knees over her body as he leaned down to peer into her face. "What are you doing?"

His threads writhed as he accessed the power he had been Made to hold to do...what?

"Now. Goddess is searching for you now."

The voice in her head rather than the one from his mouth. He wasn't touching her, but he was almost unbearably close. Unbearably because Bettina could *still feel him,* as if stitches she couldn't see wriggled between his body and hers to weave them together closer than they were already bound.

"Are you...are you hiding me from Her? Like this?"

"What do you think?" The acerbic tone would have made a smile twitch on Bettina's face if she hadn't been occupied with holding perfectly still as, somewhere, Goddess's eye passed over this place and didn't find her.

"You keep helping me. I don't have anything to give back."

"The Archives will decide what you owe eventually. Knowledge is—"

"—a taskmaster. I remember." *You, Magisend. Why are* you *helping me? If there is a "you" and not simply an extension of All...*

Bettina's head ached again. Though he hadn't moved—not an inch, even to breathe—his presence over her made her too aware and too frenetic with energy she couldn't spare. As a breeze rustling the leaves of the vineyard flora ruffled her wings where she lay, he stared down at her and let his gaze rove over her face, studying it the way only his strange eyes could.

Do not fear. I will give you all of it. He had told her that. Magisend—not the Archives. Had Bettina misinterpreted the emphasis on himself?

The desire to lift her hand to trace the severe planes of his face mingled with her curiosity whether or not the filaments would respond to her touch and how they'd feel either way. Were it not for the distant sweep of danger from Marzanna's hunting gaze she might have forgotten why he'd rolled on top of her in the first place.

"You stood on the same ship with Marzanna and She never sensed your presence. I believe in your power to hide from Her for a time, but from that close?" Bettina said. Her ears caught a faint *whir* of sound, pitched low and resonant like the drone of bumblebee wings. Magisend's outline darkened like an imitation of her Saint aureole as his power stained the Archival vineyard like a bruise.

"Goddess is less responsible for what She Creates than She imagines. Even divinities can be guided by destinies they cannot comprehend."

He waited until the sound of his power faded with a few sputtering flickers before he moved. As Magisend shifted his weight clumsily to one side, then rolled off her to land without a sound on the ground beside Bettina, something that had been nibbling at her concentration, demanding attention by destroying her focus, finally occurred to her conscious mind.

Magisend attended the Jubilee. Easoren didn't.

An alliance with the All was something she must already be duty-bound to honor, but a pact with the Priest—treacherous, unworthy adder that he was—had potential. The Archives had told her that before, when she had bargained for the knowledge either to seduce Goddess into capitulation for anointing Cristoval or a way to protect themselves if her plan failed.

"If Goddess must know all, why does She let Easoren elude Her summons? How can Her favorite whipping boy escape Her decrees without punishment?"

"Though She knows all, She cannot *hold* all. No mind that was once mortal can. Goddess craves this might, yes—but it cannot be. Something must always…" Magisend's jaw clicked shut. *"Slip."*

Somewhere in the distance, Bettina heard an echo of a much larger set of teeth snap closed like a titan of the deep tearing through a ship to sink all occupants beneath the crushing waves. It was hard to be afraid in the sun-drenched, balmy vineyard the Archives had built from her mind, but it occurred to her suddenly that if anyone could destroy a Saint besides Goddess, the Grand Archivist could. More thoroughly, more horribly, and without any way for those she loved to find the pieces she would be torn into.

He saved me, she reminded herself as she turned away, letting her unbound hair fall to cover that side of her face. *He won't destroy what he paid to recover. The Archives saved me for a reason.*

"Do you know where Easoren is?"

"Yes." *Look at me,* Magisend thought toward her.

She didn't obey. He didn't answer until, reluctantly, she turned back to him.

"The Priest is waiting for you. Goddess awaits you as well. Everyone is waiting, Swan-of-gold, and you have let them."

She hungered. Without more than an inkling of focus dedicated to the feeling, the vineyard sent vines weighed down with heavy fruit creeping across the grass-covered platform to bring her sustenance. Bettina sat up to pluck grapes from the willing vines, her mouth watering from longing for the sweet juice before she had even tasted it.

Magisend sat up with her, watching. Before she lost her nerve she offered him the first three grapes. They filled her palm they were so large; their skin threaded with minute splits to reveal the red flesh beneath. Rather than taking them from her normally, he inclined his head to eat them out of her hands like a tamed animal. While he did so, his eyes never left hers.

Knowing how great her debt to him and the Archives was, Bettina did her best not to flinch. Neither his teeth nor tongue touched her, but she observed the golden flash of fangs in his mouth and the black hue of his flesh therein, and shuddered so hard it felt like a spasm of yearning between her thighs.

231

"He's here somewhere, isn't he? The Priest. He found a way in so Marzanna can't find him. Is he in the garden, where I was?"

"The All is here as a ripple is on the water. We drift along its surface without sinking."

"So where was I? When I dreamed?"

"Deep." A word with foreboding emphasis when he said it out loud. "Enough to plumb the chasm of a soul, yet not enough to erase one. A trial and a privilege few beings can boast of."

It had been a privilege, Bettina agreed. Without the clarity given to her by her vision, part of her still might have clung to a past that had been ruined and a future that would never come to pass.

"I need to get back there." Resignation would have weakened Bettina if their conversation hadn't already exhausted what little energy she had regained. "I have asked the All for answers before with lesser results. Cristoval doesn't have time for me to waste dithering with the right questions when I can go straight to the source."

Magisend nodded. She heard the vertebrae in his neck cracking and creaking at the movement, like since she'd been asleep he had forgotten how to use the body her ichor had built for him.

"The manner in which the All grants information changes each time. The grimmer the need—"

"—the more terrible the process." His thought finished between their minds. "Our grace for this information runs low. What do you intend to do now?"

"I will be at the Archives' disposal. *After* I speak to my children."

It wasn't wise to challenge Magisend's hold on her now, but the twinkling sliver of faith she had placed in him and the Archives unsettled Bettina enough to make her want to test it. She wanted to push back at this strange need she had to believe in something outside herself like a loose milk tooth she needed to rid herself of so a proper molar could take its place.

"Go." An impassive allowance rather than a benediction.

Bettina swallowed her gratitude. For no longer than a single, fleeting moment they stared at one another. The notion that as soon as she got to her feet and walked away he would chase and bring her down froze her in place. Fear had always frozen her, or sent her fawning and crawling on her belly before her oppressors to coax them to cast their goodwill over her and make her feel worthy rather than worthless.

It had taken a lifetime for her to decide she didn't want to give into that fear anymore, or charm those who might hurt her into granting favors instead. The ability to turn the heads and hands of those in power from violence into appreciation now felt like a curse, rather than a skill she had earned.

Bettina lifted her chin to make herself grant Magisend an imperious nod of farewell before she rose, all grace and serenity, to leave. The eyes she had felt boring into her while she had danced for Marzanna spiked through her departing back again—she felt them like a chill between her shoulder-blades.

But he didn't pursue her, and she left without incident.

Then—she wasn't alone. Weight heavier than a cloak meant to weather a damp, seaside winter settled on her shoulders, around her arms, like armor around her torso. Bettina clenched her teeth as she reeled from the abrupt burden. Her balance returned as she adjusted, allowing her to proceed with a faltering stride, but haste and agility was beyond her in this state.

Magisend was invisible, intangible as anything other than a *presence*, but his mind intruded in hers anyway.

"Your connection to the Archives has strengthened during your recovery—your body cannot handle total separation at this time. This heaviness will ease the longer I remain."

"I know. Let me pretend you're not here, hm? I have things to do." Bettina grunted as she forced herself to straighten her back, correct her posture, and keep moving forward until the doors of the Archives were well behind her. *"Just keep Goddess from finding me and I'll remain grateful."*

Magisend's voice shifted into triplicate, quadrupling as he—they, the Archives—laughed before it resolved into one voice again. Some game was afoot, Bettina guessed, and it was her at her expense. Yet she didn't question it: she'd happily pay that price for safety for Cosima and Cristoval and vengeance against Marzanna.

Oh, how I loved You, Your Glory, she prayed as she climbed the path leading through the Scholar's Grave—hauntingly dark without the glow of her muffled halo—knowing Goddess would never hear her. *Yet Your "love" crafted Your worst enemy from my ravaged soul.*

Like she had been waiting for her, Cosima's aura beset Bettina the moment she emerged, blinking and dark-dazzled, from the catacombs. Cloaked in the power Magisend had taught her to wrap herself in like layers of chainmail, she picked her gauzy skirts up to run toward where her daughter's call resounded over and over from Aebbenary.

Cosima! Where are you? Bettina called as divine power lent fleetness to her feet and strength that would flag all too soon after her ordeal. It was a tricky business balancing her need to let Cosima know she was alive and well, and maintaining a firm grip on her concealment from Goddess, but she managed.

In short order a flare of violet-tinged light shot up in a fountain of rays from where Marzanna's city shone under the afternoon sun, indicating Cosima's acknowledgment. Bettina followed that sign. Though she stumbled at first, the closer she and Cosima came to each other the firmer her footing became.

Explanations and apologies swarmed in her head. *I'm sorry you had to see any of that, I'm sorry I failed, I love you and your brother so much I am broken and remade every day by the strain of it and I wouldn't change a thing about either of you.* All they did was form a lump in her throat that threatened to prevent her from voicing any of them.

Over the crest of a hill from where the glittering pinnacles and rooftops of Aebbenary emerged in architectural beauty, Cosima appeared in a flare of light and a shower of butterfly wings that twirled to the ground as she ran to Bettina.

"I've been calling you for days! Where have you been? How did…how did you…" Words failed Cosima as her wiry body went limp in Bettina's arms, like she was about to faint. But how could her rebellious, capable huntress fall apart now? After she had spent years rejecting any soft, tender hand Bettina reached out for her whenever she sensed hurt or embarrassment on her horizon?

She began to cry. Clutching Bettina tight enough to hurt, Cosima fought falling apart completely, but surrendered enough of her control to weep with muffled, shaking sobs into her mother's shoulder.

"*I couldn't make Her stop.* She trapped me on that fucking boat and I-I-I had to watch what She did to you and—"

"Oh, sweetling…" Bettina exhaled as relief flooded her. "I'm here now. Shhh, I'm going to fix all of it for you. You don't have to worry."

"Can we fix it, Mama?" With tears streaking down her face—which was grubby, like she'd been working in the fields—Cosima drew back to look at her. Aching for her pain, so much it made her chest hurt with the memory of how that same face had nursed from her breast not too many years ago, Bettina nodded.

"We can. We must. Where is—" Should she ask? She wanted to spare Cosima's feelings, but she had to know.

"He's either with me or Sovanna most of the time. I was going to meet him before I felt you come back."

"Wonderful." And it *was,* somehow. They were all in danger and Goddess still held dominion over the world, but Bettina had her daughter back. Soon she would be able to hold her son and make sure he was all right too, even if that was temporary.

Hand in hand with Cosima, with her repaired wing stiff but functional alongside the normal one, they walked under the cloak of Magisend's protection to find Cristoval.

XVIII

Sovanna

Four petulant eyes blinked, frog-like, up at Sovanna. The two ebony ones remained dry; the scarlet ones set higher in Lilias's face shed tinted tears as the child sniffled. The urge to frantically soothe the injured babe instead of focusing on the task at hand—ripping crocodile teeth out of the tender, pink flesh of their arm—hissed at the back of her mind. She ignored it, since she had learned within hours of full-time care for Fiammetta's spawn that they could compel sympathy from whoever cared for them.

"Do you see why I told you not to bait my pets? Hmm?" The last tooth pulled free with a squelching sound. Sovanna huffed her disgust and tossed it into a bowl balanced on her front stoop, where she'd plopped down with Lilias in her lap as soon as they had flown home to show her the results of their mischief. It had been difficult to pull the incisor out of their bone because their healing ability worked faster than anything she had seen before. She'd had to surgically cut the same injury open over and over to work the tooth out of their rapidly healing radius.

Lilias muttered something as they swiped their free hand over their dripping eyes. Sovanna had learned not to heed the susurrus of sound that accompanied each word a little after she had learned to ignore whenever the child cried at a certain pitch.

"I know this hurts, but you've no one but yourself to blame. That's why I made you wait while I healed the crocodile you taunted. How about you try to behave yourself for the rest of the day?" Rising from where she had seated herself, she stretched her stiff back and gathered the bowl of teeth she'd have to replace by Miraculous design for her poor swamp guardian later. When she swept inside, Lilias followed her.

"…Cristoval?"

Ugh. Sovanna would never admit that the child's natural voice was delightful. She busied herself cleansing her hands with water and Light and patting them dry with a towel instead.

"You've been so disobedient today. Why should I let you come with me to visit Cristoval?"

The red eyes dripped faster, but this time the black ones watered as well. All four wings in matching shades drooped as Lilias's shoulders slumped, adorably dejected. This time when they spoke their voice rasped with real emotion.

"…ride croc. Traded frawgs."

Oh. Relief softened Sovanna's stern demeanor despite herself. *They weren't tormenting the beasts. They just wanted to play. And why not? It must be boring to be shut in with me every day.*

When Lilias sensed her yielding they jumped around her skirts, hopping first on two feet, then on all fours, then into the air to hover on their flared wings that almost knocked down a pot of ranunculus flowers before they hurdled into her arms.

"Howsetree? Howsetree? Howse—"

"Not today. No, don't start wailing, I'm still bringing you with me to see Cristoval. But only if you promise to behave!" The brimstone smell that had begun wafting from Lilias transformed into sweet asphodel as soon as she finished speaking. The sharp tips of their feathers buffeted Sovanna's face and arms as they wriggled to be put down…then they stopped, as if they'd remembered as an afterthought to hug her neck in gratitude before plopping onto the ground to walk on their own.

They're affectionate. Sweet, even, if you handle that temper right. But what ordinary child doesn't have their tantrums? How could they throw you away? Marzanna's consorts had always been fucking useless—few knew that better than her. But Sovanna, wise as she was, had yet to find a successful inoculation against disappointment in Goddess and Her loved ones.

"If you like, you can choose a badger to come with us. They don't mind a bit of companionship now and then." Sovanna relented with a concession that made one of the snoozing trundlers resting in the corner of her cottage pick up its head and chuff. She shot a glare its way in warning for it to behave as Lilias chattered their approval and ran to vigorously pat the badger's head.

The creature didn't have anything to fear after all. As soon as she swept past them to exit the cottage, Lilias abandoned the badger and ran after her. Grey shadows that snapped like crackling fire appeared in vortices short distances ahead as she traversed the swamp to reach the regular part of the city outside. The child leapt in and out of them ahead of her, covering distance only to end up next to or behind her as they played out the puzzle their bizarre mind had made up to entertain themselves on the journey.

With them occupied, Sovanna had a moment to herself to think as she unfolded the scrap of paper where Cristoval had jotted down a time and location for her from one of the pockets in her maroon dress. His penmanship reminded her of a scholar's—precise where hers was slapdash, and elegant and well-spaced where hers was sharp and cramped together. If anything illustrated the opposing parts of their natures any better she had yet to find it.

Still—all he had to do was send word that he wanted to see her, and hence Sovanna went. Her old self would have howled at the idea of her responding to anyone's call other than Goddess's, and that only because she would have to.

When she approached the boundary of her swamp, Sovanna caught Lilias long enough to carry them through the filmy barrier that kept too many strangers from trying to spy on her property. She released them once they were through only to find some sort of pilgrimage going on from her part of Aebbenary into the rest of the city. So used to divine interactions that fringed on bizarre, the populace—distracted by whatever had persuaded them to move through the streets in groups as if they were on holiday—that no one focused on Lilias using their portals to play.

It took her a moment, standing still to observe the crowd milling by, to discern that no one was really *looking* at Lilias because they couldn't. Not only did they move too quickly to give anyone enough time to linger, but because the child had—consciously or not—altered their aureole on their own to send attention skittering away from their person.

I'll have to look into that later. Despite her nervousness over meeting Cristoval, about all the souls flowing around her for a purpose she hadn't guessed yet, Sovanna made a mental note of the phenomenon with piqued interest.

Then she turned her thoughts away from the novelty, pointed her feet in the right direction, and set off.

He said to head east. As if Aebbenary isn't big enough to swallow even me! Sovanna did not love the city like she loved the island. She could tolerate exposure to the heat and fumes the infrequent cleanses of the roads and river by divine power only helped for a time; she could appreciate the regular people just trying to survive under the blazing aura of Goddess, Her offspring, and Her chosen Saints. Yet she loved her solitude well, though her immortality promised more isolation than any other burden or boon.

Practical invisibility wouldn't have served her today. By letting herself be seen, Sovanna's aureole, horns, and height warded off anyone who might otherwise have pressed too close or forced her to walk at the point of the throng where she'd entered. A path cleared for her without any fuss other than a few murmurs and daunted stares.

"Over here!" Once she emerged, Cristoval waved, catching her attention at the front of a procession moving slightly ahead of everyone else. As soon as Sovanna spotted him and a group of compatriots standing in a line—more or less—she realized something.

Ranks of baskets, all varying in shades of straw or grass and states of shabbiness, filled with bread and fruit and morsels of chicken or pork. Sweetmeats dusted with sugar that puffed into the air like ash at the slightest breath. Sovanna didn't crave sweets often, but the airy puffs of sugary dough spotted with fermented cherries made her mouth water.

"You came." Cristoval dodged the subtle heckles of his comrades to come to her, meeting her in the middle of the street as the rest of the throng parted around them in two streams to raid the baskets. He hadn't exerted himself, but Sovanna noted with smothered alarm how short of breath he seemed, how glazed his eyes were as they crinkled at the corners with pleased surprise at her arrival, how...

He's happy to see me. She stopped herself from assessing him like a healer. *He's less likely to hide his symptoms if he trusts me...so let him enjoy it.*

"What—" Someone shoved between them; Cristoval chuckled as he plucked a bun from the overflowing basket and passed it to Sovanna. She caught sight of a rather dingy rucksack slung over his shoulders as he turned, but she had too many questions already to worry about what might be inside it. "What *is* all this?"

"Walk with me?"

You don't have to ask. Her heart briefly leapt in her throat as the weight of his full attention settled on her shoulders like folded wings. Sovanna followed the ambling pace he set eastward through Aebbenary. After a pause, he answered her question.

"My father loved this city, though he left it behind after his relationship with my mother. I love it too. I love that these people who have existed at the whims of divine beings for thousands of years are still generous in heart and spirit when they can barely afford it after all the tribute they send to Goddess. When I asked for help sending my father off after...after the Jubilee, they took pity on me. Word spread."

After Sovanna salvaged one bite, she forfeited the sweetbun to Lilias—who appeared at her side, snatched it with their teeth, and promptly vanished again. Cristoval chuckled and pilfered another from a different donation line.

"I'm a man of means thanks to my heritage. What use do I have for valuable heirlooms and gold when I can fund something the whole city can take part in? When I can help people Goddess hasn't seen fit to look at in decades?"

When you're dying. Sovanna comprehended and ached with unwanted tenderness. *When you might not be around to enjoy the fortune you inherited at your majority.*

"This is a funeral?"

"A memorial. He...he had no choice in his death or any time to prepare. I think he would have wanted people to celebrate him and the things he loved once more before time starts to forget he existed. That's what all this is for."

Sovanna had never seen a less sorrowful occasion. If the people of Aebbenary didn't know better than to worship deities who rarely considered their lives meaningful, they knew how to revel. It was quaint, she decided—in its way. The merry passing of food gifts from one set of hands to another, the homely music starting up here and there in the background behind the voices all clamoring to share news on a day they had collectively decided to rest from their labors to offer tribute to an old minstrel who had once belonged among them.

Crespin and his son, Cristoval. When she looked past his smile, genuine even though it was tinged by sadness, she saw his serenity with his lot behind it all.

"I don't understand you," she admitted. "If it was my father...well, not *mine*, but a father I could love, I would be furious at the whole world if I lost him. I couldn't possibly celebrate when..." *Idiot.* She cursed herself and pressed a hand over her mouth to crush her inconsiderate words back inside. *Vengeance is not a comfort for everyone. It's his choice to make.*

"I don't suppose anyone would mourn the former Priest's death. If that's even a possibility in Goddess's reality."

"If it is, I don't want to know it. After the Jubilee I don't want anything to do with my parents or my scattered, *useless* siblings."

Sovanna respected venom. She often gathered it from the fangs of the snakes that slunk in the shadows of her marsh to use in her studies or even some medicines. Venom had been her inheritance from the woman who hadn't really wanted or loved her, and the man who had died in agony siring her, only to be reborn into a different type of anguish that would wax unending during his boundless life. Any hurt or sorrow in her youth—she would never feel anything but old, no matter how long vitality clung to her divine body—had been transmuted into strength and purpose thanks to the vitriolic birthright she had claimed in silence before her voluntary exile.

Yet now, with Cristoval, the venom didn't taste as sweet. Though her veins ran thick with poison, Sovanna didn't want to share that with him. She didn't want him to know how rotten she was from the inside out.

"This is lovely", you should say. Or perhaps "This is a fitting gesture for your kindly father". She discarded one hollow comfort after another, knowing nothing from her lips could ever be worthy of acknowledgment from Cristoval. All she could do was dig deeper: poke her proverbial thumb into his open wound and push until fluid seeped out of the split skin.

"Have you considered the danger of an occasion this public?"

"Yes." His jaw tightened, she saw when she glanced at him as they walked. She thought he wouldn't elaborate until he did. "Goddess knows where I am if She decides my time has come. Her nature is volatile, but I don't think She would punish the whole city for having a party."

Wouldn't She? Sovanna held her tongue until she thought of something better than that. "It is likely news of what this celebration is for has already reached haloed ears. Aren't you concerned?"

"They know." Gesturing with that princely, magnanimous sweep of his arm over the people of Aebbenary, Cristoval bumped his other shoulder against hers. "There is no sedition or rebellion here. No one has helped me seek healing for my divine sickness. A funeral cannot bring back the dead, and no divine being—including Goddess—would stoop to mourn with mortalkind over a loss they will outlive by centuries."

Sovanna agreed with the truth in that. Unwilling relaxation loosened her tightly-wound muscles. What felt natural would have been tipping her head against Cristoval's shoulder, even looping her arm through his as they walked together, but she placated her buried longing with the brush of his elbow against hers and moved farther apart.

"I'll accompany you as long as you like for this. Let me know when you want me to give you a moment of privacy, or tell me when to go," she told him, granting him the blessing of her own, less brilliant smile.

Sovanna didn't pray, for she had never been under the delusion there was anyone to pray to. If she tried, though, her prayer would have been a resounding *Let that be never, never, never…*

Thankful that the *entire* city hadn't left their homes to join the walking memorial for Crespin, Sovanna breathed easier when people from the districts Cristoval had reached started to fall off at cues she would have missed if she hadn't been watching him as fixedly as she dared. Later, he told her, there would be bonfires throughout Aebbenary: little ones, nothing to provoke Goddess's or Queen Fiammetta's annoyance, and every minstrel that could be found would play the best of their repertoire in the streets. When Cristoval wistfully joked about hoping at least a few of them sang as poorly as his father, she laughed freely, before she could catch herself. Though he said little after that, she felt his eyes on her as keenly as hers were drawn over and over to stare at him.

As inevitable as the tide. As inexorable as a mayfly's death after one single day.

The eastern roads led them toward Aebbenary's docks, but a gradual turn down a southerly route led out of the city toward the cliffs that surrounded the rest of the island wherever humans hadn't multiplied. The old crowd of wealth-drenched nobility had reserved the moody cliffs for their beachside outings and summer festivals, and to Sovanna's knowledge Goddess hadn't bothered stripping any of that away during Her regime change. Her indifference had only meant most people had abandoned the steep, sand-and-rock covered hills butting up against the cold ocean waves. Especially the nobles who didn't exist anymore simply because Goddess had taken their ill-deserved wealth away from the majority of them.

Not Bettina's family, though. Not Bettina herself, since the rest of her family had been found wanting on Marzanna's judgment scale.

The climb didn't look very steep or strenuous. When Cristoval offered her his arm she almost forgot herself and took it…but Lilias arrived at just the right time, tugging on her skirts and babbling about the creatures they'd found during their portal game. She scooped them up for the cuddle they obviously wanted—while all three of them tactfully pretended that wasn't what was happening.

Halfway up, Cristoval stopped to stare out at the waves rolling against the shore far below. Sovanna guessed the direction of his thoughts—Crespin had been dumped overboard to rest forever beneath the fathoms. His mortal dust would mingle with the sand, perhaps only a short while before Cristoval joined him in death.

Never, her consciousness slithered and shied away from the awful truth. But more truths compounded on the first: Crespin was gone, and if, somehow, Bettina hadn't survived or had been changed by her ordeal into something less than humans could interact with... *Cristoval is a sensitive soul. Would he want to live without either of his parents?*

He still has Cosima. He still has me.

You? Her vainglorious ego intervened with languid savagery. *You are a Godling—one of a freakish kind at that. What could you possibly be to him? Other than a fascination with the grotesque, of course.*

While she dithered, locked in her own head and rocking Lilias on her hip, Cristoval fumbled in the pocket of his cloak, hunting for something. When he pulled it out he didn't show it to her right away; he frowned down at it, more melancholy than he had seemed since she'd met him today. Making sure she and Lilias would follow, he pressed on, clutching whatever it was tightly in his fist.

"Go, but not too far. Play *quietly,*" Sovanna murmured to Lilias as she set them down, making sure they had their feet under them and their wings in order before she let go. "This is important. You'll hurt Cristoval's feelings if you disobey."

Steam effervesced out of the child's ears, but they listened. Portals similar to the ones they had used to amuse themself popped up brimming with what had to be some sort of cold fire, since they gave off no heat. She made a mental note to study those portals later, if she ever had time. Lilias could be useful, but they were like her: an anomaly in the world, neither Godling nor Saint nor a child of mankind.

With Cristoval leading the way, Sovanna picked up the hem of her juniper-colored skirts and followed. It took several minutes to pick a path that was swift but not too hazardous to reach the summit of the rocky precipice, but she couldn't call the journey unpleasant. Not with a kindly breeze rifling the loose strands of her hair, sturdy boots she used to keep her feet safe from swamp mud to walk in, and Cristoval's broad shoulders ahead of her.

Sometimes, he paused and offered her his hand to help her climb over some tricky boulders or ground. He didn't need to, and he knew it. She didn't need to take his hand, and she knew it. By the time they reached the top, though, they had been holding hands for most of the way.

Still linked by his warm hand and her cold one—by her weakness for his affection and his inexplicable bond to her—they stood side by side and looked out from the view they'd climbed the hills to see. Like Goddess had arranged it, the afternoon was gorgeous: sunlight reflected off the turquoise water and rendered the sand in shades of whitened gold. Crested cormorants and other seabirds glided above the ocean that, at this moment, appeared harmless and welcoming to both of them, though of course they knew better.

"We meant to travel more. Our stay in Aebbenary wasn't supposed to be our last," Cristoval said after a while of silent watching. His hand flexed in Sovanna's before he let go, opening his other to pick up the object he'd been fretting over: a ring. To Sovanna's eyes it wasn't anything special: a flat, gold face surrounded by ivory and powder blue pearls...etched with a swan. *Bettina.*

"Mother gave this to him before they parted after their affair ended. Crespin said she intended for him to sell it elsewhere, in Ioggenica perhaps, to make him comfortable for a while since she had to abandon him for her arranged marriage. He told me he never had the heart to part with it—that he felt like he should save it in case he ever met her again." Bouncing it in his palm, he smoothed his thumb over the etched swan with its tiny sapphire eye and let the explanation flow from him like it would ease his pain. "He didn't know they had a son together. Me. When I got the nerve to tell him after travelling a while together, I feared he'd reject me...but he laughed like it was the best story he'd ever heard."

Wind ruffled his curls and tangled any loose strands of Sovanna's hair around her horns as she listened, and watched his eyes water. For his sake, she told herself that was only because of the bracing wind.

"He accepted me without hesitation. A wandering bard can't give his long-lost, fully-grown son much, he told me, but he passed Bettina's gift on to me and told me it was my inheritance."

"Inheritance." Sovanna repeated to show she was listening; she hesitated to speak the rest of her thoughts, but though she faltered she wanted him to hear them. "Mortals are enamored with the concept of legacy. Of having something worth bequeathing to a loved one to make sense of a transient life. I think Godlings are too. Though we aren't the same in other regards, even Goddess named an heir to follow Her."

An heir who wasn't you, though you are Her firstborn. That was a nasty, worm-riddled bone Sovanna had already chewed over enough.

"Does it help, do you think?" Cristoval asked her, still considering the ring on his palm. "Leaving something, anything, to someone you love who outlives you. I think I'm too young to tell."

"Me too." She admitted it despite her general mood of weary, middle-aged tedium regarding most of the world. "I hope it helps the ones who have to go. I can't say if the ones left to grieve feel the same."

Before she could intervene, he hurled the ring with all his might toward the sea. Gold and sapphire winked in the sunrays like they accepted the offering, though they had nothing to repay but a body they refused to surrender.

"I never wanted an inheritance! I only wanted—" Coughing stole his breath away; before Sovanna could reach out to help him, knowing there wasn't much she could do, he stifled it, half-bent over to make it stop. "It was family I wanted. A father like me—mortal. Not useless gold."

She longed to take his hand again as he straightened, stiffening his spine while tears streamed down his cheeks. He hadn't wept thus far— that she knew of—but she felt the privilege of seeing him mourn. Sovanna stood close by, her arms locked against her sides lest a single touch from her force him to crumble into her arms, and did him the decency of not looking away from the unrefined, piercing sight of his grief.

After a while, the tears passed. Cristoval mastered them and himself.

"No one was able to find his body, but I have this." The secret of Cristoval's clumsy rucksack was revealed: Sovanna watched as he pulled out a beautifully crafted, ten-string lyre. At first she thought he was going to cast it into the sea since that was ostensibly where Goddess had dumped Crespin's body, but he must have seen her aghast expression because he held up a hand to indicate his intentions.

"This is the real legacy he left me. I'm going to play his favorite composition, just like he taught me."

And he did. The privilege Sovanna felt when Cristoval began to play—awkward and fumbling at first, then more smoothly—set the melody in her mind like a firm custard. If she wasn't humming the sprightly, buoyant tune for days after, it would surprise her. She hadn't had the chance to know Crespin well—if it had ever been her habit to waste valuable time on building a rapport with mortals when she was too busy attempting to rescue them from her own kind—but this minstrel's creation still felt fitting for the occasion. For a lonely funeral with one treasured son, a Godling doing her best—and failing—not to nurture the affection that had been born when she and Cristoval had met, and, roving around the hills by flame-wreathed portals, a Saint's progeny even more uncanny than Sovanna herself.

"He didn't have a surname of note or a family of means, but *I* am his family. I bestow my name upon him and wish I'd remembered to tell him he's had a right to it since he sired me. Since we found each other again," Cristoval said after he finished playing.

The music had unwound something that had been rigid within Sovanna. Her awkwardness had vanished in the face of his exposed grief, his willingness to share all the pieces of himself with her.

"I wish you had gotten the chance to know him better," she told him.

"Well, we had a couple of years. Not enough, but…" He swallowed audibly; she wondered if it was sorrow or anger that would poison him first. "I'm glad we met. My only regret is that my recklessness brought him under Goddess's eyes and put him in danger."

"She knew he was in Aebbenary," Sovanna offered. "It's possible She would have found an excuse to...to do this anyway."

This time he didn't answer; she could tell he didn't believe her. Guilt was something they shared, and it wasn't inclined to brook any pardon.

Cristoval released a shaky exhale as he tucked the lyre back into his beat-up rucksack.

"Thank you for coming, Sovanna. This has been easier with you here."

"Me? You'd hardly notice I was here with all those people waiting for your return back in Aebbenary."

"Why do you do that?"

She blinked, losing her thread of thought as he stared out to sea, only turning to look at her when she answered. Her arms crossed over her chest, protecting her from whatever criticism he might unleash; though their heights weren't completely disparate, she still had to tilt her chin to look up at him, defiant as he turned to face her again. "Do what?"

"I want you here. I appreciate your company for the honor it is, which is why I asked you alone to climb with me. I love Aebbenary and its people, but they can't mourn with me the way I need." He took her hand easily, like it belonged in his warm, instrument-calloused one. "I am sorry if others made you doubt you were welcome in their company. I won't do that."

Her wrist sat loosely in his grip as he brought her hand to his lips to brush a kiss across her cold knuckles. Daring—Cristoval had struck Sovanna as a gentle soul, but time and time again he risked his life to protect his loved ones and his heart in hope that, someday, the thing that blossomed between them like destiny would become a future where they both survived Goddess.

"Cristoval..." A plea rather than a warning. Sovanna's self-loathing increased as, helplessly, she used their joined hands to pull them both together. She was already stronger than him, especially since his sickness and the climb over the hills had sapped his strength, but he didn't fight her.

"You'll have to forgive me. I don't know if it's the sum of everything that's happened, my illness, or just my weakness as a man that has my emotions in such a state, but…"

"No." Sovanna interrupted. This was a poison she had an antidote for. "Grief isn't weakness. It simply…it *exists*, Cristoval. It keeps us human."

Her arms slipped around his neck, his around her waist, and they embraced so tightly she could feel his heart thundering—fast, much too fast—in his chest. When he buried his face in her neck and held her like he would shatter if she let him go, she willed her heart to synchronize with his, beat for beat. Right then, if he had asked her to carve pieces of it out of her chest to ease his pain she would have done it without hesitation.

"Cristoval!" The voice which called from the sky made both of them startle, release each other, and look up. Sovanna saw the lilac shade of the Light column descending on their location and tried with all her might not to resent Cosima's showy, ill-timed arrival.

This is better, she reminded herself as she turned her back before a single ray touched the sparkling sand. Lilias materialized from a portal directly behind her, already leaping toward her arms; she caught them and swung them into a sturdy hold close to her chest to ease their fear. *I forget myself when he looks at me like that. When he says the things I've always longed to hear…*

Cosima descended, but she wasn't alone. Though Sovanna hadn't sensed her aura, Bettina landed next to her daughter with a wobble that revealed how damaged her punishment from Goddess had left her. The two of them were joined by arms linked in mother-daughter camaraderie, it appeared at first, but Bettina required Cosima's help to stumble forward up the hilltop, her eyes locked on Cristoval.

Lilias's bony legs curved around Sovanna's waist while their arms locked around her neck. Their four wings cradled them from behind, protecting in a different way: though they had feathers, they hardened like an exoskeleton as the child cowered in response to…what?

"It's only Cristoval's family," Sovanna tried to explain to Lilias between their minds as Cristoval parted from Sovanna with a single shoulder squeeze and ran to meet his mother and sister, but the child had shut her out. She tried again out loud. "It's only—"

Sovanna saw it. *Heard* it.

"..."

The midnight shadow that brooded over Bettina's sunshine figure like corvid wings and the buzzing, thrumming, muffling *pressure* that must have been what had cloaked her from Sovanna's awareness.

Nothing good can come of that. Though she prided herself on her professional curiosity and her lack of terror when it came to the unknown, dread filled Sovanna as she stood apart from the Valusius reunion and watched in silence. *Has Cosima noticed that shadow yet? How could she ignore it if she has?*

Bettina wept, holding Cristoval, or he was holding her, or Cosima was keeping all three of them upright before they sank to their knees on the sand and clutched one another like they would never let go again. It was uncomfortable to observe as an outsider, but Sovanna didn't resent them. She had only lost her home: Cristoval had lost his father, Bettina had been mutilated and abused, and Cosima's huntresses had been taken from her for an enabled tyrant's amusement.

Eventually, the deluge of tears and consolations waned to a trickle. Cristoval gestured to Sovanna and Lilias, voicing an explanation the wind carried away from even her divine ears. Cosima's face was blotchy and tear-streaked when she turned to Sovanna, and Bettina busied herself scrubbing her own eyes with the heels of her hands before she met Sovanna's gaze.

Ornamental. That was a word for Bettina as she turned her head to study her. Being raised in the Holy Tower had inundated Sovanna against dazzle and spectacle due to a surplus of divine beings—and her carnal tastes did not lean toward women—but those cerulean eyes still arrested her. Sovanna actually took a few steps back, as if she was considering throwing herself off the cliff to follow the signet ring into the sea, before she recovered her aplomb. The urge to retreat made

Lilias cling tighter to her side even though he knew Cosima and trusted her.

"How did you survive?" A bald question. Sovanna didn't consider apologizing for it.

When Bettina arched one blonde brow in response to her question, more in puzzlement than offense, the urge to look down made Sovanna flush and lift her chin in defiance of all of them.

"I had help." Ever elegant, Bettina changed the subject. "You've been looking after Cristoval?"

Even Goddess Herself, if divested of Her divine Light, could not compare to the Swan of Aebbenary's beauty. Cosima was almost a copy of Marzanna, and therefore lesser in looks but greater in strength; Cristoval's features mirrored Bettina's in some ways, but his likeness honored his sire in many ways. Guilty again, Sovanna failed to keep from glancing at him as she replied.

"Yes." *I'll always look after him. As long as he lives, as long as I can keep him on this earth I will take care of him.* Yet another thought she could never unburden to another living soul. Though...*who would understand that better than Bettina? The mother who sacrificed almost everything to save him?*

And failed. The reminder of Bettina's defeat—and Goddess's manifold victory over all of them, including Sovanna herself—was uncharitable, but she clung to it like locking her hand around a coil of blackberry brambles to remind herself that all sweetness had its cost.

When Bettina moved, gliding toward her, the doom that protected and damned her followed. Sovanna wanted to back away—a wish Lilias shared judging by the choking grip around her neck—but before she could decide how much offense she wanted to cause, Bettina was there.

Embracing her and Lilias.

"Thank you, Sovanna. I am always pleased to know someone is looking after my children when I cannot," she said. The scent of a garden—gardenias, maybe orange blossoms—fanned from her movement when she hugged her and Lilias both without hesitation.

Two reactions warred against each other as Sovanna stood awkwardly still in Bettina's arms. One: shove her away, make excuses, anything to wash herself of the unmerited honor bestowed upon her regarding Cristoval's care. *I'm selfish, Bettina. This is only for the greater good—I want to save your son, but I cannot give him anything else. I don't have it in me to lose him if I fail.*

Two: sink into the motherly, tender embrace and let someone else care for her. Sovanna had been convinced by her own lack of care from Goddess that everyone deserved a mother's love in their lifetime. Everyone except perhaps herself, since she was the unloved, bastard offspring wrought by a battle between the old divinity and the new and probably shouldn't exist anyway.

"I—" What could she say? Lilias melted in Bettina's arms before she thought of anything productive, though they clung to Sovanna while they enjoyed the affection she offered. Cristoval laughed, and he was at her side again, his hand on the small of Sovanna's back like it was an irrepressible instinct to touch her.

Bettina chuckled too, undaunted by Lilias's piercing, puppy-teeth smile, quartet of eyes, and smoky scent. Cosima had trailed after her; it wasn't her nature to laugh along or show affection without restraint, but her gaze briefly met Sovanna's, and they spoke gratitude before they slid away, avoiding her again.

The ramble up the cliff had drained Cristoval's strength. Cosima's and Bettina's arrival had sapped more still, until he swayed in place like it took all his concentration to remain upright. Conversing between themselves, Cosima and Bettina discussed arrangements for who would stay where and the logistics of evading Goddess's notice without openly defying Her while they supported Cristoval's exhausted body by propping themselves under his arms. They might not have meant to exclude her, but Sovanna assured herself again that this was for the best. She had already stumbled too much when it came to Cristoval today—given too much, received more than she deserved, and almost made promises she couldn't keep to this mortal man who had taken ownership over her venomous heart.

Don't worry, Bettina. Sovanna locked the thought in her head instead of addressing Cristoval's mother aloud. *If your guardian shadow consumes you, if Cosima buckles under Goddess's pressure, I will not fail. One way or another, Cristoval will survive.*

At long last, the weather caught up to the mood of the day: the balmy wind blew in clouds mushrooming with the energy of a vigorous storm. With Lilias still on her hip, Sovanna left the Valusius family to console each other and made her way on her own to beat the storm home.

XIX

Cosima

The specimen cringing at her feet snorted back a gob of blood, still reeling from the jab Cosima had inflicted on his portly face.

"I told you—" Red blood dribbled from his broken nose when he tried to talk; he winced, cursing before he continued. "—Her Majesty does not share her private life with the likes of servants."

"You're her chief steward! Nothing goes on in her palace that you don't manage!" Impatience made Cosima hasty, but it hadn't been a bad decision to kidnap Fiammetta's steward to try to find out where the huntresses were being kept.

"You should know, Glorious Highness, divine beings have no real need of servants. They just enjoy the possession of underlings they can crush whenever the mood strikes." Though the palace steward had the look of someone indolent, his expression was too shrewd for Cosima to miss. More blood matted the thinning hair—dyed blonde to cover the grey—on the side of his head she'd knocked when kidnapping him during his afternoon nap. He'd remembered to use her title as Marzanna's heir when addressing her, but there wasn't much of a semblance of respect for her role in his tone other than that.

He must not interact with Fiammetta personally very often, Cosima mused as she glared down at the steward, clenching the fist she had used to punch him. *She'd pluck out his eyes for his cheek.*

That insolence reminded her of the despicable nature of her task. It was *her* responsibility to free the huntresses from whatever dismal hole

Fiammetta had stashed them in. Her duty…and her guilt to bear over what she had to do to everyone who got in her way.

Cosima.

COSIMA.

Radiance burst like comets behind Cosima's eyes—it *hurt*. She teetered in place at the astonishment of the divine voice ricocheting in her skull, making her name a hymn that called like gulls screeching over the fathoms of the sea. Her hunt, the steward, the blood on her knuckles seared away as Goddess called her.

There you are, daughter. Come to Me in the Arboretum.

Cosima barely heard. Her instincts scorched every nerve as she fought to rip off the jaws of the summons digging into the back of her neck like a lion attempting to shake her into submission and death.

So afraid? It's only your Mother. I'll see you soon. Yes?

It was cruelty of a different sort to demand an answer. Cosima guessed She probably didn't realize how much it hurt to communicate under the entire burden of Miraculous presence…but she also knew it wouldn't have mattered.

Yes. She sent the word back while gnashing her teeth and jabbing her palms against her eyes to push the water streaming from the corners back in—as if that would do any good. As soon as it had come over her the tempest of Marzanna's company vanished.

The palace steward blinked up at her in awe, slack-jawed and insensate no matter how awake he appeared. Even indirect exposure to Marzanna's Light had blinded him for the foreseeable future, if not permanently. Grey and soot-black residue clung to all surfaces of the abandoned chapel that had once served as an outpost of the false god's church after Her visitation. This had been a decent place to conduct the usual crimes Cosima and her huntresses committed against the villainous Godlings and Saints…but no longer, since Goddess had found it once.

The Arboretum? Cosima wondered through her aching head, intrigued despite her irritation. *Goddess rarely goes there. Why now?*

With no time to dither, Cosima grabbed both sides of the steward's head and dug her fingertips in hard enough to feel the shape of his skull under his skin. Wiping his memory was an easy task, but also a disgusting one. The invasion left her with the taste of old, moldering food in the back of her throat and a smattering of other memories of what his body recalled of its own functions. She had an instant to learn the entirety of how his mortal flesh functioned in order to remove the kidnapping and punishment she had inflicted on him in case anyone noticed he'd gone missing and questioned him.

Cosima hadn't discovered this skill by herself. When they'd been children together, before much of the unlucky events had taken place in both their lives, Sovanna had shared this knowledge with her. She had assured Cosima that she had experimented all she needed to make this power safe: a chilling thought, but she'd been too young to question it. Only Goddess or another elevated Saint like Her consorts could reverse the forgetting.

Yet another reason Marzanna's call was such a problem. Cosima had limited time to save her ladies before word spread of her hunt and Fiammetta would act to stop her.

Cosima sent the disoriented steward toddling on his way and vanished into her Light to sail within it to the Arboretum where Goddess apparently waited for her. When she reappeared inside the insulating wall of blessed trees, she repaired her appearance with the aid of water summoned and ensorcelled into a temporary mirror. Ratty hair smoothed to a shine again; shadows under her eyes were replaced by clear skin and rosy cheeks that bespoke all health and happiness; her stale leggings, gambeson, and shirt shook out to become a plain but immaculate chiton held together by pansies gilded at the hearts rather than the petals' edges.

In an endless life, it was the *doing* of things that mattered, not just the end result. Cosima had already learned that, but few of the Godlings and Saints had bothered.

Bracing herself for pointless banter and dancing around any subject she didn't want to discuss while every other soul in the Arboretum picked and plucked at her glaring weaknesses, Cosima ventured from shadows of the trees through the gate shimmering with another barrier that prevented her from seeing inside until she'd already entered.

Marzanna waited for her—alone.

"Your Glory." Greeting Her, Cosima emerged from the shadow of the gate and bowed—formally, reverently. As if she'd had nothing better to do that day other than pine for a summons from a Mother who had done nothing but cause her loved ones pain.

"Cosima." She opened Her arms unexpectedly, waiting for an embrace. Cosima almost expected the piercing jab of a dagger thrust into her back as she obeyed and allowed Marzanna to fold her into Her arms. Instead, all she felt was two soft, warm hands stroking her back; she smelled fruit and flower and spice like none other, and felt held by incomparable Light as well as her Mother's arms.

The temptation to fall into those arms and relax—*forever*—shook her. But Cosima was strong, and Goddess had never learned what made her heart weak.

When they parted, Marzanna searched Cosima's face with Her shining brow furrowed. Their garb was similar, as were their features and bearing, but Goddess could be nothing but graceful. Even though Cosima's grace came from her skill in hunting and the agility she had trained into her divine body over the years, in her Mother's presence—even in Bettina's since she had been raised as an ornamental bride—she felt like a vulture next to a rare eagle winging its way heavenward under Goddess's sun.

"Walk these paths with Me. I had a craving for your company, and the day is superb."

She's going to ask about Mama, Cosima realized. Dread made her stiffen before she pried relaxation from the soft, welcoming atmosphere of the Arboretum. Marzanna's eyes were heavy on her as She watched Cosima stoop to pick up a passing hare from the path in front of them. The creature had ivory fur and, to her chagrin, two vestigial wings perched on its back—indigo ones like Bettina's.

Like Bettina's *had been.*

"Daughter," said Goddess, reaching for the hare, "you seem out of sorts. Won't you tell Me why?"

"Certainly. I miss my friends." A rash answer, but one she could take the punishment for. One that might distract Goddess from demanding Bettina's whereabouts, which would force Cosima to lie, which could be unforgiveable folly to Her cutting intelligence and pride...

"I know you do." Sighing, Marzanna took the hare Cosima offered and nestled it in Her arms. She stroked the velvety fur as they walked; like many mothers did for the rest of their lives after they had borne children, She swayed a little as She went as if rocking an infant. "Your separation is necessary. It's long past time for you to put away the whims of your youth and become My heir in deed as well as word."

Rebellion almost made her frown again; Cosima willed herself into calm. Another animal hopped tentatively to her side, attracted by the mingling of Goddess's halo and hers: a young antelope with briars for horns, each of which sported a number of sweet cottage roses in shades of pink and red.

Younger Cosima had appreciated and loved the growing menagerie of fantastical creatures in the Arboretum. She had wanted to love her siblings, the Saints, and the world that had bowed under Goddess's heel after such a long time suffering under the mismanagement of the elder pagan gods and the false god's heavy hand.

Don't you know, Mother? The whims of my youth got me nowhere. I rejected them long ago.

"Yes, Mother," Cosima said out loud, dismissing her thought in haste lest Goddess be tempted to snoop in her mind to root it out. "You are wise. Might You tell me why You wanted me today?"

A few beats of silence passed as they strode along the path. The rose-crowned antelope quivered in Cosima's arms, reminding her of the last young creature she had held: Lilias. The unnatural form of a deer twisted by the Miraculous will of one Godling or Saint juxtaposed against the even more warped offspring of Goddess's consorts—the only one of his kind—made her wonder, briefly, if there was something to connect there. If there was a purpose to these naturally beautiful things gone awry by the caprice of destiny and divine disregard.

"My will is law, and I am beset by many cares regarding the keeping and conquering of this world. There is none other than Goddess with My power. Yet I wish for better knowledge of you, Cosima. I would take any reprieve in the many duties that belong to Me to know you better," Marzanna said after a moment.

How can She admit Her neglect and remove Herself from even the concept of blame in one breath? Words were less efficient than the sure movements of Cosima's body, which she trusted far more. Those close to her—like Iulia, Cristoval, any friends she trusted—understood her frequent choice to avoid speaking if she could. At times, the holy music of her own voice drilled into her ears like weapons. Yet another thing Goddess as her Mother should have known about her but had never bothered to learn.

With effort, Cosima answered. "I am here as I have always been."

"Do you rebuke Me?"

"I dare not." *Thanks for the warning.* Cosima tried not to sigh as they turned a curve in the path, following it deeper into the empty Arboretum.

"If you had children of your own," Goddess started again after a short while, "what would you teach them? What would you prioritize, what would you discard?"

I wouldn't have children in the first place. Cosima hid her puzzlement and the flicker of annoyance that wanted her to hunch her shoulders and stomp away from this interview. Was there a correct answer here, or was Goddess whiling away the time until the real purpose of their meeting became clear?

"I'd teach them to be good." An insipid reply, but still better than the nothing that question deserved in Cosima's opinion.

"Good." Marzanna paused, peering at Her daughter from Her peripheral vision with eyes that could scald if She didn't control Her power. "Good how? Well-behaved and mannerly? Morally pure? Sweet, kind, gentle?"

I didn't say that. "Are those things unwelcome in Your realm?"

Goddess almost snorted—no matter what, she heard it—and twiddled the ear of the trembling hare slightly harder than petting required. Cosima clutched the antelope calf closer in sympathy as her trepidation rose.

"They're not unwelcome. They're just not of much use. Don't you have other virtues to instill in your progeny?"

Just tell me what You're fishing for and I'll say it! A slow death of uncertainty set Cosima's thoughts teetering on the edge of hysteria. Outwardly, she followed in Goddess's wake as She moved on and tried to imagine her words had been dipped in honey, sweetened to please Her palate and earn Her favor.

"I think you must indulge me, Mother. I don't think I'll be having any children for a long time. However…I had my huntresses. Many of them came to me very young, sometimes before their womanhood flowered. Not all of them needed to learn the same things, but they were all grateful for what I had to teach. Strength against adversity, discipline to ward off despair, loyalty to each other since, together, they're better equipped to face the world." Though she danced all around the pattern of logic that demanded to be spoken, Cosima couldn't avoid thinking it.

They had to be strong because in Your Aebbenary weakness is exploited. The shocks of their past were the cause of Your neglect for Your Saints and Godlings, and…oh, Mother, You built a paradise for divinities, but what is left for the mortals? What does it matter to them that a holy tyrant was slain when a new one raised Herself in his tower?

Minutes passed in silence as Goddess contemplated Cosima's answer. Apprehension gave way to boredom after the first few: Cosima's eyes roamed over the Arboretum as her mind wandered, though she still petted the antelope calf in her arms with the same distracted touch while Marzanna stroked the long ears of Her hare.

Abiding light enveloped the vivid shades of the hedges and sculpted topiaries that populated the park. A few animals roamed the stone paths gilded with shining mortar, seeking either the divine fruits fed to them by the Godlings and Saints who had conjured them from imaginations applied to nature's already lovely gifts or the velvet soft leaves and grasses grown for their grazing. The largest of these was a unicorn Cosima recognized. She knew it was strange to see it alone, but she couldn't place her finger on why.

That's Agnese's beast. I've never seen her leave it alone…

Like it had never been draped there, a veil lifted from Cosima's eyes to reveal the regular occupants of the Arboretum lounging in their usual habits and useless, pretty clothes and adornments. Every eye tracked her progress beside Goddess, who ignored them even though She must have been the one who had veiled Cosima's perception before removing the deceit at last.

This had, as always, been a *public* audience. Cosima had been the only one who hadn't known.

She did not have the luxury of reacting without preparation. Her flash of vehemence at the deceit had nowhere to go. No outlet besides the barely-there scowl she stabbed like a spear into the eyes of anyone staring at her next to Goddess, whose fault it really was.

Ormanno could have the coveted role as heir if he wanted it so badly, based on his hungry, reverent look toward Marzanna. He knelt where he was and murmured praise as he pressed his forehead against the earth in humility. The others followed suit: Giric, resplendent in gemstone-studded chainmail as if they had ever been a warrior. Druda wrapped in living water with ice crystals in her hair, other Saints arrayed around her as if they had been dancing for Goddess's approval before She had unveiled them to Her heir.

"My Holy ones need direction," Goddess told her. "Instruction the likes of which I believe you can uniquely provide as My heir *and* a talented warrior."

Cosima surveyed the Godlings and Saints with fresh eyes. All of them were accustomed to indulgence and luxury. What could she possibly do with these inept, unruly peacocks? For what reason could she, loathed and envied in equal measure with no room for better judgment, inspire them to follow her footsteps and improve themselves by labor, meditation, and anything other than vain idleness?

Her skepticism must have showed on her face; Goddess laughed. Her mirth was contagious. Whether they had heard Her speak or not, many of the Godlings laughed too, spinning and dancing in impromptu rapture at the sound.

"I chose you for this—not Sovanna. No one else. You are clever, My little butterfly. You would not singe your wings with stray cinders of ambition."

Better singed wings than mutilated ones. It didn't matter that Cosima had seen Bettina's repaired, transformed wing for herself a couple of mornings previously. The sight of Däard carving deep into her mother's back to rip one off had scarred her mind and, sometimes when she slept, the back of her eyelids so she would never forget the horror of it.

How Goddess, justified by Her sacred will, had passed the sentence and watched.

After innumerable hours of waiting for a solution to occur to her, Cosima had an idea. It grew like the fungi that had been banished from this consecrated playground of divine or blessed beings on the back of her mind as she carefully dropped to one knee before Goddess and dared clasp Her soft hands in her calloused fingers.

"It is a privilege to serve. Thank You for sharing the best way to honor You with me," Cosima said. Though she knelt in acceptance with the gravel on the ground cutting into her knees, which only a gauzy layer of fabric protected, she guessed if she surrendered too easily Marzanna might suspect another motive. "But Your Glory, am I trustworthy after I failed to care for Lilias?"

A cheap distraction, but if it would buy her a way out in exchange for the unlucky reminder of past disappointments Cosima would use it. Marzanna made a sound that couldn't possibly be a scoff, not when it came to something seemingly important to Fiammetta…or one of her petty vengeances. Cosima actually did a double-take, doubting her own ears when Goddess spoke.

"An ugly matter, but not one you should fear. I will repair the child's nature if it ever tries to threaten us. Besides…" Her hands had relaxed in Cosima's hold, neither welcoming the caress nor repelling it, but all at once She tightened Her grip and stooped slightly to make her look up. Into Her eyes, which held every color in the world yet not one shred of warmth. That She reserved for Her paramours.

"Bettina will be pleased to witness your success when she returns," Marzanna told Cosima. Her pupils shrank as the gleaming irises devoured their edges. "And you need a new purpose."

Loathing was more difficult to smother than the traitorous urge to turn a blade of grass into a dagger and cut Marzanna's throat with it. The abilities of Goddess and Her predecessors remained a mystery to the world, even for Her most beloved ones, but Cosima had tested their boundaries before. She wasn't a genius like Sovanna, nor was experimentation with natural limits a special interest for her, but this she knew: Goddess could not read every thought or feeling. Though She must by nature be omnipotent, the boundaries of reality still blocked Her from ascending past the sphere of this world.

Knowing this, Cosima manipulated her features into the prettiest, stupidest smile she could manage. She shoved happier memories to the vanguard of her thoughts and wallowed in them as she brought Goddess's left hand to her lips to kiss the antique silver ring gracing the fourth finger.

"Yes, Mama will be happy when she returns. Thank You for trusting Your children and blessèd ones to me. Is this the only purpose You have chosen for me, or will You gift me further instructions?"

Why, Mother, why? What else have You ripped out of reach because I dared care about something besides what You ordained?

Songbirds twittered overhead as Goddess sniffed and let her go, gesturing for her to stand like She didn't care one way or the other. All around them, Godlings and Saints scrambled upright and stood waiting for either Marzanna or Cosima to tell them what to do. Goddess granted them tolerant smiles as they continued their walk through the Arboretum—it was Cosima who could scarcely stand to look at them. Another time their subservience might have been amusing since they had spent years scorning her and now were forced to grant her respect no one other than Goddess and Her favorite consorts deserved.

The hare and the calf had not been dismissed, though Goddess and Cosima had set them down. With a glance from the former the hare bounded away like any moment an arrow would be sent to pierce its defenseless hide; the latter bleated at Cosima's feet, seeking further affection. She let it jump back into her arms and in her thoughts alone apologized for her inability to protect it.

Deeper into the Arboretum the path wound, and they with it, until for reasons Cosima couldn't guess Marzanna gestured to a pair of benches arranged under the shade of three middling-height trees weighed down by blue flowers and fragrant, juicy oranges rippled with that same blue. They sat, side by side—and Goddess bludgeoned her with the one tragedy she hadn't expected, not today.

"Since your ladies were so instrumental in informing your talent for leadership, I lament now that one of them has died. Fiammetta informed Me this morning over breakfast."

Cosima felt like her heart turned to lead before it dropped out of her body, deadweight. A dead heart fitting for the death of a strong, capable woman whose only crime had been that she was mortal, and that she had trusted Cosima to keep her safe.

"Who?"

"Fia assured Me it was an accident during their assigned labor in her palace. I don't think the name matters, so I didn't ask."

Even if Goddess didn't know which huntress had perished, Cosima knew. She heard it, suddenly, in the empty air of Aebbenary the island—a vacuum where a beautiful, laughing young woman who had once tempted Cosima to betray one love for another should have stood.

Konetta.

Rooted on the marble bench with her spine stiff like a rod, Cosima's arms dropped listlessly to her sides as the calf she'd cradled kicked free and bounded into the hedgerows. It stank of fear, which was justified as, suddenly, one of Evrard's hounds—thick-furred and barrel-shaped like a mountain dog—bounded after it.

All while Marzanna watched Cosima for any reaction that would betray her.

"I am sorry to hear it," she managed after what should have been a beat or two of the heart that had sunk into the abyss of her rising grief and anger. Cosima summoned coldness from the oblivion the divine beings cursed for lack of any impartial god to swear by; she cloaked herself in the slick ice and tried to make it numb her. "I am grateful, though, that You care enough to inform me personally. You know of my girlish fondness for mortalkind, Mother, but I miss You. Since responsibility beckons, and all my new charges live in Aebbenary proper…may I come home? May I live in Your tower, close to Your Light, and learn my duties here?"

Saying that felt like signing her own death warrant. Cosima's entire being thundered with anxiety, her palms tried to sweat, and it took brutal command over her every instinct to avoid running away, but outwardly she was as cool and unmoved as the marble bench beneath them.

As detached as Goddess, who accepted her request with a nod and feigned maternal care.

Was it all feigned, was it another ploy, were the rare kind moments we shared in my life an illusion? Cosima wondered as Marzanna guided her in by her shoulders to kiss her forehead.

Plans interspersed with portends within her turbulent mind. She would have to send word to Palmira to stay safe in the treehouse, to Sovanna in case she needed her for Lilias, or if Cristoval's condition worsened enough to…

Cristoval. Cosima laughed like she had forgotten her brother's name, even his existence at all, as she kissed her Mother's cheek in gratitude. *There's my key to make Her trust me.*

The Godlings were watching this tender scene unfold. Cosima's eye was drawn to the heart of their number, where a girl and her unicorn stood side by side to observe the will of Goddess decide their futures. *Cosima's* will now, for as long as she decided to play this game. As long as it took to find an escape for everyone she loved.

As much as she disdained them, none of them cared for her, especially not poisonous, cruel little Agnese. A girl born from women and Light alone, just like Cosima. She had been solitary and sweet for the brief window of childhood destiny had provided her as a divine child, Cosima recalled as Agnese slung her bare, gold-freckled arm around her unicorn's neck and leaned on it for support. All while glaring with studied dislike at the scene under the blue-veined orange trees.

I'm sorry, Agnese. Though Agnese had slain many mortals for petty slights, Cosima had never moved her name up the ladder of her huntress' priorities on who should receive their justice next. *We are all made in Her image. The best I can do is make sure She can't make any more of us to hurt.*

"Let's go home, Your Glory. We have much to prepare for when Bettina returns. Once I help You take care of…that other matter." Cosima tried her very best, summoning all the understanding that didn't come to her naturally when it came to body language and subliminal meanings to lean into Goddess's shoulder and swear fealty.

This time she felt the warmth from Marzanna's eyes as She peered at Her, assessing. Though Agnese and her unicorn—the one thing she apparently loved—lingered at the borders of her perception like an augury of her inevitable failure, Cosima emptied her entire being of anything but devotion to Goddess.

"As you wish, daughter. Let's go home."

XX

Buried in the earth, Bettina felt peace grasping at her weary soul like the first bloom of mold on fruit that grew sweeter with corruption. If she wasn't careful, here in the vineyard of the Archives, it would be too easy to lose herself to that promised peace. To unending rest that would erase the scars time and Goddess had inflicted on her.

But Bettina of today was not the one who had been in mourning for the love she had not only lost, but had never truly possessed. Today's version of herself was fueled by greater love…and greater anger.

Passion for her cause zinged through her vine-twisted veins as she lay, blinking up at the sun as her body emerged from the soil, and cursed loudly and hoarsely at another failed attempt to access the power of the Archives and return to the elusive garden where she'd had her near-death vision. Roots cut off circulation in her legs and clung to her arms, but their hold shriveled as Bettina honed her Light to cut through them. She left only one twined around her right wrist: cold and azure, it connected her arm to Magisend's as he lay next to her, as still as the dead, to facilitate her dive into the Archival depths.

"How many is that?" She spat, cursing again as a clod of sour dirt passed her lips and most likely stained them.

The Grand Archivist had been staring at the sky, half-submerged in the dirt as she was; he didn't turn as he answered. "The number does not matter. We only need one successful attempt."

"So. *Several.*" Bettina retched up more dirt. After that she mastered her body's response to her strenuous efforts to return to the garden of visions. "What did I have last time that I don't now? I'm stronger!"

"Perhaps that is the new variable."

Bettina closed her mouth as a thoughtless, heated response tried to exit. "I *have* healed. My halo wavers less by the hour. Could that really be all?"

"All?" Magisend hadn't moved, but his fingers twitched in the dry soil as he lay like a corpse beside her makeshift burial plot. "Think. If that is the variable at fault, what must you do to remove it?"

The first time she had awoken in the garden she had been broken as much as a Saint's body could be made to suffer—far past what a mortal could have endured. A hair's breadth had been all that had pulled her from the brink of madness. With Magisend's aid she had crawled back from the precipice, dragging her flesh inch by inch. The thought of going back…undoing the healing, ripping and tearing herself apart, poisoning her invulnerable body with anything that could induce a return to where there had to be answers on how to deal with Goddess waiting for her…

"There must be another way." Chasing off her apprehension like a housewife beating dust from the tapestries with a broom, Bettina hugged her knees and glanced toward Magisend. Then she stared, because he was *frowning* at her.

"Have I upset you?" she asked.

"Impossible." A word not spoken with fondness. Magisend *couldn't* feel—how could she possibly annoy him, even if she'd been sojourning in the Archival vineyard for days? The sight of his brow knotted with undeniable displeasure should only confuse her, but Bettina found herself wanting to smooth away the tension with the ease she always had when it came to charm.

Ridiculous, she scolded herself. *This is survival and work. Nothing else.*

"I've been here a while now. If the Archives are burdened by my care—"

Magisend interrupted. "Never mind. It might be your insufficient concentration. We can work on that."

I can't concentrate any harder with everything in the world at stake! Her skill at cloaking her frustration came in handy; Bettina exhaled the breaths she would have used to shout and pitched upright to stretch her legs. As she began to pace around the pleasant clearing the rune-etched platform had become at her bidding, swinging her arms to loosen the tight muscles in her shoulders, Magisend intruded in her thoughts.

"If everything in the world is holding you back, you must let it all slide through your grip like sand."

"I didn't invite you in. Please leave my head alone."

"I can't trespass in your mind unless you want me there."

Turn, pause, walk again. She used these simple movements to avoid hunching over and growling with her palms pressed over her eyes to vent exactly how irritated she was by her inability to make *anything* she needed to happen take place.

"I may not have figured out whether you're divine or accursed, but I *know* your power. That cannot possibly be true." He was helping her, she had to remember. He had been generous. If she couldn't be grateful, she could at least attempt prudent, cordial conversation.

"That is correct. It's also true that we have been sewn together by your trials and the will of the All." Magisend sat up. The movement was so smooth—so unanticipated because even she forgot sometimes that he wasn't a statue—that it made her stop in her tracks to face him. "These things are true, and one more. I cannot linger in your mind if you do not want me there. Try to shut me out if you prefer."

Bettina *did* prefer. She was through with the tension of other beings entering her mind to rifle through her thoughts like a thief raiding her estate. Scowling at Magisend's aloof bearing, she closed her eyes against him and the vineyard and envisioned a barrier against all intrusion—past, present, and future—to lock him out. A lock, and a key, as if to use for a gate...

Bah. She cursed, audibly and in her mind. *Everything comes back to the gates.*

A sound trickled past the crumbling defenses she'd built as her concentration failed. Magisend's laughter. Not the Archives—*him.*

Before Bettina could comprehend what that might mean, the vineyard rocked as if from the footfalls of an approaching giant. Or a quake in the earth that set the trees to swaying, grapes spilling to the ground from their trellises and branches, animals she had summoned for company fleeing into the unbounded horizon to escape…

"Goddess comes."

Magisend's filaments exploded into action. Dozens and then hundreds of threads shining like ribbons of steel parted from his standing figure, connected to him still only by the merest of links even her Saint's eyes couldn't see. They came from everywhere, these tendrils, from his scalp to his mouth, from his teeth and ribs and claws as his body changed into something that barely resembled a man.

Most of these threads shot for Bettina, forcing her back onto the ground—*into* the ground—and wrapping her tight. The weight of his embalming shadow covered her next. Bettina writhed in panic brought by how suddenly he had trapped her.

"Remain silent. She does not guess you are here, but She has begun to suspect the integrity of the Archives."

When Bettina panted for breath, trying to relax, a few of the threads climbed from her neck up to her lips and tried to slide into her mouth. Their touch on her tongue was a lightning shock that ripped sensations she would have never anticipated from her constricted nerves before she could blink. Her body went rigid as she lay concealed in the dirt of the vineyard. Above her, the sky and the trees all vanished as the midnight blue emptiness she had first known here swallowed it all in advance of Goddess's arrival.

Belying Her elevated nature, Marzanna entered the Archives by slipping through the doors leading from the Scholar's Grave like a late student. They closed behind Her with a puff of air that rattled motes of dust from the invisible rafters so they swirled down in their own zephyrs.

"Archivist."

"Goddess."

Radiant in Her aureole, Marzanna paced a contemplative circle around the runic platform without ascending it. A veil—worn in respect or mockery of it—covered Her sable hair along with the rest of Her. Goddess could not lose sleep or in any way experience a loss of energy or vitality as the one true divinity, but Bettina saw from the ground where she could scarcely turn her head to watch that She looked...off-color.

"What queries do You have for us today, Your Glory?"

"Something has changed here. Tell me what it is."

Bettina's heart fluttered, but a duo of filaments wrapped around her torso squeezed tight enough to crush it. The dim memory of Magisend's form—the one *her* blessèd blood had built for him, she remembered with a bizarre flush of jealousy—didn't waver from the center of the dais.

"Knowledge is not static."

"Very well. Tell Me where My swan has gone."

"Bettina Valusius? That was not who You queried after bef—"

"I said tell Me."

Teeth. Magisend exploded into a thing of black onyx flesh riddled with golden teeth, not all of them human. Bettina had to see it, since she didn't close her eyes in time to banish the image...that, and the tendrils spinning without beginning or end throughout the entire "room" of the Archives had started counting her eyelashes and might not have let her anyway.

"Has the prize slipped Your net, O hunter of treasures? We have sworn that we look not upon the petty affairs of humankind. Do You question our service again?"

Marzanna frowned at the rotating horror. Bettina couldn't tell if the change disturbed Her or not.

Curious, she probed carefully at Magisend's consciousness, reckless though it was. She regretted the impulse instantly as one of those great and terrible mouths transformed into a series of ichor-shot eyes and one of the smaller ones at the back rolled her way.

"Hush, hush," he murmured in her mind. *Crooned.* A contrast to that awful, gouging volume he'd blasted through the entire Archives to rebuke Marzanna. *"You belong under our wings until your purpose has been served."*

"That was not who You queried after before," Magisend had said. Bettina tucked the nugget of intelligence away for now, knowing it for a gift

even if she couldn't guess why. *Who had She asked about before?*

"Yesss." Magisend—his filaments only, all pieces guided by him yet not wholly dependent—crackled in response. *"This pretender seeks an abomination, worse than what She already dragged into the light."*

Revulsion soured Goddess's tranquility as She paced an unceasing circle around the platform. The hem of Her robe trailed behind Her, so close to where Bettina lay entombed.

"I will concede the point for now and allow you to keep searching, but mind your tone with Me. There is much I could inflict on you before unmaking this cursed place."

Magisend-the-horror did not visibly repent. He merely returned to the vaguely man-like shape from before, speared by and entrenched in his own threads.

Threads that wrapped like a firm hand around Bettina's neck, squeezing without the intent to kill. Her back arched—or tried to as one or two persistent filaments scraped over her mouth again.

"You said you don't concern yourself with humankind. The beings I seek knowledge of are divine. Is that phrasing more appropriate?" Goddess's voice dripped with scorn. Bettina knew Her well enough to guess She was in fine fettle today—something had pleased Her even if this conversation didn't. *What could that be?*

"Ask." Magisend told Her.

"Last time we spoke I asked who in My realm had made sacrifices besides Me. You pointed Me to Fia…and you were right."

"We learn eternally."

Bettina saw Marzanna roll Her eyes. "Yes, yes, the quest for knowledge. I confirmed your findings, though she doesn't know I'm watching her this closely. Sensitive to neglect, My Fia is. I suppose that's why she's been slaughtering every innocent soul she can get her hands on to buy My love."

"We understand sacrifices as currency to bargain with the primal authority. They are not to be trifled with for trivial gain—even by Your Saints."

"Do you threaten or warn Me?"

"Whatever You prefer. Will You handle it?"

Magisend—and Bettina, intrigued and dismayed by news of Fiammetta's rampage—waited for a concluding statement. Goddess offered nothing.

"Curiosity, Archivist? For My vain interests?"

The eyes Magisend had pointed toward Bettina slid close, fusing shut; some of the incomprehensible, lower-pitched sound filling the room quieted. "We learn eternally."

Her mind droned with the buzz of hundreds of locust wings, straining to translate the cryptic dialogue into tools she could use to bring Goddess down. If Fiammetta was buying Her love with sacrificial murder, how could Marzanna not care? That was manipulation and abuse targeted against *Her*.

"I know the Archives likes its treats—I'll indulge you." Marzanna said, but Bettina struggled to pay attention again. The longer Goddess stayed, the more Magisend's threads entangled her. The ones counting her eyelashes swept over her cheekbones while across her arms, torso, and thighs, more nettle-sharp yet painless wisps coiled over her skin.

It should have hurt. Skin or threads, Magisend was made up of needles and darkness tamed by her ichor and Goddess's will. Yet it did not. If she allowed it, if she relaxed where she lay and stopped fighting the bonds that protected her from Marzanna's awareness and let them move over her like ten thousand kisses…

"Fiammetta's time will come. So will My Priest's, though he found a wayward path to follow away from My Light. He will find there isn't far to run from My will, just as Bettina will…soon enough. Time is on My side, impatient though I am." Without preamble, Goddess's bearing shifted; Her jaw clenched, Her meander around the platform ceased, and spots of portentous color filtered through Her halo. That and Her comment expressing exactly how sure She was that She would own Bettina before long rendered even the creeping hunger invoked by Magisend's strands irrelevant. This made her want to get up and run away like Easoren must have.

"The Jubilee. I surrendered more than I wanted for *nothing*, all on your advice. I as much as hinted to Däard that I could bring *him* back the following day. His faith in Me was already…" Marzanna's

275

mannerisms had always been smooth; as enthralling as a charmer who tamed treacherous beasts before an awed crowd who never realized that, should the charmer fail, it would be their blood the animal would shed when it ran wild. Now there was an edge to them—brittle like Her beauty.

"What did you surrender?" Magisend asked. As if he didn't know.

Goddess scoffed; some of the spell over Her broke as Her former positive mood won out, and She resumed pacing. "Hearts and flesh and faith. All components of a whole I was loath to give up, and intend to reclaim with the rest. I am not willing to lose a fucking thing, Archivist. You will not fail Me again."

"We are but what You Created, Your Glory," he answered. Bettina was struck by the urge to thrash him, suddenly, for such a reckless reply. Arrogance from another, particularly targeted toward Her, was not something Goddess would tolerate.

A second later she despaired of her own intelligence for worrying. He wasn't human, and from what she could tell Marzanna needed him. She wouldn't break him in a temper like other Godlings were known to do with playthings that had disappointed them.

"You belong to Me like this island, its occupants, the sea and stars and all above and below. So *serve* Me and tell Me how to get him back."

"It is beyond all heresy, all sacrilege, all blasphemy to natural law to do what She has done."

Bettina heard Magisend's voice in her head again, but it wasn't really him. A sudden split in her skull throbbed over and over like it could rip her apart with this pulsing agony. The All spoke to her and drowned out whatever Magisend said to Goddess or what She might have snapped back.

"There is no direction in Oblivion. There is no Light, Dark, or Fire. Yet there is sin, and there are abominations. You and yours will end them."

Everything ached, Magisend's threads vibrated across her body, and Bettina tried to claim some air while a few strangled her exposed throat. Dirt crumbled into her open mouth—her only sign she was sinking again into the ground that had rejected her before this moment. Like pallbearers surrendering their charge to the black soil, Magisend's strands pulled taut and snapped, one by one, as she sank. This little death was slow already, but its pace fell to glacial as the physical pleasure she hadn't known to name dissipated with each broken cord.

It occurred to her to call for him. But that would expose both of them to Goddess, and Bettina fought to master her terror.

You wanted to go down in the first place, she thought grimly before her consciousness flickered out. *A Saint cannot die—what is there to fear?*

Neither pain nor pleasure accompanied Bettina in her fall through the vineyard dirt to whatever plane the primordial garden existed on. She sank as the sounds of Marzanna's and Magisend's voices faded and her ears, eyes, and mouth filled with dirt and the stench of turned earth. If she could have felt fear, terror might have put her into a frenzy like someone buried alive because all their loved ones thought they were dead.

Instead, nothing felt real. Not the dirt, the smell, the fall—nothing. Bettina sank…and then she sat up.

In the garden. Or just outside of it.

What gave her pause as she contemplated standing up without full awareness of her body in this shimmering, mirage-like place wasn't the emerald gates through which the vague silhouettes of trees shifted in stagnant air outside the wall. It wasn't the golden lock, crusted over with pearls that looked like they had grown there rather than been set by an eldritch jeweler. As Bettina stood, her eyes remained locked on a figure lounging like an emperor at rest on the ground before the gates as if he lay on priceless silks and furs rather than ambiguous earth.

"Priest." Bettina greeted him. It occurred to her as the syllables passed her lips, too late to be recalled, that she might have snuck past him to sneak into the garden. Then Easoren turned toward her, rotating his bare skull much, *much* too far back to look at her, and she was glad she hadn't bothered.

"Trinket." He greeted her from where he lounged, contemplating the locked gate. "Here you are, now Goddess has tired of playing with you. Will you wait for the end of days with me?"

He had demanded his skin. Expecting the impossible, he had ordered Bettina to thieve it from Marzanna and somehow bring it to him. She approached, hesitant and extremely aware of how much dirt and sap and other earthly filth covered her. Even as a skeleton Easoren had that effect: making everyone feel worthless, obscene, beneath notice whenever he entered a room.

"Goddess is looking for you."

"And you. Yet you are here, and She is not." His gilded skull angled back as a laugh rasped out of his throat, which wasn't there. "That would infuriate Her. I think we both appreciate that."

Bettina shook off her mystification and decided to play along. "We have a lot in common."

Bones creaked as he glanced away from the gate again to assess her approach for any threat. Something glittered in his skinless hand: a silver coin, which he clinked through his fingers to while away eternity. "How came you to this threshold, bauble?"

"Dirt."

He smiled at that, lipless or not. "Besides that. I know you had help."

"I am but Goddess's toy. Who would help me?"

"I, the traitorous Priest. And the Grand Archivist."

He knows about Magisend. A rush of protective instinct sent her another few steps forward; calculation steadied her clumsy lurch across the barren ground. *Who told me to use Easoren, but not trust him. What could the Archives have to fear from this bitter old relic?*

Most likely nothing, but Bettina struggled to master her alarm and keep from tearing Easoren's bones apart joint by invisible joint.

"You mean to help me? Very well. Why are you trying to get into the garden?" she said.

"I've been inside once. I'm trying to go back."

Tactfully hiding her disbelief, Bettina inched closer to the gates. "What did you see when you were inside?"

Easoren didn't answer. He snapped his neck around to watch her, effectively halting her progress under the glow of the points of Light in his sockets.

"Your warmth travels. Your Light quavers in gratification received and denied. The spark that suffering dimmed has been nurtured to a blaze." Arms that reflected her aureole reached out for her, nearly distending as Easoren lunged in slow-motion toward Bettina.

Though she compelled herself to stillness, to avoid flinching, she couldn't quite manage it. She scrambled away from Easoren at the faintest brush of his bony fingertips on her arm.

"We both wait for the garden. Why are you here?" she asked.

Recovering himself, the cold glow in his eyes returned to its usual intensity. "For you."

"You lie. You had no way of knowing—"

"I do."

"How? You—" Bettina remembered. *He did know. He told me before the Jubilee—probably right before he found a way to conceal his whereabouts from Marzanna.*

Easoren waited in silence for her to recall their last meeting. He gestured with one lithe arm toward the gates, bidding her to make her attempt with the surety of knowing she would fail. Though it rankled to obey a command—even implied rather than spoken—Bettina darted past his lounging figure to rattle the lock on the gate with both hands. She had hoped it might magically click open, or crumble to glittering dust at her touch in the way other, less waking dreams made things she wanted to happen come about.

All it did was rattle, then clunk against the smaragdine bars when she dropped it.

"You will come to me before long," Easoren quoted for her benefit when, slow in her irritation, she faced him. *"When all your tactics fail I will wait for you to crawl on your belly to beg for the keys to the garden."*

"I don't have your flesh. You know I don't, and you were foolish to ask me."

"I never required a hand to fetch it. I needed the means to keep it. Now I do." He lunged again, this time too quickly for her to dodge.

Someone screamed. Bettina heard it reverberating in the non-space lurking all around the primordial garden, barring the rest of the void from this hallowed place. Easoren knocked her to the ground with brutish strength, rolling her onto her stomach and holding her down with his weight. Fear kept her screaming, but loathing made her gag at the brittle sound of his bones rasping against her clothes and skin.

Finger bones *pulled*, not on her body or clothes, but on the midnight blue shadows that engulfed her like an aura. She hadn't known there *was* an aura enfolding her body, or that Easoren could see it. As Bettina struggled and kicked and snapped with teeth that would have broken if they were mortal he only pulled like he was unweaving a loom.

His skull grinned close enough for her to kiss his exposed teeth or the hole where his nose sometimes sat; his eyelights scorched from this nearness, but not on purpose. He was concentrating too much on his other task for that. The strands he gleaned swathed him in countless fibers by the time she gave up, exhausted and disgusted though she knew he hadn't hurt her.

Bettina heaved him off her—with all those threads he was heavier now—and watched him roll on the ground as his flesh grew over his bones and his skin shortly after. She was tempted to kick him while he was already down, clearly in pain, but she doubted avenging this latest indignity would earn any of the answers she needed.

Long, silver-white hair grew from Easoren's bare scalp, with more filling in his smooth brows, down the center of his chest, around his groin, and on his legs. Grey eyes that pierced like a lance stared up at the void instead of the sky; the Light behind them that had remained in his skeletal form faded but slightly. Bettina couldn't help but stare as he finished becoming a little more human and much less eldritch fiend. Not only because Easoren the false High Priest had been a beautiful man, but because the stolen threads he had used to stitch his flesh onto his bones to stave away rot and theft were visible in their minute thousands if she looked close enough.

Eventually, Easoren sat up. One or two of the threads burst their seams in his shoulder to wrap his nudity in a sumptuous cloak of night-dark fabric that contrasted the paleness of his skin. Then, as surely as it had appeared, his entire figure began to fade. When he was as ephemeral as fog he backed away, closer to the garden gates…then through.

"I will give you one gift for your service, trinket. Pass my greetings and gratitude to your Archivist," he said from the other side, already turning his back. "His weakness helped me after all, abomination though I am."

"What's in the garden for you?" With her heart sinking deeper than her mind and body had to travel to this dream of the garden, Bettina knew with prophetic dismay that she would lament something important if she didn't wring an answer to this suddenly important question from him.

Laughter answered as the gates rattled behind Easoren's retreating figure. Bettina pressed herself against the cold bars, hoping she could deceive them into allowing her passage, but she couldn't move fast enough. Though it made her nauseous she wondered, frivolously, if Marzanna would be able to rot Easoren's flesh off again now that—indirectly—Archival power kept him together.

Though she'd sworn to lock her mind against all intrusion even at the cost of convenience, forever, Bettina stabbed her consciousness outward to yank on the scruff of Easoren's dimming presence and bring him to heel.

"The key! You've had your flesh from me, one way or another, and I will have that key!"

"You already do." Easoren's consciousness—loftier than hers and riddled with frost and the blinding reflection of the sun over silver—stabbed back. The three words twisted like torturous screws behind her eyes; a shriek tore out of her. Bettina hadn't realized there were still—and always would be—new torments to discover at the hands of superior beings.

"It waits in your flesh. Even Goddess cannot enter without it, though She might grind Her teeth to dust on that ignoble bit trying."

The vestibule of dreaming around the garden began to dissolve the way Easoren had. Though she voiced her frustration in muted curses, though she yanked on the uncompromising lock until an improbable amount of pearls rained onto the ground from the abuse, the mirage still vanished.

"Everything else waits in the garden—death, destruction, and the truth you long for but cannot face. For Goddess too."

He sounded sad at the last: almost regretful. Like an old man aching for something he'd lost a lifetime ago, though it hurt like the sunder had happened recently. She wondered what that could mean.

Like a rat crawling out of a sewer, Bettina emerged from the burial plot that had brought her to the garden gates. Heedless of whether or not Goddess had left the Archives or not, she gulped in huge breaths and lunged out of the ground. The strands that had shielded her were gone, but the cobalt welts left in streaks all over her body remained. Her mouth tasted like sour metal and gardenias; the memory of those lightning shocks of pleasure from her temporary burial left her disoriented and wanting.

"Magisend—" She began to run through the empty vineyard— Marzanna *had* departed—searching for him. After a few turns around trees that all looked the same she found him, standing right in front of her so suddenly she crashed into him hard enough to rock both of them, though they didn't fall.

"You. I was looking for you." The uncomprehending stare couldn't warm, but the roving clicks of his faceted eyes settled to rest on Bettina.

"Goddess left, but—are you well? Did She…"

"She found something She came for. As long as that isn't you everything is fine."

"What did you give Her?" Bettina could be a fool, but she wasn't witless. *What did you pay to get Her to leave?*

He blinked down at her, unmoving. Magisend allowed her to see him as the man she had built rather than the dreadful singularities Goddess's Light had provoked from him upon Her arrival. But how could knowledge, even its avatar, hold any form? How could once-mortal Bettina behold and touch him when he could transform into white fire, or a swirling storm, or a grotesque sphere of watchful, omniscient eyes?

How could she compel him what form to take, if, according to the Archives, he wasn't meant to have one?

Am I another petitioner? Just one more pawn of the Archives meant to perpetuate itself in unbreakable balance?

No, she found herself longing for him to answer, *no, you aren't the same. You have a name I didn't give you. You have—*

"Bettina." When he said her name like that the lightning returned to ignite the fading blue scars his threads had left to heal. As she gasped, rocking back on her heels to escape the heat and the realization that dawned on her, Bettina understood with a reluctant shiver of anticipation what this and Easoren's hints had meant.

"I know how to get back to the garden. I know what the key is."

Concentration was harder than it had ever been, but Bettina managed it by picturing the gates themselves and naming each hue of green she remembered: *emerald, malachite, summer...*

"Swan-of-gold." He couldn't hear or read her—she knew he couldn't now her mental resolve had strengthened—but he paced just outside the cage around her thoughts. Restless in spirit, and restless in body, Magisend caught her as her knees wobbled and slowly pulled her into him to help her stay upright. Though she would deny it to anyone else, Bettina couldn't deny herself: she wanted to feel him. She'd grown used to the filaments that pricked her like brambles wherever she turned.

"You're going into Aebbenary again," Magisend said. Guessed.

Bettina nodded...then pulled herself away. For now.

"Not for long," she promised.

XXI

Sovanna

Aebbenary proper had never welcomed Sovanna the way it had her divine half-siblings and Goddess's Saints. If she didn't look the way she did she might have blamed them for their shivers. They were only mortals, after all. Though her beauty was undeniably divine, it possessed a daunting quality that forbade anyone from admiring too closely.

As much as they disdained or barely tolerated her, though, the people *loved* Cristoval.

His benevolence with his inheritance hadn't stopped after Crespin's funeral. After his enlightening reunion with Cosima and Bettina, he'd informed Sovanna—who hadn't wanted to pry—that his vast inheritance could be put to better use than rotting in a bank or his private family coffers. All but passing the keys into public hands, he set about undoing the neglect Goddess's indulgence had wrought in Her holy city.

He provided shelters for the vagrants bad luck and rampant poverty had punished, funded charitable institutions focused on medical care alone rather than merely shelter and food, and convinced some of the rare few members of the nobility brave enough to think for themselves now and again to fund public aid long term. Some of these already existed, but they had been so disregarded by Aebbenary's leadership that they could barely function.

Cristoval knew the likelihood that *every* project would have to be accomplished over the span of months and years he might not survive to oversee…but he didn't speak of that directly. Sovanna would be the last one to prompt him to remember.

All these things required a thoughtful, delicate touch. They could do nothing enough to aggravate Queen Fiammetta in her palace, where she had been keeping to herself more than usual. Just enough to provide something better for citizens who, perhaps, had been misguided in their swift adoration of Marzanna after the first flush of Her victory years ago.

Change had seized Aebbenary. Sovanna watched from her place at Cristoval's side whenever they met to treat his symptoms or test whatever means she had developed working feverishly during the night. She listened to him between Lilias's incomprehensible prattling and demands for attention and affection from both of them. Of all the people in the city, she and the child might have been the *only* ones to attentively listen to him talk about his past, the future he wanted to construct for Aebbenary with his wealth and labor, and anything he wanted.

Aebbenary's people loved him—generously so based on how they had been treated by divine beings and the historical nobility of their home. But they didn't know him like Sovanna knew *them*.

Like she had been able to see the shadow that hung like a shroud over Bettina, she sensed the onset of a twilight age sweeping over Goddess's realm in the advance of whatever madness gripped Her, Her blessèd ones, and Aebbenary's mortalkind. Everywhere Sovanna turned sickness surrounded her, threatening her with despair the more she focused on it.

The people: slavishly devoted to Goddess and Her chosen no matter how much Her malice or neglect hurt them.

Cristoval: a strong soul, kind as an oasis in the desert after the deceit of a mirage, sicker than any of them yet still willing to give.

Where did Sovanna fall on that scale? The more she tried to decide, perplexed as always with the question of her own identity as neither full Godling, true Saint, or simple human, the further the answer drifted away.

I will become whatever I need to be, she determined after another exhausting night that plagued her with yearning that could never be fulfilled responsibly and despair. *I will do whatever I must.*

"And you?" Cristoval asked her as he always did after a debate over architecture, which she appreciated even though it was her preference to let her swamp run mostly wild.

"What about me?" She answered as she always did.

"I want to know more about you. You seem content to let me blather on about whatever, but I don't want our time together focused on me alone. Why do you avoid letting me get to know you better?"

While I still can. Sovanna hadn't meant to intrude—and she was sure he hadn't projected that thought to her on purpose—but the words cut anyway. She opened her mouth to reassure him—

"Don't. Don't promise to save me again. That's not what I want."

He really didn't. That was what struck lasting fear into her heart—that he had already accepted his destiny to die by Goddess's will, and Sovanna was a fool for fighting the inevitable.

She wanted to shout at him to *fight back.* To do anything rather than surrender the one life everyone possessed to do what they wanted.

"What do you want?" she asked instead.

"I'm not suicidal. Life is most precious to me. I'm also not a fool—even if this sickness sown in me could be cured, I know I will die sooner than anyone I care about. You, Mother, and Cosima don't seem to understand that I've made peace with that. I did before I left Aebbenary."

"Fine. You're at peace. Why do you keep asking about me? I *will* live eternally, Cristoval. Our experiences together are already evanescent." Sovanna said.

Sensing an incoming argument, Lilias chattered in her ear—too loud—and leapt down from where Cristoval had been carrying them all over the city on his back. Any other child, even a divine one, would have given her pause to watch them mingle with and disappear into the crowded markets or residential streets. But Lilias was the only one of their kind, and she didn't worry about them for the same reasons.

"Fair enough," Cristoval conceded once Lilias's shadow-tinted wings vanished into the throng. "Maybe I will know you the least well of any man you'll meet in your life, but I still want to know you to the best of my ability in the time I have."

Left. Her spiteful mind added the last word to the end of his sentence, like a brushstroke of tarry black swiped by an envious rival over another artist's painting.

"I'm not sure I want that."

"Why not?"

"Is it fair to make me your…your obsession when you will be nothing but an experience time will wilt in my mind as countless years roll by? All leaving me unchanged."

"Fair for who? If we both choose this—" *This.* They walked together, side by side and sometimes hand in hand, and even he couldn't name the destiny that strung their hearts together.

Your selfishness might chase him away, that devilish part of her mind offered. *Try that.*

"Why should I allow this to hurt me? It's simply our natures: mortal and immortal cannot harmonize without tragedy."

"If you believed that—" Cristoval countered, stopping her in the street; abruptly, he dragged her by the hand down a secluded byway, away from the prying eyes of any city denizens who might recognize him and interrupt. "If you believe that, why try to save me at all? I *am* a dead man walking compared to you. Everyone in Aebbenary is. Why treat the plague that sickens us all?"

Sovanna knew he wouldn't let her lie. Cristoval released her hand, but then he spun her so her back was to a wall. He leaned in with one hand on the wall on the left side of her head; one of her horns caught on his sleeve, but he didn't bother shifting away. Neither did she.

Don't look at me like that. She had to speak.

"It's no good trying to make a savior out of me. I—"

He kissed her, soft, briefer than a sigh. Sweet poison began to melt the sturdy walls she'd built so carefully against him each night she spent alone working to save him.

She tried again. "I can't give you anything you want. I'm not even sure I can save—"

Another delicate kiss. "I told you not to offer that again."

"Stop it." She flinched when he did it again, her entire body shaking as she pressed her hands flat against the brick wall behind her, but she didn't push him away. *He's so breakable, and I'm so strong. How easy it would be to crush him…*

"You make me keep pushing you away. It feels like it's killing me—I, who cannot die. Is that what you want to hear?"

"No. I want to hear that you feel the same way I do. When I'm near you, Sovanna…" He tilted her chin up with his other hand. "You entrance me."

"I'm powerful. I might have cursed you."

He chuckled, tracing her bottom lip with the pad of his thumb. "Interesting. You're also beautiful. I am a man still, mortal though I am. How could I persuade you to end your power over me?"

You couldn't. There's nothing I would trade this for…except your life. Sovanna released a shudder and a sigh and leaned into his touch; she grabbed his hand and held it tight, kissing the back of it like she touched her lips to the fealty ring of her king. When she dared glance up at him, both their eyes had filled with emotion, though neither of them let the tears fall.

"We have nothing to give each other but regret that will be more bitter than sweet by the end. Regret I'll suffer alone if I fail to preserve your life."

"I'm here now. *Stay.*"

His bearing was so sure. They stood so close she could count three notches in his right eyebrow from a little scar she didn't know the origin of. His lips were a little chapped, the circles under his lagoon blue eyes were ashen, and his cheeks were haggard from Goddess's sickness taking its toll…but he was exquisite, every part of him.

I want to stay. Sovanna wished she could beg to kiss him again.

She fled from him then, winging her way by Light back to her swamp. It was a comfort in that moment to lose her body to her power, even to travel. A being of Light couldn't hurt. A heart she didn't have couldn't wring itself into a knot of dread of pain that would worsen the more she let Cristoval woo her.

More days passed. The bell tower that rang the hours that raced out of sight like wild plains horses stole more of Cristoval's remaining time. By the end of another week, Sovanna had abandoned her swamp in favor of resolute action.

She had tried to abandon Cristoval for the sake of her necessary work saving humanity from the burden of worship, but he had refused to be left behind. Her heart was too weak to reject him utterly…but more feebleness than that she would not allow. *Could* not allow if she wanted to save him from Goddess's affliction and authority together.

It's not love, she repeated as she sent her halo out in spears of sterling Light to seek, one by one, all the divine children residing in Aebbenary. *Never that.*

They weren't hard to find. Sovanna even sensed Cosima's presence in the Holy Tower, but that find had no consequence. It was better Goddess's chosen heir had no dealings with the future crimes of Her true firstborn.

After judiciously binding Lilias to the area of her house in the new marsh, she girded herself in a diaphanous boysenberry gown and travelled to where most of the Godlings and a few of the Saints had gathered for a party.

When she landed on the rooftop of one of the old cathedral's decimated strongholds where the divine beings caroused and celebrated what looked like a successful boar hunt, no one faced her right away.

"Thank you," she murmured to herself more than anyone else; the flexible, blessed silver whip in her hand creaked as she tightened her grip on its leather-wrapped handle. "Your scorn makes this much easier."

One of the Saints scoffed as Sovanna strode forward into the midst of a group of loud drinkers, wrinkling their nose at her.

"You. You may be trapped in Aebbenary for your punishment, but Her Glory never said we had to socialize—*argh!"*

Swinging her whip in an arc, Sovanna had cracked it against the Saint's cheek to halt her insults. As that one fell others came forward in disorganized protest—one clutching a goblet, another tripping over the hem of an ally's train, more still just now turning to the wake of her arrival.

She prioritized subduing the few who fumbled with conforming their slippery Light into dagger or bow-like weapons. With methodical prowess she dragged them closer with beams of Light that illuminated her skeleton in neon green luminescence from within its flesh and conquered their resistance with her whip. Some tried to run away, but she grabbed and held them with the force coursing through her—Miraculous power that left her ravenous rather than sated.

Once they were all groaning at her feet, bleeding from their shallow wounds and coughing in the poisoned aura she sent streaming from her pores to keep them down, Sovanna let the whip fall behind her and dragged it so the metallic knots clinked against the stone in ominous melody.

"This is a shock for all of you. You're used to frolicking like lambs in the shining realm Goddess made just for you." She crouched at the side of the first figure, tilting her head to examine the weal her strike had left on their exposed face and arms. Their ichor was in the process of healing them already, but that didn't deter her. Divine beings who healed quickly could withstand more hurt in the long-term.

"Consider me a snake in the grass."

Once she hauled the Godling onto their knees, ignoring their whimper, she seized their throat in one silver-clawed hand. With detachment—the product of a lifetime's practice—she noted how difficult it was not to crush their windpipe. They'd survive the injury, certainly, but their suffering would be prolonged and agonizing.

It's in me as well, this sickness, she reminded herself as, beneath the rippling surface of her calm, something blackened by fear and pain writhed. *No divine being is exempt.*

"Goddess named Cosima Her heir. Yet *I* am Her first legacy—Sovanna of the marsh, Sovanna the bastard born of a false High Priest. Swear obeisance to them if you will, but I will demand tribute from you all whenever I require it. Despise me, dread my coming: you *will* venerate and obey me as you would them."

None of them had any defenses because no one had ever bothered to teach them how to master their Light. A few had significant wells of raw power, certainly, which tickled Sovanna's brain: was it their specific parentage that granted them greater might, or was it Goddess's whim? If they had taken any interest in their own betterment besides their dissolution, could any of them have become a match for her and the silver whip she used to reduce them to meek subjects?

Using an art she wasn't sure Goddess knew she possessed—Sovanna privately theorized that this came from the false god's portion of her heritage—Sovanna weaponized her Light to consume the aureoles of the beings she'd mastered. The first one fell, then another. No one was conscious enough to protest until she came to the third Godling and channeled her Light again.

"Goddess won't let you escape punishment for this crime!" This one rasped; blood trickled out of his nostrils as she drained him, heedless of his threats. "We're Her children even if we aren't Her first—"

"Do you honestly think that matters?" Sovanna asked; she found she really was curious to hear if the Godlings believed in Her love or if they had simply been content to bask in Her favor without any doubts.

The Godling frowned at her outstretched claws. His gaze flicked between them and her impassive, blood-spattered face. Though he tried not to sneer, she still saw it.

"She cares about us enough to avenge this affront. If She doesn't intervene personally, you will find the First Saint or Her Heir at your door by the end of—"

"Däard deserted you long ago. Cosima will not challenge me. Cry to Goddess if you must, but even She won't be able to stop me from what I must do."

Regret and Sovanna were strangers, which was partially why she feared it so greatly. She pondered every decision she made hours and days before she had to make it to secure the door against the haunting of missed chances or remorse. Yet this one had slipped through the lock or under the bar across the threshold: as soon as she finished mocking the Godling's hope she regretted it. Their face formed a rictus of misery and pain as she tore their Light from them—knowing it would replenish eventually—to save the one person who would blame her for what she now did.

Maybe they're not pitiless, conceited beasts on purpose. They're sick—leaderless. Some of the ones who haven't done monstrous things yet are still children at heart. She tried to remind herself, but the mantle of nerve she had cast on herself to shore up her defenses against empathy wouldn't permit the thought to remain. She wrested the complete amount of power she needed from each of them—sending several into a slumber that might last years if Goddess didn't help them—and left.

Lilias waited where she had secured them. They circled like a hawk under the dome of the barrier she had set, their quartet of wings battered at the tips like they had passed the time slamming into the shield to escape or break it. When they saw Sovanna they mewled a greeting that shifted into a sinister, hackles-raising snarl—worse in a child's pitch—at the sight and scent of her.

"I'm back," she said. Lilias stared at her from a few paces away, visibly unsettled.

I must look frightful, Sovanna realized, belatedly picturing the shining, amber-gold ichor splattering her clothing and the whip she'd forgotten to hide. Who knew how much more the child could sense? She had absorbed so much Light from her conquest she felt full to the brim with it—like a frog squeezed until its eyes bulged. Or a wolf glutted on so much easy prey it grew too fat to hunt with her brethren.

I'm not keeping it, she wished she could tell them. *I don't want any of this for me. I don't want to do this. I...*

Dithering wouldn't help anything. She held out a hand for Lilias to take.

"Do you want to help me?" she asked. A loaded question that, perhaps, they knew they couldn't refuse.

Either way, they nodded and joined her. They walked back into the hut together, where Sovanna had already prepared everything else she'd need besides the Light she had forcefully absorbed. A sturdy table dominated the center of the room she had rigorously cleaned and sorted. Jugs and glass tubes surrounded it, expecting by presence alone that she would fill them.

Lilias cooed as she scooped them up, embracing her easily as she set them on the table. Sovanna shuddered as their four wings wrapped around her in welcome without concern for the blood spatters all over her. She didn't have it in her to hug them back, though oblivion knew the child deserved that and more.

Not what she had to do to them to save another.

"My Mother didn't speak to me much when I was your age." Why was she talking to them? Sovanna decided after a pause to think—awful for the two seconds it lasted—that it was better to talk herself through what she had to do rather than bear the silence. "She despised my father for the abuse he'd inflicted on Her before Her Ascension, and something else She never told me. Some of the Godlings that came after my birth made fun of me for resembling him, but I thought even then I look like *Her.*"

Sovanna laid Lilias down gently, atrociously aware of the last brush of their fingertips as they let go of her shoulders to lay flat. Unable to bind them on her own power, she let her Light grip their wrists and ankles to tie them down. Four eyes blinked up at her, still unsettled but not comprehending she would do anything to hurt them.

She made herself stare into their eyes. Soon they'd close forever, in a sleep of death or death itself since the child might not be Saint enough to overcome the sin she was about to commit.

"This is something She would do." A rasp; was her voice breaking? "Maybe all daughters become their mothers in the end—flaws and all. That sounds like immortality to me…though not, perhaps, for the unlucky daughters."

Unlucky. If any word described her life, Sovanna decided that was it. Misfortune had shadowed her from the hour of her birth into Goddess's Bright Age. A Saint had told her long ago that her horns had torn Marzanna apart as She'd given birth, though She had healed as soon as sobbing Fiammetta had yanked Sovanna out of Her ravaged womb.

The child kept still while she drew her forefinger's filigreed claw over the sensitive skin of her opposite wrist to let her blood drain into the nearest jar.

Divine Light. Hers and what she had stolen today. All surrendered willingly with her as the conduit. She would have given every drop of her own, but she had to be alive to complete the task. That was why she'd drained enough Light from the Godlings and Saints to make approximately enough ichor to amount to half of what a mortal would need to survive.

Abominable blood. Weakened but resolved, Sovanna picked up a knife sharpened for this purpose and held it poised over Lilias. She hadn't decided where to cut him to fit the tubes that would drain into the jars all around the table. Inspiration was supposed to come to her now, in the moment—it didn't. She stayed that way for a long time, her arms beginning to shake and cramp, staring down at a trapped child who neither struggled nor cried. Not yet.

All to replace Cristoval's blood. Three powerful ingredients to counteract Goddess's curse on Cristoval and negate the need for him to be anointed to Sainthood to become immortal. What he would become instead of a Saint even Sovanna couldn't guess. But she was still going to try.

"I will be as merciful as I can. It…I take no pleasure in your pain, child. But I will not let Cristoval—"

"Cristoval?" Lilias brightened at once, smiling with nacreous teeth that had been growing sharper by the day. As sharp as they were ever going to be, for they would grow no more.

Cristoval wouldn't know what she had done until after she'd strapped him onto her table as well and drained everything mortal from him to replace with what she would fill the jars with today. He'd hate her later, and she would lose any chance of happiness with him, but Sovanna had never counted on a blissful conclusion to her story. There were only two things that mattered for her: ridding humankind of sickness brought by divine influence and beating Goddess.

That's all, she reminded herself as she held the knife poised to cut. In the shadows of her hut only her halo and the red luminescence that surrounded Lilias gave off any Light. The tip of the knife appeared slick with red already—

"*Sovanna!*"

Power ripped the roof clean off of Sovanna's humble hut. Wings blotted out the light that poured in—Light, because it was not the sun. A Saint had come to intervene: the first Goddess had ever made.

She didn't know when she'd done it, but Sovanna had thrown herself over Lilias's body on her dissection table to protect them from crushing debris or further attack. The Godling she'd drained last had been right after all—here Däard was, eyes aglow with power.

"What—" He took stock of the situation while she watched. The tendons in his neck went taut from how hard he clenched his jaw to hide the emotion that wanted to ripple across his regal face at the sight of what she had been about to do. "What is this?"

"Can't you tell?" *How dare you. How dare you interrupt the hardest thing I've ever done with your feeble whining.* Seething beneath the numbness she had prayed to her inner self to provide, Sovanna leaned back from Lilias and gestured. "A sacrifice."

His lip started to curl, perhaps in outrage, but he stayed his sword. "For what purpose?"

She debated lying. Always, she debated which truths to hoard and which to dole out like black market currency. Däard had never cared about any of his offspring before: why should this one, tainted by Fiammetta no less, matter to him any more than the others?

They did. Lilias mattered as the others had not—or maybe those other progeny had mattered, but since Däard's duty had solely belonged to Marzanna and pleasing Her, he had not been permitted to care for any of his divine children for longer than the initial happy occasion of their birth.

"I'm going to save the son of Bettina Valusius," Sovanna answered. She had already determined he would not stop her: if he fought her, she would incapacitate him the same as she had the other Saints at their party.

"Bettina's son? Why…" He hadn't moved from where he'd landed in her (now roofless) hut, but one of his resplendent wings twitched so hard it smacked into the wall with an audible *thunk*. Sovanna started to squirm under his attention as it locked onto her, his look piercing. "You love him."

I don't want to. He's bewitched me, surely. Sudden weariness made her rise from where she had flung herself over Lilias. They both watched her, father and peculiar child, and Sovanna sighed so deeply she wondered if that was how it would feel to die: a last breath out, then nothing more.

"Please."

She'd misheard. Her hearing had inexplicably failed. There was no way on earth Däard would say that to her.

"Please don't sacrifice them."

"What do *you* care?" Genuine venom laced her tone.

She prided herself on her excellent memory. She hated it, too, because the cruelties she had endured or witnessed growing up in Goddess's tower haunted her. Maybe they always would…but some things had been shaded by the blight of passing time. As Däard fixed his gaze on her and the Light in his hazel eyes captured the reflection of her silver-grey ones, Sovanna remembered.

With her body stringy and all elbows during her adolescence, Sovanna ran away from home.

She had counted on her Light to protect her. It would have, but she hadn't known then that her immortal body could sometimes still thirst, hunger, burn, freeze, and otherwise suffer if she didn't treat it well. In the name of instilling her with womanly virtues and a worshipful attitude toward alternately absent or ardent Goddess, Fiammetta had punished her one too many times by hurting the few mortal friends she'd had before her growing divinity had begun to scare them away.

Young Sovanna had bolted without forethought from the prison of the royal palace and ventured to the coast, hoping to stowaway from Aebbenary on any passing ship that looked like it would be traveling far away on the grey-green sea. It wasn't humans who discovered her, but Fiammetta's divine servants. Saints all, and men, they had cornered her in the belly of one ship and leered as their leader described the punishment their mistress had ordained for her "if she wanted to taste the base reality of life outside Goddess's favor".

They had almost started enacting the duty they had intended to savor—one had told her this was their reward as well as her chastisement—by the time Däard had sensed the distress in her Light during a patrolling flight. He had ripped the ship apart to rescue her and beat Fiammetta's servants senseless. And, as a kindness to her…he had dulled her recollection of that night before he carried her back, asleep and oblivious, to reason with Fiammetta and buy Sovanna a respite.

"You saved me." Her voice was wooden, made deadweight by the flashback of humiliation and pain.

She should have been furious that he had compelled her to remember something so awful, but familiar numbness set in before she could summon enough outrage to shout at him. The knife she still held dropped from her nerveless fingers and clanged onto the floor. Lilias glanced back and forth between them without comprehension.

Däard nodded. "I wouldn't say I saved you. I will not order you to honor the favor you owe me, or the one you will owe me twice over for sparing you from punishment today for what you did to the Godlings and Saints. This isn't just for them, Sovanna, but for *you.*"

The numbness vanished in an internal vacuum of agony. She choked—how could that be? How could the sobs she locked in her throat feel solid enough to drown her? "I have to. *I have to.* Cristoval needs me to save him."

"Destiny lingers with her hand on the boy's shoulder. Even Goddess at Her most powerful, Her most omniscient cannot banish her or predict the end of this tale. Perhaps his death will be a catalyst—"

"Not if he doesn't die! I won't allow it, Cosima and Bettina won't let—"

"It is Cristoval's decision how to fight for his life…or not. You know this. I have stood in Cristoval's place. Another chose to save me at catastrophic cost to himself and the hearts of those who loved him. *Love* him—still. I have not forgiven him for the mistake. If the choice came back to me to save myself or spare him from martyrdom I would march into oblivion of my own free will."

Lilias blinked one eye at a time, reclining where she had bound them. Däard watched, his lustrous sword lowered by his side as the thing he'd been waiting for her to realize occurred to her.

Sovanna had bound Lilias—this unwanted brat—to her altar and *they had let her.* No one on earth, possibly not even Goddess, understood the nature or the scope of this child's powers better than her, and she had garnered next to nothing in her experiments meant to while away the resentful hours of her captivity in the sprawling city.

They could have stopped her—easily. Hurt her, killed her, whatever they saw fit to do for the crime of killing someone who faithlessly abused their trust and abandoned the responsibility of keeping them safe. Yet Lilias lay there, still, with wisdom she saw now in their quartet of black and red eyes to let her decide their destiny.

"You know Bettina's compassionate son would not allow you to sacrifice a child to grant him the possibility of a half-life."

Lilias became the face of the entire world. They were all Sovanna could see, staring down at them and hugging herself with her arms to lock the fragments of herself together before they shattered, but she heard Däard fold their wings closed and sensed him approach the table as she looked.

"Sov?"

Lilias had never once addressed her by name. It broke her—she, who had never been tamed or broken down to her soul by any hardship or years of loneliness.

At her word, the Light bindings crumbled away in lines of ash. Shaking off the remnants, Lilias sat up and lifted their arms out to Sovanna to be held. She had never refused them before; they didn't expect her to now.

Without hesitation Sovanna pulled them into her arms. Their legs wrapped around her waist, clinging tight as she started bawling with every emotion she had ever kept pent up behind the walls of her failing resilience.

"I'm sorry," she gasped between sobs, forgetting to feel shame for her outburst. Nothing else mattered but the unforgivable horror of what she had almost done—in the name of *love*, no less. "I'm sorry, baby, I'm so—"

"Cristoval." Lilias interrupted her. That was the only thing they said. In her hold their skin felt hot as flames fit to scorch any but a Godling, but she ignored the stinging ache and clutched them tight enough to absorb the honeysuckle-sweet scent of their skin and feel the soft crown of their curls pressed against her tear-streaked cheek.

I will do anything to save you, she vowed to Cristoval even though he wasn't here and would never know how far into the dark she had trespassed to save him. *Not this, though. This I cannot do.*

Däard's sword winked out of their dimension when he put out its Light. At its banishment Sovanna flicked her swimming gaze up to him, not knowing what to say or how to apologize.

What is enough? What could I possibly say?

She had never seen a man torn apart from the inside out in pain and conflict that showed in the harsh frown on his face. Enduring vigor had been granted to him by Goddess out of devotion to Her consorts, but in that moment he appeared as old as if he was a mortal man in his sixth decade. His eyes were fixed on Lilias, burning and intense, but not with anger or pain.

He has love in him still, Sovanna thought, *but no one to give it to.*

Lilias turned away from her like they had felt that gaze boring into their back. She held onto them, reluctant to let go, but her hands loosened as they pulled away and walked across the table. Toward Däard, who hesitantly opened his arms and waited for Lilias to come to him.

Sovanna wept anew when they did, but silently.

"Why do you love Bettina's son?" Däard asked when her tears started to dry up. He looked up at the sky like he was longing to be up there already; she knew it was because he was about to cry too, but refused the reprieve as if he felt he didn't deserve it. In his arms, Lilias stood silent, uncomfortable, and still. They were strangers, after all.

"Is there a reason you're asking?"

"I'm not sure. I think I'm trying to remember what that feeling is."

Contemptible pity wrenched Sovanna's heart with another tug in the wrong direction. She missed her frigid detachment and her clarity of purpose with every fiber of her being…except for those Cristoval had stolen when the stars aligned to fall to earth upon their meeting at Cosima's Jubilee. Except for those Lilias had also robbed her of while she'd been studying him.

"He's like Bettina, I've heard. A clever charmer, but as kind a man as you can find. There are many more reasons I want to save him from his destiny, but I don't know how to tell you what they are. He *needs* to stay in this world, not the next."

"When we slew the false god, Marzanna had to sacrifice almost everything. Even things that did not belong to Her." Lilias wriggled one cramped wing free from under Däard's elegant hand. Moved by the slight protest, he released them and began to back away from the table the child had been bound to.

He finally looked down, meeting Sovanna's eyes again—his own had reddened so the green portions of his hazel irises flared like summer leaves under the sun. "I cannot claim it was worth it, but I know it was necessary for *someone* to lose their life to kill that god. It had to be someone important to the usurper."

Sovanna wanted to kick and scream and gnash her teeth at the terrible, relentless truth. She wanted to slice off her ears and fling herself into a pit in the earth to avoid this hateful knowledge that would chase her no matter how far she fled from it.

Someone has to die to bring Goddess down from Her lofty seat. Someone important.

"Do you not love, Däard?" she asked. *If you did, you would not ask me this. You would not be the one to make me begin to realize what I'm about to lose—of my own free will.*

She knew he was the only one who could.

"I wish I knew."

Side by side—hand in hand—Sovanna and Lilias lifted their eyes skyward to absorb the magnificent sight of the strongest Saint in Goddess's realm flying home.

XXII

Bettina

Secrets on the sacred homeland belonging to Goddess were scarce, but Bettina had some practice hiding a few under her sleeve. With her mind firmly locked against Magisend, she used the cloak of his vague shadow to leave the Archives and go into Aebbenary not quite alone.

Funds were never out of the equation for a Valusius. Bettina had had the foresight many years ago to hide some money—as Marzanna once had, though not in the same spots—that couldn't be tracked back to an account. Under a pseudonym, with her face concealed with a few tricks of Light, she sought the second or third best pleasure house in the city and bought them out for two days. Using the impressive entirety of one stash, she began to work the magic she had intended to bring about the seduction of the Grand Archivist in her favor.

It was all titillating, in its way, but she had been here often enough to begin to resent how well she had been manipulated into this role. Bettina knew how to use her beauty: how to position herself in the light to make her skin luminous, to sway her hips just right as she moved, the power of her radiant smile or her alluring pout, how to hush or melodize her voice and laughter to ring triumphant against the senses of the object of her seduction. Her mortal past had suited her for this role along with her natural charisma. Life as Goddess's swan, existing only to be admired and petted and ravished, had increased her talents.

He could deny you, she considered as she rested during the heat of high noon and took lunch lounging on the first floor cushion that had been cleaned at her request. *He could say no and leave. He could be insulted, angry, disgusted…he might not be able to perform. He might not have that capability. Though in all other ways he resembles a man…*

You *could say no.* A reminder Bettina needed, though one she dismissed the way she spat out the water speckled with mint leaves she had used to rinse her mouth after her repast of bread and seasoned tomatoes. *This isn't something you need to do with him. Another lover might work to get you to the garden.*

Maybe, she answered her own question as she sunk into the scented bath she had ordered set up in the middle of the common area to banish any pesky shyness before the night ahead. All around her, servants and professional women hurried and flurried preparing the sensual den she had described for their proprietor. With the rest of Aebbenary in shambles—barring Cristoval's increasing legend as a generous benefactor—all it had taken were kind words, firm instruction, and a *lot* of money to buy their loyalty and discretion so word of their party didn't spread too far. The women and their discreet partners would be company enough for her plans.

She lingered on that "maybe" for as long as it took to style her golden curls with pins woven with living flowers the same pale flush as her creamy skin or the summer blue of her eyes. Aside from her hair and the blessed freckles on her face, she eschewed everything gold and clothed herself in a cut of water-smooth, gauzy amaranth silk. Secured with a matching sash, it clung to her curves but not much else; where it hung transparently, concealing nothing, it draped between her legs to prompt the eye to travel up their length to where she had all but promised access before long.

She banished the "maybe" as she studied her appearance in a mirror.

I want Magisend with me when I unlock those gates. He has to be there.

Then she shielded the rest of her troublesome thoughts even from herself. Girlish longing and naïve affection were useless trappings of innocence she somehow had to discard again and again as she aged without aging.

I need him for a purpose. Nothing else.

When every curtain over every window had been examined and each table had been laid out with a feast, when every painted belle had been washed and perfumed and instructed on the events to come, when the gentleman of Aebbenary began to come to play with these favorite ladies...*then* Bettina called Magisend.

Not two minutes passed between her summons and his arrival. Though she had half-expected him to materialize at her side thanks to her guarding shadow, it seemed the main portion of his avatar had remained elsewhere. When she heard the footfalls of his approach outside the door to her haven, she gestured for the musicians at the far end of the common room to begin softly playing the slow, luxurious music she had requested. All around the spacious room the paramours arranged as skillfully as the jewel-toned silks and cushions entered a slow dance of courtship and seduction to mirror what Bettina had set out to do to earn passage to the garden.

She stared at him. Now that they were on the cusp of it, it struck her how foolish she had been to deny the attraction she felt toward him. Her heart leapt into her mouth as the rest of her blood shot lower, between her legs where she could no longer pretend she didn't want him.

Of course you want him. Your ichor made him what he is.

Magisend *was* beautiful. Each component of the whole—olive skin, hollow cheeks under a layer of stubble she wanted to feel on her own, silken dark hair tied back into a knot, an angular yet agile body—sparked desire in her, but who could say if that was because he had plucked these traits from her mind or because he wanted them himself?

Did it matter to her enough to stay her hand when it came to making him hers, even for a night?

He spoke first. "Why did you call me?"

Bettina had stood to greet him, but she sat with flowing grace as the outer servants pulled the doors behind Magisend shut without a sound.

Without answering—he would have to earn that by coming closer—she held out her hand in beckoning for him to join her. Her smiles could be tricky, yearned-for commodities: the one she bestowed on him now was gentle, knowing, and as full of promise as her eyes, where all the candles spaced judiciously around the room flickered an answer to her Saint's glow.

Magisend's eyes traveled around the room—she hoped it wasn't to avoid looking at her. He took in the sight of the other cushions and couples through the artful haze of incense redolent of sandalwood, jasmine, and musky exotic oranges. They laughed amongst themselves and at him, some of the whores waving with friendly interest between their callers kissing their necks and bare shoulders and other places the patient removal of clothing revealed. Some of them snatched treats from the feast tables here and there, but not just to eat.

Bettina nodded in approval, then returned her focus to her outstretched hand and Magisend. Finally, after what felt like an eternity, he came to her.

"Why did you call me?" he repeated after he let her pull him down to sit beside her.

With a touch of Light, she expanded her aureole to encompass their portion of the den to ensure that while others could and would observe them, none of them could overhear whatever they might say to each other. Or remember it after, for that matter—they already couldn't recognize Bettina thanks to the groundwork she had done upon her arrival at the house.

"The garden requires a base state of mind. If I'm not on the brink of lasting agony and death…well, there are smaller deaths to seek."

"Smaller deaths?" He didn't appear to understand her, but she wondered. Testing him, she inched her hand closer, sliding it over his thigh as he sat—tensely, rigidly—on the edge of the cushion where she'd pulled him down. Quick as a cat, he grabbed her hand before she could glide it any higher or further in.

Bettina smiled, dimpling even though he wasn't looking directly at her.

"Did I startle you? You have nothing to be afraid of, you know."

"This is what you concealed from me?"

"I've found the anticipation of a surprise can have pleasant consequences." She flexed her hand, tapping the tips of her fingers against his leg.

"With Goddess. You learned that from Her."

Her smile slipped; she recovered a beat too late. "Why speak of Her now? She isn't here." Using the hand he hadn't trapped, she cupped his face and turned it toward her, making him look. While she dreaded seeing his eyes and their incalculable facets, she needed him to look at her to work her charms.

"Her presence isn't necessary for you to act like you belong to Her with every breath."

Splinters jabbed under her fingernails might have hurt less than that accusation. Bettina wrestled with the sick wrench of anger and embarrassment to master it. It was her turn in this game now, and she would *not* be put on the defensive.

"Are you jealous, Archivist?" Bettina purred as she spoke his title, purposefully leaving off the "Grand" part of it to provoke him a little more. "Shall I make amends for my distraction?"

"Amends in the form of smaller deaths?"

"Oh, absolutely. But wouldn't you like to see everything else I arranged for us first?"

Magisend didn't say yes, but when no refusal seemed forthcoming she waved at the servants standing by to proceed. They brought a table made for eating while lounging on the ground laden with all manner of fruit and sweets to her side before bowing themselves away. Bettina plucked a raspberry from an arrangement and pinched it slightly to make its juice run down her thumb.

Flicking her eyes up toward where she knew he was watching her, she licked it away and rolled the berry into her mouth. She leaned in as if she would share it with him through a kiss…then ate it alone, granting him a faint, teasing smile that would have won any award she wanted for its power.

"Will you eat with me?" She wasn't touching him now, but her knees pressed against his leg where they sat close together, and he was finally looking at her without her pleading first. Again, he offered no response other than the faint lifting of his left brow—so subtle she accused herself of imagining the change—so she proceeded as if he'd said yes.

Fruit drizzled in honey and swept through a bowl of whipped cream was impossible to resist. When she fed him quartered fig he savored it slowly; as if he knew or guessed the purpose of this game, he neglected a smear of honey that clung to the corner of his mouth. She leaned to delicately lick it off, with no more pressure or proximity than was necessary.

"I don't know much about your nature, Magisend. What do you do with yourself when I'm not with you?" Bettina asked. His acceptance—passive though it was—emboldened her. She ate some of the fruit, carefully tracing a miniscule residue of honey on her own lips so they'd shine with tantalizing sweetness in the den's smoky light.

"We learn eternally." A rote reply spoken sternly. She wanted to recoil from what felt and sounded like a dismissal...but Magisend's gaze lingered on her face. Bettina couldn't say how she knew since his eyes were not human, but she sensed his attention was fixed on her mouth.

More charm, she ordered herself, leaning close enough for him to kiss her if he was deliberating it. *More sweetness.*

"What do you like learning about?" If his proclivities followed that pattern in disposition as well as physically, Bettina knew well that men loved nothing more than talking about themselves. "All the knowledge in the world doesn't sound satisfying if you can't have any special interests."

"I was one of billions of components of the All not long ago. Until Goddess Created me from the whole to demand forbidden knowledge."

Marzanna again. Another prod at her confidence, which his muted response to her seduction steadily wore down.

Bettina accelerated her plot and swiped her finger through a layer of plum-colored frosting on a small cake; using that movement to flow into another as if this was a dance, she swung her leg over Magisend and positioned herself on his lap, with her knees on either side of his narrow hips.

Enough about Her. Bettina swore to herself that Goddess's shadow would not loom over her night with Magisend. Not for her, and not for him because she would make certain, entity of the All or not, that she would be the only thing in his thoughts for at least a few hours.

"Do you eat in the Archives? Drink? The vineyard is there, but do you partake?" She waited until his hands settled on her hips, too slow to excuse as a reflex to prevent her from sliding off, before she fed him the frosting clinging to her index finger. "Some knowledge is forbidden, but is pleasure? Even mundane amusements like eating, drinking, and…other inclinations."

Magisend's tongue flicked against her finger as he accepted the frosting; Bettina's heart skipped its next beat. She couldn't feel anything between his legs yet, but her own attraction was undeniable. In seducing him she was encouraging her own desire. She had buried it before, choosing sense and logic over abandon that always brought her trouble, but here it was: fire stoked to blazing as she rocked with methodical pace and pressure over his groin.

His hands gripped her bare hips a little tighter, and she feared he would push her off. Instead he started to guide her, rolling her in a slow grind against *something* she hadn't yet seen that had to be proof of her success so far.

"I don't require human sustenance. Knowledge sates me."

"But you enjoy it?"

"*I* do."

There it was again: that peculiar emphasis on himself as an individual. She took this as another subtle encouragement as she ground her barely covered sex against the enticing—yet frustratingly obscured—bulge between his legs. He balanced her carefully atop him, setting her pace without letting her bear down, speed up, or shift aside.

All around them, the atmosphere of lust in the pleasure den encouraged them to surrender to its lure. Timbrels and flutes and other instruments accompanied the chorus of laughter and kisses and other, wetter sounds to elevate the mood into feverish revelry.

"What other human things do you enjoy?" Was that her voice that caught on a frustrated moan? Bettina leaned into the new sensations and Magisend; she slid her left arm around his neck, holding on as he looked up at her, and twisted around to nab a slice of white pear. She slid half of it into her mouth, then leaned into him to offer the other.

His gilded teeth flashed as he bit as close as he could to her lips without more than brushing against them. Without answering, he bucked slightly higher against her, a challenge she succeeded or failed based on how he expected her to respond to more stimulation between her thighs. She didn't try to bite off the whimper that escaped her.

"What do you think?" he asked. Was it her imagination, or had his pitch lowered like she had succeeded in arousing him?

"Hmm," Bettina stalled for time as her mind scrambled for an answer—*she* was supposed to be in control here, not overwhelmed by lust before the target of her seduction had even worked up a sweat resisting her. "Honey and pears. A taste for sweet things. What could be sweeter than those?"

Play with him, she tried to remind herself as he rocked her by her hips, making whatever he balanced her against harder. Cupping his cheek in one, slightly sticky hand, she brushed the tip of her nose against his and tried to kiss him. For real this time. *Our first.*

Magisend flipped her over. One second she straddled him, open as one of the nearby whores. Then he was on top of her, shoving her down against the floor cushion with his frown an accusation. It had started to become second nature to fold or fan her wings as she moved to keep them out of the way, but she barely had time to arrange them before he pinned her down.

The only thing that would have been worse would be him laughing at her for thinking she could manipulate an unknowable entity into mundane love-making. Bettina shrank away from him all the same, humiliation burning her cheeks.

"Why did you call me?"

His weight—so much greater than anticipated, as if what made him was as dense as star matter—held her down. Everything had gone according to plan except for this. She struggled to push him off so she could get up, gather the shreds of her dignity, and run away from this awful, familiar shame of failure and rejection.

Who was she to seduce a distant avatar of knowledge? A silly, savage little swan who had never been worth anything more than a kiss or a fuck that would be used to hurt her before long…

"Bettina."

"I told you. The key to the garden is pain or pleasure—"

"That's not why you called me," he accused verbally before he plunged into her mind again. *Tell me the truth."*

"You have to make me say it?" When she struggled again, glaring up at him to conceal her contemptible hurt, he squeezed her wrists together in one hand and used his other to grab her jaw and hold it.

Then he kissed her. Pinpricks and the iron tang of her own ichor pricked her lips and brushed against her tongue. He kissed her like he had considered swallowing her whole but had decided this would be more satisfying in the long run. Bettina squirmed underneath him as the kiss stroked her desire hotter; his hand was cold fire against her face where he held it, forbidding her to move.

When he pulled away, their faces separated by mere inches, he stared with an expression so impassive she would have wondered if they had ever kissed at all if he wasn't still holding her. If he didn't shake her chin slightly, like he was scolding her.

"Tell me. Tell me why I'm here, answering your call so swiftly. *Me*, Bett. When you had your pick of anyone in the world to escort you to the garden this way."

Fuck, Bettina thought at the sound of that pet name in his voice. *I thought I hated it. Not when he says it, though.*

"I wanted you." A raw confession that reminded her of when, in her youth, she had been compelled to confess her sins to the false god in a cathedral now derelict. "I don't even know what you are and I *want* you, Magisend."

She had never seen him smile—not truly. When he did at last, showing the black void of his mouth and the sharp, golden teeth he had made for himself using the inspiration of her ichor, it took her breath away. Magisend was beautiful, awful, and enthralling to look upon. He could devour her or enter her and she would thank him profusely.

"We learn eternally," he said—then he cut through her flimsy gown with nails turned into claws and kissed her again.

Though he had most likely never known another besides her, he acted like he had expertise when he disrobed her and scraped his wintry hands—threads, nettle texture, claws and all—up and down her body. Each welt and ridge he left stung; when his head dipped toward her neck to taste the hollow of her throat she arched in his hold, gasping with readiness to be ravished no matter how cold or peculiar his touch seared.

Bettina's desires rarely frightened her. Only after Goddess had taught her to doubt and fear the traitorous longings of her weak flesh and shown her the consequences of surrender had she learned to reject them. *This* should have scared her to death: the greedy hungers it would have been better for her to banish, never to feel again. Desire this intense for anyone with power greater than hers could only bring heartache in the end, most likely for her alone and not her partner.

I'm supposed to do this, she reminded herself as the temptation to balk faded. She had squeezed her eyes shut during Magisend's devoted attention to the sensitive, erogenous points on her neck. When she opened them he drew back, lifting himself off her so they could look at one another.

She would have helped him take off his clothes—eagerly, hurriedly—but she blinked and they were gone. Her eyes traveled down Magisend's nude body, appreciating what they saw but really looking for the source of the swelling she had grinded against. All over, cobalt, gold, and traces of black metal locked the plates of his flesh together—including his generous cock, already rigid and ready for her.

Something about her expression beyond her panting desire must have given him pause. He sat back, unflinching, and let her look.

"Am I less than you expected?"

Bettina could have laughed, but she didn't. She couldn't completely banish a smile, though.

"More, actually. More and different. I'm planning my attack, you see." Sitting up with him, she took gentle hold of his penis and stroked it, circling her thumb under the base of its head. She had thought he didn't need to breathe, but because she was looking for any subtle reaction she noticed how it caught and the rise and fall of his lean chest at her touch.

"I planned *such* an eventful night for us. All around us, practitioners of love play for our amusement. I know you like to learn, Magisend—would you like to watch them while I please you?"

"Why watch them when I can look at you?" It was her turn to lose her breath. Then she blushed—*actually* blushed like a shy milkmaid—as he continued. "You're beautiful, Bett, but your splendor will defy words when I see your lips wrapped around my cock."

Magisend's head tilted sideways as he watched her flush and stutter, as if she fascinated him.

"Wh-Where did you learn *that?*"

"I'm learning you."

What is there to discover but more of my vanity? "I'm not sure I want you to."

"What do you want, then?" Magisend reclined on his elbows, his posture inviting. Flirtation from him, directed without screen or sieve at Bettina, had *devastating* consequences. His smooth voice stirred her desire such that her halo radiated like the sun, her shield against the den observers near solid. They were in their own world now—protected from all but each other.

"Let me," she entreated before she laid herself down on her stomach between his legs, propping herself up on her own arms so she could do her work. "I want to."

The moment she slid his tip into her mouth she tasted her own ichor again, fainter this time…then forgot to think about that as she swallowed more of him and the strands on his cock responded to her attention.

Nettles punctured her tongue and the roof of her mouth. They didn't hurt, but they lingered. The texture was unsettling at first and she wasn't sure if she should keep going, but Magisend hadn't reacted and she took the risk. As soon as she moved, she realized what he'd done: her clitoris throbbed as if she had moved over herself.

It had been a long time since Bettina had enjoyed a man. Her last lover had been—*no, I won't think of Her. Not with him.* She discovered the art of pleasing one hadn't much changed, though Magisend's nature transformed a sacrificial gift of pleasure into something mutual. When she traced the tip of her tongue in careful loops around his cock, miniscule threads diffused his pleasure through her tongue down to her vagina, which throbbed with sweet emptiness she knew he would sate later if she conquered her impatience. When she opened wider to guide him to the back of her tongue and throat, first gradually then faster, she heard him groan and felt his hand slide into her hair to grip it and help her set the pace that worked best for him.

He lasted longer than most might have, but Bettina won before long. When he came it hit both of them hard—he thrust as he held her head in both hands, making her take it. Near finishing herself, she moaned around his cock as her own saliva dripped out of the corners of her mouth from her efforts…then coughed, gagging as something that *wasn't* normal seed scraped her throat. She ripped out of his hold, shuddering and choking—

—then stopped as whatever it was dissolved. Metallic black liquid slithered down her chin—a remnant of his first climax. It savored of nothing Bettina could compare it to or name—certainly not human— but her tongue cautiously darted out anyway to taste it again.

She glanced down at Magisend as she sat back on her haunches and wiped her face with the shreds of her discarded clothes. She could breathe again, and he hadn't hurt her. There was no reason, really, to ignore the agonizing desire that made her limbs shake and her flesh burn the longer he took to sate her.

"Are you—"

"That was—" Bettina interrupted and then left off. Her desire was so intense she shook with it, from head to toe to the tips of her wings.

"Up," Magisend commanded. He didn't wait for her to comply; defying even divine speed, he pulled her up over him and started to roll her under him.

Bettina pressed her hands against his chest, shaking her head; her hair, tangled now where his hand had woven through it, fanned back against the cushion in a river of yellow gold and remnants of jasmine oil. "Wait. I want to ride you. We both have to achieve ecstasy if we want to reach the garden."

"Will you command me the entire night?" If he teased her he didn't look amused, but she taunted him in return anyway.

"Tonight? Yes." Self-preservation made her add something else as she positioned herself over his cock and slid him into her. "After we get what we need from the garden we can revisit the chain of command."

Fuck. If he answered with a jibe or anything else Bettina didn't hear him. His strands extended to connect deeper the second his arousal slid home in her entrance, lashing them together and searching for her clit and any other tender place to stimulate. Her back arched as she leaned back, guiding him—and them—deeper. *How can this feel so good? He's not human or divine, yet I'm already undone—*

"I don't know," he answered the question she hadn't asked aloud. "I don't know how you feel like silk and taste like honey when you kiss me. I don't know why I can't think of anything but how you'll sound when you come for me. *Soon.*"

"F-flatterer." That was the absolute last thing she could say before her conscious thoughts shattered under his attention. Magisend's hands cruised up from her hips to her waist to start her moving; one slid higher still, cupping the base of an ample breast. When she looked down, marveling at the textured feel of his strange skin, she saw more strands rising from their settings to tease her exposed nipple and bring it to a peak.

Similar to what had happened to him when Goddess had called on the Archives, his form shifted and altered in pieces. Plates like armor—some of them no bigger than a coin—turned lusterless black behind the gleaming filaments before changing back to their usual shade; a few burgeoning eyes formed closed slits over his face, arms, and chest, but none of them opened, and they melted back into his flesh soon enough. Bettina was almost disappointed.

I don't know. There was frustration in that deeper than anything Bettina had heard from anyone in those three words. Could it be, she wondered, that it *wasn't* just because she had helped construct his form that their attraction was undeniable? That something more had come into play to personify the avatar of the Archives more than her meager sacrifice of ichor already had?

No, she decided before his threads snaked around her ribcage and helped steady her so she could move how she liked. The expected strain in her legs from lifting herself off his cock so she could slide its entirety back in again, over and over as long as it took to bring them to finishing, didn't come as the threads augmented her strength as well as helping her up.

When she looked down—avoiding Magisend's eyes for some reason—she saw that thousands of tiny needles had pierced her, sinking in without drawing blood.

"Look at you," Magisend said as he admired her. Something twisted between them, inside her—the threads that lined his cock rotating, perhaps. Not a sensation she could pinpoint exactly, but the added friction and additional lubrication felt blissful.

"What about me?" she asked after her resultant sigh of delight made her blush again. She'd had plenty of lovers admire her for hundreds of reasons they had named during their hours of lovemaking. *How is this any different?*

He sat up smoothly, bracing her with his hands against her back; more and more of his strands propped them up and helped them move together. "You feel incredible in my hands. Fuck, Bettina…how are you doing this to me?"

He'd never sounded like this before: he'd never *looked* at her like this before, even when—as she knew now—he had thought of her as someone who desires another when he'd watched her dance at the Jubilee.

Firm against her back, Magisend's hands moved to stretch out the wings she had kept tame and still behind and beneath her during this session. Both of them flared out, their tips poking out of the sphere of her aureole's protection. Nettles and pins poked the tender nerves at the base of each wing, even the one he had stitched back on.

Within moments Bettina came, *hard*, with a scream that echoed surprise as well as delight. When she tried to bend forward, seeking to bury her face in his neck, a black, corvine wing more membrane than feathers brushed against her forehead, making her look up.

How am I doing this to you? What have you done to me, Magisend?

He may have heard; he might not have. While she stared at him, panting in recovery from her orgasm as he slowed their continued pace to a lazy, pleasurable roll, he gazed into her eyes and waited for…what?

They didn't hurry again. Though they shared a goal, Bettina let herself forget it and hoped Magisend did too. In the carnal nest she had organized for their tryst, they engaged in a leisurely, passionate dance more intensely enjoyable than anything she'd experienced in years. The longer they fucked, the further they strayed on the path of abandon required to find the garden again and unlock its gates.

With him guiding her, knowing the Archives remained always with their avatar, Aebbenary vanished into midnight mist, deeper with each passing second. It took a few tries—which Bettina was thrilled to practice—but as soon as they managed to come together the mist shrouded them completely.

She'd wound up on top of him again; he helped both of them up as soon as they could command their sated limbs to obey. Suddenly his touch was alien again, almost hostile. He could not be a man here, not even for her. She yanked her arm away from him and pretended it meant nothing, though sudden melancholy wrenched her heart more than her shoulder.

Bettina reminded herself that didn't matter, for they had succeeded. Beneath her feet lay the diminishing dust of the void before the gates of the prophetic garden. Ahead of her, the green gates creaked open, swinging inwards and leaving divots in the earth beneath their bars.

At last, she thought, satisfied enough to forget she was naked and tousled by hours of sex. That felt right, in a way: entering the garden without veil or pretense. Bettina steeled her courage and walked through the gates without a backward glance.

XXIII

Cosima

As a child Cosima had loved Fiammetta's palace. Not its occupants, though she had no qualms with the lower servants; the ones dedicated to the upper levels didn't value kindness to children. Even divine ones.

Now she had to stay there once again until she found and rescued the huntresses. She had Godlings and Saints to train up according to Goddess's design between her wanderings during the heat of the day when all but the servants rested, or the cool nights when the divine beings of the palace occupied themselves with debauchery or solitude. Among all of that, Goddess insisted Her heir keep Her company and learn from *Her* what it meant to lead Aebbenary from behind Fiammetta's garish throne.

Obedience was like a rusty tool Cosima had discarded in antipathy only to find, when she picked it up again out of necessity, it was still shiny and useful under the grit of her neglect. Cosima's days of being seen and not heard lest she disturb Goddess's serenity or revelries still served her the veneer of humble gentility Marzanna and Her favorites appreciated. Especially Fiammetta, who didn't care for any Godlings or Saints besides Goddess.

Marzanna's mood was a fickle one. She came and went more than Cosima remembered from her youth. Once or twice She was pleased as punch when She returned, but that satisfaction quickly faded when She held court alongside Fiammetta.

The other instances She returned from Her journeys, Goddess was in such a foul humor that everyone fled from Her sight to spare themselves Her ferocity. Everyone but Cosima—who made regular reports with every relevant detail of her training program for the Godlings and Saints to stay on Marzanna's good side—and Fiammetta, who was too blind to the changing winds to do otherwise.

She's looking for something, Cosima mused, her own mood darker by the day no matter how brightly she forced her aureole to glow with contentment. It was what she had told Bettina the day she'd arrived on Aebbenary. *Something besides Bettina and Cristoval.*

She had also told Bettina when she'd arrived back in Aebbenary that the whole realm felt the pressure of Goddess's unmet desire. Stymied by the puzzle, Cosima had even gone down to the Archives herself. Frustration had been the only thing she'd gained, since the specters ignored her questions and eventual insults, and at the time she hadn't felt things were urgent enough to storm the Archives to force them to interact with her.

That hadn't been wise, hindsight told her. Though Bettina hadn't been able to discover the details of what Marzanna wanted—and her attempts to woo Goddess into a passion of blessing had failed spectacularly—Cosima wondered if she could have earned an anointing to Sainthood for Cristoval if she had fought harder.

An even more foolish observation. Goddess would brook no distractions from any other life to come between Her and Bettina.

Maybe her bored wishing was foolish, but Fiammetta's folly was something to behold that defied even Cosima's poor expectations. After Cosima had returned to the Holy Tower with Goddess, Marzanna had sent her to stay in the palace right away to "keep Fia's spirits up" and mold the blessèd flock in Her will.

Crowned in a laurel garnished with candied lemon that dripped sugar onto her flaming tresses, wrapped in pale yellow silk, Fiammetta had hurled the bouquet of daisies she had brought for Marzanna down the stairs and shrieked her tantrum like a harpy.

Cosima might have laughed at her if it wasn't for the threat that Fiammetta would order the huntresses punished for her disgrace right then. She thought of following her in secret to see if that's what she would do…but the risk was too great. Fiammetta was mean-spirited and stupid, but she had a villain's cunning, years of maturity beyond Cosima, and great, undeserved power from Goddess.

Someday, Cosima vowed behind the barred doors of her consciousness, *soon, I think, I will kill you. A Saint cannot die*—Goddess *cannot die. But I am going to change that.*

She didn't know how. But she was going to find a way.

Goddess wanted Her progeny and blessèd ones made useful rather than ornamental. Thus Cosima did her utmost to make something of the reluctant whole rather than each obstinate individual. She transformed several acres of the Arboretum into a training ground, brought them all together each morning at dawn, and set them to work using the holy bodies and powers granted by Marzanna and their destinies. Each of them shone with health and strength under the sun, their skin glowing brighter than their aureoles at times; when she armed them with non-lethal weapons even a bare club looked majestic in whichever hand grasped it.

Outside the Arboretum and the bubble of havens Marzanna had claimed in the first days of Her Ascendance, Aebbenary stagnated and starved almost as badly as it had during the false god's reign. The only difference now was that *this* rendition of a divine overlord had known the importance of compelling their love alongside mandating their worship and adoration.

Cosima could scarcely stand in one place whenever she thought of the injustice of it. She had to pace wherever she was, shaking out her agitation bodily or jumping into as fair of an unequal sparring session as she could manage.

For punishments if the Godlings and Saints wouldn't comply, she commanded them to disguise themselves with their Light and go into the city as a mortal to find someone to help. That could mean many things from repairing a dilapidated residence without payment, assisting elderly citizens in the market, or anything that helped someone out of the appearance of generosity if not a willing spirit.

Tokens fashioned from flower petals claimed from their source and transformed by her Light to track their obedience would turn from nature's shades to pure gold once their keeper followed her command. Anyone who brought back a colorful petal would receive harsher punishment, like long periods of physical labor or a period of isolation and imprisonment wherever Fiammetta usually stashed her prisoners.

Though most of them despised her, no one returned without a golden petal after she told them that.

It will be a long time before my huntresses have another challenge, Cosima thought as she strode amongst them on the training field, correcting this or that one and breaking up a frequent squabble with a whack from a quarterstaff she'd taken a liking to. *They're all so proud and sensitive to the tiniest insult. Giving such peacocks physical weapons along with their Light might not be a good idea…*

Her ladies were always in her thoughts. The distraction of missing them made her a poor supervisor and ill-tempered by the end of each day. The lack of progress with the Godlings and Saints brought each of the huntresses to mind, like whenever Giric fumbled a shot—even with a crossbow—or Druda tried to cut a newer Saint's throat again.

Grisel had a temper like that, but she'd never hit that hard, or *Palmira would love to try swinging that flail around,* and, *Ricla would have won that match against both of them and helped them up after,* tormented her each day. *Iulia—*

Konetta—

Those thoughts swam away from her with all haste, their tails flashing an inscrutable reflection in the daylight that waited patiently for her to open her eyes again. Cosima had disappointed Iulia: loving her then still hadn't changed her for the better or expunged the greed blemished throughout by divine sway.

Konetta had sacrificed herself for Palmira's safety and Lilias—*Lilias* of all beings, their Saintly tormenter's abominable issue—and possibly her life. Cosima wondered if Fiammetta had sniffed out their relationship somehow, or if she had targeted Konetta because she sensed the kindness in her.

She's our weakest, Cosima's thoughts nudged her as she floated miserably through her days while circumstance forced her to appear at all times like she was enjoying her life more than she ever had before. *So frail. Fiammetta would have pounced on that the moment she noticed.*

Sovanna's attack did nothing to raise the wounded spirits of her trainees; Cosima's insistence that the ones well enough to train still did so angered them further. More Godlings trudged into Aebbenary in dejection, chafing under her orders to make use of themselves in some way in Goddess's city. Only the news that Däard had returned triumphant from chastising Sovanna for her rabid grab for more power—"to run back to that fetid bog", one Godling spat during his sparring with a Saint who had more natural talent than her—made all of them smile and crow for hours as if *they* had taken their vengeance and not one of their minders.

Cosima had her doubts. She watched Däard for the rest of the day and through the celebration that night where Marzanna expected him to take his turn as Her companion. To her eyes the First Saint looked pallid, distracted, and most of all unenthusiastic about anything going on in the world outside his melancholic thoughts.

If it was anyone else she would have sympathized. Cosima couldn't help blaming Däard in part for everything her family had endured and what her huntresses must be enduring now in the bowels of the palace, in Fiammetta's private wing where very few guests were allowed to tread. Surely if Goddess loved him as much as She claimed there was something he could have done to stop the tragic events of her Jubilee.

Her holy charges ignored their parents or benefactors and cavorted the same as they always had with boasting, bored wantonness, and disregard for any pleasure but their own. Cosima surveyed them in anxious despair, hoping Goddess was too captivated by Däard to notice the lack of change in their behavior. That Fiammetta—who pouted in her finery while Marzanna snubbed her—would be too absorbed by trying to force Goddess to acknowledge her to be catty about the Godlings and Saints.

That was her own folly, though. When had those three ever paid attention to anyone but each other? Barring Goddess's frequent, meaningless affairs She had at random with all types of mortals and Her sick obsession with owning Bettina down to her soul, of course.

This thought made Cosima sit up straight, the cup in her hand more of a temptation than ever rather than an annoying prop she had to keep track of to look like she was trying to have a good time with the others.

Of course these divine beings are wicked. Why wouldn't they be? All their experience is either indulgent neglect or harsh retribution for mistakes that barely matter. Cosima battled her sympathies with every mental weapon she could think of, to the point of distracting herself from the reality staring her in the face the longer she spent in the company of the Godlings. *And I've been treating them worse than ever to force them to become more than they know how to be without meaningful guidance.*

Now that she looked rather than bemoaned her own existence, the signs of change shone everywhere she surveyed. There, in the corner of the room: two Saints running drills with each other rather than drinking themselves as sick as a divine child could get or skirt chasing. Two or three Godlings patrolled the entrances: not due to fear since Goddess could protect all of them with no effort, but because Cosima had ordered them to ostensibly keep eyes out for Sovanna in case she wanted to make mischief again. (Not that she cared greatly what Sovanna might ruin, but because it would look better for her in Marzanna's eyes if word reached Her about these precautions.)

Agnese caught her attention from afar, though Cosima was sure she hadn't meant to. More than her halo shone in the amber torchlight illuminating the palace courtyard. To match the unsullied flanks of her unicorn, she had transformed her auburn hair to cherry blossom pink with a pearly sheen; unlike the lesser of her mothers, most of her skin sported thousands of freckles, many of which she'd willed by Miraculous whim into the same luster as her hair.

She murmured soothing things to her beast while coaxing it to eat handfuls of grain from her palms—good, solid food rather than the wasteful fluff most divine beings fed their Miraculous pets. When she felt Cosima's gaze she whipped around to look at her...but she didn't frown. She didn't mouth a curse word or stab her middle finger up at Cosima for daring to perceive her.

Agnese nodded. *Respectfully.* When Cosima answered with an

awkward wave of acknowledgement, she nodded again and went back to caring for her beast with what looked like genuine consideration and responsibility.

Some of them can be saved. With time, care, and close supervision, someone could make decent people out of these idle lions.

Goddess's words carried on the evening breeze, muted but audible. She hadn't addressed anyone but Däard, so Cosima knew she wasn't meant to hear what she was about to.

"…too long, I know. These wasteful laws of nature require delicate circumvention. I haven't forgotten My promise."

Cosima considered the eggplant-colored liquid in her cup and pretended to be absorbed by it so she could continue eavesdropping.

"It's not that." Däard's reply sounded curt.

"Then what is it? Did Sovanna wound My peerless swordsman?"

"She would not."

Cosima turned in her seat—a throne-like settee where she was supposed to recline alongside her Mother and Her consorts—to watch Goddess frown and sit up from Her own lounge.

"Talk to me. I ache at the sight of your discomfort," She said to Däard. The braid She or Her attendants had twisted a blue sash through dropped over Her shoulder as She leaned toward his seat— right beside Her own—and turned him tenderly to look at Her. He obediently followed Her will, but Cosima saw his eyes drop to his lap after a few seconds of peering into those terrible, treacherous golden eyes.

"Your Priest is still missing. I am worried for Your sake."

"That." Chuckling, Marzanna patted Däard's stretched-out leg fondly. "You know he runs off as he wills. He'll crawl back on his bony knees any day now."

"He's been gone longer than usual. Do You know where he is?"

The conversation paused as Goddess thought about it.

"…No. Hm."

"That last time You couldn't find him—"

"There is *nothing* he can do to Me. Even if he stole his skin away from Me in a moment of passion—"

Däard risked interruption. "He has his flesh *and* You can't find him? How could You not tell me? It's my job to—*Marzanna.*"

The last word was a hiss of annoyance blended with desire. Goddess had glided Her beringed hand to the joint between his muscular thighs and began to rub him there. Cosima rolled her eyes in disgust and turned away, but she continued to listen.

"You worry too much. I promised you I'd always take care of you a long time ago. Don't you trust Me?"

Däard didn't say anything else. Marzanna massaged him, slow and practiced based on the little sounds he made and the creaking of his lounge as he arched closer to Her hand. Cosima was revolted but compelled to look one last time—and perceived with a sinking feeling that his responses were purely physical. Goddess played him like a lyre but he felt nothing but what his body had to.

He stared up at the sky with empty hazel eyes. *How can't She see he doesn't want this?*

Cosima hadn't been the only one listening. Fiammetta whined something under her breath, her lovely face broken by a heartrending twist of loss and confusion. *Even she doesn't know why Goddess has all but discarded her. How can that be?*

Fiammetta was mad by origin. It worsened the longer Goddess played with how long She could ignore her before romantic duty bid Her tolerate Fiammetta's smothering adoration again. Däard was *miserable* and had been so for years. Cosima wondered how She'd missed that. If even he suffered so deeply in the bosom of Goddess's love, if the most favored woman in the realm had lost Goddess's regard without knowing why, what hope was there for the rest of them?

Drinking did the trick for the rest of the celebration. Alcohol flowed readily in the palace, poured by pretty, scantily-clad servants who existed only to pour Aebbenary's famous wines, liquors, or aged brews into whichever hand and cup lounged their way as they walked circuits through the eternal gatherings. Cosima hadn't drank this much since well before she had fled the city to escape her Mother's intermittent fawning or displeasure as well as the gaping absence Bettina's self-imposed exile had left in her former home.

Drunkenness promised to erase the guilt that ripped her to shreds inside whenever she had a pause in serving, celebrating, or cheerfully obeying Goddess or Fiammetta to remember that one of her huntresses was dead. Murdered by the red-haired harpy she smiled and conversed with to please Marzanna.

They'll all be distracted tonight, Cosima mused to herself as she bade her farewells to the gathering and Goddess as soberly as she could appear to be, with the excuse of an early morning to grant her permission to leave. *I should look for the others once things loosen up here. This will be a pleasure party soon enough.*

Marzanna didn't care; She was probably about to fuck Däard in public again as soon as Her daughter left. Cosima supposed she was lucky enough to foresee the outcome of their conversation and take her leave before Goddess forgot she was present.

She searched. Every room, every crevice, down to the depths. Bold in her inebriation—prepared to arm herself with it as an excuse if Fiammetta retired earlier than usual—she raided Fiammetta's room with her physical presence and her Miraculous will to seek her friends.

As always, she found nothing. No trace of them. Fiammetta had begged Goddess to give her the huntresses for "handmaidens", but none of them had probably ever been in this room.

Cosima's power flared. Everything was too much. She remembered that drinking like this stimulated her senses beyond belief. She could hear the music from the celebration a couple miles away pounding in her ears like the surf; the breeze on her skin blowing in from windows open to the air during this summer night scratched like nails. The stone walls stank of damp and salt and every body that had walked through this hall earlier that day.

The overstimulation sent her fleeing as a spear of Light to her old room in the Holy Tower, far and away from the noise of the palace. Goddess had kept it in good condition, as if waiting for Cosima to inevitably return to live here. The furniture and linens were as impeccable as if they were new; pansies spilled over their painted vases on vines that weren't their nature, equally preserved.

Slamming the door behind her, Cosima collapsed on the queenly bed at the center of the circular room and stared up at the ceiling as it wavered before her eyes. Not from tears this time—from the wine.

This is it. I've failed, she thought. *Even if I find a way to remove Goddess from this world I won't find them in time. Fiammetta will kill them first—*

A new, strange sound reached her through the tempest. Something digging into the outer wall, bit by bit, climbing higher. None but divine ears would have been able to catch it. Cosima would have been afraid if she didn't recognize the presence accompanying the sound in its rash ascent from the ground up to her window.

She had granted an artifact of blessed claws meant to climb any wall to Iulia at one of her birthday celebrations the huntresses had thrown a few years ago. They had come in handy for hunting divine beings and in the forest, since they worked well on trees as well as buildings.

What are you *doing here?* Cosima's interest stirred. Her jaw hung, loose and relaxed as the rest of her, before everything tightened and she leapt off the bed to stare at Iulia as she appeared outside the radial window.

Hanging from the tower window with her climbing hooks embedded in the rock, Iulia gaped at her in equal shock.

"You're here," she mouthed from outside.

The window between them offended her by existing: Cosima ran to it and lifted her fist to smash it to pieces before she reconsidered. Anyone outside might overhear; the shards might cut Iulia.

All this power is good for something, Cosima thought—definitely euphoric from the wine as well as this new arrival—and used her Light to haul Iulia bodily through the window like it was water that left both of them dry.

Well, not *dry*. Cosima surveyed Iulia's trim muscles and the suggestion of curves she was well-acquainted with and felt desire curl low in her belly, more demanding by the second.

Iulia stood a little apart from her, gingerly holding herself away. After what felt like the slow crawl of an eon spent alone or in this viper nest, Iulia was *here,* and she smelled like leather and sweat and the cinnamon pastries she must have eaten for a terrible dinner. Weariness deepened the faint lines around her eyes, and stress had put dark circles beneath them, but other than that she was as healthy as Cosima had left her in the treehouse.

"You're *here!* Thank oblivion—I thought I'd have to ransack the whole tower to get to you. We should talk—"

"I don't want to." Cosima didn't let her go. Iulia sniffed her hair: a remnant of a lover's familiarity.

"You're drunk. I didn't know you could even get tipsy anym—hey!" Iulia's protest smothered away as Cosima pushed her against the window she'd transformed from glass to water and back again to kiss her. Iulia had always had the softest lips she'd ever kissed.

There was another prize here—even while fighting, even when either of them had casually romanced other people before their relationship, Iulia had never been able to turn down a proper kiss. She tried this time, her muffled protests dying quick deaths against Cosima's mouth as she pressed her against the window with her own weight, but ultimately failed.

Come on, Cosima found herself thinking through the suddenly cheerful haze of the wine, *make that noise I like, Iulia. The one that breaks both of us.*

"I have something to tell you," Iulia told her around their kisses, fighting hard for self-control. "I came…to rescue you…Goddess sent word through the city that you're home for good a-and…*mmm,* wait…"

Cosima broke away with a huff of frustration. "I don't want to talk. Please, I am *done* with talking. All day I've had to—" Here she was, engaging in more *hated* conversation, when she could be…

Iulia protested again with an annoyed grunt as Cosima went to work undoing the straps of her tight leathers. When she went to slap her hands away Cosima grabbed both of them and kissed the ridges of her knuckles, heedless of the climbing claws still secured around her fingers. She banished them—temporarily—with her will.

"You want this. *Badly.* I do too. Why fight it?"

"Because." Iulia answered peevishly. When Cosima looked at her with one eyebrow quirked, she flicked her eyes up to the ceiling and huffed.

"Give me my gear back."

"After."

Fairly snarling with impatience, she yanked the rest of Iulia's clothes off with Miraculous help and nudged her legs apart with her knee. Iulia's sex was right there, though she balanced at a hover to avoid resting it on Cosima's knee. Cosima felt her legs shake with resistance neither of them wanted before she slid her hand between Iulia's legs to glide her fingers against her. Inside her, slipping in and out with ease.

Wet, she thought, satisfied and smiling. *Already so wet for me.*

"There's no after. We can't—Cosima, we *can't*—"

In answer, Cosima withdrew her playful fingers…and balanced her knee a little higher against the window between Iulia's legs, knowing she wouldn't resist. As soon as she moved Iulia did too, already starting to grind her pubic area against Cosima for the friction she craved.

"I'll stop if you tell me no again," Cosima promised. "I'll let you go that instant."

Her surrender was gruff but still so, so delicious. Cosima could feast on this satisfaction for days.

"One time. Once."

"You'll only come once? That doesn't show much faith in me."

"I'm not coming for you. It's for me."

"I see. You're using me for your own pleasure."

"Mmm…fuck you."

"Did I say you couldn't?" Cosima teased. This should have surprised her—she'd never been good at this, or any skill she'd learned with painstaking effort had been lost the longer she went without a bedmate—but Iulia ate it up. She distracted her with her rocking, the scent of her, the exposed arch of her throat as she rested the back of her head against the window and let Cosima completely support her weight.

Cosima was wet by now too—yearning for Iulia's familiar tongue between her legs, aching to feel something more than the delightful torture of helping someone else reach the peak of pleasure while waiting for them to carry you up later. She couldn't say if it was the lingering effects of the divine wine or the urges of her lust that made her break a taboo she had put on herself and dive into Iulia's hectic, orgasmic thoughts.

"Use me then, Iulia. I know you're desperate. I know you've wanted me every single night since we've been apart. You probably slid your busy little hand down there and fucked it, wishing it was mine."

"Get out of my head!" Iulia gasped, rocking her hips faster. Though Cosima wasn't fond of talking, she knew how much Iulia loved it during love-making…and, suddenly, pleasing her had become the most important thing in the world. It hadn't been like this before: Sovanna had been trapped in her own head, too aware of how one misuse of her strength could break Iulia before time naturally separated them forever.

What had changed now? Despite her distraction and lust, Cosima stored her curiosity for later.

Iulia came, shuddering and gasping on her knee. Wetness slicked Cosima's leg, but she was nowhere near done.

"We need to talk. I have new—"

"This first." Cosima let her drop, gently; Iulia clung to her shoulders for balance and barely protested when Cosima turned her around and guided her hands to balance against the window so she could bend over. Before she could protest the position, Cosima grabbed one of her hips—after kissing the little stretch marks she spotted there—and slid her other hand back between Iulia's legs.

"Fuck. *Fuck,* someone might see or, *ahhh*…hear…" Gasping around the steady thrusts of Cosima's fingers inside her, Iulia matched her rhythm without consciously trying.

"I don't care who sees or hears or stands under this window to watch. You're going to keep coming for me until I decide it's my turn. Say yes," Cosima ordered. When Iulia pretended not to hear her she dropped to her knees and nestled her face between Iulia's legs.

She moaned at the first flick of Cosima's tongue against her clit. "Ahh…*fine.* Yes, yes, I'll keep coming for you."

"You taste *incredible.*" It took Cosima a second to realize she'd moaned this into Iulia's folds so it was unintelligible; she repeated it in

Iulia's mind. Somehow, Iulia still had some pride. When Cosima felt her hesitate she worked to bend it, sucking purposefully on her clit and circling two fingers against the sensitive ridges inside her as long as it took to make her relax again…then tighten, close to another climax.

Her own core pined for touch. While Iulia came, loud as ever, Cosima pushed her palm against herself and rubbed, still licking and sucking on Iulia to make her delight last as long as possible. After the tide ebbed, by mutual agreement they moved together—Cosima lay on the ground and Iulia crouched over her, riding her face with luscious dominance as she worked up to another orgasm.

Out of kindness, perhaps, she *did* lean back a little to feel how wet Cosima was. Before Cosima could protest—this was supposed to be all for Iulia, she hadn't asked for pleasure for herself—Iulia rotated and pulled up Cosima's flimsy celebration dress to kiss her below as well. Neither of them calculated the time that passed while they pleased each other this way: they kept going because neither of them wanted to stop.

When Iulia's fatigue caught up with her she rolled off, hoarse from the sounds she'd made. Cosima pursued, undaunted, but limited herself to dragging one last orgasm out of her with her fingers and mouth before she collapsed on the ground next to her. They caught their breath together without conversation.

After a while, Cosima sat up on her elbows and turned to her. Iulia matched and met her with a chaste kiss after she swiped her forearm across her mouth to clean some of Cosima's residue off.

"That was *one* way to welcome me into the belly of the beast."

"I missed you." To Cosima's ears her unrefined confession sounded like she was referring to the weather; she couldn't let that stand. "I finally realized what I've done by hurting you. You might not want to hear this apology again, but I will say it. I'm sorry, Iulia."

Konetta's specter lay between them. Who would speak her name first? Cosima imagined she could see it turning like a bauble on a string in Iulia's mind, unwanted but unforgettable.

"I hear you," she said with gruff finality that signaled how reluctant she was to continue in this vein; she changed the subject. "I found out where Fiammetta is keeping our girls."

The rest of them. Whoever is left. Iulia didn't add that: Cosima's spite did.

"Mother hid the girls from my senses. I didn't get to one of them in time...so, even if I can wrest them from Fiammetta's hold, *you* will be their savior."

Iulia took a long time to respond to that. She rolled onto all fours then stood up, reaching her arms above her head to stretch and work the kinks out of her back. Cosima heard the familiar *pop* of her hip cracking. She started to pace toward the window, realized she was still completely nude, and sighed as she stole a velvety blanket from the bed they hadn't bothered using to wrap around herself.

"Well. Even you wouldn't have found anything while drinking yourself into a ditch," Iulia said with a sideways glance at Cosima as she arranged the blanket. The unshaven side of her hair was half-pulled out of its sloppy braid; tufts near the part line stuck straight up.

She's adorable, Cosima thought.

She didn't mean to laugh, she really didn't. It frothed out of her anyway. She wanted to choke it back down at the look on Iulia's face. They'd just been holding each other in passion, Iulia made a dig at her to provoke a fight, and she *laughed...*

"I deserve that." Cosima nodded; she tried to stop, but it took wiping her face with her hands to smear fresh tears away to still the movement. "You caught me at a bad minute. But I haven't been idle here. Can we—"

"Right. Let's worry about that." Iulia cut her off. Seeing past the stony look on Cosima's face, that rigid cloak of purpose that looked so at odds on her after everything they'd done in this room softened. "I missed you too. You know I did."

Enough to forgive me? Enough to take me as I am—monstrous divinity, hunger, and selfishness—and stay with me forever? Cosima couldn't say that. She had been the one begging her to focus on greater matters. Besides—deep in her heart, she knew forever meant something greater to Iulia as a mortal. What meant "forever" for her was but one lifetime in the hundreds Cosima might experience.

If Goddess didn't slaughter all of them before this was over.

"I didn't get to them in time either. I stayed with Palmira in the treehouse to comfort her after you took Lilias away. She's been keeping things tidy to prepare for us all to return…and I'm not so calloused I wouldn't help." Iulia said. She looked like she wanted to relent in the face of her discomfort, but Cosima's disloyalty had shut the door against the risk of further hurt and her affectionate nature.

"Who…" Cosima swallowed; since she had remained sitting up on the floor she moved to stand as well. "Who did we lose?"

"Ricla."

Not Konetta. At least she wasn't so far gone as to savor the reprieve in her sorrow more than she honored the sense of loss that speared through her at the name Iulia spoke. Shame crawled beneath her skin, though, too hot to bear. Cosima took her time arranging her dress around her body to mostly cover it again and switched to pacing from one dresser or chair and back to keep focus.

"I've waited to save them because I knew I'd need your power to get them out. Cosima, they're in the cathedral. *Inside it.*" Iulia failed to hide her dismay any longer. Cosima gave her a moment to say the rest. "That bitch changed them. No one else could transform humans into stone but *keep them alive inside it.*"

No…it can't be! She went to Iulia—figuratively floating across the room as if trapped in a nightmare—and tapped on her forehead, asking for access.

Iulia showed her the last ancient relic of the false god's realm, derelict but for the portions Goddess had reserved for Her Shining Court. Desperate for any new lead, Iulia had decided to explore the ruins on her own to find her friends. The memories shifted, blurring in the shuddering aftermath of lasting trauma, but then faces appeared before Cosima's mental eyes.

Stone faces. Elegant statues of nude women curved and swirled together from marble no natural phenomenon had built from the earth. The longer Cosima looked, the more she recognized the frozen faces of Grisel, Piera, Konetta, all the others through Iulia's appalled eyes…while beneath the stone the spark of their life wavered with pain and awareness of their prison, reaching out for anyone nearby so they could sense their presence...

When she flung herself mentally and bodily out of Iulia's memory she stumbled, pacing backwards from the bed she waited on with her hands over her eyes. If it would help to erase the dread Iulia had shared with her she would pluck them out now.

For all Cosima's constant fears and anxieties, she had forgotten to anticipate the chaos divine power could breed.

XXIV

Bettina

The dust of a dying world transformed into a lush landscape untouched by decay as Bettina passed through the gates. All around, in every direction she looked, a jungle of fertile land brimming with vivid, tropical hues overwhelmed her senses even more than her experience with Magisend in her sensual den had. Musk and sandalwood dulled into lively, exhilarating floral scents from the thousands of different blooms that opened to welcome her.

Us. She remembered. *Magisend?*

He'd been at her side the whole time she'd stood still, naked and ogling the wonders in sight. She had last seen him beneath her, felt him thrusting up into her while his sinuous threads both held her up and hypnotized her with their weird grace.

Now he had changed again. Armor that looked decorative but surely wasn't clung to his slender form, highlighting the lean muscles that had moved and flexed beneath her. It looked black at first, but it was green under the spears of sunlight that stabbed through the leaves as invisible wind shifted them now and again in time with the garden's own living, breathing cadence.

Nothing of his skin showed other than some of his neck and his face; his hair was pulled back into a knot on his head, sterile and subdued.

It was him as she knew him, as part of her had brought parts of him into reality—and it *was not*.

"Swan-of-gold. You've come." His voice carried a layered quality similar to when the Archives used him to convey knowledge. Nothing black lingered in his eyes or his shadow: everything glowed enticing emerald or malachite.

Abruptly ashamed, Bettina folded her wings—one around her torso, the other against her backside. Gooseflesh rose on her skin at the brush of her own feathers, but it was better than proceeding nude next to this unfamiliar warrior.

"I came for knowledge and truth." The notion of addressing him by the name he'd given her never crossed her mind. This wasn't Magisend anymore.

"You did not. You came to save your son from his own destiny. And—" The censure in his gaze flickered; surprise almost lightened his apathetic features before resolution smothered it. "This Archivist. You want him as well."

There could be many meanings to that word. Bettina considered all but the one she wanted nothing to do with and answered for the others.

"I *had* to want him to get here. That or try to hurt myself unto death again. Is it too much to ask you to understand why I chose the want rather than the pain, Speaker?"

"You cannot lie here."

Flowers folded into themselves, reeking of mildew and carrion. Singing birds dropped from their branches stone dead while snakes by the dozens slithered from the foliage littering the ground to devour them whole.

"I didn't lie! I—" Bettina backed away, lifting her hands in surrender, but the gate behind her had closed.

Locking her in.

"Last chance," The Speaker said, speaking in a low rumble punctuated by that *other* that possessed him.

Bettina licked her dry lips nervously.

"Fine. I want him for more than pleasure. Is that enough?"

No reply—splendid and uncanny in his armor, he waited for her to offer more.

"Is Magisend...still with you? In that body?"

"I'm here, Bettina."

Amazement pulled her in to investigate the sound of his voice. Just his.

"What happened to you? Why can't you—"

The Speaker approached her. He didn't come too close before he held out his hand—gloved and gauntlet-clad for battle—and waited for her to take it. "The garden is willing to show you what you need to see. Walk with me."

Bettina lingered by the entrance, trying not to wring her hands. This was the offer she'd worked for, the means to defeat Goddess and protect Cristoval and Cosima forever might be in her grasp, but...Magisend had helped her get here. If she didn't make sure he wasn't hurt or lost that would put her at a level of heartlessness she scorned in other divine beings.

"Tell me he's all right in there first."

All the animals, familiar or twisted and bizarre, fled from The Speaker's wrath, but he only looked at her without blinking until— ashamed again—Bettina lowered her gaze.

"You will see what you need to see. Walk with me."

"Which way?" She looked up instead of ahead. "The canopy is too thick to see the sky, let alone fly above."

The garden hearkened to her human requirements and reallocated its flora and fauna in a hypnotic swirl of color that made her brain shrink away from the commotion. Seconds after she'd finished protesting, a cobblestone path led far and away through the garden that might not ever end. The Speaker yet waited for her to take his hand: when she did, he led her onto the path.

It wasn't cobblestones that constructed the path—it was pearls. Thousands or millions of lustrous pearls laid out for her journey through this secret, forbidden sanctuary. Bettina had to wonder if it was her own preference for pearls that had influenced the garden, or if its appearance was mere coincidence.

Magisend's—The Speaker's—hand closed tight around her fingers as if he would yank her around like an irate mother with a naughty child, but he led her impassively and without force along the path. His piercing skin could not prick her through his gloves.

"This garden is older than mankind. More ancient than most gods, current or lost to the vacuity of the ages. What you see here might not have any context you will be able to comprehend, but truth will not be a stranger to you by the end of this pilgrimage."

Though Bettina was a Saint and accustomed to being in the presence of the Miraculous, even she could never convince herself that anything about this garden was ordinary. She nodded along to The Speaker's explanation and surveyed the jungle utopia with child-like wonder and unease.

The canopy above didn't allow much sun down to the ground, but the area was lit from so far within it should have been total darkness at the outskirts of the garden where she had entered. Yet her eyes were not darkened by the untold distance. The lack of celestial warmth didn't leave her freezing and alone in this realm out of what even divine beings could comprehend of space and time.

Something dropped in front of Bettina and rolled away, bouncing ahead on the path they walked. When she looked up, startled, another fell—her reflexes helped her catch this one. The gift of a fuzzy, fragrant apricot tempted her with its scent and its promising flesh.

Apricots symbolize beauty, Bettina thought. *What message is here?*

She didn't have to wait long to find out. Above her and The Speaker, birds began to caw and swarm. Wings flapped in ominous thunder—Bettina thought she heard *real* thunder from whatever sky hung above the confining trees—and descended in a spiral of dozens toward the fruit she held. She held it out to them, thinking nothing of it…then yanked her hand back as the first bird to reach her snapped its beak at her fingers and revealed ghastly little teeth that would've drawn blood.

The Speaker watched impassively as she hurled the apricot into the farthest copse of bushes she saw and frowned at the shrieks from the avian cluster above as they followed it…and vanished.

"What did you learn?" he asked as the garden quieted.

"Nothing new." Disappointment didn't dull her hunger; she'd

worked up an appetite before this. "Goddess craves me for my beauty and will do anything to have me forever. At least the garden knows what I'm asking."

Bettina shrugged and bit into the next apricot that fell. She felt it changing her as juice dripped down her gullet. Nearby, to the right of the path, condensation from the leaves as if from recent rainfall gathered and swirled into a mirror to show her what had changed.

From one bite, Bettina's youth had bled away. She was not elderly by mortal standards for the years she'd lived, but her skin sagged and creased, her womanly shape softened from its taut curves, and the hair flowing down her back changed almost completely to grey.

She felt it all before the sweetness of the apricot had diminished. The sight that greeted her eyes barely gave her pause. *Is this the worst the garden can do?*

Meeting her own faded yet still matchless blue eyes, Bettina bit into the apricot again and watched her vitality return the same way it had gone. A quarter century of wear dropped from her like an unwanted veil.

"I know I am old. Or I *should* be. Beauty can be given and taken away by Goddess, is that what the garden is trying to tell me?"

"That's one possible interpretation." The Speaker plucked the watery mirror from mid-air and molded it into a less reflective sphere. He blew on its surface and watched intently as the sphere became a diamond the size of a child's ball.

Then he hurled it away from him without warning or emotion, and Bettina wondered if there was a message in that too.

"Goddess should not have made us," she pondered aloud, "like She made all those Godlings and Saints to admire briefly before She casts their priceless presence away like it means nothing. Am I right?"

The Speaker did not reply. He gestured for them to proceed on the path, so she did. *After* tossing the twice-bitten apricot into the bushes.

They had nothing to occupy them while they walked. Bettina waited impatiently for her next encounter to reveal something she could use. Her hand wilted in The Speaker's firm grip, but he did not let her go.

"You cannot wander," he assured her after her second attempt to politely extract herself. "It is not permitted."

"What *is* permitted?"

A sideways look, but one without the comprehension or wit of Magisend's usual guise. This version of the Archivist was devastatingly desirable and tantalizingly different, but she did not trust her instincts when it came to meeting that stern gaze.

"You may ask a few questions of us. Not every answer requires a vision or prophecy."

"Thank you." Bettina dove right in. "Does Goddess know of this place? Or how to get in? What or who has She been searching for in the Archives?"

Some of these things Bettina had already begun to guess. But she had been wrong—grievously wrong—before. There were no spare chances waiting for her in this disturbing branch of paradise.

"Goddess knows of this dimension. We fed Her this knowledge to keep you a while longer. She does not have the keys, not yet, and the garden has placed greater demands on Her as the price of entry. Greater than anything She has paid so far to commit Her sins." The Speaker paused, considering. "We do not think She will pay. She seems to be hunting for any way around the garden's requirements."

As they proceeded along the curvilinear path she had a sense that they were moving toward the source of luminescence at the heart of the garden. She was curious enough to want to ask about it, but reserved that question for a later she hoped would come. Currently all she could think about was the question The Speaker had evaded.

Patience, she reminded herself again.

"Is the Priest here?"

"He walked a different path." He sounded indifferent at first, but something washed beneath the surface of The Speaker's face that made Bettina grow cold beneath the comfort of her wings. "*Very* different. He must atone for his own sins."

The opportunity for more questions had to wait. Bettina stopped when The Speaker did; she peered into the unrelenting trees to search for her next revelation. A question popped in her mind, vowing she'd regret bringing it into this all-knowing dimension, as the rest of the garden vanished in fog to highlight the grove that arrested her gaze with its sights.

If our existence is a sin, she thought as her feathers and bones began to tremble, *what can any of us do to atone but end our existences?*

A girl resembling Cosima played with butterflies in the clearing. Others joined her, laughing when they caught one and released it, or scolding when another child was too possessive or rough with the fragile creatures. They were all children, but Bettina began to recognize them: Marzanna, Easoren, and their first, horned offspring Sovanna. Däard and Fiammetta. Cristoval and Crespin and then herself. The sight of them all playing in harmony made something twinge in her soul.

The butterflies increased by hundreds the more of them the children caught, but their numbers tapered off about the same time as the children began to leave, divide into groups, or fall.

The slender red-head that was Fiammetta began to howl like an entire pack of wolves and ran away from the group to disappear in the jungle. Sovanna and Cristoval carried Crespin into the bushes after he collapsed under the weight of innumerable, white and gold butterflies. Not as many butterflies as Easoren, though, who shrieked like an unholy beast and fought against gossamer wings that wouldn't tear until he collapsed at the center of the clearing, disappearing entirely. Marzanna still danced and leapt about happily, Her grip on Däard's arm iron as She forced him to play with Her until long past silver tears streaked down his boyish cheeks.

Cosima played alone until she noticed at last that something had gone horribly wrong with her innocent game. She moved to run to her mother—though they were both the same juvenile age—but Bettina had pursued Cristoval. Cosima hesitated, looking from one playmate to another to torturously decide who to help and who to abandon. By the time she decided, she was alone in the grove, and the consequences had already been meted out.

That hurt. *Both* of her children needed her. Bettina had spent too long fretting over Cristoval while trusting Cosima to her independence. Some things she couldn't change, even as her mother, but others…

"Watch," The Speaker commanded her. Bettina hadn't realized she'd closed her eyes until the word pried them open.

The beginning of this vision played out the same minus Crespin, but as the butterflies consumed Easoren, more children entered the grove. A living flame wearing the vague shape of a human toddler floated from Däard—who looked but did not embrace it—to Marzanna. Her holy delight turned ugly as She spat in its direction. It found Cosima next: she welcomed it for a while, but then sorrowfully gestured toward Sovanna, who made the same face Marzanna had...then embraced it, somehow knowing it wouldn't burn her.

A northern wind gusted away all the butterflies while adult Bettina watched her younger self dance frenetically before Marzanna, who didn't look at her as She focused on the entity that blew in with the icy breath of destiny.

When younger Goddess dashed toward the seething shadows of the new arrival, the Light in Her wake tumbled everyone else onto the ground. While the entity ran from her, circling the butterfly grove without leaving its boundaries, childish Bettina crawled to the others but collapsed before she made it to either of them. Blood oozed from her spine in a river that turned the soil red-gold.

While Fiammetta howled like a dozen wolves all around, matching the groaning wind that began to strip the leaves from the garden's tropical foliage, Marzanna caught the entity. It took the shape of a child the way the flame-child from Däard resembled fire; it struggled beneath Her claws.

She held on. Winter tempests shredded the clearing down to bare earth and cut everyone but Goddess and Her prey down to nothing as the flame-child flickered out in Sovanna's vanishing arms. Before long, nothing remained. Bettina was left staring into a terrible void that *looked* back in condemnation as if a portion of this—or all of it—was her fault.

"Come," The Speaker said beside her, startling her back into her current reality. "There will be more."

How many times must I watch my children die? Feel them *expire in one vision or another?* Bettina wondered. The anger she had felt at Goddess after the Jubilee and Magisend's healing sparked again, waylaying the patience she had promised to keep.

"Speaker."

Nothing.

"What did I just see? I think I understand some of it, but it was so much that I—"

"It is what might yet come to pass if you do not allow destiny to take its course."

This dire portend was all he offered for what felt like another few miles of walking along the pearl-strewn path. Outside of the razed grove Bettina had observed, endless life carried on without concern for the visions tailored to her search for truth.

When she started to glance behind, curious, The Speaker's hand yanked her closer and grabbed the back of her neck to stop her. He squeezed hard enough to hurt—hard enough for her to imagine her vertebrae snapping with one flex of his fingers.

"You cannot look back," he ordered her in the same tone he'd used to tell her she couldn't lie without consequences in the sacred primordial garden.

Bettina rasped her compliance and tried to push The Speaker away to regain her composure. He wouldn't go; before she could order how it had happened they were walking again, her hand in his.

"It's the Scholar She wants, isn't it? She wants to bring him back."

Then why hasn't She? Why doesn't Goddess yank him from his grave the same way She resurrected Easoren at the dawn of Her age?

"Goddess's urges are gluttonous. She would reclaim the very sacrificial force that purchased Her divinity and retain Her entitlement to that power in the same breath. Even this would not satisfy Her appetite. Even you would not—but you might be the bait that leads to Her unmaking."

"Is that my destiny? To bait Her into Her own destruction?" She didn't want to die, just as she didn't want to age alone, but Bettina tallied up the cost in her head and decided it would be worth it to buy eternal protection for her children. "Tell me how. Consider it done—I won't fight the All's will."

"Part of you is mortal yet to consider this a simple matter. Wait and see."

The trees ahead of them distorted. She feared another dizzying transformation that threatened the boundaries of her sanity with loss, but all they did was sway from the distant storm from the winter-blasted clearing. Swayed, and danced, and *walked alongside them*. Bettina was so taken aback she swerved closer to The Speaker—to Magisend—for what little protection he might offer.

"Speaker, where are we going?"

"Toward the basin." His reply was a long time coming. His gaze did not venture to either side, where the trees walked and began to hum in a susurrus that sounded like a choir of the old cathedral in Aebbenary. "You will not be permitted to enter—yet."

"Then why do we have to go there?"

"You will need to understand how to reach it so you can return."

The trees began to bring her things. Bettina supposed each item had meaning, but she was too unsettled to parse more than a rudimentary, overall understanding of each gift: a muslin cloth as white as snow, two golden coins sporting the likeness of a swan, rope dyed blood red, sticks of incense smelling of copal, and palmfuls of fresh basil leaves to crush for their aroma.

She began to guess what these things were for after the coins. She knew for certain by the time a tree studded with bioluminescent mushrooms in violet shades lunged from the light-washed shadows to press the basil leaves into her last free hand. Bettina partially unfolded the white cloth to hold everything like a sack and felt part of her beginning to break away to avoid what the rest of her knew was coming.

"These are burial trappings. Whose?"

The Speaker did not answer. He guided her to a stop before another clearing—larger than the last—and pointed ominously toward its heart for her to look and see.

She did, reluctant but resigned. This was why she'd come.

The trees that had come alive had gathered in the clearing and sunk roots in a random array all around it. Cooing, their leaves bustling, they extended their branches toward one another to link themselves into one creature. New fruit grew from the sprouts that flourished where they joined, shining peach or gold or red as the blossoms matured.

It looked so appetizing that Bettina's mouth watered. She almost drooled with desire to taste it, overcome with ravishing hunger and inexplicable thirst. The Speaker's iron grip held her fast as she lunged toward the fruit.

Shortly, after she struggled to leave him and wander toward the linked trees still singing after their faces had melded into their bark, she wanted to thank him. The fruit had inspired overpowering envy in other beings as well. One after another, they came from far and wide in the garden to steal the trees' bounty.

A multicolored horde of rats converged on the fruit from above. They couldn't eat all of them, but they made a significant dent in the abundance. They even wasted some while squabbling and fighting over one bulb or another. The abused fruit rolled on the ground below; the trees cried piteously at the sight.

A hooded serpent flashed silver scales in the light of the garden and roved around the trees with devastating haste, biting each rat and devouring it down to the last, who saw what was coming but failed to stop the inevitable. There were still many fruits left: the serpent savored the first two or three it swallowed to sate its bottomless hunger, but then it too began to waste what it had earned consuming its predecessors.

While it curled around a branch, hidden by foliage, something burst from one of the fallen fruits and the last rat the serpent had rejected rather than swallowing. Black and slimed from its cocoon of rot, it was grotesque to look upon, and Bettina wanted to turn away. The trees' suffering moved her, though, and the music of their tears changing into brittle laughter kept her interest.

A scorpion drenched in blackened fruit juice climbed the base of the joined trees and crept up behind the snake before it could bite into another fruit; it was fat and swollen by now, like it would burst any moment. After priming itself with growth to match the serpent's size, the scorpion leapt...and impaled it with its tail. Venom spewed from its chelicerae as it sank its fangs into the snake's neck and sucked all the undeserved bounty from its body.

It didn't stop until it left the serpent a shriveled husk. Then and only then did the scorpion begin to taste the fruit. The Speaker shifted his weight next to Bettina as, with systematic cunning none of the other animals had displayed, it spun golden webs like a spider throughout the clearing to eat each and every fruit down to its last drop.

Bettina clapped her hands over her ears, jerking backwards and away from her guide as the trees started to moan, louder than ever, and then scream. Without her touch the burial gifts they had passed to her vanished.

The trees' grief went on, and on, and *on*—the green life of the grove drained with only bare golden webs and the glossy scorpion left. Still the scorpion labored; still she ate, and ate, and ate. She did not waste, yet she took so much more than she needed after her destined foe— the serpent—had perished that more scorpions followed. They ate too, though not as greedily as their mother.

The snake stopped the rats, and the scorpion stopped the snake, Bettina thought from where she stood in safety. *Who will stop the scorpion?*

"Who indeed?" The Speaker said. He hadn't moved from where he had stood, pointing at the place of her vision, but he slanted his head down now to meet her startled gaze. "Who indeed, Swan-of-gold?"

"Your parables are transparent enough. Tell me how to stop Marzanna and I will!" Bettina dropped to her knees before him, clasping her hands in earnest reverence. "All I ask—"

"What you ask is impossible."

A tree broke away from the joined horde. It was so withered and twisted by rot that it barely resembled a tree. Bettina might have mistaken it for a human crone if she hadn't known better. It shuffled toward her, leaving the scene behind to proceed without interference.

"Impossible?" Bettina echoed, refusing to stand; she ignored the approaching crone even though it unsettled her. "That can't be. This garden let me in! I know the secret to saving Cristoval is here."

The Speaker bade her look toward the hamadryad crone. Bettina shook her head so violently tendrils of her hair struck her face. She spread her wings broad in offering and to block the sight of the decaying grove.

When she heard the sounds of trumpeting swans, though, she had to look.

A mother swan and her cygnets waddled into the heart of the clearing, shaded by the few remaining green leaves of the suffering trees. The mother had only one wing; one cygnet was weak, barely walking, and the other fretted endlessly over both of them, warbling her desolation.

The chief scorpion noticed them and looked away from one of its fruits high in the canopy to spin webs down to catch them. Alone they were vulnerable, but the swan and her cygnets huddled close and snapped sharp beaks at the webs before the strands stuck to their white feathers. Juice from the fruits dripped onto all of them but the sickly cygnet, strengthening them and helping them resist...but the webs were inevitable, and with most of the fruit gone and the trees going silent in sleep or death there was little else to be done.

The mother swan wrapped the cygnets in her remaining wing. Then she pushed the weak one into the closest web, just out of her reach, and moved to hide. So focused on the offering was the ruling scorpion that it hurried down to claim it, black dripping from its jaws...and when it pounced and started to feed on the dying cygnet, the mother and her remaining offspring jumped on the scorpion to peck it to pieces.

When it was done and their beaks were streaked with tarry gore, the rest of the scorpions fled. The fruit grew in peace—different than it was, smaller and all red rather than gold-touched, but still sweet. It took what felt like an age, but the trees began to wake and bloom again. New beings—badgers and deer and strange, winged lizards—ventured cautiously into the grove, but they did not abuse the privilege of tasting the fruit or overstaying their welcome.

The Speaker watched with her as the vision dissolved into vapor. He lowered his arm from its condemning point and slowly, softly rested it on her forehead in benediction.

349

"You have been deemed worthy and honorable, Bettina Valusius. We know you will accomplish what must be done of your own free will," he said to her.

"I won't!" Bettina shook her head again, rejecting his kindly touch; she was still on her knees, so she rushed to her feet to face him like a contender rather than a supplicant. "You cannot demand I do this. There is no mother on earth who would sacrifice a child, even for the whole world."

The green Light behind his eyes flared, and the crone she had studiously ignored emerged from the dissipating mist. Bettina flouted the obvious implication to pay attention to her and jabbed her finger at The Speaker's armored chest.

"You showed me a path where the sacrifice of my only son leads to victory over Goddess. I cannot pay that price!" Her voice started to break; tears filled her eyes, threatening to overflow.

"What of your boy? Is he your property, your pet? Do you decide his destiny to the end of the world along with dooming all creation to the rot of divine Light?"

"My…my children belong to themselves, yes—I've learned this. But—"

The accusing hamadryad got in her face, close enough for Bettina to trace the crack in the bark across her nose with a finger. Evidently the garden would make her acknowledge the crone rather than let that vision go.

"Every soul belongs to everything that made it. To everything it makes and has the potential to make. Your son is yours and not yours."

"He's mine enough to save! I'd give any—"

"Even if you did, little fruit, Goddess would not accept it in replacement of your bondage to Her. At odds with the divine Sinner, even destiny would not accept the offerings you would present. The only way forward is to lose the boy," said the crone.

No. Bettina utterly rejected this truth. She shouted her refusal. *"No!"*

"His life has been claimed. All that's left is the taking of it." The hamadryad smiled at her with mossy teeth—was it pity or a savor for the premature grief shredding Bettina's soul? "The taking of it, coveted apricot. The taking is what you can change."

Bettina tangled her fingers in her own hair and pulled so hard she ripped some out; it prickled as it grew back, fueled like vines by the garden's power. "Take me, then! I would make a better sacrifice anyway!"

"Goddess's Light and desire have marked you irrevocably. You will have your purpose after the deed is done—someone must lead Her to where Her power can be restrained." With the ravages of the trees' misery on her body, the crone stared at Bettina and provoked her into seeing all that had been done to her as a symbol of what the world would suffer if Goddess continued to grow in power and rule unchallenged. "Your son and daughter have their own parts. Even that madcap Priest has his role in what it will take to end Her dominion."

The worst of all was that Bettina could *see it*. Her mind's eye held the images of what was to come like the most vivid of prophecies—she would kill Cristoval. Gently, reverently, for he was already marked for death without cure by Goddess's vindictive punishment. Cosima—her pearl, her cygnet—would help her, but never forgive either of them.

Then Bettina would run. Fly, fleeing like she never had in her life, when Magisend's concealment vanished and Goddess pursued her all the way down here. To the garden basin where the trees and their destinies would be waiting. Marzanna might catch her, might flay or embrace her with that deadly golden touch, but Bettina would endure it. She could not unlearn what this garden had showed her, and she would regret it forever.

Falling, sinking onto her knees bruised from the path, Bettina covered her face in her hands and wept.

"No more," she moaned, rocking where she had collapsed. "I cannot bear another prophecy."

"Bettina."

She sniffed, looking up through her fingers at him before she dared lower her hands from her face. The crone was gone, vapor once more.

"Magisend?"

"..."

He couldn't say more than that, then. The Grand Archivist was not a being she should have sought succor from, yet she couldn't stop. She pulled herself up by clinging to his armor-clad legs and into a one-sided embrace. Solid warmth greeted her, but nothing else. He stood like stone while she sobbed into his shoulder, grateful for a bulwark against the garden even if for all intents and purposes she was alone.

When she was done, he changed. The Speaker had been the garden's means for conversing with her, as Magisend was the mouthpiece for the Archives, but the being that addressed her when she stepped back to look at him was neither one nor the other.

"We would mitigate your loss if we could, Swan-of-gold, but we cannot give you this vessel to keep. He will aid you during this trial, but after—"

"I do not want him." *A lie, a lie! You crave him like wine. You care for him down to your soul.*

Green eyes bored into hers. Bettina held her ground, still sniffling, daring the garden to contradict or threaten her again. Everything she had seen and heard already had wrung her dry…for now.

Magisend "the vessel" walked away. His armor made no sound, his passage did not move the bushes, trees, or vines as he left the path to venture into the garden. Bettina started to follow, but caught herself.

"Where are you…" she started, but the mists swallowed his figure. "…going."

The path wound on as far as she could see. He had told her not to look back; thus far she had obeyed. With The Speaker and Magisend gone, though, Bettina risked the quickest of backward glances to surmise how she should return to her reality.

There was nothing. Worse than nothing: the void that had eaten everything she'd encountered and still consumed all that did not encompass the place she stood.

Forward, she decided. *They need me alive. This is not my end.*

Bettina allowed herself a brief pause to wish wholeheartedly that this *was* her chance to rest forever rather than do the most assured thing to rip her soul apart. Then she followed the path all the way back to the gates of this accursed garden.

XXV

Cosima

Konetta was waiting for her in the dilapidated cathedral.

She had been ossified into a stone replica of herself. Beautiful, serene, but still solid rock. A statue could not wait with bated breath in the hushed, stagnant reverence of the old foundation of worship belonging to a god conquered long ago. Yet she did—Cosima felt her fluttering mind the moment she crept down through the crumbling roof of the sanctuary with Iulia right behind.

This had been a haven for the church's devout. Remnants of that decadent era lingered before Cosima's eyes as she looked around from where she stood in the center of the sanctuary. Silver candelabras, rosewood kneelers padded by torn blue velvet, and hundreds of other obscure artifacts Goddess must have been intimately familiar with in her days as a Fount.

Cosima imagined now, seeing these vestiges for herself, that Marzanna must *hate* that anyone knew of Her humble origins. She wouldn't put it past Her to look forward to the inevitability of the eternal years hereafter erasing any mortal knowledge of a time outside Her dominion.

"*You've come,*" Konetta said into her mind when Cosima could bear to look at her again. "*I bet the others you would.*"

"Can you do anything?" Iulia interrupted the beginning of their exchange with an impatient grunt as she kicked the corner of a rat-nibbled, faded blue runner lining the center aisle out of her way.

Cosima felt her stare like a javelin between her shoulder blades as she waited for her Light to flash in a surge of divine power. She didn't answer immediately. Cautious over the risk they'd taken, she scanned the wards of Light she'd positioned around Fiammetta's laughable idea of her own sphere of blinding, concealing illumination. Iulia huffed and grumbled a curse before she threw herself onto one of the pews nearest the rest of the statues.

"How did Ricla die?" Cosima asked out loud with one mental ear still cocked to listen for Konetta again. "Before this curse, or…"

Iulia pointed to a statue near the end, closest to the dais where Priests of the false god had spent centuries lecturing their flock on the tenets and practical applications of their religion. One statue in the line had fallen and shattered. The outer layers were as polished as the rest, but the fault lines of its collapse were stained like mortal blood.

Oh, brave huntress, I am sorry…

Cosima took a seat beside Iulia on her pew, not trusting her legs to hold her. They leaned against each other for solace.

Iulia filled her silence in like an old habit.

"I paid a forgotten old gravetender to say what he overheard. He was half-crazy—babbling about Light and the old false god. I got him to tell me Fiammetta was *"persecuting"* a few of the huntresses in her lair in the abandoned wing. She was trying to cast something, or perform some mad ritual: he heard women shouting angrily and pleading. Then Light blasted from the windows." Iulia's eyes closed briefly. "He's blind now. Must have been too ignorant to look away."

Another casualty. When will she answer for any of this? Cosima asked herself: the deeper self she rarely trusted answered.

Only if someone makes her.

It was Iulia's turn to get up and start pacing. "Can you undo this?"

"Fiammetta's power exceeds mine. Not by much…but enough."

"You just told me she was an idiot when it came to warding."

"She is: she focused on blinding me to their presence here, not keeping me out. But she has enough raw energy to prevent me from restoring their human forms."

"So we give up? Leave them stuck forever?"

"Of course not." Cosima wrung her hands where she sat. The pain on her joints from that encouraged her, and she dug her nails into her cuticles to provoke enough to stay grounded. "I can't overpower her, not with Goddess's backing, but I might trick her."

"Is it dawn?" Konetta asked. The sudden return of her voice provoked Cosima to stand and rush to the base of her statue. She hadn't dared touch the cool stone of her hem at first in case Fiammetta had been wiser than she appeared, but the magnetic pull of Konetta's quiet distress guided her there anyway.

"Dawn is soon. I'm going to find a way to rescue you."

She shouldn't keep Iulia in the dark any longer. Cosima drew in a deep breath and caught Iulia's attention from where she'd thrown herself into another pew as if determined to wreak destruction on anything left in the sanctuary.

"Konetta is here."

"Obviously, she's right—"

"She greeted us when we came in."

"Oh." A muscle twitched in Iulia's jaw. Konetta was probably the last person she wanted to hear from. "How is she? Under all that rock."

Cosima hunched her shoulders, then tried not to so her posture wouldn't look so guilty. "I'm not sure how she's even conscious…or if she's in pain."

"The sun is warm when it peers at us through these windows. I can't see anymore, but I feel those rays. It's so cold without them," Konetta said. Without preamble, she launched into whatever speech she had planned for when she'd anticipated Cosima's arrival. *"Tell Iulia I never meant to claim a heart that belonged to her when you see her again. Tell her my heart has always been open, and that it is open to her as it is to you, Cosima."*

"Iulia's here, Konetta!"

There couldn't be joy in this forbidding place. Even when congregants had strolled these ancient halls this holy ground had been tainted by the abysmal regret of the native occupants before Ioggenica's conquering boot had stamped most of them out. Cosima gleaned a pinch of relief from being able to share something that would bring solace to Konetta in her suffering.

"Tell her. One of us is always awake in here, sometimes two, and I never know how long my turn will last…"

Cosima repeated the original message. As Iulia listened, several emotions passed across her face: flushed discomfort, downturned brows of annoyance, and, lastly…

She approached the statue prison where Konetta beseeched her from within. "You pursued her without honor. She allowed it—I'm still thinking up something nasty for her. Now you want my blessing?"

"Not just your blessing. I admire you, Iulia. I think I could easily love you. I should have told you before."

Cosima winced. Konetta prompted her with a dull nudge to repeat her message to Iulia, who took a physical step back from the bold assertion like she wanted to bodily fight it off.

"Do you think that's funny? You seduced Cosima so you'll tolerate the noisy dog she comes with? *Ugh.* The sheer gall."

"You're not my dog. You're just…"

Iulia's face started to fall, but she tried to hide it. "If you have to add a "just" that means the just-ee is expendable. If you th—"

"You're mine. *She's* mine."

As she started to speak, it occurred to Cosima—like Iulia had told her during their confrontation after the Jubilee—that she should have started with something like this. That she could have had both of them, the right way, and wasn't it always better for more love to be born in the world?

Goddess loves Her consorts, Cosima's conscience whispered, *more than anything. Anyone. Isn't it love like that that caused your family and Aebbenary's suffering?*

Marzanna *did* place the highest of values on the concept of "more"—being more, doing more, *having* more. During their tentative sisterly visits during these dark days of huntress seeking, Sovanna and Cristoval had both theorized to her about the nature of the sickness that stemmed from divine beings to pollute the world. It subjugated mortal minds, seeping obedience and devotion from their comparatively frail bodies, often to the point of giving them physical symptoms that wasted them to bones.

For Godlings and Saints the indicators of the taint were more subtle. Down to the smallest grain of their being they could not conceive of decay or loss of any part of themselves. Thus, Sovanna had theorized solemnly—with Lilias laying stomach-down across her lap in a doze and Cristoval taking notes across the cluttered table—what the sickness claimed from them were the parts that kept them human, if not mortal. Their empathy; their charity; even some higher forms of knowledge that blurred the barrier between thinking person and instinctive beast.

"I am proof," Sovanna had murmured as she stroked Lilias's bath-damp hair, *"that even a Godling has something bestial within their soul that the right set of circumstances can unveil."*

Unease had constrained Cosima's attention despite the serene view of firelight from the cozy hearth flickering against the tall horns that protruded from Sovanna's head.

They might never know if Goddess had intended this rot to corrupt the world. If She was even aware of how She, changeless and undying, had performed the paradox of this bleak transformation. Cosima was resentful enough to lay the blame at Her feet regardless.

Pick, pick, pick went her nails against her skin after she reluctantly let go of Konetta's effigy; blood dripped on her dress. The ichor gleamed, echoing the aureole that illuminated Cosima at all times unless she concentrated on hiding it.

Warm, rough hands closed over hers, forcing her to stop. Cosima stared down at them until Iulia angled her face up to look at her where she stood stalwart in the ruined cathedral. She had waited, watchful, as Cosima worried out the rest of what she wanted to say and thought herself into a corner.

"I loved being yours. I'm not sure now that you were ever mine, though. What is in your heart, Cosima, that you cannot let me see?" Iulia asked.

They had made love, clinging to each other, briefly joyful, not long ago. What marred their connection hadn't been solved, but Iulia had never been able to stay away long. She made another offering of steadiness by resting her hands on Cosima's shoulders.

Iulia's compassion for her eccentricities had been such an incredible responsibility to answer. Had that been the problem before, Cosima wondered? Had she fled her honest heart in quest of something else—someone else—as a safeguard against the time when Iulia would eventually turn her back? Who could want a strange, brooding woman, Godling or not, benefactor of the huntresses aside, like Cosima?

These epiphanies made Cosima wonder if there was still something magical about the cathedral. Despite all the woe, the former god's greed, and the march of time that allowed this sacred hall to be forgotten, there must have been something that had tenderly wicked away the cobwebs strewn across her thoughts to let clarified air reveal the wishes of a heart she had never been familiar with.

No more silence, Cosima commanded herself. *Not with her.*

"Goddess maimed my mother and put a price on my brother's head that I've all but promised to fulfill to buy time to think of something else. Sovanna is taking care of the little monster entrusted to my care by Aebbenary's rabid queen. I'm..." The words stopped coming for a while. "I'm as bad as they are. I'm just as greedy and vicious and spiteful—more, sometimes. I helped you avenge a dark past, but I didn't do much to uphold any future where you could be happy and safe. I'm sorry for that. More than I can say. All I know is that I'm not going to lose you. Either of you, Iulia, Konetta—any of you!"

The other huntresses couldn't hear her speech—or communicate if they could—but Cosima threw her arms wide as if to gather each woman beneath intangible wings and hold them close forever.

Then she wrapped Iulia in them, Iulia alone, and embraced her tight enough to bruise her ribs as if the pressure alone would convey how much had changed in the last few minutes. Longer—Cosima's transformation had begun an age ago, with Bettina's return and the reminder of how much she had to lose if she never fought for it.

Iulia answered with her own bear-like strength. An embrace, then a kiss as full of passion as the arms that wrapped around Cosima and tugged her closer still. There was forgiveness in that which Cosima marveled to experience. It humbled her how faithful her companion was—had ever been—no matter how she'd shamefully taken her for granted.

"Good," Konetta sighed like the wind that stirred the branches of the treehouse; it sounded like the effort cost her. *"Be happy, Cosima. Even if you can't set us free. You gave us a little more life when destiny would have let us suffer and die alone."*

When they paused their kiss Cosima repeated what Konetta had said. Nodding, Iulia let her go and crossed her arms. Somehow, though the statue was several feet taller on its pedestal, she managed to glower *down* at Konetta's effigy.

"Tell you what: when you're human again, I'll deck you once for going after my girl, and we'll be even. You can court us like a proper suitor if you want. Though I'll not promise to tell you yes." Iulia whipped her head around to answer Cosima's helpless chuckle, still glaring but without vehemence. "That all right with you?"

"Whatever you say," Cosima promised. Konetta wheezed a laugh in her head. She was in earnest, but Iulia laughed and kissed the tip of Cosima's nose again before the business at hand forced them to get serious.

"What about them?" She jerked her chin at the others.

"It will take more power than I have to undo the will of a favorite consort," Cosima said, *"But."*

"Don't say "but.""

"I don't know what to do other than hunt—it's the only thing I'm good at."

"Don't say that either." A saucy joke accompanied by a crooked smile should have made her smile, but the spiders had returned to Cosima's thoughts and were spinning their befuddling webs once more; smiling back took effort. Iulia sensed the change in her mood. "Let's hunt, then."

Cosima gazed into the faithful strength in her firm jaw, the purposed line of her brows, and started to feel her Light reaching out to embrace her even though there wasn't time for it. Her wards would warn her of anyone's approach, but the longer they stayed the greater the risk of discovery…and punishment.

"Hunt Fiammetta? Under Goddess's eye and the wings of Her sword? It's madness." But it was the beginning of a plan, and Cosima's mind ran with its potential.

I could lure her to a secret place with a promise to meet Goddess full of apologies for ignoring her, then subdue her…

The plan was the easy part. Subduing one of the most powerful beings in the world—an insane one at that—would be another story. Cosima knew her martial strength, great though her talents were, was no match for the brutal frenzy Fiammetta could unleash in revenge based on the spark of her Saint's Light.

Iulia had remained silent to let her think. Her thumb stroked Cosima's flushed cheek, summoning her back out of her head.

"It *is* madness. Fiammetta could call Goddess to aid her before you're done. She might know how to fight better than you somehow. But I have faith, Cosima. I believe we can do this. *You* can do this."

Dawn shone through the window; the morning Konetta had longed for from her effigy. Though she was mortal, the sun granted Iulia a halo. Though the shadows darkened on her face, they vanished as she looked toward the east to watch its first rays illuminate the sanctuary.

The ruined relics took on sublime significance and a measure of their former glory in that light.

I don't know if I can live up to your expectations, Cosima thought, keeping her own counsel one more time, *but I'm going to try.*

With nothing else to debate, Iulia deigned to remain with her in the lonely tomb of a dead faith and watch the rest of the sunrise through the smudged, cracked windows.

Dreams bloomed in Cosima's mind and heart as she rested in the protection of her tower room. Iulia had gone, for now, to ensure Goddess never found her and assumed Cosima's ties to useless mortals were still too strong to be proper. Godlings required less sleep than mortals, but she rested with her eyes closed and felt the dream find her anyway.

She saw Cristoval.

Denial was something her mind was good at. This was an ordinary dream, she told herself. A commonplace grove in a familiar vineyard where the air smelled like grapes and wine and Bettina's fading perfume. Cosima had visited the Valusius estate often during Bettina's exile, though it pained her to see it forsaken. It hurt to be abandoned: Bettina had fled partially for her sake and partially for Cristoval's, but she had gone nonetheless.

After pleading with Cosima to come with her. Stubbornness and a longing for independence and peace—most of which had never come to her as she hoped—had kept her in Aebbenary. Spite too, if she was honest.

Cristoval was easy to love, but impossible to protect. Even he accepted that all mortals were supposed to die eventually. Cosima had understood—or thought she had—Bettina's relentless urge to save him from his destiny, but at the cost of her daughter? Was a son worth more than a daughter? She'd never found an answer.

Denial was easier.

The specter of Cristoval waited. Down the path toward the hedge maze, with tiny chrysanthemums blooming in echo of his steps, he led her on. Cosima didn't realize she had followed until she walked right behind him, staring at the linen shirt on his back where sweat had plastered it.

In an old habit, he reached behind him to take her hand. Cosima took it and let him lead the way he had when she'd been a child, though divine grace had protected her from the awkward clumsiness mortal children had to go through to walk. His hand was dry as straw and cold—just like his sweat, like he was sick.

He is sick, Cosima reminded herself. *Goddess cursed him. She cursed all of us.*

The maze went on longer than it should. It was nighttime, and her divine eyes weren't working like they should in this dream, but she counted the familiar turns and found dozens too many. Denial staved off any fear along with the bizarre sense that with her elder brother here she would be all right. They both would.

"I understand what I must do," Cristoval began to murmur as they walked, *"but oh, I fear what is to come. If your will is merciful, you will take this yoke from my neck …"*

Her ears failed too. Cosima was helpless aside from his guiding grip on her hand as they travelled deeper and deeper into the maze.

"Take what from you?" she asked of the figure she could no longer see, no matter the moonlight pouring down on them. "What do you need? Tell me, I will do it!"

"You can't save them," he told her.

"I can and I *will*," Cosima answered. "What is this, Cristoval? This place—"

The maze ended. They passed through light as if at the end of a chasm tunnel and came into the Arboretum. No Godlings or Saints populated the beautiful haven; there weren't any animals or creatures left to greet them. Cosima scanned the vast lake that had swallowed the bulk of the Arboretum like a colossal, world-ending flood had wiped any signs of civilization clean from the world.

Cristoval let her go. They could both see now, after all. He strode purposefully toward the shoreline of the new lake and knelt in the sand.

"I have been brought here several times. I don't know if this is Goddess's doing." Reaching out with a limb that extended a little farther than it should have, as if distorted, he nudged a bizarre paper boat deeper into the pond. "I tend to think not. But this place shows me things. Like what you mean to do to Fiammetta to free your friends. You won't defeat her."

Cosima winced, her hands flying up to cover her mouth as Cristoval lifted his head to look up at her. Deep furrows ravaged his skin, like he'd clawed them there. The moonlight of the garden was serene, but as soon as she clapped her eyes on that horrible sight it changed. The orb reddened like mortal blood in the sky. His eyes looked black in that, and flat.

Dead already, she thought.

"You can't save them," he said, solemn and sad. "Only I can."

"You're sick. You're dying." *You're mortal.* She almost said it. Two words of the truth that had almost broken their mother and had brought him to this state of ruin. *How could someone like you save my huntresses from Goddess Herself?*

"I am. I will be—forever. Goddess lied when She told Mama I would eventually expire on my own. This place told me She will keep me alive until Bettina is ready to sacrifice me to Her. That's the offering She wants."

"That cannot be."

Cannot, her denial echoed.

"It is. I am."

"I can save them, and you *will not die.*"

"I am," he repeated.

Cosima grabbed him. She dropped beside him from where she had stood, a listless doll in this nightmare, and shook him by his shoulders.

"I am a Godling! If I say you shall live, and my huntresses will survive after I put a spear through their monstrous keeper, *then it will be so!"*

A denial wasn't significant no matter how many times she said it, or how firmly she believed it. Thrice and thrice again changed nothing.

"I am dying," he whispered to her, hushed, mouth closed and his face a wreck of the handsome youth he had been before Goddess's curse.

Cristoval fell…then the moon followed. Still crimson, still a sphere of blood that churned like liquid trapped in a crystal ball, it crashed into the lake and sent a tidal wave of icy water over where Cosima stood alone on the shore.

She'd collapsed onto her knees after her strong legs gave out beneath her, but she barely noticed. Panic and water running down from her soaked hair clouded her vision, but she dug into the silt and sand with both hands to drag her brother's sinking corpse up from oblivion. The moon rose, slowly, thrumming with power that promised to undo her as well like divine hands tearing asunder a sacred veil...

He's gone, Cosima thought as she sat back. Hurting, sobbing, and aware of the sand that had turned to glassy dust and burrowed into her skin and hands to forever cut her to pieces. *He's dying, he's almost gone, and the only way to save my huntresses is to let him.*

Something rose from the lake. The water rippled and rolled off the glossy sphere of the landed moon as multitudinous wings peeled out of its surface to bear it aloft. It moved toward the shore, toward *her*, and looked with eyes as big as she was or as small as the rotting grapes that littered the ground of the vineyard.

Who are you? She asked.

"*I am Magisend of the Archives. You sought me not long ago and warned Bettina of my existence when she returned to Aebbenary.*"

Mama told me a little about you. You're her friend. You've been helping her.

That ball of eyes blinked *s l o w l y* where it hovered over her. The eyes were so large from this angle they resembled feathered moons or planets about to crash where she lay and leave the entire world a crater signaling it had been there.

The sphere shut three-quarters of its eyes. Only the green ones, Cosima noticed.

"*Her friend. I am her friend.*" He said it like he was realizing it for the first time now someone else had voiced the thought. "*That's why I'm here. There are things you need to know and a role you need to play. Destiny does not need you the way it needs the others, but it* can *use you. And you can benefit from the inevitable.*"

My brother is dead. Is that what you're here to tell me?

"*He suffers an agony few can claim to know. He may appear close to death, but Goddess has writ his mortal destiny to spell out such anguish for him that no one in the history of your world has ever experienced its like. In lasting death, you and your sister and your mother can free him and use your gift to do what you must. Save your huntresses from this pact of destruction and rid Aebbenary of its tyrants once and for all. Protect Bettina from ever being hunted and owned again—perhaps the abandoned Godlings and Saints can be rehabilitated under your care. All it will cost—"*

Cristoval. You're telling me to kill him too! You're no better than Goddess! Any of you! Without anyone else but the sphere to witness, Cosima threw herself into a stormy tantrum. Her human shape melted away in the lake; she became the salt water, the tide, the waves that crashed against the jagged rocks to whittle them away with time on her side.

Magisend waited her out. He didn't chide or try to persuade her.

"It is the way of things," he said. *"If I knew of any other way,"* he assured her before he tucked her consciousness back into her body and steered her toward wakefulness, *"I would share it. All the knowledge that exists has availed me nothing."*

Cosima resisted. She could hear the gloom in the moon's voice— the moon named Magisend, who was Bettina's trusted friend despite his strangeness—and felt it too. It caught in her teeth like sand and in her streaming eyes like ash and in the air like fumes. They all had something to lose from Cristoval's destiny, she realized as the material world sank hooks into her again from where unknown force had dragged her into this waking dream.

My brother and my mother's heart, my sister's true love, Cosima comprehended, *or my huntresses. My friends and lovers, mortal and trapped.*

She had always been selfish, she knew. Now destiny had all but told her to honor that.

367

XXVI

Bettina

The moon over Aebbenary was round and full and utterly above scrutiny. As Bettina spent another sleepless night in the Archives she turned her shoulder with a lunar mien of disdain for the miserable swan Goddess coveted.

Magisend hadn't reappeared after he had walked away from Bettina in the garden. The truths she had heard all jabbed her out of any rest like rocks digging into her soft back from spending the night on the ground. (Not a frequent opportunity or choice for an influential nobleman's daughter like herself, but the uncompromising ground had been good enough during the first days of her exile from the island.)

One kernel of knowledge had been seared into her mind and heart like a brand of molten metal. That scar had only begun to hurt—when Cristoval died it would unmake her. She would never be Bettina again.

That was the second blistering truth that scorched her awake from dreams of the altars and pungent incense of her younger days. Magisend had gone, he might never be himself again, and no matter where she turned Bettina would end up alone or in Marzanna's tower. Cosima had forgiven her other failures, but she wouldn't let the death of her brother—willing or not—pass.

The Archives had reverted to their default state: midnight mists popped with brilliant stars there and again. The sigils of the platform carved reliefs on Bettina's back where she lay; she had been too listless to summon more than a cozy feather blanket and a cotton wrap as white as milk. If she needed more warmth her wings helped, but she left them flat no matter how much her muscles stung.

I should find them, she thought as she watched the faintly real moon she had eventually called to track the hours proceed through the firmament. *The hourglass has already turned for our time together. I should tell them the sand is almost gone...*

Cristoval, her doomed baby. Cosima, the endangered adder in Marzanna's burrow set to avenge her family and rescue her huntresses at the first opportunity. Sovanna...that odd, lonesome creature completely in love with the Saintspawn that had been passed down to her and even more completely in love with Cristoval.

Bettina couldn't guess why the idea of Marzanna's and Easoren's progeny claiming the role of daughter-in-law didn't bother her, but all she felt at the prospect was a sense of bittersweet joy. The destiny that would tear her family asunder, that had chosen her line specifically to cleanse Goddess's stain on Aebbenary, had at least granted her son a perfect, predestined romance, even if it was doomed. She knew him like a mother should: he would take what comfort he could before he went to meet his end.

After all, the vision in the garden had shown the feeble cygnet lying quietly to wait for its doom. It hadn't fought its mother and sibling at all—it had understood.

The Archives had offered no hospitality so far, but the wheeling stars multiplied as she watched them dance amidst the infinite, misty atmosphere above her platform. Bettina sat up and pressed her palms over her stone-dry eyes.

It's time I stopped wallowing. My children need me.

Only, she didn't know for certain if she still had Magisend's protection outside the Archives. Her revelations in the garden had implied they would protect her until the moment she became bait for Goddess after the sacrifice, but no one had been explicit. With Magisend gone...

They need me, she repeated, and stood to leave.

Once she was resolved, the mists around her converged and assembled the door leading out toward the Scholar's Grave through the library wing of the Archives. Calling a sash from the ether, Bettina fashioned herself a semblance of decent garments and left.

When no beacon in the material world or in her guarded mind went off to signal Goddess flew on wings of Light to punish and claim her, Bettina exhaled her relief and hurried past rows of bookshelves to leave.

The door didn't retreat, but she came no closer to it. She elevated her walk to a trot, then a sprint as consternation wrung a dry heave of alarm from her battered spirit. She hadn't been as determined to go about her business as she should have been upon leaving the garden, yes, but for the Archives to actively keep her from it when time was already so short was harshness she refused to endure.

Let me go! She called in her head, slowing her pace and throwing her hands skyward in exasperation. *I vow to come back. I know my duty. You cannot keep me here forev—*

"You're still here."

She didn't recognize the consciousness that stormed her mental barriers at first. Layer upon layer of power cradled it in such intense Archival will Bettina guessed this had to be the garden's doing. The fright sent her scurrying backwards and around the less than protective corner of the nearest shelf.

"Magisend?" Caution prevented her from emerging from her dubious hiding place. Her knuckles accidentally brushed against the sleek spine of a book when she leaned around to scan the aisle for the intruder. Its knowledge blasted through her thoughts as if by catapult before she pulled away with a shudder. "Where are you?"

She saw him when the Archives permitted it. One moment he stood still, leaning against the doorframe and staring wild-eyed at her shocked face. The next he materialized in front of her, already lifting her into his arms to kiss her like a man returned from war.

No needles, now. A high, nearly inaudible whine of power set her teeth on edge. Bettina cupped his face in her hands and kissed him back with incredible relief coursing through her.

She had things to do. Affairs to arrange—she had doubted from the moment she learned of Cristoval's inevitable ruin that her survival was guaranteed. When Magisend kissed her, though, fully himself or not…everything else was hard to remember.

Bettina tried: the yoke of her responsibilities demanded some effort. "How are you here? You left—"

"To return. This one time, I meant to come back." He was everywhere, all over her. Bettina had experienced a thousand and one kisses from many skilled lovers—none of them compared to this. Magisend fit her figure against his and held her both like she was precious to him and like he wanted to peel her apart just so he'd have more pieces to admire.

One time. There wasn't enough pain in the world to fill the well of what Bettina must endure. It mingled with her pleasure instead of tainting it, making it sweeter.

He resisted her attempts to pull back so she could look at him; from the glimpse she had seen he had looked as hale and eerie as ever. His usual midnight blue and black had replaced the garden's all-encompassing green; he wore the clothes she had imagined for him rather than the imperious armor reflecting the garden's beating heart of Light.

When he began to drag kisses down from her jaw to her sensitive neck she almost lost the battle to confront him about what she had seen in the garden and what he must have endured as The Speaker's possession. He defeated her with the ravenous roaming of his hands as they squeezed where they wanted.

"Wait, *wait*—" she moaned into his mouth as he kissed it again; her breasts throbbed with longing for more of the rough, starving pressure he had showered on them. "How are you *you* again? What hap—*oof!*"

He shoved her body against a bookshelf—miraculously, it didn't tip over and only a few books fell on the other side. The breath that puffed out of Bettina became a smothered whimper as he lifted her higher and tore apart her makeshift dress with his sharp golden teeth. They grazed the skin of her abdomen and sent a shock of want down to the coiled lust inside her.

"Talk to me, please. Here if you must." Taking a risk, Bettina opened her thoughts to him. Bashfulness tried to follow as Magisend stopped,

freezing in place where he had all but chained her to the bookshelf by strength and wisps of his power.

No threads, she observed, surprise lifting her brows. *Just him. Well, mostly him.*

Slowly, he looked up. The edges of his form had been honed by whatever had happened to him. Bettina hadn't been able to perceive the whole of his form before, when the edges blurred or his gilded filaments rearranged portions of his physique to suit the mysterious workings of his power, but she could now. His dusk dark, multifaceted eyes locked on hers and stayed there as his tongue darted out to taste her kiss where it lingered on his lips.

He was not a man, but he resembled one. And he did *not* look like he would let her stop him again.

"I gave myself last time," she reminded him. *It was supposed to be the only time. What's happened to us?* "Are you going to demand what should only be given freely?"

"Only if the command from me will increase your pleasure," he said; she felt his nails dig into her ribs as he leaned in and sucked one of her nipples into his mouth. When she moaned, her hand lifting by reflex to tangle in his hair, he withdrew and grinned with dazzling and—deeply, fundamentally unsettling—satisfaction.

This isn't wise, she thought, unable to look away. *Attachments like this always hurt. The more intense the flare, the deeper the damage.*

Hands gripped her skull from above and yanked it backwards, forcing her to look back and up toward the midnight abyss of the ceiling. An even more demanding hold seized her arms at the wrists and spread out her arms to parallel her wings and more assuredly lock her in place.

Magisend stood in front of her. And above her. And, she saw as her eyes darted around the room in a frantic hunt, all around her. Numerous like the facets in his eyes, wraiths bearing his likeness became his identical copies.

Every one she saw was fixated on her to the exclusion of all else.

"They're me," he answered the question she hadn't asked yet. "They're All."

"You're—"

"An instrument. Nothing more."

And yet. And yet. And yet. Heartbeats of doubt resounded with her own. *You. You.*

"How can an instrument desire like this?"

"I know not. I care not. I will keep you as long as I can."

He didn't let her stall any longer. Magisend buried his face between her thighs and began to taste.

Bettina clawed at the shelves behind her, her back arching; her wings knocked more books and scrolls off and snapped full width as his tongue stroked her clit. And her labia, and inside…his tongue had been mostly normal when they'd kissed, but she bet it wasn't any more than the rest of him was now.

Pleasure zagged through her veins as she balanced on his shoulders, her position precarious only if she tried to escape. Which was out of the question: he nipped at one of her lower lips while his ink-black tongue still worked somehow and Bettina bucked into his mouth in delight.

The specters he'd summoned weren't idle. Barely constrained by the boundaries of the physical world, they played with her without ceasing. Hands kneaded her breasts and mouths kissed their aching tips. Fingers and claws petted and rifled through the feathers of her wings, searching for sensitive spots she didn't know she had. The first time she came was due in part to a particularly slow stroke from the textured pressure of Magisend's tongue between her legs *and* a duo of specters finding a place on her spine between her wings that responded like living lightning to the right combination of touch.

They didn't stop after the first time. Or after a few more of the cataclysmic quakes they extracted from her body. Bettina lost count like she lost herself to their caresses; the only significant action in her world was the paradise Magisend wrought betwixt her thighs with his split-tongued magic. She heard him too, moaning in time with her like indulging her brought him the same level of intense gratification she felt.

"Magisend…" He and they dragged his name from her in a silken

sigh of bliss. "Oh, Magisend…"

Everything stopped. Bettina slid to the ground, aided by his specters. Her knees were weak, and her form was wrung out from their efforts.

Though they were gentle enough, Magisend wasn't. He dragged her to one of the study tables and cleared it off with a snap of his fingers. His hand closed around her throat and he slammed her onto the table. It hurt, but not much; she didn't think he meant it to. The specters confirmed her suspicions when they released her wings, which they had carefully pre-arranged so he wouldn't injure them.

Magisend balanced on his knees above her—one hand squeezed her throat to make her gasp while the other fucked her in rhythm with her writhing hips. She came between clenched teeth as she stared up at his intent, almost glazed expression of lust that made her *burn* amidst her rising apprehension.

"That's the last one I'll let you have for a while. Would you like to thank me?" he said to her.

"I have a feeling I might not want to thank you for what you're about to do to me."

He laughed; the specters chuckled, waiting for his will to guide them into pleasing her again. Bettina turned her head to look around at them, trying to keep count. Their numbers had decreased to just a few.

"Give me something sweet to sustain me. Well…" he circled his thumb around her clit, listening to her breaths hitch while he contemplated her face. "Something *else* sweet."

Bettina resisted. Her defiance became futile when he started gently fucking her again, slow but deep the way they had the first time. It was hard to resist anything when she wanted this, wanted *him* inside her so badly she writhed on the table and sighed her longing and joy.

"I want to take you apart and examine you." He fanned out her hair between his hands like it was woven gold; she caught her scent on his dominant hand. "I want to stitch you back together just to enjoy your gratitude."

"You've done that already." Bettina's reminder amused him further; her sewn-on wing twitched when she tried to lift it to show him. One of the specters leaned back to allow her movement. She lifted it, curling it around Magisend above her to brush indigo feathers against the harsh line of his cheek.

"Then I want to do it again."

Tinged the same blue smoke as Archival energy, the replicas surrounded Bettina and the table and resumed their work as their source positioned himself above her and slid his cock inside where she had already parted her legs to welcome him. Both of them groaned as he slid home, deep and fast; Magisend captured her mouth in his again and kissed her with the same care he'd used on her sex. When he started to pull away Bettina rose halfway to balance on her elbows in pursuit, the rhythm of his thrusts already unraveling the tension their flirtatious conversation and the pauses between orgasms had built back up.

His replicas took up new positions all around the table where she lay, accepting whatever they would give. Magisend set a steady pace he knew would tease her as he continued.

"I know why Goddess hunts you. *Yearns* for you. The sight of you spoiled by pleasure, still begging for more…"

The wingplay resumed, much more sporadic and specific now they had learned where to touch to tantalize but not finish her. One of the more corporeal replicas tilted her head back toward itself to kiss her, fulfilling one need while increasing others.

Your taste, your scent…

The multiplied echoes of himself came and went while the source took his pleasure from hers. Magisend's demands increased—to Bettina's delight—and the others revealed it. The one that had been kissing her tilted her head farther back and guided his cock into her mouth to fuck her there, quick and fast without worry for a quick release. There were others to come after him, and Bettina wanted all of them.

He praised her when she gagged on his essence—each time, since the others wanted their turn. Her aureole of Saint's Light banked brighter and stronger as if this joining healed something broken so deep inside her spirit that she had only lately discovered the chronic bruise making her life a misery. All aspects of Magisend possessed her, held her in their hands like a cherished lover rather than mere treasure. Bettina gloried in each stroke and caress though the release they fanned for the satisfaction of denial frustrated her to pleading.

When they finally let her come, they had positioned Bettina on all fours between three of them: the true Magisend lay beneath, balancing and fucking her hard enough to make her scream around a replica's cock in her mouth, and another replica behind and higher to slide in and out of her anus with possessive strokes she'd rarely allowed anyone to enjoy from her. By that time she was a mess of reflexive tears, shadow-slick seed dripping down her chin, and knotted hair pulled into the hind replica's fist to make her arch her back so Magisend could lavish attention on her breasts.

A reminiscence of fatigue stirred after a while. After Magisend himself finally came in her the specters blinked out one by one until only he and Bettina were left. The Archives were oppressively silent. It should have been cold since they were naked and vulnerable in this forbidding plane, but they still lay pressed together so it wasn't.

By mutual agreement, they reached for each other again. Magisend cradled her in his arms and rocked her over him as she leaned down for a kiss that tasted more holy than anything she had ever done with or urged on by Goddess. They made love, sensually and silently, gazing into each other's eyes with unflinching devotion and knowledge of each other that no denial would honorably serve.

When it was over, Bettina rolled off to lie beside him; the table shouldn't have survived their weight or supported their width, but it had and it continued because their will made it suit them. Magisend stared at her awhile—not dazed, but certainly not as present as ever—before he sat up and bent until his elbows rested on his knees. The knobs of his spine were stark under his skin, as were the filaments binding the plates of his body together.

Bettina sat up—slow in case she was sore—and impatiently shoved her tousled hair out of her face. All she had to look at was his lone back now he was the only Magisend left. Would her departure hurt him after a joining as intense as what they had done? Could he feel the loss already as keenly as she did?

"I will keep you as long as I can", he had told her. Bettina's heart skipped again at the simple assertion that he was himself and that he wanted to keep her. It made her want to speak softly to him. To whisper pledges of her own devotion while she still had the chance.

She crawled to the edge of the study table where he sat and threw her arms around him, pulling herself as close as she could manage.

"I'd stay if I could."

"I know," he repeated, and that was all. He didn't move to pat her embracing arms with absentminded fondness.

"You're not going to make it easy for me, are you?"

Magisend didn't look at her until she guided him her way by a gentle hand on his chin.

"I would never make things difficult for you. You have enough sorrow in store without any addition on my part," he said. He might not have meant the reminder of her upcoming trials to injure, but it did. Bettina scraped her thumb across his smooth cheek to ground herself in the present rather than the bleak future waiting outside the Archives.

Bleak except for this sequestered jewel that had been borne of their connection.

"You'll be with me, won't you? To keep hiding me from Goddess?"

"You have the garden's protection now. I am needed here."

Bettina scanned the Archives surrounding them, looking around and up at the poorly concealed void behind the bookshelves and study alcoves. "To do what?"

"When Goddess is no more, there won't be a place left on this earth for these Archives. I must select which aspects of knowledge to leave on this plane before I go."

"Go?"

"We would mitigate your loss if we could, Swan-of-gold," the garden had told her—she had been too busy denying Magisend's claim on her to listen. *"We cannot give you this vessel to keep."*

"Defeating Goddess means losing you." *Too.* Along with her only son she would lose Magisend. "That's why you insisted on…then this day could be the last time we…"

"No, not yet." He took hold of her hand and held it against his cheek. "Soon, though. Cristoval's time is very close now. At his side, the huntress and the outcast have already realized what it will take to free this realm from Goddess's avarice. You must go to them to see it done."

"To say goodbye," he added to her mind for her benefit since he must have guessed hearing that word spoken out loud would prompt her grief to overflow.

"I…" What speech would be sufficient to describe how intensely she wished to throw off the shackles of her duty to save her incurable son and give Magisend a life of his own? Bettina couldn't surrender her life to fulfill this hated destiny because—other than to Goddess—it had no value.

She was leaving. He would remain locked away in this exterior realm laying out plans for his own winking out of existence if they succeeded in their quest. Bettina thought of what she had to offer—the only thing that had ever belonged to her—and gave it.

"I will mourn you, Magisend," she promised. "My lament for my son will resound through this world wherever I go, but I will not forget you in the midst of it. I swear I will grieve your loss alongside his as long as I live…however short those days may be."

She couldn't say more once her voice cracked with emotion. Their lovemaking had distracted her in a perfect pattern of affection and release her very soul had craved. Bettina wanted to thank him for the gift of holding her together with every piece of himself, but she had no more strength in her voice.

I have never loved like this. I have never been loved like this.

And I had never been, Magisend answered her errant thought, touching their foreheads together, *until you shared your life with me and taught me its purpose.*

"Existence is a temporary gift for all beings. Even constructs and avatars," he told her out loud as she grabbed onto his waist and held on tight; he let her pull them closer together so her wings could shield them from all but each other. "Mine might be shorter than most, but I am glad I spent it with you, Bettina."

Some time passed after that, but not much. Magisend extricated himself from her embrace, and she made herself rise and return to the path leading out of the Archives through the Scholar's Grave.

XXVII

Sovanna

In the ephemeral last days of the age, Sovanna spent every moment with Cristoval and still couldn't determine how to tell him he was doomed. Confessing she had failed—and would fail again—to save him felt like she would inflict a grievous, mortal wound the instant she opened her mouth to declare the truth.

The final week progressed in shining moments of joy interspersed with sinister purports of the death stalking Cristoval. There was something miserable, forever isolated, within Sovanna that refused to let him court her with pretty words and flowers gathered from the currently vacant Valusius estate…but he wooed her without hesitation. Bold by nature and brash with the haste of a condemned man, he stole smiles and even the occasional kiss from her during the rare hours he felt well enough to move about on his own or conduct his last business providing hope for the hopeless in Aebbenary.

He sang, too, though not often. While Sovanna cared for or entertained Lilias and pretended to labor at her studies—her findings were pointless now she knew there was nothing to be done about Cristoval's destiny—he would hum or sing a tune. He still had his father's ten-string lyre, along with a vibrant voice leaning to a tenor's pitch. She hadn't heard him sing much before his illness, but after its symptoms had begun to take their toll she heard the changes in his voice. The complexity of added depth and a rasp from long hours of wheezing lent poignancy to lyrics he composed at will.

Some were about her. About them; subtle, not pointed enough to mortify her, but a gift packaged for her nonetheless. Sovanna memorized every word. A memorial cache set aside for the immeasurable years she would have to live without him.

She *had* to talk to him. Confess that there was no hope of saving him because he needed to die to dethrone Goddess. Other matters pressed against the tight knot of the lament caught in her throat all hours of the day, like the one of her tattered heart and who it belonged to, but she couldn't speak.

The other women in his life came to her by and by. Cosima arrived during the golden hours flowing slow like honey in the afternoon, accompanied by her favorite huntress—and obvious lover—with news of how Fiammetta had been treating her other ladies. Sovanna hoped she manufactured enough dismay for Cosima's benefit, but that felt pointless too.

Someone has to die to bring Goddess down from Her lofty seat. Someone important. Let Cosima fret over her friends: Sovanna had a greater loss to prepare for.

Because she was looking for it, or because their fortunes had dovetailed into one desolation yet to come, Sovanna had met Cosima's eyes and scrutinized the exposed soul behind them. Though she could have retreated, or contested the offense, Cosima had let her look. Like she had come to break the news anyway, and Sovanna's discourteous investigation of her thoughts saved her from speaking.

"You know. How?" Sovanna's voice sounded far away to her own ears. Cosima nodded; a ways off, the huntress she'd brought with her in her Light was staring down one of the badgers who lived in the garden.

"A prophetic dream, I think. Brought by the Archivist."

She knew a little about the Archives Marzanna had made, but not much. Sovanna had attempted to visit a long time ago: there had been nothing to see and no books or scrolls for her knowledge-hungry mind to devour.

Cosima hadn't asked, but Sovanna told her how she had gained the same burden of Cristoval's destiny.

"I was going to use Lilias to cure him. Or try to. I'm not certain it would have worked anymore. Däard came to stay my hand...but I don't know now if I could have done it." The urge to apologize struck. Cosima had never wanted Lilias or any children of her own. Whose life had more value to her? Cristoval's, or an unloved abomination rejected by everyone who saw them?

Everyone but them. Cosima's attention shifted to Lilias, who stalked Iulia as she contemplated the badgers snuffling through their burrows in the swamp grass and pretended not to notice them. Winged, chattering, child Lilias who had been a forlorn babe sleeping in her treehouse not very long ago.

"Thank you," Cosima said. "Cristoval wouldn't have accepted that. I know I don't."

Sovanna couldn't stand it. Any of it. Not watching Cristoval die, slowly and with only one foreseeable end, not Cosima's gratitude for Sovanna failing to become the monster that could have saved him— the villain her conception had damned her to become. Cosima sensed her changing mood and departed without another word.

Bettina arrived last. Alone, forsaken by her shadow guardian reeking of an unknown calamity Sovanna wanted to defeat. Divine beings surpassed the depredations of mortal weariness unless they expended too much of their Light, but Sovanna saw her signs of exhaustion and sorrow because she was looking for them. Loss clung to her like a shroud, dulling her golden hair, dimming her aureole, hunching her shoulders like she was as old as her years numbered.

Cosima had known: she'd blamed a dream and her mother's shadow. How could Bettina not know as well?

"He's asleep." Sovanna prodded the simmering pot hanging over the sickly yet serviceable fire she had conjured on her front lawn to cook her stew; it was a strong recipe and smoky as could be, not suitable for indoor cooking. "That comes rarely enough I won't tolerate anyone waking him."

"I understand." Though she peered longingly at the closed door of Sovanna's hut, Bettina accepted her authority and sidled closer to breathe in the medicinal aroma of the soup. "It looks like he's eating well."

"He isn't. His appetite wastes away. That terrible cough gets worse and worse, sinking deeper into his lungs, but will he hear of gallivanting less and resting more? No."

It was too late to take all that complaining back or mute her frustration with a detached tone, but Sovanna's dissatisfaction had been getting harder and harder to tame. To her own ears she sounded aggravated and spiteful toward the role others' decisions had locked her into: a powerless, *ineffectual* caretaker. Good for nothing but reminding the world by her horns and the remnants of Silver's power clinging to her blessed flesh that every bright age might have a dark end.

She stirred the pot so forcefully some of the salted broth sloshed out and made the flames beneath it sputter. Bettina studied her a while; Sovanna pretended not to notice how that lance of perception pierced her.

"You know," Bettina proclaimed after Sovanna finished dumping several chopped herbs into the stew. "I was told you would."

The notches of her kitchen knife skidded against the wooden cutting board she'd used to prepare the herbs. Sovanna jerked her chin up and down once to convey her confirmation.

"Do you know if Cosima—"

"We all know except Cristoval."

Bettina sucked in shaky breath at that; her eyes slid closed as she sat heavily beside Sovanna on the log some of the marsh crocodiles had brought for her little camp.

Sovanna recalled the way she had hugged her when they had all met again after the Jubilee. Welcoming arms had enfolded her like this was the start of a new habit. Like they had at least one lifetime to become family if Sovanna and Cristoval were destined for happiness rather than grief.

"I can tell him when he wakes up." An offer that would ease some of Sovanna's burden, but not one she wanted.

She's his mother, she reminded herself as she studied the simmering surface of the cooking pot. *She might want to. It's her right.*

"No," Sovanna said to Bettina, risking her disappointment or anger. "I've been caring for him while you and Cosima have been…away. I will tell him."

Bettina said nothing. She sat next to Sovanna, and they watched the pot together as the scent of the herbs mingled with the garlic and wafted an appetizing aroma into the open air. After a moment, her hand slipped into Sovanna's lap to hold one of hers; a wing that drooped slightly lower than the other lifted high enough to wrap around her shoulder in an extra offering of solace.

"All right," Bettina said, calm and soothing. That was all it took to persuade Sovanna to pull at the ties of the knot in her heart that defied every attempt at subjugating it.

"I don't understand what the point is. Why…" She would *not* cry. When he was alert Cristoval paid such close attention to every minute change in her expressions or shift in her moods that she couldn't risk it. "Why *me?* Anyone else could have been compelled to care enough about him to make a worthy sacrifice. Destiny didn't need to ruin me to bring this plot to fruition."

"You care. On an island with only a handful of people left who still do, you care."

I don't want to! I beg you, or anyone else who might be listening, to take this cup from me and pass it to another! Even in her thoughts the plea for liberation debased Sovanna in her own eyes. From the moment she had met Cristoval, through their letters then in person, she had willingly swallowed the poison of her own undoing.

Not poison, she realized: seeds. Seeds that had dropped into the cavity of her chest to take root and grow the unwanted organ she wished she had the strength to carve out and throw away.

"I'm not supposed to be like this." Shifting away from Bettina's tender wing, but not quite brave enough to stop allowing their hands to hold each other, Sovanna tilted her head back to stare up at the grey skies her Miraculous will had conjured to block out Goddess's eternal, balmy blue. "I'm not supposed to be the one who feels this."

"Your heart isn't cold. Not like Hers."

"What use is a heart that can break? I never wanted one."

Bettina had no answer for that. They sat together on the mossy log under the Miraculous trees of her new marsh and listened to the stew bubbling and boiling to cook the savory lamb Sovanna had selected so carefully for Cristoval knowing it would be quite the task to convince him to eat today.

Bread, she thought with a wave of fresh, foolish despair. *Hot, crisp bread slathered in sweet butter. I forgot to make some.*

They sat together long enough for the stew at the bottom of the pot to start burning. Bettina leaned over before Sovanna could to stir it. She let Sovanna cling to her—there was no pretending she wasn't— with the practice of a woman who knew what it was to be a mother with children hanging onto her skirts or running underfoot.

As she stirred, Bettina tried to answer her.

"The powers that move the world have shown me that it is necessary to excise Goddess from its weaving by trimming the thread of my son's life too soon. My son, who I carried and bore in pain and blood. Who I nourished, taught to walk, and raised to manhood. Not perfectly, but with all the love in the fibers of my being, either mortal or blessed. I have wondered…"

The words Sovanna needed to hear were not a magic spell or a Miracle. They did not exist, since there was nothing anyone could say to assuage an already grieving soul, and the cure of time's passage was out of reach. But this helped: Bettina helped. The last encasement of armor around Sovanna's bleak spirit splintered and fell away as she listened.

"I don't think it matters if there's a point to any of it. It is meaningful to us, therefore it is meaningful to the world. Everyone belongs to everything, so I've been told. Extravagant, reckless, wasteful love is part of that. That's why I want this world to continue, free—for the sake of everyone who hasn't felt that sufficiently or at all."

Mindful of her sharp horns, Sovanna heaved a sigh that felt like it billowed out of her soul and leaned against Bettina's shoulder to cry. She couldn't heal from a wound that had yet to be inflicted, but the knowledge that someone understood her and what she was about to go through—a rare experience in her young life—healed something different that, repaired, might help her survive this ordeal to see Goddess's demise through.

Rocking them side to side on the log bench, cradling Sovanna closer, Bettina let her cry and joined her as their haloes formed a prism of Light around their figures.

They gave each other that time and the gift of understanding, as much as anyone else could, what they would go through together. Bettina whispered comfort, and a threadbare recounting of who else she'd lose besides Cristoval to let nature curb Goddess's ambition. She really *did* understand, Sovanna decided.

They separated after their tears dried along with their conversation. Bettina's nails were well-rounded and immaculate without appearing sharp, but her forefinger sliced a line in her bare wrist like a knife through butter. Before she concealed it with the bell of her sleeve again Sovanna spotted the scars of older cuts.

When Bettina held her arm over the steaming pot, a thin stream of ichor dripped into the stew.

"I've tried giving him my ichor," Sovanna said.

"I used to give him mine when he was young. Even recently I tried to sneak some into his victuals to fortify him while I persuaded Goddess to make him a Saint…but it must have drained away since then. There's no sign of it left in him that I can sense." Under the gloomy clouds and canopy she'd built to hide her pocket of Aebbenary from Goddess's relentless sun, her ichor sparkled like gems as it continued to flow into the stew. "It should sustain him like it used to when he wasn't well…for a time, at least. Make sure he drinks as much as he can stand."

"Aren't you staying? He'll want to see you."

"I'm going to return in the morning. I think the rest of this day should belong to the two of you."

"You're his mother—"

There was nothing lighthearted about their situation, but when Bettina cast an amused, sideways look her way Sovanna's lips twitched in a ghost of an answering smile.

"And I might as well be yours now. I think he'd want that. So I charge you, daughter, to treasure these hours before they fade. Tell him what you wish or need him to hear before he…goes." Bettina rubbed her arms as if chilled by the appalling transgression destiny would compel them to commit before long.

Then she left. Sovanna couldn't hurry fast enough to cool the stew with her will and bring it inside to wake Cristoval.

He stirred on the bed she'd crafted for him in her kitchen. The hut expanded or retracted according to her needs, just like her old one in the swamp Goddess had destroyed. It had made room for him the instant she wished it. Sovanna set the stew beside the door and served a bowl while he blinked in the late afternoon light peeping through her windows and the cracks of the door

"Who was out there? Cosima again?" he asked.

She shook her head. "Bettina."

"Mother came?" He started to rise, but the cough that overcame him collapsed him back onto the bed she'd constructed in the wall of the hut's main area so she could keep an eye on him. "I should see her—"

"She'll be back first thing in the morning. You need to rest a while longer and *eat.*"

Though he was foggy and disheveled from sleep, fitful or not, Cristoval nodded and stifled a cough as he shuffled around to rinse his mouth with a cup of water. The rest he dabbed up with a spare cloth from a laundered basket hanging from the ceiling to wipe his face to freshen it. Only after that did he sit at her table to thank her for the food and slowly, reluctantly try to eat it.

Her attempt at patience tormented Sovanna as she watched with a hawk's focus to see if the enhanced stew tempted his waning appetite. She was almost disappointed when his eyes widened at the taste and he began to shovel it in like he'd been starving—which he had. It would be mean and selfish to tell him everything she needed to before he'd finished, but she could barely stand the wait. Her foot tapped anxiously against the ground; she folded and unfolded her hands in her lap as she watched.

"Where's Lilias?" he asked between spoonfuls. This was the longest stretch of minutes where he hadn't been assaulted by a coughing fit in days.

"Cosima took them to see Palmira. I cautioned her, but the girl is alone in that treehouse. Iulia promised to help look after them while…" Sovanna paused. She couldn't tell him the middle of the tale before confessing the beginning.

"I love you, Cristoval."

His spoon clattered into the bowl where he dropped it; she ignored that.

"I love you. I know destiny must have arranged our connection, perhaps at the dawn of the stars or an era before that, but that's not why. I did not think anyone could ever move this heavy stone trapped in my chest. It beats like a heart. Sometimes it hurts. But it never lived until I found you and you found me. I love you," she repeated, her voice breaking, "but I'm not going to save you. I can't."

Cristoval knew her. He had guessed she wouldn't want to be interrupted. He had let her talk herself up to this confession of love and the betrayal that had to come after, without moving an inch in his seat at her table with the half-finished bowl of stew growing cold between them.

"I know," he told her, just like Cosima had, before he sat back and wiped his face on his sleeve. Then he stood, and pulled her up and into his arms to kiss her with every ounce of ardor he'd been holding back since they'd met.

They had never kissed like this. Sovanna had never kissed *anyone* like this, and she did kiss him back. There was no question of not moving her mouth against his, linking her arms around his neck, letting him mold their bodies together so her leg instinctively started to wrap around his like he'd pick her up any second.

The stories were true: she thought she heard birds singing. Twittering outside the window like the sun would always be shining on them—because it wished to, not because Goddess compelled it—and the only task that remained was promising their undying love to one another.

Promising...and acting. Cristoval didn't hesitate after she'd given him permission to love her by admitting she loved him. Though he'd been weak for a long time, the ichor-bolstered stew he'd eaten sustained the tide of vigor that helped him lift her off the ground, carry her to the nearest table, and set her on it.

The way he held her...her face cradled in his hands so he could kiss her gently. His hands creeping back into her hair to hold her tighter, tip her head back to deepen that same kiss with a taste of desperation in the brush of his tongue against her own. All Sovanna could do was match him—placing her hands over his, sliding them to his shoulders when he moved, leaning back when he half-climbed over her like he couldn't get close enough—until what he'd said distracted her from what had to be the most incredible kiss in the universe.

"How do you know?"

"I have had dreams since Goddess set this affliction upon me. Dreams, nightmares, prophecies...one after another." His tone dipped into brooding territory, but he wouldn't suffer it to stay there. He resumed kissing her like the conversation had ended until Sovanna thumped her fist against his shoulder to make him pause.

"Tell me what you saw." There was nothing there to contradict everything she had been told, but even prophecies could be wrong...

"I am meant to die to save mortalkind. Mother and Cosima are meant to kill me...and you, I think. I know you're supposed to be there."

"And you accepted? Just like that?"

"What is one, brief life compared to the health and happiness of uncountable people living or yet to be born?" He leaned over her on the table, hungry for her as if she was the meal he wanted, but the sadness in his eyes contrasted the noble purpose he had accepted.

"It's *your* one, brief life. And mine." Talking with Bettina had inspired Sovanna's courage. "It's my happiness too. I can never be happy again if you're not at my side."

"Because you love me?"

"And you love me." He hadn't said it yet. Her desire to hear those words from him—wasteful or not—flowed so strongly in her veins she trembled in his arms from the force of her longing.

Tenderly, with the reverence of a man who believed in her divinity and its right to be venerated by praise, Cristoval backed away from her. Not far—just enough to rest his hands on either side of her hips on the table and look into her face with sad, searching eyes like her features might hold the answers to every question he'd ever asked.

"I don't want to die, Sovanna, but that's not my greatest sorrow. It's not quite enough to tempt me into the utmost indulgence that would damn humanity to Goddess's care forever." He caught her hands when she reached out to capture his face between her palms and brought them together to clasp in one of his own. "This burden is mine: I accept it. But I wish to whatever power that exists that it was not. The life I could have had with you, even mortal, even sick, would have been the most sacred bliss any man on earth has ever received. I *do* love you. I will into whatever life waits beyond my death."

Once more they leaned into each other, allowing their lips to meet again. The shattering that had begun with Bettina's conversation by the cooking fire outside enfolded more and more of Sovanna as she kissed him like that simple act would bind them together and transform him into what she was. Immortal, divine; abiding forever on this earth.

That same kiss evolved in response to the desperate, despondent hunger with which they clung to one another. Cristoval picked her up again and guided her legs around his waist to carry her to a more comfortable place to lie down. During the temporary lull, their attention wandered to the makeshift resting cubby her will had carved into the paneled wall of her hut.

"Not there." His nostrils flared in revulsion as he glanced at the bed. His *sickbed*, which did smell medicinal and stale now Sovanna thought about it.

"Here, then." Holding him tight, Sovanna transported them in a flash of her Light to her bedroom on the second level. Ordinarily it would be strewn with clutter and befuddled by visiting fauna, but lately she'd barely spent time in it. Aside from some rude, overgrown vines and a little dust, her simple bed was clean and inviting welcoming.

Cristoval laid her down there and began to show her how much thought he had spared for the hour she would finally surrender to the fixture that joined their hearts in love as well as the promise of pain. He had become known these last days for his unstinting benevolence with the less fortunate denizens of Aebbenary, but Sovanna knew he had always been that way. Open-handed with friends and strangers in need, kind without previous cause, and willing to laugh at himself despite the vanity he sometimes shared with her.

She had not allowed him to be generous to her until now. Cristoval's leg hitched up slightly under her thigh as he leaned over her on her bed. That made her wonder why she'd squandered all that time fighting this; her exasperation with herself increased as he kissed a path across her cheeks and nose, down to taste the shadows under her jaw and the delicate skin of her arched neck.

He undressed her without hurry. Sovanna tried not to squirm as he studied her body—kissing and caressing at will but always, always studying—and the ways it must differ from any mortal girls he'd made love to. Silver streaks as if from a divine painter's brushstrokes decorated her flesh here and there; in the eternal glow of her Light she could not hide what she was or the beauty that had been granted to her, even if the manner of her conception and birth had rendered her different from any other being in the world.

"You are a Godling," he murmured as he gazed down at her where she laid, her dark hair a tangle on her pillow, "yet I have not honored you as you deserve. I haven't paid homage to your beauty and wisdom."

"Stop…" *Please don't.*

His smile as he removed his own clothes promised he wouldn't dream of it. In the illumination of her Light he couldn't hide from her either: his body was lithe, his grace cat-like enough to remind her of Aebbenary's famous duelists of old, but he was pale under that, and skinnier than a healthy man should be. Her eyes tracked the trail of dark hair on his chest down to the prominent vee of his hips and the marked arousal that showed how intensely he wanted her.

She shivered, not from exposure, but from the force of her own want. *I could make him mine forever. I could brand him with my Light and show him to the world as my companion. I could eat him up, drink him down and—*

"Tell me what you're thinking," he said. "You look hungry."

Guiding her legs apart he pushed between them and then inside her. He paused, hissing something like a curse or a prayer between his teeth; he tilted his head back, his eyes closing in pleasure at the slick feel of her clenched around him.

Sovanna buried her face in his shoulder when he smiled down at her, charming even in this; the ridged base of her horns scraped against his skin. "You have to stop looking at me like that. You're outrageous."

"Ah, you can't give me commands I must disobey." He teased her, he made love to her so slowly and tenderly but with mischievous intention that stoked her impatient lust higher.

All they could take from each other, gifted willingly and without reserve, would amount to these twilight hours waiting for night to fall. The love they made changed Sovanna on a fundamental level: she felt it swirling through the human shell that encased her blessed soul, breaking ground on new furrows that would crack her open like a vein of ore the moment she had to lose him.

Cristoval whispered sweet somethings and nothings in her ear, over her heart, between her thighs. Vows of ceaseless devotion and promises of fidelity she knew he would honor the way he venerated her body and beguiled a chain of orgasms from her to make this a night they would never forget. He wouldn't let her return the favor more than a couple of times, laughingly pleading his mortality and the indisputable fact that pleasuring her gave him just as much delight as the feel of her riding him or giving valiant effort to the prospect of eating him up.

The ichor didn't last as long as Sovanna hoped. Bettina had promised it would only help him, not cure him, but the eventual drag of Marzanna's curse sapped the passing flush of health from his skin, rendering it ashen once more. It filmed over his beautiful eyes with the glassy sheen of fever; it opened the gates to the unwanted mess trapped in his lungs so his drowning alive resumed its evil rattle in his chest.

Morning had always been a surety rather than an empty promise.

For one night only Sovanna and Cristoval had held destiny at bay to rejoice in what they meant to each other.

XXVIII

Cosima

The morning she was meant to kill her brother, Cosima knelt before Marzanna's brilliant throne and reported everything she knew would bring Her joy.

"The Godlings and Saints have shown promise. Your word is the only one that matters, Your Glory, yet I am confident in their progress to earning Your pride given enough time in my care." Cosima's voice rang with assured authority. She had taken great care arranging for this audience so she could play her part as the honored, thankful daughter and throw Goddess off any scent of subterfuge before the deed was done.

She'd worn her hunting leathers. Cleaned, polished, free of scratches and blemishes…and transformed from brown to ivory. It wasn't beasts Cosima stalked; the huntress's forest was not her hunting ground. The prey she promised Goddess would see her coming and open his arms to welcome the traitor's kiss of her blade.

Däard and Fiammetta were present in body but not in thought. Though Goddess couldn't have failed to notice, She permitted their distraction. Däard had leaned his head back against his throne and looked like he was asleep, though his brow furrowed unhappily. Fiammetta fidgeted and fretted with her garments in her seat, glaring at Cosima or pouting at Goddess spasmodically. Never had it been more apparent that she was mentally disturbed.

Goddess drummed Her lacquered fingertips against the arm of Her throne while She measured Cosima with a critical, unnervingly blank stare. It looked like She hadn't listened with more than half an ear. Cosima waited Her out and stood straight with a commander's posture to convey her lack of fear.

"You have not taken a consort."

A consort? Cosima's mind raced. *Of all things…why the fuck would I?*

"Should I have, Your Glory?"

"It is fitting for you to take an official partner in the coming days. Are there not numerous, favored Saints enough in our city to appeal to your tastes?" Marzanna gestured to the thrones on either side of Her own. "A consort is a steady bulwark to present to a watching, anticipating world…as is a strong ancestry. You are My heir—I would have you boast about that."

Cosima had been prepared for a whip of disappointment in her progress with the progeny training. A lash of motivation to try harder, do better, show more loyalty even if it meant groveling in the dust outside the Holy tower one who had failed as she had wasn't fit to ascend. Not her Mother's urging to bed and essentially wed someone to carry on a divine dynasty.

It had been whispered for most of the early years of the Bright Age that Goddess had ambitions for conquest that echoed the path of the former tyrant. In Cosima's youth most of those rumors had dissolved into stale speculation since Marzanna's attention had reverted inward, exclusively on Her pleasures in Aebbenary.

On the elusive prize She had been searching for, seeking with all Her thought and energy, to the exclusion of everything but Bettina and her children.

"A consort," Cosima repeated. She had not entered Goddess's presence armed, but she was grateful for the grounding sensation of the seams of her leather gloves creaking as she clenched her hands into loose fists. "I will obey You as always, yet I admit my astonishment. May I have time to consider—"

"Cosima, I didn't mean today!" Peals of Goddess's laughter rang throughout the room, sparkling and buoyant. "Your compliance pleases Me. Say what you have to say since you requested this audience. I will reward you after."

This mood of Hers is strange. Perilous. Quicksand would be preferable to this pockmarked arena of favor versus disfavor Cosima had to navigate.

"Your Glory," she began; smiling back at Goddess felt like it twisted her features into a grisly mask, but she managed it, "I grow impatient to see Your wish fulfilled. I know You seek Bettina: I know Your generous heart pines for her affection despite her wayward spirit. When I asked to live in the Holy tower at Your side, I all but promised You I would deliver Your will wherever I could. Though You granted me responsibilities here, over my fellow Godlings and the Saints, I humbly request temporary freedom from them to hunt."

Fiammetta grumbled where she slouched. "Hunt what?"

Goddess knew. She was the only one who mattered. Cosima nodded an excruciating, humiliating acknowledgment toward Fiammetta as hatred simmered below her surface, and waited for Marzanna to give her leave.

Golden eyes, immaculate in their thousandfold hues, pinned Cosima in place as the ruthless hooks of Her mind and will abraded the surface of her mind to seek any signs of deception or disloyalty. Marzanna jabbed and sliced at her mind—all without so much as a breath of effort expelled from Her lungs. Despite the ripping sensation of a tusk gored through her brain, Cosima recited the façade of her intentions with just enough truth to convince Marzanna of her faithfulness.

I am going to my brother, she repeated as long as it took for Goddess to believe her, *to draw Bettina out of hiding. Then I'm going to kill him and present his head to You on a platter. Let this be done.*

The worst part was that most of it wasn't a lie. With Magisend's help, Bettina *had* managed to hide from Goddess all this time. It was believable that Bettina hadn't contacted Cosima or Cristoval to protect them from further disfavor.

Cosima *was* going to kill Cristoval. Though the plan was sound, though the finger of destiny had dipped into their pool of time to send ripples out in rings over the world, nothing changed what her hands were about to do to her beloved brother.

"When you return, dearest daughter," Goddess said in a voice like rolling thunder, "I will honor you beyond compare. I will grant you the conquest of the world in My name."

Cosima had seen horrors before. She had found some of her huntresses who had endured divine abuse that had distorted their bodies almost beyond her healing capabilities. Her imagination had shown her unbearable nightmares in her restless childhood. Recently, she had dreamed of the eldritch, awful shape of personified knowledge that had told her what destiny had written for her family. When she closed her eyes, each time, she pictured Cristoval's body splayed out in undignified death; she heard Bettina's wail of despair whenever her surroundings fell too silent.

None of these would compare—none of them could—to what the earth would become once Marzanna decided all of it should belong to Her. Cosima couldn't wrap her mind around what the world would look like, subject to Goddess's full, occupying focus. Aebbenary had never even had that, not since the newborn weeks of the Bright Age.

"Her?" Fiammetta said. "What about Däard?"

She leaned toward Goddess with her gilded claws outstretched as if the mere brush of Her hem would be the boon of a lifetime. Her plaintive tone made Cosima want to close the distance between them to rip her hair out of her scalp. The pathetic *"What about meee?"* implied by the schooled echo of a whine in her protest couldn't have been louder.

Marzanna did not grant Fiammetta more than a passing glance, though She did allow her the chance to rest her pawing hand on Her arm. Fiammetta pounced on the offered tolerance like a kitten on a ball of twine and leaned her head on Goddess's shoulder to rub her cheek against Her exposed skin.

"Däard belongs at My side," Marzanna declared. "He will have another, happier matter to attend to. I have promised."

Däard's gaze flicked toward her, then away. That was all. The way Goddess ignored him was markedly different from the veiled disdain she showed Fiammetta: like these two, embodied power and highest Saint, had argued enough and wouldn't risk another quarrel.

Fiammetta's unspoken question remained unanswered. Cosima wanted to jeer at her in malicious glee. Throw stones at her and kick dust over her wicked heart. Anyone could see that Aebbenary's queen had fallen out of grace and couldn't slither back up to the high place she'd been cast down from.

The only question was *how* someone so elevated had tripped off their pedestal to land on mortal ground.

Goddess didn't view either of Her consorts' clearly desperate issues important enough to sway Her notice. She fixed Cosima in Her attention and charged her with a grinding thumb of authority to do her duty and return. Obedient in every aspect but the one that mattered, Cosima bowed in her murder-ready leathers so her coiled braid fell over her shoulder and dared approach to kiss her Mother's cheek in filial piety.

Once she had walked well outside the throne room, Cosima began to run. Physical, maximum effort sprinting as far as she could from the suffocation of Goddess's presence and the doom promised to every being in existence if Cristoval didn't die today. Bare of conscious direction but aware of her purpose, she fled both in her Light shape and sputtering out of it away from the tower and through the main thoroughfares and outskirts of the city to where Iulia waited for her.

Since Cosima could be compromised at any time, the others had waited to inform her where to meet for the sacrifice. Iulia had volunteered to carry the discreet, common scrap of paper that held Sovanna's instructions on where to join them. Divine beings, particularly supreme ones like Goddess and Her cohort, had all but forgotten the ordinary, necessary means of life and communication that mortals were ruled by. They were set to meet behind a candlemaker's shop and an apothecary; the scent of beeswax and the tiny seasonal fruits Aebbenary's city trees produced mingled to make a scent that should have been comforting.

She landed with secrecy she barely maintained in case of pursuit. Iulia had been seated on a wine-stained barrel in the backstreet. Her intimidating posture discouraged questions or intervention from anyone who didn't want someone who looked like a mercenary outside their business.

She stood as Cosima bent her knees to fall on them. Not hard, not like she'd really collapsed, but accepting the reality that they wouldn't hold her.

"I've got you." Iulia towed her up and enveloped her in a tight hold that couldn't be considered just a hug. She wore her hunting leathers too, but hers were not pristine ivory. "You're with me."

They'd said everything else before her audience. After making love that morning in the secrecy of one of Aebbenary's poor but respectable inns to avoid discovery.

"Take me with you?" Iulia had asked her. *"You shouldn't do this without someone who understands you best at your side."*

She knew Bettina would be there, and Sovanna. She knew Cosima loved them and didn't begrudge more people in her heart. But Iulia *did* understand her on a level no one but a huntress and a lover could match. For that moment in time Cosima loved her best of all.

"I will need you," Cosima had promised her, *"after."*

"You need me during. I can't let you do this alone." Iulia understood—she had almost always understood Cosima no matter how much her own heart sabotaged her—and hadn't judged. Neither did she diminish the difficulty, the *agony* of what Cosima had to do to defeat Goddess and Fiammetta and rescue the huntresses.

Cristoval was alive. Three blades would cut him on an altar somewhere Sovanna had arranged...then he would be no more. And Cosima would have eternity to mourn him.

"After." Cosima had repeated.

Iulia obeyed: with one last rib-crushing hug she departed to wait for Cosima near the abandoned cathedral. If something happened and Cosima didn't come, she had orders to travel in all haste back to the treehouse to pick up Palmira and Lilias and get them out of Aebbenary by any means necessary. It was possible someone would be sent to pursue them...but Cosima hoped Goddess's general disregard of mortals meant She might forget one or two long enough for them to flee to the other ends of the world and live their lives well before She came to conquer those distant lands.

Two curt sentences written in code had been etched on the paper Iulia had guarded. Cosima read them and ignited the missive to destroy the secret. She called her Light again and hurried away.

It troubled her that Goddess had not seen fit to have her followed. She wouldn't put it past Fiammetta either, but the caprice of a madwoman—though she could be cunning on occasion—supported itself in Cosima's mind. Did Marzanna really trust her? Had her performance, enhanced by the mask she had learned to wear and the presentations she had mimed skillfully since childhood, been convincing enough to assure a paradoxically omniscient being of her allegiance?

Or, Cosima thought with enough mental weight to sink her, *has She decided it doesn't matter if I'm really loyal or not?*

The Jubilee haunted her. Goddess had orchestrated that from the very beginning. What other grave theater might She have in store for them now if Cosima had failed to lie well enough?

Cosima chased these presages of doom away with all her strength of thought. All that mattered now was saying farewell to Cristoval and taking his life. She flew with the imaginary beating of wings she had never been granted—and saw now as a jinx—thundering in her ears toward the public gardens.

Blood loss would be the kindest death: they had agreed. Even Sovanna with her poisons had told them there was nothing kind or gentle about any of them, not for certain. Besides—ancient, dreadful lore whispered of blood's intrinsic value as a synonym for life itself. The act of spilling it on an altar once sacred—perhaps still sacred to the memory of god or gods long dead—had the potential to earn greater favor from the will of that which ordered the world and kept their globe spinning on its axis in the cosmos.

After she landed and wrapped her Light back into its usual halo like a cloak no longer needed, Cosima walked with delicate progress across the green toward her family. The long grass sighed as she passed as if in gratitude for the care she took not to crush their substance under her boots. It was impossible to see flowers or other colors at first. The only vision Cosima had in her mind showed the steel edge of her knife and the fountain it would release before the sun set over this consoling garden.

Aebbenary's public gardens were meant to be a refuge for city folk who tired of their lives spent in the lumber and stone island capital. The nobility had their private gardens—or vineyards in the case of the Valusius estate or a few rival sommeliers—but one Saint or another had taken pity on the populace to build something for them as well.

The urge had passed over a decade ago for whoever's idea this had been. The last thing Cosima had heard about these gardens had been a string of complaints about how ugly, overrun with vermin, and overgrown with bizarre plant manifestations it was. Cristoval had been the one to fund a renewal for these reserved acres: when he'd been stronger, he'd come himself to clear out rubbish, nurture any old plants that could be salvaged, and plant new bulbs and seeds that would blossom in years he would not live to see.

Bettina sat on the ground at Cristoval's feet in the center of a new grove lined with interesting stones and other relics purloined from destroyed architecture and smoothed into something useful. She rested her head on his knee as he played. She looked up at him with all a mother's love, shining brightly in spirit and halo. His were closed, though, in weariness revealed in the shadows beneath them and the slumped posture of someone a long time dying.

Behind them, Sovanna paced. Warlike in her wrath and misery, visibly ready to fight an entire pantheon of deities to cut them all loose from destiny's ugly net if given half a chance, her visage struck Cosima with the realization again that *this* was who Marzanna should have named heir.

Sovanna had chosen to side with them: the first Godling had chosen compassion rather than ambition. But it *had* been a choice. Faced with her now, Cosima wondered how fucked they would have been if Sovanna had decided Goddess was a better master than her own conscience.

Others were here. Though their grief and the wreckage of its lasting power would be devastating, neither Bettina, Sovanna, nor Cristoval had banished any visitors. The longer Cosima studied the scene the more convinced she was that word had gone out that this was the day the world would lose Cristoval. And somehow, incredibly, the people of Aebbenary trapped by the necessity of worship cared deeply about their doomed son and brother.

"Was it wise to begin here?" Cosima asked. Eyes cut her apart from all around, from mortalkind who had yet to judge if she would match Goddess's indifferent cruelty as well as Her likeness as heir.

Bettina turned, slowly, as if looking away from Cristoval hurt. Sovanna answered before she could.

"Aebbenary has grown to love him. We can spare a moment for him to take proper leave." If Cosima's expressions were masks, hers were set like the gemstone sculptures of Goddess and Her consorts erected all over the city. "Besides—Marzanna already sent Her dog to prowl among us."

Cosima grimaced: *she* was the dog. Tales of the favor she had garnered as dutiful heir had spread. The peasants and layfolk had heard…and they feared her.

She looked around at Sovanna's last bitter condemnation—though of course she understood Cosima had only played the role out of necessity—and watched as citizens and nobility alike shrunk against the edges of the round garden walls. Most had already begun to leave, in small groups and larger ones that didn't quite conceal their departure being a mass exodus away from the danger she posed by walking among them.

In Cristoval's hands the melodies and harmonies of Crespin's lyre were joyful rather than dejected. He didn't brood over an elegy for his short life or the ravages of the sickness starving and choking him in his last days. Bettina listened, the only one silent enough to memorize the tune, while Cosima and Sovanna traded verbal shots to avoid confronting their grief.

"Let her be, my love." Cristoval spoke up for her. "She did what she had to."

"I know."

When he smiled up at her where she stood beside him, Cosima watched and wished she could unsee this. Unsee Sovanna meeting his gaze without any of her usual aloof, stinging ice to cool her eerie beauty into a siren's treacherous lure. Somehow in the weeks since the Jubilee she had learned to love: Lilias the abomination and Cristoval the doomed.

Cosima closed her eyes to gather herself and summon whatever divine disregard she could lay claim to. Someone colder and harder might be able to work the sacrifice to greater affect than the whimpering ball of emotion resembling a human heart that she was.

"Cosima." Bettina didn't say her name often. She'd always had an endearment as a placeholder, though Cosima had sometimes cringed away at the intolerable affection in those titles. *My pearl, sweetling...*

"Yes, mama?" *How different they are, Mother and Mama, yet they both belong to me and I to them.* The concept of legacy boggled Cosima's mind if she thought about it too long.

"I'm happy to see you. I need you to know, though, that I wish even more powerfully that you weren't here. I would do everything for you—both of you—and it hurts me to my soul that I have not been permitted that chance."

Bettina didn't resemble a woman falling apart at the prospect of losing a child. She had finally looked away from Cristoval to address Cosima: serenity smoothed her expression to sleek glass, empty as a window. Purposefully so. When Cosima knelt beside her and tentatively pulled them together in a hug the tears that began to fall were silent. Like they had overflowed despite her best efforts to make the rest of her body delay its mourning.

A final moment passed. Cristoval played his lyre, Sovanna stood watch, and mother and daughter embraced and leaned against the rock where he sat for the last time.

Cosima couldn't bear to be the one to end that timeless respite before the duty that had conspired to unite them called. But the minutes ticking by were precious for more reasons than being Cristoval's last.

Goddess would not wait forever.

"When…"

"Now. We were only waiting for you," Cristoval answered her. Before any of them could stop him, he stood and set his instrument on the rock where he'd perched without any intention of picking it up again. When he staggered, unable to stave off the gurgling wet of vile fluid in his lungs, he waved them off between hacking coughs.

"Let me—"

"No. They'll be looking for me, to say their goodbyes." He paused to catch his breath; there was a blue tinge to his skin, Cosima noted, and a sheen like fish scales under the moon to his cheeks. "Goddess is going to have me, but I will not go to Her in secret. I will meet my end as a man."

He accomplished a few steps toward the open gates on his own, but not many. He didn't make a sound—other than a puff of a forced exhale—as he collapsed.

None of them could bear this alone. Not him, not even Sovanna, though of the three of them she would have been cold enough to accomplish the task and break later.

So they undertook this together: Bettina and Cosima propped Cristoval up by arranging themselves under each of his arms to help him walk on his own feet. Sovanna led the way from the tranquil, almost vacant park out into the city. She carried nothing but herself; with a regal lift of her chin she glided with effortless grace toward the streets that would lead them out of Aebbenary.

Ahead of them, citizens continued to flee. Though word of some of these events must have spread, if only among mortalkind, they all knew better than to risk their plausible deniability against any interrogator—even Däard himself—by lingering to see where Cristoval and his divine companions went. The boy was sick, wretched and marked for an ugly death, and everything else about that wasn't the business of poor mortals.

Some of them stayed long enough to cast fronds illegally cut from Aebbenary's blessed, cultivated trees before Cristoval on the path as they went. Glossy, deep green leaves fragrant with vitality that leaked from the places they'd been cut or twisted off their branches littered their way as all manner of people—dressed in humble clothes or rags and drawn with hunger—used these offerings to bid farewell to the man who had tried to help them.

Cosima listened for the thoughts that had persuaded so many people to gift this gracious farewell to her brother. According to Cristoval's studies with Sovanna—conducted by letter over a number of years—the mortals had been declining in health and mental stability since Goddess's Ascension and Her infamous sin. How could people reduced to slaves to Marzanna's will revere a mortal man in this way?

Could it be that they aren't really sick? There might be no need for this— Cosima's inspiration of hope made her Light flicker around her. _If there's any way we could be mistaken—_

"They are sick." Sovanna interrupted gently; Cosima hadn't realized she'd been casting out her hope like a contagion in her excitement. "Most of them could not defy a direct command or request even if they longed to refuse. I have read their hearts, now and again. Few now remain who do not think of Goddess and Her will every other moment. But they love Cristoval."

Who could not? Her brother had always been the apple of everyone's eye. Cosima could scarcely remember the years she'd spent envying his natural talent for making friends and earning affection.

"They've come to say goodbye in their own way." Bettina was paying more attention than she seemed, with her head bowed as if in prayer as they bore Cristoval onward down the streets.

"Some of them have reasoned that Goddess would not care about this temporal scrap of events. What does a rebel matter after he's…" Sovanna bit her tongue. Cosima heard her grind her teeth as if in rage.

Anger would, she agreed, be preferable to this knotted mess of other feelings the three of them shared.

I've been foolish again, Cosima realized. _We could have flown him where we're going. He must have known his people would want to say goodbye, no matter what would have been easier for him._

"Thank them for me," said Cristoval. With his head hanging in exhaustion it was hard to tell, but Cosima used the pretense of adjusting her stance to see his face. He stared at the fronds where they fell, as if memorizing the minute details of each leaf, and smiled as if this was the greatest tribute he had received in his life.

"Later," he added, sounding almost amused, like he was trying to lighten their mood.

Later. After. Meaningless measurements to Cosima—the world they knew would end the moment Cristoval died.

He fell before they made it to the seaside portion of the city. Divine beings like them could have supported him all the way, but if Cosima could feel him shaking and sweating while he concentrated everything he had on putting one foot in front of the other, so could Bettina.

No! Her thoughts railed against the indignity. He hadn't made demands of destiny or set his one mere life on a pedestal above all of humanity. *He just wanted to walk under the sun while he could. Even that...*

Bettina crouched beside where they had lowered him to let him catch his breath.

"I held you more times than I could count. I taught you to walk, talk, dance…everything. And I was honored to do all of it." Gently, so tenderly, she lifted her grown son into her Saint-strong arms and cradled him within their blessed Light. "Will you honor me again by letting me carry you?"

Cosima heard the distant sound of wailing that began from afar. Aebbenary couldn't—shouldn't—mourn Cristoval. It was treason to all-mighty Goddess. But who of the surrounding citizens lined up in surreptitious, shifting rows possessed a hard enough heart to refrain from weeping as they watched Cristoval nod and Bettina stand and carry him to his destined end?

The fronds continued to drop over their path with the people's manifestation of farewell. Though he was taller and larger than her, Bettina walked without faltering or tiring with her son in her arms, her daughter at her side, and Cristoval's beloved ahead of them.

He said something. Muttered to himself like he was invoking powers he didn't possess. Cosima leaned in to listen, watching for him to look at her, but even her senses didn't catch what he said. He slipped back into silence as they continued.

They reached the entrance to the docks; their path had brought them through the greater part of the city, which had taken as long as it had because more people than Cosima expected had come to say goodbye. Sovanna let them observe their pilgrimage to their chosen altar, but the moment they stepped from cobbled streets onto the wood of the docks she linked her Light with theirs to transport them to their destination.

It wasn't far, but it would have taken them several hours and a spot of sailing to reach the cove that appeared before Cosima's eyes when the dazzle of their own aureoles dimmed. No trappings of fishermen or wanderers littered the beach. Not far from where they landed, just around the jutting shoreline and a monument of boulders, a cave sat waiting for their arrival.

Her realm of choice was either the plains or forests of the island; even a desert would be preferable to the cold damp of Aebbenary's beaches and looming cliffs. Bettina cuddled Cristoval closer, as if she remembered swaddling him as an infant, as she caught Cosima's eye while they surveyed the coast.

Sovanna stared out toward the sea. She'd waded slightly into the shallow waves drumming against the shore, restless and greedy with the tide. The burgundy dress she wore clung to her legs in the damp; Cosima imagined the crusty feeling of salt drying on the layers of fabric and wanted to scratch her arms and legs to banish the idea.

Under the sun, her silver-ringed horns shone and distorted the reflection that appeared as the water smoothed to glass around where she stood. Appreciation for Sovanna's intense nature and the quiet, sisterly bond that had struggled up out of fallow soil to unite them struck Cosima as she watched.

The memory of how she'd struck up their link again after years of silence embarrassed her now. How could she have dragged Lilias to her to throw them away like rubbish? Like Sovanna had been discarded, she had intended to abandon a child who had never asked to be brought into the world rather than care for it for a while.

"Here?" Cristoval asked. He'd awoken from his stupor; the effort of turning his head toward Sovanna looked like it would do him in before they could.

She turned back, facing him without turning her whole body his way. The reason she had paused so close to their purpose became clear when Cosima saw the tears that had stolen past Sovanna's armor to trickle down her cheeks. She pointed to the cave, indicating it in case they had somehow failed to notice, and started to walk toward the entrance.

"This island suffered more gods before Marzanna and the tyrant She usurped. The records I found don't trace back to humanity's dawn, but...power dwelt here, long ago." Her voice stayed even though the rest of her must be in turmoil.

"And you will need all the power you can claim," he said, voicing the rest of her notion like they shared the same mind.

You, he said. Not we. Cosima kept forgetting he wouldn't be there to share in whatever future they clawed out of Goddess's blessed future.

The cave beckoned. The ground was sand and salt-crusted shells washed up from the sea that crashed against the shore in high tide. Their destination was barely out of reach of the icy fingers of the ocean that, perhaps, would claim Cristoval's body as it had claimed Crespin's.

Sunlight still yellow with late morning hues pierced the dark maw of the opening. When they entered, their aureoles provided similar luminescence to the stale air of the passage they traversed to reach the end. Ancient peoples had hollowed this cliff for their own purposes. They had no need to pretend anything else was here but the round, torch-studded room and a plain altar.

Cosima stared at it, unable to look away. Sovanna had been here before, so she didn't wince at the sight of the pitted slab stained here and there with moss or old blood. It was wider than the breadth of a man and longer—as if other beings different from mortal men had been sacrificed to old powers in those distant ages of blood. When tongues of Sovanna's Light set fire flickering in the ancient sconces, the illumination made it appear more terrible, not less.

This isn't the place for him, Cosima thought, lingering at the end of the passageway. Her hands were empty, and she despaired. She should have brought something besides the knife sheathed in its scabbard on her hip. Coins to place on his eyes, basil to crush for its scent of mourning, sandalwood to prepare his body for…for…

Bettina laid Cristoval down on the weather-carved altar. Cosima approached, swiped her hand across its misty surface, and shivered at its frigid, slick feel. Cristoval shivered too, but he couldn't stop shaking. More racked him and chattered his slightly crooked teeth.

He still tried to comfort her.

"I see you agonizing, Cosima. Always worrying."

"You make me worry. You and Mama."

He couldn't laugh, not shivering like that, but his wry smile was familiar even though pain and his permanent struggle to draw breath marred it. "I'm sorry for that. I wish…we were able to spend more time together without you both worrying about me."

That fault lay at Bettina's door, and she knew it, but Cosima couldn't find it in her to withhold forgiveness for those anxieties. In the end, was there anything they could have done to stave off the destiny that had dragged all four of them into this cave to trade Cristoval's life for the hope of salvation? For everyone else even if peace would elude their family.

"We don't know what powers rule the world beyond this one," Bettina said suddenly, thoughtfully. Her arms looked empty; her face had fallen like it felt empty too. She leaned against the altar as if still wondering how she could make anyone understand how intensely she wanted to lay herself upon it rather than her son. "Maybe we'll meet again in another place. Another life."

"I hope so." Cosima could not think of hope, or of a life beyond this accursed immortal existence that had rarely brought her joy, but she granted Bettina and Cristoval the promise of it anyway.

"It's time." Sovanna laid a hand on his chest and, with a thought, let her power disintegrate his shirt. Cosima's arm jerked as she fought the protective urge to slap her hand away—he was cold! Couldn't she *see* that? Didn't she have any pity left to give?

It will be harder to clean his body afterwards if she left it on, Cosima reminded herself.

They stretched out his arms to either side like wings. Cosima stared at the blue lacing of veins at the vulnerable places under his arms, fluttering in his throat, darker than usual under his fever-bright eyes. He had felt hot when she had first helped him walk out of the public park, but the gooseflesh that ridged his skin now showed that he would never be warm again.

"I love you." Cosima offered her love like it would mean something.

"I love you," he repeated back to her. A ghost of a smile at her awkwardness—which he'd professed eternal fondness for—played around his pale lips as he accepted the clumsy hug she gave his reclined figure.

He looked toward his mother.

"I…" Bettina covered her face with her hands, almost cutting her own forehead with the knife, before she recovered. When she lowered her hands she was smiling, *radiantly,* as she stooped to kiss Cristoval's forehead and each cheek. "I love you, angel."

"I love you," he replied again. His voice cracked that time; Bettina's silent tears leaked over the smile she couldn't maintain to make his last sight of her joyful, and she embraced him where he lay.

Cristoval looked toward Sovanna. Who gazed down on him without flinching, with aught but steel in her thunderous expression. She was so angry Cosima saw the knife point carving a tiny circle in the air as she clutched it tight.

Then, like a gift, she softened. Cosima admired from the other side of the altar as Sovanna mastered her grief and rage and banished it for his sake. It was a gift of her own, they all knew it because they knew *her* better now, to let her sorrow show. Her tears began to fall—only two or three—as she stroked Cristoval's hair back from his forehead and tenderly cupped his chin with her free hand to kiss his lips with unrestrained love.

"I love you," she swore like a vow. "Cristoval, I am *always* going to love you."

"I am grateful I knew you in the time I was granted. I love you with everything in me, Sovanna."

Staring with all devotion into his eyes, Sovanna pressed her knife to the prominent vein in his neck and sliced a rope of red there. A gasp shuddered out of him, too low for a cry…then the awful gurgling started.

End it! Cosima shrieked in her mind, aching and wounded unto death like it was herself she cut as she raised her wooden arms and cut another vein under Cristoval's arm.

Bettina cut under the other arm, where Sovanna showed her. Cosima already knew how to end a man's life, but she followed her instructions anyway to carve more streams to end his suffering as quickly as they could.

His eyes closed. His blood flowed out, over the altar and onto the ground. They listened to the silence of the cave, broken only by Cristoval's fading gasps, until enough had left his body to sink him into sleep.

He had lived; he had died because they had taken his life for their own. Cosima offered this despicable truth to whatever power wanted it, cursing the name she didn't know as she thrust her bloodied knife high above her head. Her defiance was symbolic, but the only thing worse than this would be the realization that it had been for nothing.

Bettina didn't even glance at her knife before she hurled it toward the back of the cave. She threw herself over Cristoval, keening a lament punctuated by tears she had no further need to restrain.

Sovanna didn't move. When her hair began to float up in an invisible breeze, when the energy summoned by the death they had brought sweetly and gently to their son, brother, and beloved, she looked up at the shadowed roof of the cave and gripped her knife tighter.

I cannot bear it. Cosima's thoughts were barely coherent as she watched. The urge to pluck out her own eyes brought her hands to her eyes in fists to block everything out. *What have we done? Nothing in the world can be worth this—*

Objects began to fall, appearing from nothing. Cosima realized they were pearls as she watched a few of them roll under the base of the pitted altar and stick in the tide of blood pooled there. Confusion captured her; she looked up, lowering her hands to seek whatever had dropped the pearls.

Bettina slowly stood up straight while the cave began to quake all around them. More pearls rolled off his corpse.

Her tears had transformed into blessèd, bountiful treasure. A symbol of favor only one being would grant.

Goddess is coming. Cosima, Sovanna, and Bettina stared at each other and braced themselves against the earth rocking beneath them.

XXIX

Sovanna

To beings conceived outside of the rules of time, the passage of it meant nothing. It could be bent or folded neatly according to Miraculous will with enough power and a divine constitution. The past was a closed door: some deities had already attempted to explore it out of curiosity or other nefarious reasons. Though they had bragged to others they had seen the shimmering figment of a hole or a door through time, no one had ever confirmed their claims.

Besides, who could possibly want to leave Marzanna's Bright Age?

Goddess was coming. Before Cristoval's body had begun to cool, stiffen, or bloat, She flew through time and Light to come to the place where Bettina's shield of concealment melted away. They had, the three of them, released profound power on this altar. Either the benefactors she had told Sovanna about had not empowered her shield strongly enough, or they had dropped it to allow Bettina to serve her role as bait.

They had planned this. Sovanna saw panic and terror rounding Bettina's eyes anyway. It wrenched a cry from her throat as she turned, glittering under her son's blood, and threw herself backwards from the altar. Pearls clattered all around in her wake.

Something caught Bettina. The phantasm of a hole or a dream-like gate materialized behind her and sucked her in while the world quaked like it would shake itself apart under the onslaught of Goddess's haste to capture her.

Sovanna didn't have time to shout a warning before the last sight of Bettina—blood-spattered hand reaching out toward Cosima as if to drag her into flight with her—vanished into the portal.

Before the sacrifice, in advance of Cosima's arrival, Sovanna and Bettina had discussed much. She knew Goddess would follow Bettina into the fabled garden where the Archivist and the All using him would be waiting.

Cosima ducked; Sovanna waited until the last second to do the same. Like sisters, they reached for each other across Cristoval's body and knotted their bloody fingers together to anchor themselves under Goddess's torrent of unchecked radiance.

She came. Streaking across the island, Her approach a dire serenade of victory sung by an accursed choir within Her manifold Light, Marzanna arrived. Without vacating Her Light, without even looking toward the altar, She stabbed a spear of Miraculous will into the place the portal had been and *pried* it open.

The sound was like steel grinding against steel. Brick and plaster crumbling on a colossal scale. An avalanche beyond the high mountains or a landslide beneath the sea that sent mighty waves racing to the shore to swallow civilization as they knew it. Goddess paid no heed—Her thoughts were fixed on Bettina and invading the garden to plunder its power.

Bettina dancing around the spear in the ship, Bettina flying on wings that She had granted and ripped away. Travails and tricks to break into the garden where, deep within its secretive heart, a scholar with empty eye sockets and a generous smile held out his arms for Her to fall into...

Sovanna collapsed, rolling on the ground and clutching her head in agony as images struck her mind in waves.

At last!

No thought had ever been more triumphant. The two words obliterated the paltry defenses Sovanna's psyche had thrown up like shored walls in a siege in her panic. She wasn't screaming anymore, but Cosima had yet to stop.

Goddess's Light screamed overhead and through the portal with chaos under Her wings and incredible power at Her back. With the same finality of Cristoval's existence trickling out of his body, She was gone. Bettina would be on her own during whatever lay in store for her in the garden.

Half-blind and still trembling, Sovanna rolled onto all fours and leaned on the altar to heave herself up. The edge of her knife scraped against the stone; she winced. Nearby, Cosima lurched to stand as well. Grains of sand adhered to where Cristoval's blood had spattered her ivory leathers.

"Did Goddess know about this place?" she asked.

"I'm not sure. I gambled on Her contempt for the old ways or ignoring their relevance when I chose this spot for…" Sovanna's attention drifted down to the motionless figure on the altar. She swallowed, hard, willing her eyes to stay dry.

The deed was done. There was no undoing that.

They had no time at all to spare, but Sovanna and Cosima lingered together in the cave. The darkness crowded close after the brilliant comet of Bettina's departure and Goddess's pursuit. The torches had been blown out during the chaos. In their grief, after the shock of it all, their aureoles darkened so even blessed eyes might struggle to see.

Cosima smoothed Cristoval's curls back from his clammy forehead and kissed his brow. In farewell.

"I'm going."

Sovanna tried to understand. She knew Cosima had other people to look after.

"The huntresses are waiting for me. While Goddess is distracted, I'm going to make Fiammetta—"

"Go." If Sovanna gave the order herself would it hurt less when she stood vigil over her lover's body? The same obligations that had brought this tragedy about still hounded each of them.

They had done this together. It was no more in Cosima's nature to show affection than Sovanna's, but she surprised both of them when she hurried around the table to embrace Sovanna.

Before knowing any of them she would have assumed she was a stand-in for Bettina and the huntresses: there was no one else here to hold onto during this tempest other than each other. But Sovanna had grown in ways she hadn't dreamed were possible. She *liked* Cosima. She thought if their futures were less bleak they could be friends, and knew Cosima shared her idea when she ended the embrace.

She didn't speak. After the searing path of Goddess's chase, Cosima's transportation of Light was as mild as a spring shower. Sovanna was alone.

Alone.

Cristoval's corpse was her only company. Sovanna had no choice but to admit that his body disconcerted her despite her love for him and her familiarity with corpses. Her knife was still in her hand. The patters of Cristoval's blood dripped off the altar to mimic delayed rainfall. After Bettina's flight, the pearls she'd cried remained stuck where they had fallen, mired on the ground or glued to Cristoval's skin like barnacles.

She hadn't brought any burial weeds. Back in her hut, Sovanna had written a list of what to buy or steal to prepare Cristoval's body for its resting place, but indecision had prevailed. She'd forgotten to ask before she sacrificed him if he would rather be burned on a pyre, buried in the earth, or sunk to the ocean depths.

It's the taking of it that matters.

Sovanna contemplated that for a while. The cave swallowed any notion of time she still had. It would be easy to take something else, now: something just hers. What was the life of an abomination like herself after any of this? Would its worth amount to even a quarter of Cristoval's?

She had been loved. *He* had loved her with everything he had. The hour had long since passed when she had resented how that love had changed her or what it might still cost. But he was the first one who had truly felt any affection for her, and the list of others who might was short. Part of what had made his martyrdom worth it was because of how much his family and his city had loved him.

Besides, her practical side needled her as she ruminated and— obeying a ghoulish urge—plucked the pearls off Cristoval to toss them aside, *you don't know how to die.* Godlings *can't even do that, let alone an atrocity like you.*

They had their new power. Sovanna knew what Bettina would do with hers—what she *had* to do—and guessed how Cosima would use hers. If Cristoval had managed to accomplish anything in his last moments of life he would have granted whatever gift his willingness to die had left him to the people of Aebbenary to cure their ingrained dependence on divine dominance.

What could she do with hers? What did Sovanna desire beyond life restored to her beloved?

"Sovanna." A voice from the depths of the cave. Thinking it a manifestation of her grief, she ignored it.

You can't bring him back. That's how Marzanna sinned—that's what necessitated all of this.

"I don't know how to join you, wherever you are." It felt right to speak to Cristoval. She didn't believe in human specters, she wasn't sure if he could really hear her, but speaking her wish into existence must give it power if she had anything worthy for this. "I'm going to try something else first. If I don't succeed—"

"Sovanna."

She knew who it was. When he was around, flesh or bones but rarely both, she always sensed his presence. He was here now, creeping around the altar like he had been here the entire time, waiting for the evil prophecies he had been privy to to bear fruit.

"Do not disturb my grief, father. Tempting my wrath will not be difficult."

"Sov?"

Sovanna's neck cracked as she whipped her head to the side at the sound of Lilias's voice. Only once she looked did Easoren emerge from the shadows, carrying Lilias in his flesh-clad arms. It hadn't been the darkness sidling close, supple as a serpent preparing to strike: it had been the former Priest, cloaked in his own skin by his own machinations despite his rebellion against Goddess.

She'd been holding herself together remarkably well given the circumstances, Sovanna thought. She had physically wrapped herself in her arms as she'd considered how to prepare Cristoval's body for his

419

eternal sleep. She flew to where Easoren stood with Lilias, who reached out for her with their strange little face eager and happy.

I can't let them see Cristoval. Not like this…

Easoren let her rip Lilias out of his arms. He stood, watchful as a cemetery sentinel, as she launched herself back toward the altar, ready to defend herself against any trickery or attack.

"Don't look!" Sovanna shouted. The wrath she'd boasted of swelled in her heart. "How could you bring them here? They're a child. *They loved him too.* You—"

"They wanted to come."

"Wh—"

Lilias wriggled their arms and legs and four wings with uncanny strength to make her loosen her grip. Their usual babbling was silent, but they peeked over her shoulder toward the altar with all four of their eyes open in what could only be named…curiosity. Even once they recognized Cristoval laying there they didn't wince or fuss.

Their wings flared. One of their eyes—a red one—closed as they cocked their head and leaned down, half out of her arms, to splash their small, clawed hands in the blood on the altar.

Though she should have felt disgust, all the emotion Sovanna could rally was exhaustion. Of all beings, Cristoval wouldn't mind Lilias misbehaving in his mortal coil's vicinity. It was disturbing, but not a sin she wanted to waste effort punishing.

"What are you doing here? *How* can you be here? Did you kill Cosima's girls to steal this child?"

"The garden has no limit of paths. I go where I please and take what I must," Easoren answered, cryptic as ever. When Sovanna glared at him and hefted her stained knife in a threat he sighed with theatric impatience. "The child knew to come to me after the martyr died. I merely had to help them find you."

This was the most normal Easoren had ever looked. She examined him from head to foot since he posed no immediate threat, assessing the danger his presence might bring. It had been years since she had seen him, let alone seen him wrapped in his own skin and not rotting slowly for failing to please Marzanna well enough.

She saw the means that knotted him into one piece if she looked close enough: midnight blue threads, too tiny for mortal eyes to notice, crisscrossed all over his body with precise stitches. Thousands and thousands of them.

"What will you demand for your sacrifice?" he asked.

"Does it matter?" Sovanna huffed as she chuckled—a schoolmaster amused with a former student. "Goddess's downfall. All the power we have must go to that."

Tetchy, Lilias beat their wings. Sovanna released them to let them hover in the air by their own power. All around the altar they flew, crossing their stained hands over their chest as they studied Cristoval's body with curious mutters emitting by fluting harmony from their mouth.

Easoren approached: slowly, with his hands lifted to show he wasn't a threat. Sovanna didn't trust him for a second.

"Must it?" he asked.

The two words plucked at the bridle Sovanna kept on her hope. A bridle, a cruel bit, *anything* wicked or harsh she could think of to strangle that useless prize in its cradle.

"You've come here for a purpose." That much was true: Sovanna knew Easoren *always* had something nefarious cooking in that usually empty skull of his. "You have no right to interrupt my mourning. Say what you came to tell me and *get out*."

"I know you tried to sacrifice the brat to save your martyr."

He's proud of me. Renewed shame made Sovanna duck her head; she didn't want to see his face. In the fortifying Light of her halo the shadow of her horns cast slender darkness over Cristoval's body. *Who could be proud of a monster but the one who helped conceive it?*

"You failed," Easoren continued. "Perhaps you were meant to. I have found that destiny can be blind to beings outside the compass of its foretold patterns. Did you not consider that you did not need to kill the child to make use of it?"

Lilias had let her bind them to her table to steal their blood to heal Cristoval. They were inherently good, noble, even if their existence was bizarre. Sovanna had been the selfish one, though a ray of something as holy as maternal love had persuaded her to stay her hand at the last second.

How could I ask it of them?

"Look." Easoren told her, because she hadn't.

She looked up. Lilias straddled Cristoval's chest and leaned over his face to pry open his vacant eyes. Their other red eye closed; their sable wings folded closed around their body as they pressed their nose against Cristoval's and let their red wings broaden further than their span ordinarily allowed.

They *breathed*. Into Cristoval's slack mouth as the power beginning to *thrum, thrum, thrum* in reverberation inside the cave's walls made Sovanna's hair stand on end. She watched, aghast but enthralled, as stained blood trickled out of Lilas's mouth and into Cristoval's.

A gift. Grotesque, maybe in vain, but an offering nonetheless.

"A sacrifice such as Cristoval's is without equal, without parallel. Even the implicit rules that order the world can be persuaded to yield by the crooked means of a bargain. You cannot bring him back…not *entirely."* said Easoren. He stood beside her now, beside the altar where Lilias did what they had come to do.

Sovanna watched. She hadn't noticed her father step close enough to whisper lies—they had to be lies—in her ear. She hadn't noticed when her hope sprang from its chains and coursed unchecked through her soul.

Her knife fell from her nerveless fingers.

"Why help me?" She could not conceive of an answer. Neither Easoren, the High Priest of Aebbenary, nor Easoren, prisoner and plaything of Goddess, had ever cared about her as a daughter or as anyone remotely useful to his schemes.

"I know that same binding that tied you to the martyr."

"You kn—" Surprise was a weapon in his hands. She didn't want to hand him one. "You and Goddess. Your bond. *That's* why She kept you all this time."

"I took something from Her before Her Ascension. She came to get it back—Her Scholar. Even if I had the power, I would have refused."

"You refused many things She might have wanted."

422

I needed an ally. Could a daughter ever escape the longing for a father's affection? Horned and considered hideous due to her origins, Sovanna had built up her strength and her vanity all alone in the hollow court of a Goddess who had denied her every connection that mattered. Easoren's neglect had been expected, as she had never been enough of a fool to anticipate anything else, but the wound had been struck. It would always be there.

Yet he had come to deliver this to her. Hope in the black pit of despair when her world had come crashing down around her ears and there was still work to be done to make this sacrifice mean anything at all.

"You gave more than a life—he gave more than his own. You surrendered the sacred, destined connection that linked you for enough power to change providence itself. Would that I could do the same with my own millstone…" He let the sentence lag and fall off without conclusion.

He never had to love me back. He just had to live, mortal and kind, and be happy. Sovanna would have been grateful for that. If Goddess had let that happen, she would have traded her dignity in for eternal shackles and danced as Bettina had for Her Shining Court.

"I won't thank you." Sovanna made her decision while she spoke, not before. "Though you sired me, I don't know you. Something tells me you don't deserve my gratitude or anything else but an end to the too-abundant suffering Goddess inflicted on you all this time."

Easoren's skeletal frame shifted as he bowed his head in acknowledgment bordering on respect. A note too late his skin moved with him.

"You have given enough. I only sired you in place of the god I once served, but I recognize my likeness in you. I cannot atone for whatever harm that has caused."

Was there anything she could say to that? They were not father and daughter in any sense but blood, and that just barely. Sovanna had wondered before, knowing what she did, how much time she had squandered dreaming of a family she would never have. Two parents— whatever their origins or temperaments—who were united in their love for her. Siblings who didn't revile her for her differences. A home with people she loved, and one who loved her more than anything or anyone else.

All of that had passed out of her reach, now. Every futile wish.

Lilias finished their donation. They sat back on Cristoval's solid chest and watched expectantly for it to rise and fall with life restored.

Sovanna watched too: talk of millstones, sacrifices, and rewards swirled in her mind along with every memory she had ever shared with Cristoval. Däard's words after he had prevented her from sacrificing his child with Fiammetta—how that could have happened when he clearly despised her, Sovanna didn't know—returned again and again to the comforting darkness that covered her eyes with each slow blink.

"Do you not love, Däard?"

"I wish I knew."

She knew. The revelation that struck her made her aureole blaze high and hot in the abandoned cave. The moisture clinging to the walls and shards of shells in the sands sparkled as she burned with the knowledge that her clever mind finally put together.

Easoren studied her. He had been this entire time, waiting with uncharacteristic patience for her to conquer her grief long enough to make the connections she needed to. When she turned to him, frenetic and half feral with the urge to act, to *save Cristoval...*

He was melting. Already—she hadn't had to ask.

"Strange blood. Living flesh cleansed of all traces of rot." There was a poignant tone in Easoren's voice as the threads binding his skin to his bones snapped piece by piece to leave him naked to the world once more. "I gained something back during this twilight hour of Goddess's reign. To grant unto you."

Gilded bones swarmed with filaments that snapped and writhed like centipedes as they tried to compensate for the loss of anything to bind. Sovanna stepped back, wary and already reaching for Lilias to put him behind her, as Easoren's skeletal hands lifted to cover his lidless sockets and lipless teeth.

"Pick up the flesh. Cover the boy before it claims me again—it longs to return to me, always," Easoren commanded from behind his hands. Sovanna hurried to obey and steeled herself to scoop the puddle of mortal matter off the sand and lay it on the altar. Nothing else in the universe could feel like this: she could barely analyze it. Warm, smooth, ridged like snake scales, it didn't look like what it was anymore. A bundle of white-and-silver stone neither alive nor dead.

When she laid it on Cristoval's body and tried to spread it over him—gagging on revulsion she couldn't quite banish—it sank *into* him and vanished. Light—untouched by gold—swathed the body on the altar like fine burial cloth. Where it touched the artifacts gifted from Sovanna, Lilias, and Easoren, Lilias's scarlet and brimstone offering of blood stained it red. Sovanna told herself this was a good sign rather than an unsettling omen.

"Good. The sacrifice is already in motion. Your wishes have been made known." Easoren panted the words from a body gripped by threads stretched tight to imitate the flesh he'd given up for Sovanna's use. He looked like his mostly-human self, but a shadow of his former mortality.

"You…" She had already vowed not to thank him. He was one of the architects of her loneliness still, despite his gift now. A gift he'd all but said he was donating to bring Goddess low, not to honor a daughter he had barely acknowledged all these years.

Easoren's pale brows lifted as he sniffed out her conflict. "These trimmings will hold as long as they need to. Do what you must."

Was an amalgamation of gifts enough to rebuild a man from the ground up? Lilias's blood, Easoren's flesh, the will of her sacrifice to call as much of him back as she could…Sovanna ticked off the list to herself as she dared reach into the augmented Light surrounding Cristoval and plucked a discarded pearl-tear from where it had gotten lost in his hair.

She met Lilias's eyes across the altar. Sweet and disconcerting, the child propped their arms on the stone—they had to be standing tiptoe—and beat their wings gently in time with the slow winking of their ebony eyes. Waiting for her to act.

Will Cristoval be anything like he was with other fragments lost to the void? How much did Sovanna care?

"Maybe this is part of our destiny." Sovanna reached up to grip her left horn just above her head. "He would not have defeated Goddess before. All he could do was die."

"That was his role. He knew it," Easoren agreed. He must have guessed what was coming, what she would do.

He watched without blinking his piercing, sea mist eyes as she braced herself against the altar with one hand and used all her strength to break one of her horns off with her other.

You were too kind, my love. Too good. Blood spurted from the jagged stump high on her forehead. Sovanna groaned, her consciousness wavering, but that was all. *If I cannot bring you back as yourself, I will make you stronger than you ever were. More powerful than you ever could be when you belonged to others.*

"He completed that task." Sovanna's resolve didn't waver as she swallowed the torment that clawed at her throat as the horn she had broken spattered the altar with more blood, this addition silver rather than crimson. "But I think he has another."

"It might not be him," Easoren cautioned where he stood at her right hand. "It most likely won't be him at all."

Sovanna laughed. The sound was as dead as her lover. Her destined companion, granted by a power and order that could not comprehend the nature of anything but itself. They had been connected, had passed each other like ships in the night, and the thing that bound them had frayed and snapped once death had cut it asunder.

"It doesn't have to be," she answered, and cracked Cristoval's ribs under her hands.

XXX

Bettina

She stank of copper and iron and mortal salt. Would it cling to her forever, this horrendous sin that she had been tasked with to save every other mother's children?

Even her right to mourn had been stolen from her. Ripped away like the wing Goddess had granted for the purpose of taking away. Yet this loss could not be allayed with the skilled stitches of an Archivist.

Bettina ran from the blaze of Goddess's quest. The garden that had extracted her from the cave where her son had breathed his last opened like a storybook as she fled through gates that were wide-open on a shadowed path. They closed behind her…just in time to block Marzanna and give her a head start.

The way ahead presented only darkness. Her blessed eyes could make out the vague shapes of trees and fleeing beasts. The sounds that assaulted her ears were loud and frightening, but all the light from her first visits to this place was being devoured by the awesome might of the being who followed her from the outer world.

Frailty after her ordeals became but a memory. Even if she had enjoyed the luxury of ignoring the ways her divine body could still fail her, either Goddess, Bettina's sacrifice, or the garden itself empowered her limbs with strength and speed to outlast pursuit. Though Marzanna had entered almost right behind her, Bettina's elusion was a success.

She staggered to a halt what felt like several miles down the lone path in the murky garden. She couldn't lose her breath, but she panted from the effort of everything since she'd met Cristoval that morning—had it only been a day?

He lived, she mused; thinking was difficult with each thought scrambling for escape that couldn't be found. *He lived until we cut away his life to spare everyone else.*

A better mother would have spared her son and damned the world. As a favorite of eternal Goddess, Bettina had suffered too much to pretend anything would be better for those unlucky enough to enjoy Marzanna's partiality.

"Bettina!" Someone called ahead. A familiar voice she wasn't sure she trusted given the garden's taste for manipulating her with unwanted prophecies and visions.

Trust it or not, Bettina hastened to its source. Maybe the garden would see fit to grant her one final gift before everything else ended...

Magisend was here. He had waited for her.

Bettina flung herself into his arms knowing he would catch her before she let herself collapse. Even if The Speaker had already absorbed him, there would surely be enough of him left in there to hold her close, even for a moment...

"It's done!" she sobbed into his shoulder. "We killed him. *I killed him.* Cristoval is dead!"

Jewels poured from her mouth in echo of her words, one gemstone per syllable. Rubies and sapphires and topaz and emeralds. Bettina tried to shove Magisend away from her in complete irritation, stomping on the jewels to crush them into dust with all her divine strength.

Magisend caught her by her waist and crushed her to his chest. It really *was* him with her still, but she couldn't appreciate it when all her tears became pearls and every word she uttered transformed into gems flickering with sacred Light under their facets.

"Fuck You, Marzanna!" she screamed as loud as she could. She beat her fists against Magisend's chest, and he let her. "Fuck Your blessings and Your *love* and everything You claim that was never Yours!"

All the gems were garnet now. Red like mortal blood. Bettina choked on one and spat it out in defeat, watching tear-pearls follow its fall.

"I'm here, I'm here…" Magisend offered the only comfort he could as she wept.

It was foolish to stand on this path with Goddess on Her way, bogged down temporarily by the gates that would confound Her until might prevailed against the locks, but neither one of them could release the other. Not when these were their last moments together.

"You have been brave beyond compare. Noble without equal." Magisend released her long enough to cup her face in his hands and make her look at him. "I cannot pretend to understand the extent of your loss, but I grieve with you. I can offer that."

And he did. Bettina laid her hands over his on her blotchy cheeks and watched tears like green sap trickle down his gaunt face. When they kissed again, hearts breaking together, she tasted a hint of vibrant summer greens and grape must vinegar.

He wore The Speaker's armor and visage. *How can that be when he belongs to me? When I sacrificed pieces of myself to give him this body and he prides himself on the soul he must have grown?*

"Thank you." Two words instead of the three she should have said, but their need felt stronger. Bettina kissed Magisend again and whispered her gratitude against his cold lips. The needles that filled his pores pierced her again, but it had been some time since she'd loathed that sensation.

"Thank you." He offered the words back. "I learned to become myself from you. There is no greater gift I know of."

The garden began to shift all around them—like it had been waiting for Bettina and Magisend to meet—transforming the landscape into what was to come with Goddess' arrival. She flung her arms around his neck one last time and then made herself let go. Bettina pried herself away from him when all she wanted to do was hold on and sink to sleep on the downy grass together for a repose that would last an age.

The Speaker inclined his head in acknowledgment of her continued dedication to their cause as Bettina backed a few steps away.

"Where should I go?" she asked. "The way is dark. I don't know if the path forks."

He answered without offering more than a little valuable

information. "Goddess will pursue you to the ends of the garden. She will chase high and low, above and beneath to make you Hers. There is only one who could stay Her hunger long enough to let the powers we have all conjured to end Her reign work."

"The Scholar. Lior Betilienus. But he's dead. Even She could not—"

"She could have if She had willingly surrendered the power that his death and other sacrifices bought Her. Very little moves the powers beyond to relinquish their dead…but the price they named was in Her hand. She did not pay it."

Bettina understood with a dour bloom of victory amidst the deep well of her grief. "I did."

"She comes," he reminded her as behind him, beyond the gates the howling uproar of Goddess in full glory seethed. "When decisions come, I will be there to guide you. Flee with all haste."

Bettina scanned the road ahead and shivered. She feared the hot, conscious darkness more than she had when she was a mortal child left to sleep alone in her nursery.

"To the ends of the garden?"

The Speaker pointed with measured, unhurried veneration. "To the basin of the world."

Bettina spread her wings and took flight down the path.

Trees bent slender limbs toward her. They creaked and snapped if they stretched too far. They mourned with her as she cried, unable to cease the tears that streamed from her eyes as the distress from what she had done and had yet to do accelerated her flight.

Goddess attempted to lock her down with a myriad of blessings meant to reward her for the terrible sin no mother should commit against her child. The wind that should have soared under her wings ruffled her feathers like hands petting and plucking in rough affection. Bettina's halo brightened to fantastic hues that, while beautiful enough to inspire tears and awe, dazzled her eyes so she couldn't see.

I refuse these and all other gifts, she sent the thought on the profane wind back to Marzanna with a bejeweled curse to accompany it. *You will never have me. I will never love You as I once did.*

If, in the distance, Goddess heard her message, She did not

respond. The wind might have screeched in Bettina's ears like laughter, like a spider spinning a web just for her, but that was all.

As if her capture and subjugation was too inevitable to argue.

The first fork in the path split the road into four channels. The fruit trees, conifers, and deciduous watchers wilted low enough to force Bettina to land or risk impalement on bare, spear-like branches. Her heels skidded on the stone as she landed with inexpert steadiness.

They all looked the same. Some were darker, some rockier, but none of them were different enough to make an educated guess where to go. As Bettina hesitantly approached one of the two middle paths, the animals in the garden began to whisper or hiss.

They spoke to her, these owls and bears and other beasts twisted like the pets of the Godlings' Arboretum but in less aesthetically pleasing manners. Their speech was awful to hear and worse to behold as they emerged with lips and tongues twisting and folding to address her with words that, try though she might, she would never understand.

"Which way?" Bettina asked the garden; rubies cascaded from her lips. "I don't know what you're saying. Please, please just tell me!"

Snakes with white scales and scarlet bellies slithered toward her. When they fanned their hoods and hissed at her in their unnerving speech, their faces shuffled through those belonging to Bettina's children and anyone else she had ever loved. She flapped her wings to escape them, hovering above the ground, but the verdure canopy pushed her to the ground like an invisible hand.

I traded everything to be here! I gave, and gave, to you and everyone else. Bettina savored her anger for the gift it was and kicked the nearest snake—this one vacillating between Crespin's face and her old nursemaid's—away from her. *I'm done. I will give nothing else.*

Something roared in the darkness. Goddess was close—it was *Her* aura tainting this sacred place. Transforming creatures who, while not benign, were entities unto themselves and served the will of the garden that shepherded this world through each age.

The Speaker walked toward her from the rightmost path. He carried a sword that banished darkness from its length like Bettina's aureole illuminated her body. With one sweep, then another, he cleaved the serpents into pieces and sent the other traitorous animals scurrying for cover in the jungle-like tangle outside the road.

Bettina shook her agitated wings out to stretch them. His sword paused mid-air, mid-strike at the sound and the sight of the golden dust that flickered like embers on the shadowed road. He cut a striking figure as he stood, like an avenging Saint, but there was nothing of Magisend in him when he turned to observe her.

Wisps of midnight blue filaments dissipated around him as she watched.

"It costs you something to show me this. To lead me."

"Yes," he replied.

"Don't, then. I will find my own way."

The smile he offered her, while crooked and very like one Magisend would present, displayed sadness that put a lump in her throat. During these seconds transposing in and out of the time bent by Goddess to hunt Bettina he shifted between his two selves with the same chaotic turns.

"This is my role. I was Created by Goddess, molded by you, but oblivion arranged my conception and birth as an outpouring of itself. I will see this done."

Bettina had no arguments. She had been given roles to play as well. She had been a pretty swan born for Goddess to admire. She had been a willing mother destined to become an ugly blade for the purpose of cutting her eldest from the fabric of Marzanna's world so the rest of the tapestry could survive. With everything coming full circle, she had become the beguiler that would lead Goddess to the basin. After that...

She shook off these thoughts and took off again down the rightmost path The Speaker had cleared for her.

Her perception altered as veils of mist and water swept aside as she flew along the road ahead. It took her longer than it should have to realize The Speaker—*Magisend*—soared invisible at her side the whole time. He overtook her speed when she approached new parts of the garden further in. Ever, always further in.

The more he helped her, the more of himself he lost. While Marzanna's relentless chase stole Bettina's fortitude, wisps and facets of her Archivist shattered and left the man a wreckage of his former self as the path went on.

Into the unknown descent of oblivion where the All waited to welcome them.

I'm glad you're here, she thought toward Magisend, not daring to take her eyes from the way ahead as branches slunk low with the shadows.

Soon, the basin gaped like a jaw ripped half away from the face it belonged to. There, a mirror image of the garden twinkled with beauty strong enough to wreak havoc on a fragile mind. With Goddess close enough behind for Her wind to blister Bettina's neck she dared not stop, but her wings betrayed her purpose and slowed her down.

"Not far now. You're almost there."

Bettina heard the finality beneath his encouragement. He wouldn't show himself to her—not even as The Speaker's armored vessel—but she raked her eyes over the illuminating movement in the dark to find his filaments.

I'm not ready to do this alone! You have to come with me—in there.

Neither being answered. Bettina soared to a—more practiced— pause in front of the basin's opening and turned her back to it, seeking Magisend. When she saw what he had been reduced to, fresh pearls fell from her reddened eyes.

A shade in the likeness of a man stood at the end of the walkway, illumined by the glow coming off the portal. Green irradiated his customary Archival cobalt: The Speaker's hue, but he had been lost further back on their trail.

I can't go further. The will of the basin is meant for those with souls or avatars of the All. I am that no longer.

"No!" A child's protest. Bettina wanted to stomp her blood-stained feet and rage, but neither of them had the energy or time. "I can't leave you alone to—"

Other threads—foreign but familiar—pounced from outside the portal. Blue-white like dead flesh, they snapped barbed shoots toward where the specter of Magisend stood at the edge of the garden. She lunged, trying to catch them before they ensnared their target, but the spurs sliced her palms and slipped out of her hold streaked with her ichor. Touching them granted her the realization of who had joined them.

Bettina shuddered. *Easoren!*

I would see this forbidden paradise. I would greet this power that can master death and divinity above all other beings.

Strands knotted together, not by nature, but by force. Gold and midnight blue bled emerald sap that dripped ominously on the inky stone of the garden path. Before she could reach Magisend—the shade that he had become—the threads wrapped him up alongside Easoren and blocked her view.

You did not aid me willingly, Easoren's voice jabbed her mind like nettles, but maliciously, as Magisend's had when they had first met, *but you did nonetheless. Let us work together again this doomed hour.*

"If you lie—"

"Peace, bauble." She heard the former Priest's mocking name for her in a voice that twinned his and Magisend's into a bastardization of both. "Bring us in."

Bettina stared at the being that staggered from the shadows surrounding the basin portal. Light, shadow, and fleshy threads stolen and corrupted spread over an indestructible cage of gilded bones. Both forms and features struggled for dominance before her eyes, weaving and swaying where the bricks merged with the soil before the basin.

Easoren smiled behind Magisend's shell. Then he seized her shoulder and jumped into the basin, dragging her with him. Cold clutched them as they passed through the darkness…

…and vanished, leeching from Bettina and her frosted wings like morning mist as she stepped out of the portal into new light.

She saw a vineyard. A realm of rapture no longer dark, no longer consumed by the power sucked up by Marzanna's gluttony.

Bettina's mouth opened in wonder as she moved, entranced beyond her will, deeper into the basin. Her wings draggled behind her as she walked. The petals from the flowers that blossomed beneath her feet and failed to die as she stepped on them tickled her skin as she stared around and around at the most beautiful place in the soul of the universe.

She had expected horrors. She had expected something worse than the prophetic dread of the outer garden and the ancient cruelty of the salt-washed cave of sacrifices back in Aebbenary. Even the garden where she had foolishly sought truth had shown her wonders before the ugliness her sanity could barely handle. It would be just as foolish now to trust any delights she saw or was allowed to see by this abyssal realm beneath the rest.

"The basin is a pool for all the outer energy in the world. It's a reservoir for the All while it tarries in this realm, seeking to restore stability to what Goddess and the former gods consumed," Magisend said through a mouth that wasn't entirely his. The hand that lifted to pluck a bunch of resplendent grapes from the nearest tree in wonder was Easoren's, and moved by his will, not his own.

Bettina heard their gilded teeth shear through the golden flesh of the grape. She did not look, though, since the center of the vineyard held something far more important.

A cylindrical prism, covered in sharp edges, reflected its surroundings and more like a mirror. It showed Cristoval's sleeping face.

The prism summoned. Its many facets were scintillating in ways no mind once mortal could grasp. Bettina stared into them, enthralled, as its magnetic force beckoned her closer. It was difficult to remember what she was here to do when faced with the embodiment of eternity—here, in a place very like the home she had loved but never truly had freedom to enjoy.

Her heartbeats resounded in her ears, slow now compared to the bird-fast tempo her haste had required. *Cristoval. Cosima. Cristoval…*

Magisend. He was here, joined with Easoren's cage of bones so he could be with her at the end. Bettina turned halfway to the prism, seeking where she had left him, but he hadn't moved. He stared at her with helpless yearning as Easoren began to devour the grapes he had plucked in earnest.

"Go," Magisend reminded her. *"Do what you must."*

435

Cristoval's face was gone when she looked back. Bettina hunted for any trace of his reflection, but saw only her own. Beautiful, sorrowful, a pretty picture with only one use left in her divine body.

Empowered by the prism and her own sense of what was proper, Bettina reached into her chest, slipping her hands into her flesh like it was another misty veil, and gripped her aching heart tight. She pulled it out and, with the strands beaded with water and pearls, split it open by digging in her nails and separating the two halves like stone fruit.

It hurt. It didn't. Relief like the promise of rest coursed through her as she gazed down with detached fascination at the golden Light of her heart and saw the red aura pulsing beneath it. Within that, her divine eyes glimpsed traces of all the love she had grown within her soul.

It would be easy to rip it out. Pull the pit from the peach and offer it to the prism so she would never grieve again. That would hurt too, but not as badly as her grief.

I offered one mortal life, treasure though it was. I did not offer the pieces that keep me human. Bettina sighed and pressed the halves of her heart together again once the prism had seen what lived within it. *I love you, Cristoval. And I thank you.*

She tucked her precious heart away for safe-keeping. Its need would wait for…after. If Goddess did not prove more powerful than destiny itself.

"Lior," said Bettina, calling the name out through the vineyard as she approached the prism. "You who were never meant to die as you did. Come back and come forth, Scholar of Aebbenary."

Revolving and immaculate, radiating heat that should have flayed flesh from bone but instead fed into Bettina's aureole like synthesis, the prism answered. The facets molded together and apart and fashioned the shape of a man amidst the Light…

…and Lior stepped out of it. The very image of the Scholar's monument in Aebbenary's catacombs, as if he had scooped the sculpture out of the earth and breathed life into it since he could not reclaim his buried, decayed flesh.

"It is a privilege to meet you again, Bettina Valusius," he said, granting her a gentle smile.

Behind her, Goddess's chaos shrieked in the gateway of the basin.

XXXI

Cosima

Aebbenary did not welcome her victorious return. Sick with wrath and armed with Light more powerful than any she had felt course through her divine body before, Cosima failed to care.

Time had bent under the might of Goddess's hunt for Bettina. Between the ordained sacrifice she, Sovanna, and Bettina had accomplished in the ancient seaside cave, three days had passed. Three days Cosima had spent circling Aebbenary's borders as a pillar of violet light, seeking purchase against the Miraculous walls Marzanna's consorts had erected by their own power to protect the city during Goddess's absence.

Three days since Cristoval's death. Did Sovanna still stand vigil over his body?

Three more nights her huntresses had been trapped in their stone prisons, poised on the cusp of consciousness and mortality.

They had planned for this to an extent, she and Iulia. Somehow, Cosima would break their curse and distract Fiammetta and whoever else got in her way from noticing while Iulia led them to safety. A ship from distant climes—rare in these unsettled days after word of Goddess's vicious temperament and the menace of Sovanna's swamp in the city—waited in port to bear them away in exchange for gold Cosima had stolen from the palace over time rather than dip into her allowance and alert Goddess to her intentions.

That plan meant *nothing* if Cosima was wedged out of Aebbenary in whatever form she took by power greater than her own. Goddess's power, ultimately. Her consorts would be nothing without it.

Cosima's sacrifice was a leaden weight in her body. A stone to sink her from the skies and drown her in the sea. She had meant to use it to free her huntresses, but now she and her power were here, both completely locked out of the city, she had no use for it.

It was all down to her wits and fortitude again. Cosima hated to bet on those terrible odds.

At dawn on the third day, Cosima took to the sky again in her Light. All Godlings could fly, but they knew one and all that transporting themselves via Miraculous will was nothing compared to flight undertaken by the strength of their own blessed wings. Goddess had denied such a gift to all but a few of Her cherished ones: Däard, Bettina, a few scattered Saints who had pleased Her over the years, and of course Herself.

No one loved Marzanna more than Marzanna.

Ascending above Aebbenary with her power gathered around her, Cosima tried not to overthink the mad plot that had come to her no earlier than a few minutes previously.

If I cannot enter, she had decided, *I will force them to join me up here. I will make them sorry they ever bowed to Goddess or took my ladies from me.*

It would feel wrong to use Cristoval's sacrifice to cause more death. The taking of his short, praiseworthy life in its flowering youth had been transgression enough. Cosima could never atone for the part she had chosen to play so she would have leverage to save her huntresses rather than her doomed brother. She had wanted to make something beautiful amidst the repulsive, appalling deed her hands had wrought alongside Bettina's and Sovanna's.

Yet her role as protector of her huntresses—and everyone else in the city beaten down by divine rule—mattered more. If she had to save them by being the first person since Marzanna to kill Saints, she would do it and smile as they fell.

She didn't have wings, but she didn't need them to take her corporeal form and fly above Aebbenary's tallest spire. Light consumed her human eyes; she felt them melding together in her sockets. Her ivory leather garb melted in the searing, sun-hot might as she forged it into weightless plate armor. The plates and chain were neither steel, silver, nor bronze; she eschewed pure gold as well.

Cosima had slain her beloved brother to get here: his blood had spilt a fountain of red on her hands. That same red tainted her inherited gold and stained it forever.

"Face me, First Saint!" Cosima magnified her voice with her will. "Let us find out now who is stronger—an old wolf too comfortable in its den, or a hound thirsty for justice!"

Clinging to the spire with a gauntleted hand, Cosima hefted her favorite spear and screamed another challenge, this one wordless.

Let all eyes see this. Let every person here witness their downfall, she thought, bracing herself for battle she anticipated and dreaded. Power coursed through her. She hadn't summoned it yet, but it was ready like oil waiting for fire to obliterate everything in its path.

Minutes passed, but not many. Cosima heard the swish of Däard's beating wings before he appeared, rising from the guarding web over the city in full splendor.

He wore a pure white sash tied around his body without adornment. He had abandoned his crown and any generous gifts of jewels from Marzanna. All he carried was his sword of glorious Light, forged exclusively from a sliver of Goddess's aura, and the only color that differed from his unalloyed white and gold were his ruby red wings unfurled splendidly at his back.

Others would have bowed. Surrendered; groveled to be spared and embraced by those gleaming, muscular arms. Cosima bared her teeth and shifted her grip on her spear to impale his heart if he attacked first.

"Before we begin, look," he said, and pointed down.

Portions of the golden web scrolled back. Cosima gazed through the opening to see what Fiammetta had somehow concealed from her by enhancing Goddess's protection over Aebbenary. Enhanced so she could…

One stained wooden altar that would have been prepared in haste for Fiammetta's demands. A queue of people weeping but progressing by their own free will with trepidation up to where their queen under

Goddess stood, jeweled scythe in hand, arranging them on her altar for black sacrifices.

She's killing them, Cosima covered her mouth with her free hand, unable to conceal her abhorrence. Tears she didn't know she had left pricked her stinging eyes. *She's trotting them up to her altars and killing them to make Goddess come back to her. And they're going willingly!*

It was a gruesome abuse of power. The full extent of the divine sickness Sovanna and Cristoval had labored so long to diagnose and treat before blessèd beings—also tainted with the blight—took advantage of every mortal in Aebbenary. Fiammetta killed efficiently, without delay, but she spared no one—women, the elderly, even children—from her banquet of offerings she intended to use to buy Marzanna's devotion.

These sacrifices won't even work. Goddess can't be bought any longer, not with Bettina found and hunted. All this blood and waste…

Cosima had not heard her say it, but every soul on the island knew Aebbenary's queen cared for naught else but Goddess. Fiammetta lived at Her discretion to cause harm and suffering wherever she went. Däard lived to serve, no matter what his role had been before any divine hands had chosen to lift him up.

As she recovered herself, he closed the web before it occurred to her to dive inside and waited for the condemnation he seemed to guess she would hurl at him.

"*You* look, Däard. You have nothing worth guarding in Her name."

"I have made vows I will honor. I merely wanted you to know what should not have been concealed from you—from any Godling or Saint—in the first place."

"Why?" Cosima let her mask slip: desperate confusion smoothed her furious brows, her spear was a deadweight in her hand, and the sun shining down on their duel-to-come could blind her if she let it. "You know what Fiammetta is. Goddess allows it!"

He nodded; a stiff, jerky movement. "She does."

"You had honor once. Can't you remember what that felt like?"

"Honor is for those who have never surrendered to love or anything else. Though I have been rich in Marzanna's regard, I cannot afford it."

"Why not?"

"She is the only one who can let me die. Let me go to him if he cannot be brought to me."

The Scholar. Cosima was no longer a child: she comprehended the consequences of one meager human death that had shaped the world they must live in now. Unfortunately for both of them, she also understood the sorrow in that. Were it not for her huntresses—Iulia, Konetta, beyond them to her closest friends—she would feel the same.

What good is eternal life if you don't have the ones you love to share it with? That question demanded another. *If the ones you love have lost themselves to greed or madness, leaving you alone with your empty honor and pointless ethics, do you have anything worth keeping?*

"Did She promise you She could bring him back?"

"A long time ago."

"Has She kept Her promises?"

He laughed. It sounded like it hurt. "Not if you ask Fiammetta."

"If you let me pass, Fiammetta will not live to hear another question by the end of this day."

His red wings beat honey-slow as he considered her threat and offer. She had been right; there was no love lost between those two judging by the disgusted curl of his lip and the impatient flick of his glittering sword.

"I cannot. Do what you must."

Cosima launched herself off the tower, her spear shining in the sun.

Elusive, sacrifice-purchased power churned within her breast and goaded Cosima to new heights. She refrained from calling on it as the rose-gilded haft of her spear spun and battered against Däard's sword. She hoped she might not need to as he matched her blows with swipes of his own, to and fro, ensuring she could not cut him down while he didn't yet strike her from the skies with his superior strength.

I'm sorry, Cristoval, she apologized preemptively as Däard's wings buffeted her with hot wind and forced her back onto the curvature of the Holy tower rooftop. *I wanted to use the sacrifice to make this all better. I never wanted to use it to kill a Saint...even this one.*

She flew at him, in and out of her Light, again and again. Each time he batted her away like a parent tiger swipes at its young with its claws sheathed. Cosima was a Godling, not a Saint, and the battle skills she had worked on most of her life were succeeded only by her natural talent for weapon arts, yet she could not wound him. She could not even touch him, for his skills paralleled hers and he had been famous—infamous too—in his time as a man only for the talents destiny and joyful practice had granted him.

Then he had her. She knew it before his sword pierced and shattered her ribs and pinned her down against the roof while her ichor burned around his sacred blade.

"You're not fighting me as an equal." She hacked a bloody cough and instantly remembered the slow, suffocating death Cristoval had suffered before they'd cut his misery short. "Y-you're trying to put me down. Like a rabid beast."

If she used her sacrifice, she might be able to fight back. She might have won against the greatest Saint in Goddess's Creation. Cristoval would not have judged her for that. He hadn't been judgmental or uncharitable the way Cosima often thought of herself. He hadn't been perfect—what human could be?—but he had been her brother and she had loved him.

Should my love for him and his for me, for Mama and Sovanna, buy paltry death? If we had to make him a martyr, is that all his life was worth?

Cosima would rather die here than concede that. She tipped her head back against the roof to look up at the sunrise hues she could barely glimpse because of her ever-shining aureole and laughed—at Cristoval, herself, and miserable Däard.

"I did wonder if you could be the one to end all this. My bet was on Sovanna. If that is not to be, if you can be swept aside like morning dew, I must hope for another…someday."

He could end this. I could die. He could make a present of her to Goddess upon Her triumphant return if Bettina didn't succeed in the garden. He might even be able to kill her. Cosima didn't put much store in faith, but this she believed with all her soul.

I might see you soon, brother. If there is any room for pathetic Godling souls wherever yours has gone.

Two consorts. Two beings blessed with all Marzanna's love and glory beyond what any of Her other Saints or progeny had inherited. What was one heir, favored or not, compared to them?

Before Däard could toy with her further or attempt to kill her for her betrayal of Marzanna's trust, a clarion call from the depths of the world sent a shockwave through Aebbenary. Cosima felt it more profoundly than the flaming sword that scorched her divine shell. It rattled her teeth and cooled the fire burning her up with a dousing of frost.

Däard turned. The golden champion with his face inches from her own shifted his focus long enough for her to shove him away with his sword still locked between her ribs as she gasped and choked around the obstruction. He'd *let it go.*

He stared at her—assessed her. Perhaps it had been most of the Bright Age since Däard Ranieri had shown this much interest in another living soul. Everything about his person was glorious during their battle—already won in his favor by but a tenth of his skill—but no joy lit his princely features. Wind ruffled his flaxen hair and his magnificent wings—like Lilias's, Cosima noticed with another pang—but he only studied her.

His distraction ended with the last notes of Goddess's summons. Blood and froth wheezed from Cosima's mouth as he watched his sword dissolve the blemish of her ichor into smoke with pensive deliberation. His tortured disappointment in her efforts was so plain, so palpable, that she considered apologizing for it before she decided to grip her spear tighter instead.

Aebbenary's distant clock chimed the hour. Cosima dropped her spear—she no longer needed it—and grasped the sword lodged in her body. She didn't scream as she ripped it out, all at once rather than inch by inch, and concentrated on healing her damaged body from the inside out.

Though he watched her struggle with Marzanna's holy sword, he did not move to reclaim it. Däard would not strike the killing or maiming blow she knew he could…but he would not let her enter

Aebbenary to conquer Fiammetta and save her huntresses. Save everyone.

If he won't fight me…

Cosima wrapped her stained fingers around the glassy hilt of the Light sword and dashed past Däard to leap off the roof to fall. Wingless, streaking ichor in a stream that filled the air rushing by her ears with the scent of sacred lilies, she fell down with her arms flung wide and flames from the sword burning her passage like a comet.

The web disintegrated beneath her when she burned through it, still high above the city. Däard's sword had bought her purchase against the Miraculous binding trapping Aebbenary's populace inside with Fiammetta on her rampage. Now she was aware of them, Cosima caught the malodorous stench of her vain sacrifices burning on the pyres where her servants cast the bodies.

She slowed; hovered. Scorched and broken beyond what a Godling could heal quickly. Moisture wicked from her eyes and skin as she broke down the carefully guarded walls of her mind and heart once and for all and reached for every blessèd being in the city besides Marzanna's consorts.

Power too great for any one being to deserve aided Cosima. Great enough to capture the consciousness of every Godling and Saint and yank it into her will like plucking stalks of wheat from a bountiful field.

Godlings! She cried in her mind and outside of it. *Saints of Marzanna! Goddess has deserted you in your hour of need. Goddess, who Made you, abandoned you, and punished you for your natures.*

Insight passed through her more easily than the sword she clutched close to her ruined body. Her sacrifice had meant something for the mortals she had always pitied—and envied—for their short, purpose-seeking lives. But why should it mean something only for them? Did only mortals deserve her pity when everyone had endured Marzanna's selfish reign?

I cannot assure a happy future for any of us. Not even a sacrifice like mine can accomplish that. I cannot make any of you worthy or good by force. But I can promise if you swear allegiance to me I will teach you how to live better lives. I will never abandon you.

Somewhere, in a garden lost to time, Bettina had split her heart open to know what lay within it. Cosima saw this in a fleeting vision and mirrored that act of devotion to look within herself.

Her heart was a swarming ball of butterfly wings steeped in wonder for the world, made fragile by the strength of her hope. Wings of all colors fluttered and closed over her soul as she mentally cupped it in her ichor-tainted hands and *willed* the wings to part so she could see inside.

Love—that she'd keep, no matter how much it hurt. Cosima decided she would always have room for it to grow. To welcome in whoever she needed and wanted, but also to let them go so she didn't let this beautiful, intangible gem within herself rot like Marzanna's had.

The rest, though…all her power and divinity and the stain of her sacrifice…

Cosima plucked it out and tossed it up into the air.

*I give this to you. Iulia, Konetta, Grisel, Palmira…*she listed her huntresses names and went on. *Agnese. Druda. Ormanno, all of you Godlings and Saints who want a second chance. We can all make this life mean more.*

A few of them refused. Because she allowed it, they cut their connection to her with dull shears of hate or fear or whatever they decided was more important than the life of meaning she offered. Agnese was one, but her rejection was the most curious one of all: her amused whisper of thanks pushed back the tide of Cosima's favor and snatched a few shreds out of the whole to squirrel away like a talisman against bad luck.

Curiosity prompted her to look closer, but greater matters beckoned. Cosima nested the fluttering wings of her hopeful heart back inside her body and lifted her arms to the power and incarnation of her sacrifice to guide it. Like she had split her heart, she dug her fingers into the underside of the hovering sphere and ripped it apart.

Into enough pieces to transform everyone who had chosen her.

She did not consciously choose the forms they would share. Grasping for anything to hold onto in the maelstrom of her new, unleashed power, Cosima contemplated what she valued most in her decelerated fall beneath the golden web protecting Aebbenary from her wrath. Love, of course, but what else...?

Loyalty, but not just to power. To justice and a cause beyond oneself. She plummeted through the web—how could it ever have locked her out or kept her back? Cosima laughed wildly as she spun in the air above the streets.

Faithfulness. Charity for loved ones and empathy for suffering. Marzanna's chosen had gone without either for too long. What magnificent force could they be, she wondered, if she gave them the chance to learn to be human?

And granted her beloved mortal sisters the chance to protect themselves from all the hurts Aebbenary's divinities had made them suffer?

With all senses human and divine opened to receive as well as give, Cosima *felt* the huntresses' stone returning to flesh as the knot of her terrible sacrifice dispersed throughout the city. She felt the power she surrendered infuse her huntresses with divine Light equally among their numbers, so they could fly her way in beams of their own once they tripped off their pedestals and remembered how to breathe with human lungs.

It was gone. Everything she'd had to give and more. Cosima landed upright with her Light diminished but still strong at the edge of the central square where Fiammetta had destroyed a fountain to perform her sacrifices. Her corporeal hands gripped the sacred sword in a two-handed hold.

Goddess's second summons was a screech that corroded reality. The web Cosima had fallen through shivered and pulsed with the energy from beyond their plane that pulled the leashes of Her consorts taut and struck them for their delay besides.

Fiammetta had ignored Cosima, hastening her murders, but that call made her pause even as it caused Däard to wing his way down from the roof of the Holy tower to join her. All the mortals lined up to die in submission to Goddess began to break ranks when the call shattered Fiammetta's influence on their spirits.

Fiammetta shrieked. Glaring up at the sky, she flung her latest kill off the altar before she covered her face with her elegant, gold-speckled hands and *screamed* in frustration.

"I'm not ready!"

"Go!" Cosima shouted to the mothers and fathers, children and grandparents, laborers and merchants; her voice cracked like the chords she used to speak had been partially shredded. "I will protect you now. *Go!"*

They stampeded, prompted by her command and their panic. Like rats fleeing a sinking ship, they streamed around the searing aureole around Cosima toward the main and side streets in uncanny silence. Like one audible breath from them would remind Fiammetta that she could steal their will with mere thought.

"Marzanna, *wait!"* Still screaming, Fiammetta hurled her scythe on the altar that dripped blood under the morning sun and dissolved into Light to fly toward where Goddess summoned her. She skirted around Cosima, faster than she expected, too quick to haul back by her hair to cut her to pieces as justice demanded.

"She's going to let me kill you now. All of you. These offerings will be enough," she cackled as she dodged Cosima's belated swipe with the shining sword and departed in a ray of Light that streaked bruised red up and across the azure sky above Aebbenary.

When she looked up, Cosima watched Däard's unhurried arrival as his wide wings carried him down.

He stared at her. He gazed into her defiant, blazing eyes and held her in his own while he floated above Aebbenary, unarmed but formidable.

"Will you go?" Cosima asked, her chest heaving as the impact of what she had given absorbed into her altered body. "Still, now, will you go to Her?"

She couldn't think about what had changed, not yet. Not until this was over for good.

Cosima wondered if he remembered a time when he had been Aebbenary's champion, not just Marzanna's. She had heard stories of the man who had fought for ordinary people at the end of the false god's age. Who had defied the power-hungry elite of Silver's church and dissolute royalty and sought justice and safety for everyone.

Däard smiled. Cosima loved women, not men, but even her heart stirred at the sight of something as heart-rending and beautiful as that last smile.

"I don't know if you will survive to protect Aebbenary as you promised. I cannot foretell any destiny that does not end with Goddess on Her throne, but child…you are worthy beyond compare for the honor I gave up," he said. His praise rang through the sky like the singing of steel against steel.

"You can get it back again. You can—"

"No. This is not my hour of redemption. I do not want it."

Cosima remained alone in the square at the site of Fiammetta's carnage. She was armed and armored, but there was no one left to fight here as he lifted his hand in farewell and dissolved into Light to answer Marzanna's summons.

Cosima's huntresses soared by their new powerful will toward her presence. It would be terrible to let them see what horrors had been shaped here, but she was too late to send them off. Along with the distant sparks of the Godlings and Saints who had promised themselves to her cause of meaning.

Cosima saw Konetta and Iulia through the mental eyes of her horde. Plaster and stone clung to Konetta's dusty, rag-clad figure as it did to all the huntresses. She had a bruise blooming on her jaw, from one solid punch; in parallel, Iulia's knuckles on her non-dominant hand were bruised when Cosima looked for that evidence.

But they were coming to her, and they held each other's hands as they ran.

I'm going, Cosima told them in their minds before they could run to her. Her Light might still burn; her armor at least would be forge-hot. Däard's sword might blind any who looked upon it but did not hold it. *Mama will need me if those two are on their way to help Goddess. And I owe Fiammetta a debt of violence.*

You're not going alone! Iulia said. Bellowed, really, at a spiritual volume difficult for mortals to achieve without practice.

The huntresses were still joined with Cosima's mind, as were the Godlings and Saints who had sworn themselves to her claim. They clamored like a flock in her thoughts—all at once, loud, and panicked at the idea of separating from her.

We're almost together now. We already lost Ricla. That was Konetta.

You're not going alone. Not when you have us. Iulia repeated in synchronization with the other ladies. *We owe Fiammetta for Ricla too.*

Emotion pricked the wings of the butterflies surrounding— guarding—Cosima's true heart. With the heat of battle coursing through her she had not been able to push back the Miraculous energy burning her alive.

"Together," Cosima agreed out loud and in her mind, surrendering in joy. "This we do together."

Gathering them up in her Light by the tiny, winking flames her sacrifice and splitting her own essence had bought for them, Cosima shouted her victory like it had already taken place and followed Däard and Fiammetta's comet with her own stars at her side.

XXXII

Bettina

"You remember me?" Bettina asked Lior Betilienus, the Scholar of Aebbenary.

"Yes. I was a prince of your city, once. You were famed even then as a beauty and a wit."

Pleasantries. Goddess was all but here to claim her entire being by force, and the dignified ghost of a dead—but treasured—scholar engaged in social niceties with her.

Bettina peered past him, toward the prism. She hadn't known what to expect, but this large and fairly mild-mannered replica of an ordinary man didn't seem like enough to conquer the supreme being that dominated the outer world.

"You're supposed to tell me how to defeat Goddess. I want to wrest Her ill-used power from Her claws before She reaches this place to capture me."

"And use it how?"

"To…" She started to splutter before she stopped and made herself dwell on his question. "I don't know. I haven't thought about what we'll do with it or Her once we collar Her ambition."

"Thank you for your honesty. We did not expect you to know the furthest ends of what happens here, in these stardust remnants of destiny already accomplished, or that the powers granted to Goddess must always have a vessel."

"Must they?" Bettina asked. "Can't they just be…dispersed elsewhere?"

Lior sighed; patiently, wistfully. "I have missed teaching. A quarter century as part of the All and I forgot the sharing of knowledge is just as diverting as absorbing it."

Bettina wrapped her wings around herself, chilled despite the illusion of the vineyard's familiar façade of summer's warmth. A lifetime ago she had dreamed of a time when her children were young in this illusory paradise. Mothers were as different from each other as the women who carried the role across the world, but which of them would not share Bettina's longing to hold her children at every stage and know they were happy, independent, and living well?

"Is that where we go when we…is Cristoval with you?"

Is he safe now? Has he been healed? Can he be happy, in whatever way souls are, beyond life's warm touch? Bettina could not voice the rest of her thoughts, but she fixed her pleading eyes on Lior and hoped he would understand and answer everything.

"I cannot speak to whatever end destiny foretold when I traded my mortal life for Däard's. I know only that I expired, then awoke in the Archive's embrace with All knowledge within my grasp to learn. I do not think that destiny was granted to your son: he is not here," Lior answered. When he trailed off, hesitating, the prism behind him altered its gradual rotation where it hung in empty space, changing directions.

Bettina's eyes leaked pearls again to form a humiliating heap of gemstones at her feet. She didn't want to bring more into this world, but Goddess wouldn't let her stop. She ached to be held, cradled without any hunger or possessiveness from someone who cared about her without reserve, but she was the only one here.

Her own arms wrapped around her torso as she shivered again. "Do you think I might find him again someday? In any world, in any life, will we meet again? Is that something the All can answer?"

"I have not been sanctioned to tell you more than this: my path ends here, today. As do many others. I have argued that my path ended before this age began, but… oblivion had need of me since Marzanna refused to let my death stand."

There might have been a message in that. Bettina tried to receive it in good grace. It was not a son Marzanna had lost, but Her proclivity for greed had led them here. To this basin at the bottom of existence where Bettina pleaded for any lingering trace of Cristoval to ease the anguish of his death.

Goddess was too close. The portal hadn't confounded Her for long since the garden meant Her to proceed. The power searing Bettina's wings and back could only mean She was almost through. All around, grapes swung wildly on their vines and fell, rolling into the dirt. Counteractive Light from the prism that had spat out Lior clashed with Marzanna's golden tempest as it transported Her gigantic power through the portal.

"Tell me what to do! There has to be—" Jewels clattered on the ground to join all the ones Bettina had spoken already.

"Hush now, hush now," Magisend's voice soothed her mind while his twisted flesh and Easoren's bones melted into the shadows behind and slightly under the basin prism. He had been silent during her exchange with Lior; she hadn't known he could even still speak. *"You have passed your torch to another."*

What does that mean? Tell me, please, Magisend...

Flowers rained from the sky in hues of ivory and white, yellow gold and lush violet. Their fragrance mingled with a heady savor of excellent wine before Goddess's aureole singed their petals into smoke like incense.

Too late, Bettina's animal mind crowed with absurd humor. *She's here, She's here! Goddess has come!*

Strange vapor clung to the molecules of the vineyard's air like dust motes. It changed as the flowers fell and Marzanna resonated with incomparable joy as She emerged from the portal. The atmospheric residue that clung to Bettina's skin like dew on rose petals transformed to glittering condensation that washed any trace of old blood away.

"Blessèd be My swan, My splendid Bettina."

Bettina didn't turn. She couldn't. Her eyes closed against her better judgment as she shuddered under the oppression of Goddess's aura. She fought to maintain her own weak halo just so she'd remember her own name.

When she opened them, Lior was gone. *Vanished.*

"You fled from Me like a thief from My tower. How could you fear *Me,* precious swan, when you obeyed My will? How could you run from Me, and run *here?*"

Bettina covered her mouth with both hands to stifle a sob as Goddess's radiance spilled over her and lengthened her shadow to monstrous proportions. As Her voice had altered, resonating with unrestrained power that enriched the syrupy quality, Bettina stared at the stretched, enlarged silhouette looming over her like a magnificent vulture.

Of course I ran from You. But for Cosima, I wish You had never noticed me all those years ago.

What might hurt Goddess enough to make this quick? Bettina couldn't stand the tension that felt like it frayed the atoms of her body apart.

"I don't love You. I will never love You again."

"Don't worry, dearest. I expected your ire." Goddess sighed with tolerant affection and forced Bettina to turn to Her with claws She sunk into her shoulders like fish hooks. "This mortal attachment will fade. You will feel as you should before long, and I will hold you in My arms."

She tilted Bettina's chin up with a nonverbal command, compelling her to gaze upon Her glory. As Her hooks burrowed deeper in her shoulders, Bettina gaped at the sight of Goddess at full power that should have melted her eyes in their sockets.

Golden mist surrounded a woman supported by dozens of wings, all of varying sizes, some feathered and others bare. Her skin had transformed into metallic gold, like an idol erected to appease Her wrath after a mortal sin. Huge eyes—more than two, though Her normal eyes were brightest and remained where they should—swallowed up everything they saw, eating Bettina alive. When Goddess leaned in to kiss Bettina, the lips that brushed hers were furnace hot and blackened like ash.

"Do You see it now, beloved? There is nothing else besides Me. Nothing but—"

"Marzanna."

Her head snapped up from where Her sacred form had stooped over Bettina. Golden eyes stabbed past her to study the prism; Goddess had known it was there, but Her triumph had delayed Her.

"Who speaks?"

"Don't You know me? We were heretics together before You became Goddess."

Marzanna's sense of victory deferred to the suspicion Bettina heard in Her melodious voice. It would have been touching, once upon a time, during her dreams of Goddess's eternal love and bountiful favor. Now the only thing she felt as she shrank under the weight of Goddess's hands on her shoulders was aversion and fury.

We all lose loved ones. Some we lose because of beings like You. *Who are You to decide who lives and who dies?* Bettina didn't guard her thoughts, not a word, but Goddess wasn't listening.

"This game stinks of the Priest's humor. Easoren, if you have defied Me this far it will not just be your skin I—"

"You know my name. You fear to utter it because of what my presence means. *Say it.*" Lior had seemed mild in nature when he had greeted Bettina with politeness and pity for her situation, but there was indisputable accusation in his voice as he addressed Goddess.

Who considered both Bettina—still pinned under Her dagger-length claws—and the prism where Lior waited for a long while before Her surrender. When She suddenly threw Her head back on a neck that bent too far, Her river of black hair streaming behind Her, She cried out a corrosive series of notes Bettina had a bad feeling was a call for something or someone to join Her in the basin.

The scream seemed to go on forever. Bettina's hands over her ears couldn't block out what felt like acid washing over her eardrums, but her aureole healed any damage before the pain could sink in.

Marzanna released her and approached the prism.

"Because I owe it to you. Come and greet Me, Lior. I have missed you."

"I am here." He emerged from the prism once more, unsmiling and glittering with the cold fire of one dead but not gone.

Bettina hoped he had more of a plan than that. As Goddess rushed to him in a flurry of wings and Light, she prayed to oblivion that he would stab Her in the back with a divinity-slaying blade or some other mythical weapon to end Her tyranny forever.

Soon, Cristoval. We will avenge you soon…

Lior opened his alabaster arms. Wrapping Herself up in them, Marzanna laughed with tears streaking down Her face and clung to his body.

What is he doing? Why won't he destroy Her? Bettina wondered. She could do nothing else—Goddess was not so foolish as to let her walk free. Even without the claws that trapped her, Bettina could only stand and watch until Marzanna released her.

"Destroy?" Magisend-Easoren susurrated in her thoughts, as illicit as an affair. *"No one can do that. No one but Her."*

What do you mean?

They failed to answer.

Goddess laughed with child-like delight. "After all this time…I can't believe you're here! I've been searching for you, I've sacrificed so much—"

"You have not given the things oblivion would have required. If You loved me enough, You knew how to bring me back."

Whatever greeting She had expected, that wasn't it. Visibly hurt, Goddess drew back with Her hand resting over Her heart as if to protect it from another blow.

"That's not fair. You can't ask that of Me."

"Why not? Few have paid a price higher for love than me, Marzanna." Lior did not reach for Her again. He stood as statue-like as if he had never returned to speak with the living; though he glittered amongst the detritus of Goddess's glory and Bettina's bejeweled tears and words, the warmth he had shown Her had drained away to leave Marzanna wanting.

"The dead should stay dead. You know this in Your soul. You know, too, that the power You have is greater than Silver's. That it should never have belonged to You alone."

"It doesn't! I shared—"

Lior interrupted. "Aebbenary is bloated with evil sourced in Your design. You bore dozens of divine progeny with them and others and sent a blight of Saints into the mortal world to claim more power in Your name. None of that eased your hunger for more."

"Where is this coming from? What matters more than all of us being together again?" Goddess gestured with an irritated flick of all the wings on the side of Her body closest to Bettina. "I've called Däard. Perhaps I can forgive Fiammetta in time, if she repents, but if not I have chosen to love Bettina, and she loves Me. Now you've come back I can keep you too, Lior! I can have all of it! The world at our feet and you beside Me on My throne!"

"You should have let me go. Let Silver's High Priest lay cold in his tomb. Death will not answer to Your whip without consequences."

He had presented a stern, forbidding mien thus far, but Bettina watched Lior waver even if his heart had literally turned to stone.

They were lovers, once, she thought. *He must love Her still, even beyond life.*

"*You* were the one who taught Me to want more! To *become* more!"

"More," Lior agreed, his statue-flat eyes sorrowful in a way Bettina marveled to understand. "Not everything. Not all that exists."

He and Marzanna faced each other. Opposed in what felt like a cruel joke destiny had played on all of them. Bettina glanced away from the scene that felt too private for her eyes to watch the ichor dripping from the holes in her shoulders transform into puddles of honey on the ground.

"So." Goddess's happiness had evaporated with Her triumphant entry; whatever She had expected to find in Lior, either gratitude or jubilation, She had found blame no one alive would lay at Her feet. "You would have Me give up everything I fought for. Relinquish every single power I earned by blood and death when I fucked Silver and killed him by My own right and what I inherited from the eldritch gods. What was the point of all this, then? Who exists to deny Me anything I desire?"

"Who are *You*," argued Lior, "to demand more than You ever deserved at the expense of everyone who serves or loved You? Are

You no better than Your predecessors that You would trample the will of every soul beneath Yours for selfish greed?"

"I am Goddess!" The undertone of that caustic call reverberated through the vineyard like a blast of volcanic pressure. Marzanna screamed Her defiance…and cut Herself off as, all through the vineyard, someone began to laugh.

She could not pale. Goddess was a being of heat and wrath and oncoming death for Her foes. Yet Bettina watched the color drain from Her lovely face and relished, trapped as she was, Her clear apprehension.

"I will not beseech thee, Goddess, for favor…for I need it no longer."

The being that encapsulated Magisend and Easoren slithered in liquid, curling Light up from the ground like a hooded snake rising to strike. Though Bettina struggled in the bonds Marzanna had enmeshed around her both to free herself and see how much of Magisend remained in that abomination of a mortal shape, she remained caught. She heard nothing but Easoren's exultant taunt.

"There you are," Marzanna answered, scornful to hide Her distress. "Your hand has been in this from the beginning. Though you've pleased Me with it now and then, I think I will take it from you for good by day's end."

"I have nothing left for You to claim. I have found rich reward in giving away all ties of my flesh to stand before You, untethered, one more time." Easoren-Magisend laughed again.

"Do you stand? There aren't enough pieces of you here to do that."

"It may be that I deserved some years of torment under Your will, my heretic," Easoren continued, watching as Marzanna flinched at the old endearment, "and the rapture we shared in each other's arms we earned too. But You have become what I never could as Silver's vassal. Your sins have surpassed mine at last."

"You're not alone." Sniffing his aura, Goddess's proud lips curled. "My Archivist. I Made you from My own will. How could you be here, traitor? Can a Creation now defy its Creator?"

Magisend scarcely existed. He was a wisp, a memory with hardly any substance to link his consciousness to Easoren's flaking shell. Yet he was *hers*—Bettina would not let any being denounce that. The tigress's wrath that unfurled in Bettina's heart prompted her to speak at last.

"He's not Yours anymore. He's *mine.*"

Marzanna flung Her arm back with another shriek, flinging power toward Bettina to punish her defiance. Her will knocked Bettina though the empty space between those gathered around the basin's prism to land hard against a tree bursting with ripe grapes.

Goddess closed the distance between Herself and Bettina as juice from burst fruits flowed from the bark as it split to scream in her face.

"You have nothing but what I will or will not give. *Nothing*—none of you!"

"What are these, then?" Though they ached, though the wing that had been torn from her hung by tenuous threads, Bettina flexed both of them against the tree at her back and laughed like she was about to burn eternally for it. "You tried to punish me with these. You manipulated me, abused me, and destroyed my family. I would rather die now then spend another ounce of eternity in Your love and favor."

An age ago, when they had met as two mortal women at Bettina's arranged wedding, she had invited Marzanna closer to spit on her as a representative of the false god. They had fallen in love after that…at least Bettina had. A lifetime later, she spat with vicious hatred in Goddess's face and laughed even while she cried cathartic, human tears over how far they had fallen.

They weren't pearls anymore. Her words did not beguile or beseech.

"Dearest Bettina, it was your hand that slayed your son, not Mine." Goddess smiled wide, wider than anyone should be able to, as She licked a trail of juice from Bettina's bare arm. "As enticing as Your insolence is, nothing will change what you did to earn My indulgence. There is no invective harsh enough to erase that."

She couldn't move, but Bettina's tongue was still sharp. "You don't…I can't believe it. You don't know why we killed him. You assumed it was all for You."

Marzanna's eyes narrowed, all of them confused.

The portal whirling in a clash of Light with darkness rumbled as it ejected two more figures from its center. Everyone in the vineyard turned to see who had come except for Goddess, who kept Her baleful stare on Bettina until Däard's audible, shaky gasp bade Her look toward him instead.

"It cannot be." Bettina heard him choke on the astonishment. "I dream while awake after all these years—"

"My love."

Two simple words for lovers. Lior addressed Däard with them and a fond smile from his sculptured body…and caught Däard as he ran to him like Marzanna had.

As First Saint he had always been the strongest under Goddess. Immaculate, dangerous to any who would defy Marzanna's whims, a living legend and handsome enough to make every lover in Aebbenary sigh with longing for a look from his solemn eyes. Bettina had not been immune to his legend or his charms, and she had known the man beneath them for much of her life. They had made love with Goddess's sanction over the years, even, though in Her shameless court that did not carry much meaning.

It was Däard the man, simple and grieving, who clung to Lior and kissed his smooth lips between sobs. They held each other as childhood friends who had learned to love one another through betrayal, fire, and one misunderstanding after another. Lior smoothed Däard's wild flaxen hair out of his face, unable to weep but with his eyes bright like he would be if he had living flesh. He kissed his brow in greeting and apology.

"Däard…"

"You're not back. I know that."

Lior nodded; slowly, sorrowfully. "That cannot be. But I can take you home with me, Däard. Our stories can end at the same time."

"Please. I have walked as if through a nightmare since I lost you. Any delights have been fleeting; any joys burned to ash in my mouth, dust in my eyes. Any love I had but what belongs to you has faded. I *ache* for a release from this torment. An eternity of sleep at your side is…I wish for *nothing else."*

"How could you?"

Bettina had never seen Marzanna soften so much. Something as glorious as Goddess could never suffer mortal weakness, never endure the pangs of heartbreak, never wither under neglect or cruelty. Now, like a passing shadow, she saw genuine pain twist Goddess's shining visage with loss.

"How could you unite to abandon Me forever? I love both of you too!"

Lior had allowed everything before him to transpire without intervention until Däard's arrival. Hand in hand with his swordsman, humble again despite his Saintly luminescence, he opened his other palm to Marzanna to beckon Her closer.

"It is not beyond Your power to join us. Give up what You have taken, and come be with us forever."

"In death."

"Yes. In what should have been before, and what must happen to all beings eventually. Your time to enjoy divine power is over."

In fairness to Her Bettina hated to acknowledge, she watched Goddess consider Lior's offer. She trembled where She stood in full divinity before everyone She had ever loved and stared at Lior's marble hand and Däard's head slumped on his shoulder in contemplative silence.

"No!" Fiammetta had arrived first, but she had watched in a predatory assessment of what would work best to her advantage in the unfolding drama in the basin before she interceded. "'Zanna, 'Zanna, You love *me!* You promised to love me *always.* Stay with me!"

Racing across the swaying grass toward where Marzanna pinned Bettina, Fiammetta skidded to a stop on her knees and clung like a damp cloth to Her skirts. Her pleas were mournful, like a dove's, but the sideways frown she passed Bettina for the briefest instant held nothing of virtue under her pretty visage.

Whatever few mercies Goddess had stored up during Her reign had run dry. When She looked down on Fiammetta's kneeling figure, her radiant, doe-like beauty and red hair shining under the stain of mortal blood, She frowned without pity.

"I'm not going anywhere, Fia. But I will not keep My vows to you after what you've done."

"Me? What have I…" Feigning innocence with a lifetime's worth of practice, Fiammetta looked up at Goddess with clasped hands and a reverent fanatic's lust and love in her empty eyes. "I have loved You. I have *loved You beyond compare.* You cannot discard me after all we have shared!"

"The forgiveness I have extended to you since before I made you My consort should have been enough. I loved you in earnest. Why, then, did you try to buy Me with idle sacrifices? You have lied by omission and direct influence over and over. I cannot permit that."

"Your Glory, I was sick with envy, I admit it! All Aebbenary loved and worshipped You when for many years *I* had been your only disciple. You loved others, and others still, when I thought I was Your true heart…"

Marzanna did not dignify that with a response. Contemptuous now, as if the veil she had draped over Her eyes regarding Fiammetta's malice and madness had been stripped away by the garden basin's penchant to reveal truths, She shook Fia off with a kick that sent her sprawling on the ground.

Grapeskins and juice stuck to Fiammetta's face and hair as she lay, stunned, for no more than a moment. Bettina wanted to mock and spit on her too, but she was trapped, and all her energy needed to go to defeating Goddess.

Destiny had promised her this was possible. She had killed Cristoval to make it so. Lior was here, now, ready to welcome Goddess to Her death…

Fiammetta's fury turned on Bettina.

"It's her. That traitorous bitch has poisoned our love! Without her You *will* adore me again, Your Glory!" She launched herself toward Bettina, fingers hooked into claws to tear her apart.

She had no opportunity to dodge or fight back since all Goddess's Saints were as infants in strength compared to Her consorts. With Magisend all but gone, with her son dead and her daughter safe and powerful in her own right, Bettina watched as if from outside her own body as golden claws opened her throat as she had bled Cristoval in a sacrifice for the world.

It is fitting, Bettina thought toward wherever Cristoval's soul had gone, *that I bleed for this cause again. I hope to meet you soon, my angel.*

Magisend's consciousness wrapped around her in spider-thin threads, layering over and over themselves, as she slumped back against the tree and waited for her wasted life to drain out of her opened veins.

XXXIII

Cosima

Her stars fell deep into the world. Sinking into the dark to seek the Light of Goddess's consorts they had tracked to the end. Baying as they pursued, howling in the forms that coalesced around their shining souls as they landed beyond the portal others had passed through, Cosima let their essences fly and allowed the change to come over her own body to join them.

Fur like silk in the wind. Lean, stunning bodies with teeth meant for ripping and tearing. Four paws to run faster than Light itself if need required it. Voices communicating devotion and loyalty to one another in communion and barks that reverberated around the vineyard they entered to bring justice to one who had long deserved it.

Through dozens of eyes, linked in love and fidelity, Cosima surveyed the scene they had interrupted.

Goddess dominated every tableau She graced and drew all eyes first. Cosima was drawn to Her presence in reluctance, though at least linked with the others she saw more than she would have as a mere Godling.

Outside of Goddess's musing figure, Cosima witnessed Fiammetta lunge toward Bettina and slash her throat with her blood-crusted talons.

"Mama!" Dogs, even ones crafted from shared divinity, could not speak. The word came out as a howl from her strange new throat.

The others echoed the spirit of it as, hounds one and all, they streamed out of the portal to surround Fiammetta. Bettina slumped against the tree where Goddess had pinned her, her veins spurting ichor from her many wounds, and watched without comprehension at first as the pack of hunting hounds haloed each in their own Light saved her.

Some of them chewed at the trappings of Light tying Bettina to the tree; their transformed Light disintegrated Goddess's inattentive bonds. The rest dragged Fiammetta a ways off to punish her for everything she had wrought.

Goddess let them. She stood in silence, Her face turned away from the carnage as if in regret, and looked toward where Däard and the sculpted man Cosima recognized as the Scholar waited...for what?

"Goddess!" Fiammetta shrieked. "*Marzanna!* Make them st—"

One clever hound leaped toward her mouth and clamped down on her tongue to rip it out. Fiammetta's screams died to a gurgle.

For Ricla! For Ricla! The huntresses barked and howled in their joined minds as they each claimed a piece of shrieking Fiammetta in their jaws and began to pull her apart.

For us! The Godlings sworn to Cosima did not have the same noble cause to venerate, but she listened to their woeful memories of secret suffering as ichor sprayed and spattered them from Fiammetta's death. Even the ones Fiammetta had borne from her own body had not been much spared from her malevolence and despicable taste for torture.

Fiammetta survived where she lay on the grass, dismembered and foul with the indignity of her death, long enough for Cosima to stand over her and open her novel dog's mouth over her throat.

Die, Cosima told her when she opened the floodgates of her pack's minds to spill what they had suffered back on her tenfold, *and know you never meant anything. We will forget you after this, one and all.*

We forget you, the hounds echoed with flesh and ichor blotchy on their teeth, and tore Fiammetta completely apart.

Bettina slumped to the ground, blanketed by her limp wings. Her divinity worked to heal her, but it was sluggish in the chaotic atmosphere of oblivion clashing with Goddess's might. Cosima wanted to go to her...but she refrained because her bloodlust did not wane. She snarled, trembling, over the pieces of their prey and fought to master herself before she turned on someone she loved. Not her pack—*never* them.

But Bettina was here, clinging to life after yet another painful indignity, and Cosima *needed* to protect her. Lior was a stone effigy who probably didn't require a guarding hound to keep him safe; Däard had half-killed her before they had all fallen down to decide the destiny of their world, but she didn't want to kill him. One look at him from every eye of every one of her dogs showed he had been suffering every minute since the Scholar had died.

They had united in a similar way to Cosima and her pack. One arm from each wrapped around the other's waist; Däard slumped against Lior for support, his magnificent wings dragging on the ground like he couldn't wait to get rid of them.

His eyes, sorrowful and eager for rest, lifted to where she was dithering over who to fight next.

"I didn't know about Fiammetta for a long time. They hid her sins from me. By the time I knew it felt too late…everything felt too late. I have been living as a man already dead for the length of this age."

Who am I to decide if you are forgiven? Clarity had come to Cosima sometime between sacrificing Cristoval and falling from Aebbenary's skies with a sacred sword burrowed between her ribs. *I have enacted justice on a monster who deserved it. Your wrongs have been great, First Saint, and you have been negligent…but you are not a monster. You may yet be redeemed.*

The prism hummed as it rotated on an invisible axis. The fragmented Light it cast over the vineyard dazzled and befuddled all eyes, but Cosima withstood the onslaught and ordered her companions to keep watch.

She is not beaten yet, my friends, she warned them as she stalked on four bloody paws over the grapes and dying grass of the vineyard. Two others prowled close behind, then joined her to stand side by side.

In front of Bettina as she stumbled upright, between Goddess and her remaining consorts. Between Her and the shrinking, fluxing figure of verdant Light and golden bones that Cosima didn't recognize but knew, somehow, Bettina needed to save.

I'm here, Mama, she thought toward her. *I've come to save you this time.*

"There is nothing left for You here, Marzanna. Your treacherous dove has paid for her sins. If You atone for Yours You might write Yourself a different destiny. A better one—mayhap even one that should have been from the very beginning of Your age." Lior's persuasion hypnotized Goddess.

Cosima understood as she waited and observed why everything from the time of Bettina's return had come down to bringing the Scholar back long enough to induce Marzanna to surrender the power She had abused.

"A different destiny. What of the one I paid so dearly to obtain? The years I have spent building this world in a better design: *My* design. Is there nothing you would return for, hale and whole, to rule as My right hand?"

"You cannot bring me back without destroying the world You schemed to conquer. Is Your heart so riddled with rot You would allow that?"

"Never mind that. If you wish to live with Me, Lior, I will make it so. Däard will be himself again as long as you join us."

Cosima paced, flicking her tail, uneasy and thirsty for more blood. Justice had only partially been served in this uncanny realm. Bettina knelt on the grass beside her, holding her close like a pet; Cosima forced herself to breathe deep and stay patient.

Lior lowered his marble hand; Däard did the same.

"No. It would be an evil: it cannot be. The only way ahead is for You to surrender what You have stolen and sink into oblivion with us."

Hearing the grief in his voice, Cosima whimpered with involuntary pity. Not for Goddess, her first mother. For the young woman and young men the three of them had been before all of this had begun. For what a zealot Priest had set in motion to lure his false god down to enslave all earth. For the greed and lust for power that had brought everyone and everything to this point where all they could do was beg Marzanna and appeal to whatever humanity She had left to spare them all.

They appealed in vain.

"I am Goddess. I will not part with any of you—not you, My twofaced swan. Not Lior, Däard, or My sacrilegious Priest."

Marzanna took a wide stance and raised Her arms up and far apart toward the sky. She threw Her head back to gaze up at the pinpoint stars of the outer world. When they started to fall, summoned by Her hunger like a web pulled closer by a jubilant spider, She fashioned them with taloned hands into chains. She hurled one around each of her prizes, faster than Light, and yanked them closer.

Cosima lunged at these chains, followed by her loyal pack. Power flung them aside, blasting them out of reach, but not her. She was their leader, she was justice incarnate, and her fangs could not be denied.

Goddess's manifestation of authority sliced the tender skin of her houndish mouth when she seized the chain that snared Bettina before it reached her. Cosima clamped down with the full force of her bite. She channeled her whimper of pain into a snarl as she shook the sizzling chain as if to break its neck.

You have hurt us enough! No more!

Bettina ran to her, her expression determined but despairing as she laid her hand over Cosima's muzzle to try to heal the damage being done to her. Around them, Marzanna worked with silent rage to conquer Her prodigal consorts.

Lior and Däard clung to each other as they fell, one on his knees and the other on all fours, to try to crawl back to the prism so they could end their existences together. The shell of Easoren and Magisend was barely corporeal enough to be held by Goddess: Light fluctuating between brilliant hues of emerald, midnight blue, and solid gold formed a shape similar to the teardrop prism and failed to move closer or further away.

"Daughter, daughter," Goddess said, mocking Cosima as She pulled tighter on the chain. "You were right. I should have named Sovanna My heir. I see now you are too rebellious and too strong in spirit to serve under Me. Don't fret—your greatest achievement is yet to come. I will trade *you* for Lior."

The hounds began to sing their refrain of loyalty as Goddess reeled Cosima toward Her. Though she dug her paws into the dirt and ripped at the chain she couldn't let go of, though Bettina held her tight and screamed, Marzanna's power was inexorable. Her victory had been inevitable from the start no matter how many sacrifices they made to tear down Her throne.

Cosima's ears heard what happened next before her mind could absorb it: the voice of a new being in this basin beneath everything that had ever existed.

"Goddess, who rules on high."

Reality had broken. Cosima's mind had melted under the awesome radiance Goddess called on to ruin everyone who had ever defied Her.

The Light that Magisend-Easoren had turned into dawdled by the basin prism. Surrounding it.

Opening it.

"As You supplanted the old order, I am here to supplant You."

"Who are you?" Goddess's grip slackened. Real fear—that brought Cosima savage joy—marred Her perfect aspect.

"I am who I am."

Cosima knew. It didn't sound like him, not entirely, and that power exuding from his voice and the inevitability of his purpose…

The prism spun, faster and faster as the beings that had taken refuge in its heart left its protection behind to face Marzanna.

Sovanna walked at the right hand of an imposing figure, silent and pitiless as she stared Goddess down. Oleaginous blood streaked and spattered her face along with what looked like soot. One of her horns had been broken beyond repair, leaving an array of silver spikes where the horn had been. Though she seemed like she had been through a battle fought on the losing side, her poise remained unmatched, and her grey eyes revealed nothing but satisfaction.

Left of the central shape, still undefined other than a monstrous outline, Lilias arrived. They had grown again: circumstances must have forced them to adapt one more time to a world that hadn't been ready for them. Adolescent and lanky with fresh growth, the Saintling lurked with cunning, charming glee in their quartet of eyes and two more wings budding from their shoulders; these were white rather than black or crimson.

When they looked up at the figure, then around toward Sovanna, Cosima witnessed the love that shone from their strange features and recognized the affectionate infant she had been given to raise by a heartless mother. Her own spirit ached with nostalgia she never imagined she would experience in her entire lengthy life.

Prismatic or golden, Light fled from the darkness of the figure in the center as red fire swallowed it up. Only when it overthrew every stray spark but its own did the darkness unveil the man who had come to subjugate Goddess.

"*Cristoval!*" Bettina shouted.

XXXIV

Bettina

He had died at their hands, but he lived. It was him…and it wasn't.

Bettina crouched over Cosima in her hound form as, one and all, they stared at the being who sounded like Cristoval, who bore his general shape, but with gifts the world had never seen before.

He stood head and shoulders above them all; the horns on his brow curled up and around his head like a markhor's twisting crown, shining like abalone where the prism reflected. The blood he had willingly shed had dyed his pale skin that selfsame color over a body that was broad and strong enough to fight or run for days on end without tiring.

Scaled wings arched behind him, tipped at the spar by sharp silver joints like exposed bone. The gift that Goddess had granted Her favorites, the very thing that had become a curse for Bettina, rose proudly from his robust back in mockery of the blessings She had polluted with spiteful pride.

Bettina looked into his eyes when he glanced her way—searching for her deliberately—and gasped at the change. Her baby's eyes had been blue, like his mortal father's. This being's eyes held some of his old self, but the sclera had darkened to black as glossy as his horns. His snake-like pupils pierced darkness as well as light, and the color his irises displayed was as faceted as the prism he had emerged from.

My son, her heart skipped in pain and longing, *yet not. I know you, I would know you anywhere…but I don't know this. Not for certain.*

He looked away, back toward Goddess. Sovanna laid a hand on his arm, as did Lilias on the other side, before they let him go.

Friend or fiend, stranger or son, the being with colossal strength and Cristoval's face interceded to save them. He closed the gap between himself and Goddess's splintering form and grabbed the chains that linked all of them to Her to split them in two. Where Her Light touched his skin it vanished into his ember-speckled darkness without branding his crimson skin from the heat.

"You died!" Marzanna gasped, Her voice a caw as Her aureole forfeited dominance to the grip of his crimson hands and black claws. "I made sure of it. All these stars aligned for Me to take what I want from this chaos."

"There are some ends you cannot prophesy even as Goddess." Cristoval's answer was calm, but because Bettina knew him she heard the current of rage beneath the rest that had been strengthened by the suffering he had witnessed at Her order and the brush of death's scythe at his throat. In his grip, with the veins on his forearms stark beneath the red skin, the sundered chains forged by power and captured stars writhed like snakes while Goddess wailed at Her approaching defeat.

She let go. Of *everything.*

Flames consumed the vineyard and everything living or pretending at life in the basin belonging to the All except for Bettina, her loved ones, and their allies. Everything except the prism that droned its final song as it anchored them to this reality while the fire expended by Goddess melted away every shield, every pretext.

Smoke did not befuddle the rotting core of Goddess's spirit. While Bettina flinched away from the ugly result of divine greed enacted on a soul that had not entered the world this corrupt, she saw even more.

One tongue of midnight-blue energy lingered without his consciousness—like a human soul but infinitely more fragile. Soon the prism would claim it with the rest.

"Magisend, *wait—*"

It wasn't him. It hadn't been for several minutes. Bettina could have spent a hundred years asking him to wait for her, to hold on longer, and given anything to keep him…but he was gone.

She had no time to grieve. Her eyes were drawn to another phenomenon: dozens of souls sharing Cosima's mark, with her at the center of the array.

Oh, Cosima.

Cosima had become mortal. Bettina heard it in the pumping of her mortal heart, linked with all the huntresses and the crowd of Godlings and Saints that had arrived in her procession. She smelled it in the iron and salt of humanity. There was something like magic flowing around and between the molecules of mortal stuff, shining like rosy gold, but ultimately Cosima had doomed herself to mortality.

Why? The despair Bettina felt pierced her like a spear through her side…but she had bled too much for anything but water to spill out. *My pearl. What have you done?*

I gave it for love, Cosima answered in their minds; she sounded serene instead of tumultuous, mature in a way Bettina had not heard from her before. *I don't regret it. It will be all right.*

Sovanna came to stand by her, hand in hand with Lilias. When she reached to her Bettina freed one hand from holding Cosima to take her hand. Cristoval claimed Lilias's open hand while Cosima leaned her dog-shape against his leg to link them all. She was enough to secure the other hounds to their unit since it was her divinity that linked them.

Bettina flinched when the Light tethered in Cristoval's unbreakable grip thrashed, resisting all taming, but he didn't let go. It belonged to him.

Goddess materialized once more—still brilliant, still grotesque to behold behind Her human façade, but present. She had eyes enough to watch as Lior and Däard vanished into the prism, their faces immaculate with relief and love so profound Her eyes pricked with scalding tears.

"How can your pointless, temporary life be restored, but none that I value? How are you here while I am alone?" She asked.

Sovanna answered. Her voice was pitched low, but the anger beneath it coupled with her loss gave it dignity Goddess could not match. "I used my portion of our sacrifice to forge him from one fleeting soul into the only monster who could best You. I Made him in this matchless shape and brought him here to finish You."

Though Marzanna heard, She ignored her. Her attention was fixed on Cristoval with anguish bare on Her twisted features.

"You did not value them higher than Yourself. That isn't a sin, not according to oblivion, but a simple truth. Besides…" Cristoval's ruthless expression did not soften. "I have been made whole by the love of another. Who remains to care for You after You sacrificed their hearts for power?"

NO ONE. Marzanna's shriek of abandonment resonated though them all. *NO ONE IS LEFT!*

Goddess collapsed, in and in again over Herself until She resembled something like the woman Bettina had met before the dawn of the new age. She covered Her face and wept, loudly and without restraint, sobbing the names of Her consorts who had gone.

Bettina thought she had nothing left to say to Goddess. She had wasted enough air in affection, pleas, or fury, to last her for eternity.

"It is done now." She hesitated before she crouched, merciful the way only she could be as she rested a hand on Marzanna's shining hair. "You have lost all of us. But there is relief in store for You, if you seek it."

Goddess jerked away from her, lifting Her head. "Solace in death. That is all you can offer."

"Yes. More than You deserve."

"How do you know this?"

"I was never just a bauble for You to toy with, or the pretty swan You coveted. This place…the garden…" *How to explain?* Bettina barely understood it herself. Another meaning behind her visions in the garden came to her as she considered. "Life goes on with time. Nothing is ever really the end. Some paths end in the dark that even divine beings cannot comprehend. I think that's what waits for You, if I'm honest…but I don't know. There might be hope for You to start again ten thousand years or worlds away."

They all waited as Marzanna wept, quiet now, and contemplated what Bettina said. She didn't look at any of them as She bowed Her head and breathed out. And breathed…*breathed*…

…Her Light. As Bettina had once danced for Her favor and shed her Saint's Light, Goddess exhaled Her *self* out toward the prism in the last offering She would ever make.

At the end, at the last possible second, Marzanna sought what remained of Easoren with Her eyes.

He had stayed. As Magisend had not been able to, for he had never truly been alive, the Priest had lingered. Waiting for Goddess to surrender.

"You waited. For Me."

He didn't answer. Bettina wondered how little of him remained after the prism was almost done sucking in whatever Light had lingered in that pitiful cage of gilded bones.

"If you come with me, Priest…" Marzanna began.

Easoren finished. *"We were meant for this."*

"We are meant for this," Goddess agreed.

Her pulsing, golden rot in the form of dying Light mingled with the diminished silver of Easoren's aura as they followed the passage into oblivion where Lior and Däard had already tread.

If the All is just, that would be the end of both of them. Bettina imagined the everlasting sleep of non-existence that still did not seem painful enough to justify what all of them had gone through or what mortalkind had suffered under the dominion Silver or Marzanna had held over the past millennia.

But who am I to say? Perhaps life begins anew after each turn, again and again.

Cristoval stood where the prism had spun the end of their story. They dangled in a tapestry of divine aureoles, suspended in the empty space of the world's depths where oblivion waited for one of them to set events in motion again. The chains of power Marzanna had tried to enslave them with had gone silent…but they stirred again. Seethed, writhed…*demanded* someone use them.

Before their heat and noise grew and grew to devour all existence in their vacuum.

"We have to do something with it!" Cristoval shouted as he stared warily at the seething mass, his claws sunk in to gouge whatever stuff constructed the chains.

"What do you mean?" That was Sovanna.

"Cristoval has to control this power!" Bettina remembered. At her feet, Cosima growled with her tainted gold hackles raised as one of the chains flailed and left a streak of soot against her muzzle. "We can't let it go, it'll destroy everything!"

Shouting at him when he hesitated, Sovanna let go of the others to grab Cristoval's arm. "Do it. I know you can. It's what you are meant for!"

Still, he hesitated. He looked down at his closed fist to deliberate the untold power he held without burning or dissolving in its presence, cloaked in the immortal body Sovanna had built for him with pieces garnered from herself and others. His prismatic eyes reflected the chains and everything he might do with their power embedded in his flesh.

He could do it, Bettina thought, awestruck but uneasy. *He was made to rule this world.*

They would praise and sing his hymns far and wide in the world for a long age of dark. This Cristoval…

Is it him? Somewhere in there, does he remain?

"I don't want to do this alone. What was all this for if we just begin the cycle again?" Cristoval loosened his grip on the chains, but they didn't slither away with that grace. "I don't trust myself or any one person with corrupting power. I cannot allow mortalkind to suffer under this grinding stone again."

Sovanna didn't question him. She had been tense, stern at Cristoval's side like one of her toothy swamp guardians, but her ominous expression mellowed and then accepted.

"We'll find another way. We can take it apart and remake it."

What did Lior say? Before we came here? Did he tell you the power had *to go to one alone?* Cosima asked in their heads, her fur stained by Fiammetta's gore.

"Lior said…" Bettina tried to remember. Elation had her fighting a wry smile as she recalled the beginning of their conversation. *He never answered me!*

Cristoval's smile revealed the boy she had raised in the man he had become. It was contagious, though she saw his teeth were sharper than all of theirs. Sovanna smiled, then Bettina, then Lilias, who laughed with childlike triumph. Even Cosima chuffed a laugh. Light flared around her as she returned to her human shape, shifting from hound to woman.

Cord by cord, Cristoval divided the chains evenly between them. Bettina's felt like Magisend's threads in her palm. The longing for his embrace filled her so purely she ached with it all the way down to her exposed, divine soul.

As they had contemplated what to do with the power their sacrifice of Cristoval had earned, the three of them decided one more time how to disperse Goddess's divinity.

Sovanna cured mortalkind of the sickness that had enslaved them time and again to divinities. Bettina watched her wave of healing snow on the glassy sea around their island spread out from Aebbenary to wrap the world in the will to stand for itself. With Lilias at her side, as much her child now as Cristoval was Bettina's, she carved a place for benign abominations like them into the weave of reality.

Cosima worked her will next. Where she had spread her divinity amongst her followers, she siphoned the Light from the beings who hadn't followed her lead to ensure they worked no mischief on vulnerable mortalkind during their long lives. They had those—nothing else, and little to no chance for their progeny to populate the world with divinity. As Goddess's named heir, she fixed all the destinies of immortalkind, including her huntresses, on a wheel they could not exploit.

Cristoval eased some of the hurts Goddess's regime had inflicted on the world: erasing sickness, filling empty coffers with a second chance at security, giving the downtrodden the strength and courage to protect themselves from any who would take advantage of their bodies or time on earth. So many details others would have missed, he tended to like a shepherd. Bettina couldn't be prouder...but sorrow tainted her pride.

Her children's roles had turned on their heads. Cristoval would be safe forevermore, as immortal as Bettina had schemed, prayed, and debased herself for. Cosima was the one in danger now. By the state of the diminished aureole she still possessed her life would be youthful and longer than a mortal's by many spans, but...

Bettina picked up her share of the chains. The links clung to her skin like mesh and cinched around her dominant hand like a glove. While she pondered what to do, her attention captured each of them in her eyes and heart, filling her to the brim with love she might soon feel safe enough to enjoy.

I could save her. Her first impulse.

Time had reclaimed Cosima. She and her huntresses would leave this world the way all humans did. Bettina had the means in her hand now to save one condemned life...just one. Claiming more would make her little better than Goddess.

Don't, Mama. Please. This is what I want. Cosima pleaded with her in their minds. *I love my pack. We belong to each other...and it is not your choice to make, whether I live forever or only as long as they do.*

Aebbenary had welcomed Bettina home within the past year, but she was not the same desperate mother who had been compelled back to her shores by divine command. Choices mattered, for everyone, and some were not even a loving mother's decision to make.

I love you, Cosima. I would never take your happiness from you...even if it won't be forever.

Her smile was brilliant, unashamed, less restrained than Bettina had ever seen. That was reward enough, though in some years hence there would be a time when she would have to mourn her.

What was there for Bettina to do? The others had arranged it so beautifully.

You matter too, Cosima replied.

You matter for yourself, Sovanna elaborated.

What do you want? Cristoval next. *If anyone has earned the right to claim it...there might be someone you can save.*

As he had gone, Easoren had ejected the fragments that did not belong to him from his spirit. The silvers that had belonged to the once-powerful Grand Archivist hovered in the void around the prism, green and midnight and green again as they slowly vanished.

"*He loved you,*" the All whispered to Bettina in one final offering. "*His existence is not one you will ever comprehend...but he loved you.*"

But he existed! Bettina shook off Cosima's hand and lunged toward the prism. She didn't care if it cut her; part of her, the sections dying with the loss of Magisend, hoped it would.

Bettina embraced the prism with her entire being and Light and called.

He did not live...so he cannot die.

She screamed for Magisend by name and pressed her forehead against the lustrous surface of the All's prism hard enough to leave a bruise. She beckoned every sliver of ichor and Light she had ever traded to him, every mote of flesh and desire and pain they had ever endured, and stamped her brand on each piece as her desire lured or dragged it back.

See, this is mine! It belongs to me! Bettina's thoughts burned with acid and it felt like needles pierced every facet of her divine body, but she clung to the rock as tightly as if she was trying to meld with it. More ready for battle than she had ever been, she infested the tranquil absence within the prism with her human lusts, hurts, hates, and loves.

Magisend lying beside her on the platform in the Archives, Magisend on top of her to protect her from Goddess's roving notice, Magisend stitching her wing back on its stump with threads ripped from his own borrowed flesh, Magisend kissing her, thrusting in her, Magisend in triplicate and in singular form telling her he never wanted her to sorrow again...holding her as she wept for Cristoval at the end of the world...

Magisend, Magisend, her *Magisend...*

The prism cut her then. It fought off her memories and outpouring of herself with all its will, but not in cruelty. Not in malice, for oblivion knew what it owed her generous heart and nurturing spirit.

"Give it something from you!" Sovanna shouted from what sounded like a hundred miles away. "A piece of yourself might—"

Bettina didn't need further prompting. But what to give? She could stand the loss of one wing...but that would mean less, since they had been a gift, not something that had come with her into the world. Magisend deserved something that had always been hers.

Bracing herself against the prism, she reached into her chest around her heart, through her Light, and prised one of her ribs out of its cage to break it off. The pain barely registered compared to what the prism was doing to her the longer she held on.

Is it enough? I will give more. Her rib scraped against the prism as she pressed it against the adamant surface with her ichor-drenched hand. *I will give almost anything to bring him home to me.*

Let him go, it murmured to her as it restrained her railing against its surface like strong arms preventing her from injuring herself further. *Live in your freedom, Bettina Valusius. Live as only you can.*

Her rib vanished into the prism, making her gasp with shuddering hope…when she pulled her hand back, it and the ichor she had given was gone. Her wounds healed in her battered body, but nothing else happened.

As Bettina guessed, her efforts failed. The All had already told her they couldn't give back a person who had never existed as more than a construct of profane desire and lovesick hope.

For one brief instant, she considered following Marzanna and Her consorts into oblivion. That wouldn't hurt as bad as this, surely. Perhaps, in ten thousand years like she had told Goddess, whatever stuff made her and Magisend up would exist again. They might meet. They might love one another in happiness…someday.

But.

Cristoval. Cosima. Sovanna, Lilias. They need me. Bettina dropped her reaching arms and dimmed her precious Light.

We want you with us, they said in her mind, and embraced her in their midst. *Don't go.*

"I'm not," she promised them, smiling because she knew it would help heal her to enjoy the devotion of her favorite people in the universe.

The atmosphere around them changed. Though her wings were wrapped close around her, Bettina felt like all of them were flying as they rose rapidly up from the basin of the world as tendrils of Light to surface in the garden of paradise on earth.

Epilogue

Sovanna

After Goddess, Aebbenary became Sovanna's home again. She wasn't sure she had it in her to leave it behind…not yet. When she had returned—alone—after the marvel they had wrought in the heart of the world, she had revisited her hut because she had nothing better to do.

She couldn't face Cristoval. She couldn't face any of them after everything that had happened: the hurts were still too raw, her grief present and near like a thunderhead over her endless life.

Her animals had gathered on her doorstep to wait for her. Marsh badgers and crocodiles and toads and rodents, all polished and clean as she liked them so they could be there for her. Sovanna had plopped at the center of their huddle in the moss and mud and wept until every terrible feeling she had suffered gave way to numb acceptance.

She remained there for many days. Let others tend the garden that had materialized in this plane by the mellowed sea around Aebbenary. Let others manage this strange world in the infant days of humanity's first age not dominated by any divine presence. All Sovanna did was sleep, clean her work-ravaged cottage, and do her best to not experience a single unwanted thought while she worked.

A missive came to her from her favorite badger, carried in Lilias's teenage arms in resignation if not comfort. The child brought it to her with smug pride and grunted a few words of explanation that ultimately conveyed who the note was from.

Cristoval.

When you're ready, it said when she unfolded the letter that felt like crisp parchment and smelled of woodsmoke, *I will wait for you at the cathedral. Only think of me, and imagine a time, and I will be there.*

His power had yet to be defined. The prospect inspired Sovanna when it should have given her pause…but, well, how could she experience fear again after she'd lost her true love and defeated Goddess with the creature she raised in his place?

Another day had passed. Two. By nightfall on the second, while Sovanna contemplated the moon from her front stoop, she decided it was time to get this over with. She sent Cristoval her stray thought on the wind.

What answered also smelled of forest fires and an enticing resin like frankincense. It didn't intrude on her privacy for more time than it took to blink…but Sovanna could not deny the thrill that gave her too.

The next morning, after a few hours of fitful sleep, she woke up a little refreshed. She girded herself in a sage-colored dress embroidered around the waist and hem with other greens, and dared attempt cosmetics on her peerless face. It was difficult to avoid looking at the stump left of her donated horn, but she managed…until she didn't.

I gave this for him. She compelled herself to study the silvered, ridged remnants. *We defeated Goddess with my help. Let it remind me of my strength.*

Journeying by Light, she travelled through the city toward the grave of the religions Aebbenary had abandoned to serve its own people. Already, a change in power had altered the city, Sovanna noted: Cosima and her huntresses had been present and active to continue Cristoval's programs for aid and betterment of the citizens.

After the basin, some of the huntresses had brought word out of courtesy to share Cosima's invitation to join them in helping restore Aebbenary to a reasonable shade of its former glory before they set up a council of mortals to oversee the wellbeing of the city for the future. Sovanna had read the letters, listened to the impassioned speeches from the huntresses when she refused to write a reply, but nothing else. It was impossible to think of anything when her business with Cristoval had yet to be closed.

Someday, maybe, she'd like to help. Sovanna had been working behind the scenes to preserve mortalkind for so many years she hadn't the faintest clue what to do with herself now she wasn't the only one who cared. Now all of them had a chance to build a better world for the people who labored on land, sea, or anywhere humans could eke out a meaningful existence.

She didn't stop to greet them today, though.

When she reached the cathedral, Cristoval wasn't there. Sovanna had half-dreaded, half-hoped he would be standing outside the smashed in yet still imposing doors across the massive bridge, waiting where he had promised. But he wasn't.

She paced a while, taking the opportunity to gather her thoughts before she remembered.

I gave him wings, Sovanna thought, and looked up.

Sure enough, there he was. Cristoval, the savior of Aebbenary, balanced on the edge of the derelict cathedral's roof with his bare wings spread out for balance.

He had sensed her or seen her Light; he looked down, his horns glossy like oil under the sun. The stars of the heavens wheeled an eon as they stared at each other, one above and one below. Her divine eyes watched a muscle feather in his jaw as he simply looked.

Without further preamble, he sprang down to a lower roof, hung with claws embedded in the nearest wall, and glided down to stand in front of her. The air filled with a scent both dry as smoke and sweet as honeysuckle nectar and made Sovanna's mouth water.

"You've been avoiding me."

She nodded. "Yes."

"Tell me why."

An order, even if he didn't mean it to be.

"I—" *I'm not sure I know you anymore. I'm not sure I owe you this. I—*

"Wait." Cristoval cocked his head, watching closely as he picked her up by the waist and splayed his wings to fly them back to the roof.

Sovanna had flown in her Light, but not as herself. The rush of being bodily picked up and winged upward enticed a gasp of pleased surprise out of her.

When he set her down and stalked away to lean back against a window, folding his wings and crossing his arms, she was sorry for it. He wore black clothing that clung to his muscular legs, but the shirt he wore hung open, sleeveless, and loose to leave his large wings room to flex.

"Things are easier up here. I don't know why."

"I…" Her tongue had always been called silver. Why was she so awkward now? Sovanna tried to shake it off. "I hope so."

"I missed you." He blurted; his prism eyes blinked twice as he visibly concealed a wince. "We haven't seen one another in a fortnight. Since the basin."

"I had responsibilities." Sovanna didn't elaborate.

He waited. And waited.

"These—"

"I have things to tell you, Cristoval." Her turn to blurt some clumsy words before she had the courage to say the rest. It didn't help that she had made him handsome: she had liked him before, mortal or not, but her tastes had trickled into this new body she had slaved over in the twilight realm of the sacrificial cave with her father whispering guidance in her ears.

I broke your bones in my hands and molded your flesh with my will. I am responsible for everything about you but whatever spark brought part of you back. I hope you don't think it was a mistake after everything is done…

He waited again. Sovanna flushed and twisted her skirt in her hands at her sides and fought the urge to hide her broken horn.

"Won't you tell me?" he asked, staring at her like he couldn't look away. That gaze was arresting: an unstoppable force, yet one she knew in her heart of hearts she owned.

"I'm not sure I can…"

"Try. Please."

Sovanna ached at the sound of his kindness. He would not force her to explain herself—she had come here ready to destroy him, one way or another, if he proved himself a ghoulish villain bearing her dead lover's features. His example in the basin had set a precedent for trust, but she had been fooled before.

"You have to live with the changes I made," Sovanna began. "It must look like I didn't love him for who he is...was."

Cristoval exhaled, like what he heard was a relief. When he leaned forward, off the window he'd tilted back against, his approach felt like the most delicious threat in the world.

"Not all my memories are fresh. They are like undisturbed grave soil in my mind."

She frowned; an odd thrill tickled the hairs on the back of her neck. "I never buried you."

He smiled—that was Cristoval's, but the teeth were whiter and the canines sharp. "Ah. That must be my imagination."

"I wanted you to be strong. I gave you a better shape than what you had rather than the one I loved." Out of habit, Sovanna catalogued how many changes she had made as she scanned Cristoval's body.

Horns, muscles on a strong frame, and height to tower over any ordinary man. Flesh impervious to fire or decay, eyes to pierce darkness and Light, wings that cannot be hacked away or plucked to cause pain...

"Can't say I mind." Lifting his hand—still as elegant as a born musician's despite the claws—Cristoval turned it this way and that to study it. "It seems I am a practical sort."

The laugh that startled out of her was shaky.

He's a paradox, this one, she thought, cynical yet undeniably attracted. When he stopped in front of her she managed *not* to back away. *Dangerous, but gentle as spring when its sweet...*

Hope made her foolish again. "How much of him is in there with...whoever you are now?"

"The connection you had with this soul was lost. Irretrievably. I am sorry."

She had known it. That thread had been cut with so many others—perhaps it had been the first to go. It didn't hurt to hear as much as Sovanna had imagined, but the ache that made itself a home in her chest would linger forever.

"It..." Her voice shook again: that wouldn't do. "It was an honor to experience the love we shared."

One step closer. He looked down on her—how tall he was!—and

dared her to back away. She didn't.

"Tell me the rest. Then I will speak."

"I know what I'm worth now. I know neither one of us deserves to live in the past now he is gone…in the shadow of our genuine love." Sovanna could see he had thought he'd guessed what she was going to say; he hadn't.

"That's what you came to tell me?"

Sovanna nodded; everything hurt, especially her heart, but she couldn't stop now. "I release you from any obligation that might linger from Cristoval's remains toward me. I release—"

"Sovanna. Stop."

She had to. This was the hardest thing she had ever done aside from sacrificing Cristoval in the first place.

"I will not be released. Not for those reasons. The pieces of what make me are from all of you: Lilias, Easoren, my mother who bore me, your horn and your heart's desire for me." Cristoval wrapped her hand in his and pressed it to the bare skin on his chest, over his heart. "I am willing to learn what that means. I'm willing to re-learn the secrets of this soul I carry. I am *grateful* for the chance to love you to distraction if you allow it, Sovanna."

"We…we barely knew each other. How do I know the connection we had would have lasted? How could we know it was love?"

"Because it was," he answered, as if nothing was simpler, "and it will be again." Though they stood close together, he held out his hand in offering as he stood. "You don't have to lose this again. I will cleave to you forever; I will never forsake you. Only promise me the same."

She couldn't—not out loud. Sovanna shook her head, choked by emotion. She laid her hand in his and watched as his clawed fingers closed gently, *so* softly, around hers.

I promise, Cristoval, she said between their minds, and tipped her head back for him to kiss her.

Cosima

"Lilias, Lilias, you cannot do that on your own!"

Palmira's scolding carried across the clearing under the huntress' treehouse. Cosima heard it all the way from the outskirts where she was helping some of the Godlings and Saints arrange the tables for the feast.

While she ignored it, so did Lilias. The imp flared all six of his wings and flew away with an entire bucket of newly-caught saltwater fish…until they smacked right into Ormanno, who had positioned himself to catch them midair. A brief tussle ensued, but not a hostile one. Cosima chuckled when Lilias tripped Ormanno over his own feet and zoomed away, babbling insults. Palmira ran after them in pursuit.

"Just *look* at them. They're useless. *Hopeless.*" Grisel's grumbling had been going on for hours. "That oaf might be the worst of the lot. Most of them have never lifted a finger to do *anything* before. How can you trust them to set table or cook or—"

"Give them a chance," Cosima sighed, bumping Grisel's stiff shoulder with her own. "They want to be helpful these days. I think they like being nice to each other, and others being nice to them. They don't have to be vicious to survive anymore."

They'd been working side by side to manage the food, but Grisel shouted a rude curse and scurried to tell one of them off. (Evrard— he'd brought his dogs to the clearing and they'd scattered as soon as he arrived in his Light, chasing deer and knocking floral arrangements over.)

Cosima knew she wasn't wrong. It would be many years before any Godling or defunct Saint's first instincts pointed toward fairness or justice rather than self-interest and egoism.

They were here. They were trying to help, attempting to bond with their fellow hounds and build connections that weren't founded on rivalry. Cosima had already told them she was only herself—not

Goddess, not their ruler. They could earn her favor as friends, but nothing more.

They could lose it too, if they didn't change, but despite their flaws now Cosima didn't imagine any of them would fail. She had given up a large portion of her heart to see theirs: they wanted this life of service and camaraderie, one and all.

This was the start. This feast was for more than celebrating their victory and all their hard work to restore Aebbenary so far. It was for more than the love that had joined Cosima, Iulia, and Konetta after all was said and done and she had tied her life to theirs.

The party had been Iulia's idea. The reason for it had been Konetta's. And Cosima...

While she pared bitter skin from sweet pears, Cosima's thoughts must have summoned her loves. They had finished their tasks, she gathered as they approached her with smiles and tools to help her finish hers.

"When will the others arrive?" Konetta asked.

"Soon. Sovanna wanted to meet Cristoval, and—"

"Meet him?" Iulia eavesdropped as she lumbered over with a basket full of seasoned venison balanced in her burly arms. "They're lovers, aren't they? Haven't they—"

"Don't!" Cosima fought off a laugh as she traded Konetta her pears for a tray of peaches to slice. "Cristoval sent word they'll be late, but they'll make it. *Together.*"

Any huntresses close enough to hear ooo-ed in raucous, bawdy amusement, sounding very much like the hound shapes they could take whenever they wanted.

Iulia located a free cutting board on a nearby preparation table and began to carve the large chunks of meat into bite-sized pieces. The scent of herbs wafting through the air along with the zest and sweetness of different fruits made Cosima's stomach rumble.

"Do you think they want to exchange vows too? The more the merrier."

"Mm," Cosima answered Iulia, "Sovanna is private. She'll want whatever they share to be theirs alone, I think."

"Not like us." Konetta popped a sliver of pear into her mouth—cheating since they weren't supposed to eat until everyone had gathered—and wriggled between Iulia and Cosima to kiss each of them on the cheek.

Contentment sang through Cosima at her touch. At the easy companionship not fraught with jealousy or anxiety they shared now and would for a long time. Even if it was only *their* forever rather than eternity.

They're learning to love each other because they love me, she thought as she dropped her paring knife and the peach she'd been slicing to pull Konetta and Iulia into a spontaneous embrace. *Is anything more perfect than that?*

"My heart is almost overflowing because of you, and you," Cosima told them as Konetta laughed and Iulia wiped her hands on her tunic so she could hold both of them in the span of her arms. "I still can't believe you're with me for good."

"You'll believe it soon enough," Iulia promised; Konetta laughed, giggling without any trace of the cough that had poisoned her since she had met Cosima long ago. Not all hurts could be erased by Miraculous will, but that one's source had been in her weakness to suffer divine presence. Others throughout Aebbenary had already recovered from this particular illness, though mortals could never be immune to everything.

When all the preparation was done and the huntress's clearing had been decorated with all sorts of garlands and delicious but simple fare for everyone to enjoy, her hounds in human shape cleaned themselves up in the nearest river. They adorned themselves in bright but practical clothing and waited for the other guests of honor to arrive.

Cristoval and Sovanna arrived by wing rather than Light. Sovanna nestled comfortably in Cristoval's arms, cradled like precious treasure and set on her feet like a true queen. When he approached Cosima and they embraced, there was no awkwardness between them. They had already met after the basin to talk through any uncomfortable truths they needed the other to know.

Cosima had apologized for her role in sacrificing him, and thanked him for the duty he had accomplished. This strange, demonic shape of her brother was still her brother: she had told him so.

"I don't care what face you wear," she had said. *"I know the soul you kept, even in pieces. You are always welcome in my life, Cristoval."*

Divine beings had little to no use for a family tree. Lineage rarely mattered in cases of eternal life. Yet it wasn't lost on Cosima that she and Sovanna were sisters twice over, once through blood and now through whatever means of marriage she and Cristoval accepted.

Lilias emerged in a *pop* of sulfurous smoke and a portal that quickly *squinched* shut behind them when they saw Sovanna and Cristoval together. They rarely spoke now even though they understood far more than they let on—for the convenience of mischief, Cosima had guessed—but she heard the three of them whispering to each other with all their horned heads inclined together to share something that looked like family business.

Her heart did overflow then, into her eyes. To see Lilias—the last unloved, forgotten child in a line of offspring birthed for pure selfishness—loved and appreciated by a family unit that clearly understood their needs and how they communicated…Cosima had learned to appreciate that. It had never been in her to mother the child, but Sovanna had risen to the challenge.

Bettina was the last to arrive.

"Is she well?" asked Konetta, observing from afar while Cosima secured a few briar roses in the kinks of the curls on her head. "She's so pale—"

"Saints can't have poor health. But Cosima…she does look pale."

Cosima twisted her beringed hands together in inattentive fretting as she watched Bettina fan her wings to stretch them before she folded them closed. In the seconds before she knew she would have to be observed and social, Bettina's face looked drawn and tight with an ocean of grief.

"She lost her heart in the basin. I don't know when she'll learn to live without it or wait for it to come back to life for someone else," Cosima murmured to the others, low enough for only their trio to hear.

"We should be extra kind to her. So she knows she doesn't ever have to be alone," Iulia suggested. Cosima was happy to honor it.

They went to Bettina then, pouring their joy over her with happy greetings and hugs that Cosima hoped conveyed how grateful she was for her mother's presence. How glad she was that they had, sometime at the end of the last divine age, overcome their differences to love each other as themselves.

Bettina's smile was radiant as she held Cosima's face in both hands and kissed her forehead in blessing. "Cosima. You are lovely."

Officiated by the eldest huntress (besides Iulia) and the next oldest Godling (under Cosima and Sovanna) Iulia, Konetta, and Cosima were wed by the old ways Aebbenary had all but forgotten under the canopy of flower-bedecked leaves protecting their treehouse. The words they exchanged were nothing ostentatious or particularly formal; the promises they vowed to each other carried significance but did not bind beyond what each of their free wills would tolerate. They were observed, they spoke to one another with an audience, and then it was done: they were wed.

All the huntresses, Godlings, Saints, and the trio that had become Cristoval's family cheered when Cosima, Iulia, and Konetta inclined their faces together over their linked hands and kissed between giddy laughter.

After, illuminated one and all by their various aureoles, they feasted by that same Light. Other weddings between royalty or important persons might have been fancier, with entertainers, music, and all sorts of divine amusements, but Cosima preferred this. A few Saints practiced on instruments they had brought that they didn't use their power to play: their music was earnest and not unpleasant, but distinctly human in quality. Troubadours and jesters didn't flock between tables to titillate the guests, but the huntresses were a hilarious group. Together they had most of the camp roaring with laughter from the stories they told or jumped to their feet to enact.

Cosima enjoyed all of it where she sat at her table—exactly like the rest—beside her loves…and watched Bettina. She sat next to her, between Cosima and Cristoval, but her attention wandered.

I'm sorry, Mama. Tonight may be for me, but I'm not going to let you be sad forever. We're going to find something to bring you joy if it's the last thing I do.

Cosima banged her empty cup against her table several times to get everyone's attention. When that didn't work, Iulia whistled so loudly with her fingers that Cosima could have sworn she heard something shatter back in the city. She stood, then, filled her cup with wine, and lifted it to address her guests: a feast table full of her hounds in human shape, Godlings and Saints diminished after Goddess's demise but happier for it, a handful of abominations, and her mother.

"I know this is a different wedding than you're used to. All of this is a change from one age to the next…and I'm happier than I can say that all of you have joined us to celebrate it. After what we've been through, I think we deserve to drink ourselves sodden!"

That was all she had to say. That was all she *could* say as she gazed around at all the faces she loved or knew she would soon come to love as friends and comrades in arms.

Bettina, clapping and laughing as Iulia thumped Cosima on the back and stood to publically drain her tankard; Konetta, leaning in to kiss Cosima and whisper how proud she was of her. Cristoval hauled protesting Sovanna into his lap to kiss her; Cosima expected her to protest, but she reclined into his arms without a care in the world.

Lilias perched in a tree nearby, high, high up. Occasionally, one of the Godlings would carry food to them since they didn't want to mingle in the boisterous crowd for more than a few minutes at a time. They descended when Cosima beckoned—bolstered by a good-natured order from Sovanna—and took a seat on the ground in the center of all the tables as Bettina stood to speak her own toast.

Bettina

Her cup of celebratory dandelion wine—preserved at the bottom of the treehouse years ago by a huntress with a hobby—swirled in her cup as she stood to make her speech. She hadn't prepared anything even though it had occurred to her she would need to as she busied herself at her estate or in the garden by the shore. It had taken ages to clean up after...

After.

"You don't know what pleasure it gives me to stand with my daughter's friends and cherished ones and commemorate their union under the stars," Bettina began, because what else could she do? The words of her heart would be more meaningful than any artificial formality her courtly upbringing would have helped her compose. "Hope has teased us for such a long while...it's good to see something wonderful bloom in my children's lives. After all we had to do to reach this happy evening."

Lose. She had almost said "lose" instead of "do". Everything was worth it, even losing Magisend, if her children were safe and happy. That had been her goal all along, though she had lost her footing and drowned in the sea with one wing to reach it.

Bettina would not show the grief that weighed down her soul and threatened to sink it every moment she didn't fight back. She lifted her wooden goblet higher and fixed the fondest smile she could on her face as she shared her attention between Cosima, sat at the head of the largest table, and Cristoval and Sovanna to her right.

"My beautiful, wise daughter, I give you a mother's blessing on your matrimony and wish you forever happiness with Iulia and Konetta. If either of you ever need a mother for...well, motherly things, I am here for you."

She toasted the three of them and sipped her wine with the rest of the gathering before she continued. Some were surprised enough to hastily lunge for the nearest pitcher to refill the cups they'd quaffed; Bettina smiled and pretended not to notice.

"Cristoval. We already spoke when you visited me after..." *After I failed.* "I knew you before I bore you and I will always, always know you for yourself. I just wanted to share before everyone who knows or cares about you and our family that this is true. I love you, my son. Because of that, I love your beloved too. It is an honor to be connected with a woman who is brave as well as clever, and kindhearted as well as strong."

The assembly accepted the second and final toast she offered. Cristoval's one-of-a-kind eyes might not have been able to water, but Bettina knew him: he would have shed a few affectionate tears when he stood to kiss her cheek in gratitude before they all sat down again.

I wish you could see this, she thought to someone who was no longer there. Though it had healed, the rib she'd donated to save Magisend was lost forever. Her habit of massaging the place it had been was hard to fight, but she did. Cosima was already watching her too closely for what Bettina wanted: her children focusing on their joy in one another, not worrying about her.

Not long after, she left the young ones to their revels and flew home alone. The stars were as much company for her as they were for the others…but their light was cold.

Bettina had promised Magisend she would mourn him. The obligation weighed on her soul, but nothing like how burdens in her past had hurt her. She was glad to do this for him, though he was gone…well, as glad as she could be in her grief. Her children were thriving, joined by companions she approved of and admired, and building lives of their own out of the shadow of Marzanna's reign. It was a kinder destiny than she had ever known to wish for.

The garden by the sea had, somehow, become her responsibility. It was there Bettina walked whenever the lingering trauma from her ordeals drove her from sleep or beset her with nightmares. Though elements of the garden's origin had been eldritch and beyond strange, much of that power had diminished on this plane. The gates that had blocked out guests had been lost in the basin. Citizens from the city hadn't dared approach, not yet, but Bettina guessed their curiosity must be growing.

She waited to welcome them. To prepare, she set to work in ways that challenged her still holy body. Mapping the miles of land the garden had claimed from land and sea and transfigured for its own claim, categorizing the beasts she saw or the fauna she came to recognize as she walked or flew under the trees. These were not skills that came naturally to her, but she was willing to learn. The occupation of her mind kept her busy and, almost, happy.

Aebbenary's bells rang the passage of time into weeks while she strove for contentment in her solitude. Her children broke her lonesome vigil in the paradise garden occasionally. They conversed with their joy apparent in their eyes shining with love toward Bettina and each other and a distinct lack of the fear they had been raised with in their bearing.

Cristoval and Sovanna, joined by Lilias, claimed the Valusius estate when Bettina bequeathed it to them without accepting any possible refusal. Though Cosima should have been the busiest among them, she was Bettina's most frequent companion. In comfortable understanding, the two of them would walk side by side—as women or with Cosima in her hound shape—as Bettina tracked one path to its end or picked fruit for her dinner.

Gratitude was not a rich enough word to describe what Bettina felt toward Cosima for that gift.

Seasons came and went as they and the world they had saved healed. Winter storms blew in from the ocean as they once had before Marzanna had molded the atmosphere to Her orders, but the citizens prepared for and weathered the damage without much loss. Spring bloomed in beauty that was better because it was natural and not compelled from the land and skies. Bettina had heard it was still forever spring in the divine Arboretum, but she didn't begrudge the Godlings a last haven away from mortality as long as they weren't abusing others. Summer waxed hot, with enough balmy days to grow abundant crops.

By autumn's first flush of amber and cool gusts, Bettina had done almost everything she could in the garden. As spring lingered in the Arboretum and winter had claimed the empty husk of the Holy tower and cathedral, her garden did not cycle through more than one season. She had to return to the Valusius estate if she wanted to experience autumn for herself…but the tropical garden had become her home, surprisingly. One she had chosen and commissioned a few Saints to help her build a modest house in the most secluded clearing she could find in this disinclined jungle.

In all this time, she had never tried to return to the Archives. Cristoval had gone, once, looking for something to comfort her during a week in winter when the grief had been too unkind to Bettina's loving heart...but it had been empty. The Scholar's statue had crumbled to dust, and there was no sign the Archives had ever existed.

The garden had been Magisend's gift, in a way. Or the All's—recompense for refusing to bring him back to stay with Bettina.

Cosima visited her the day she signed her name to the last official document opening the garden to Aebbenary. There was a lot of that now, Bettina mused with a dry smile. Cristoval and Sovanna were both more fond of paper documentation of everyone's efforts to provide Aebbenary with the best rulership in the world than anyone else. Even Cosima's hounds were less dedicated to the cause if they had to provide records for whatever changes they made or petty transgressors they handled.

They went for a walk together, arm in arm, their hair tamed with matching scarves to prevent the breeze from tangling it. Cosima had cut hers shorter, up to her shoulders; Bettina contemplated doing the same to her own as she listened to Cosima describe the latest mischief Lilias had done according to Sovanna.

She had laughed, her thoughts far away from sadness and grief, when Cosima's face turned white from shock.

"Mama!" Cosima's her shout halted Bettina's merriment.

Alarm made Bettina whirl to look where Cosima pointed; her dangling earrings swayed as she turned, looking for old ghosts.

Marzanna has come back. She's here to kill us all—

With her wings splayed and her entire being ready to fight to death and beyond—again—Bettina realized her huntress daughter hadn't shouted out of fear. She did not change her shape or pull her divine blade out of her Light.

Is that...It cannot be...

Far away by a mile or more, slinking underneath and in between the trees, green luminescence like undersea caves flickered. It waited, took a shape like a man…then walked away.

"Go, mother." Cosima told her. "Go to him."

"But—"

"*Go*, Mama," Cosima ordered.

Bettina obeyed. She fled the tasks she had been focused on and followed the green flame shining in the darkness on feet that grew wings.

Wait! Wait for me!

The ghost led her on. Bettina stumbled through the garden in such haste one of her wings almost knocked her back because she didn't side-step a tree deftly enough.

Magisend, is it you? She flung the thought ahead, pursuing the shadow that instilled her with hope she prayed was not in vain. *Have you come to say goodbye? Is this all that's left of you?*

The luminescence glimmered, reflecting against the foliage in a way it shouldn't have been able to without rain or dew.

"I'm here," it said in her mind in Magisend's voice, *"do not weep for me."*

Bettina did: she couldn't help it. She stumbled to a stop and fell to one knee in the soft dirt that would stain her gown. Her flattering but practical gown she had been so proud of since she did not have to dress herself to entice Goddess for favor anymore.

"You're here, yet you cannot show yourself to me. Tell me how that's fair! You helped us accomplish its bidding, and it just swallows you up after—"

"I'm here, Bettina. Don't cry."

From where she knelt, Bettina looked up. Between her fingers before she lowered her hands, struck by wonder at who—or what— she glimpsed.

The column of Light, similar to a divinity's aureole, wavered and solidified from the mere suggestion of a human shape into a man. Magisend inspected himself with the threads that wandered over his form. They were different, Bettina noticed: thinner, greener, like living vines rather than filaments of a construct. As she watched, as he looked at her again, flowers the size of thimbles sprouted here and there on his body.

Him—and not him.

"How are you here?" she asked. She had suffered too much to not be wary, but nothing of this encounter made her feel afraid. The only fear that clutched her by the soul was that she was imagining this. That she had fallen asleep in her lonely bed, or on a pillow of flowers and moss in the garden, and dreamed of a destiny for them that hadn't ended in separation.

"I don't know."

"Is…is it you?"

"I don't know. I awoke in the dark. I saw your Light, so I followed it."

She listened for more, but that was all he offered. Bettina righted herself from leaning on the tree to bolster her amazement and crippling hope and walked toward him with hesitance slowing her pace.

"Do you remember anything? You know me, but are you…" She couldn't ask. He leveled her with that all-knowing gaze…though, now she studied him, she caught the difference.

His eyes had shape. Iris, pupil, sclera. The hues twisted together, her gold and the garden's green and the extinct Archive's glossy blue-black shine, but she could tell when he was looking at her for certain. Beneath all of it…

"You gave of yourself to bring me back. Your very bones. You tempted every piece of me you could save out of the All and claimed me with your own blood. I remember…it took the Archives a long time to decide whether or not to let me go. To build me back up with everything you swore belonged to you."

She heard it. A heart in his chest, threaded or vine-wreathed or something else, beat and pumped life through his veins and marked him as a man of flesh and bone rather than a temporary shell for the All.

Life. He lived. He had come back to her.

Bettina threw herself toward him and knocked them down in the meadow grass.

"You're going to stay?"

"I'm yours. For—"

"No!" Protesting, Bettina slapped her hand over his mouth to cut him off. "I want you to belong to you. I just have the important parts—like your love."

"I do love you," Magisend agreed once she lowered her hand. "I loved you enough to return."

"Then stay. Come with me to meet my children, their friends…as yourself."

Words came less easily to him than they had before. She would have to teach him to be human, Bettina realized, but that didn't prevent him from nodding an agreement. From smiling at her, with teeth that were still gold in a black mouth. There was nothing to mourn anymore even if most of what had othered him as a construct had vanished into the past. Into oblivion.

As always, his threads—vines as alive as he was now—twined around her in longing for more communion between them. A shoot snared her ankle while others grew into her hair and sprouted more strange flowers that smelled of Magisend himself and her hopes fulfilled.

"I don't care how you came back. I don't care whether it was the All's pity that sent you home to me or only chaotic nature. I will love you in whatever form you take for whatever life we can make together," Bettina said.

She had told reborn Cristoval, who had fully died and fully lived in a shape that had never been touched by Marzanna's greed, much the same. After this, she realized as she and Magisend kissed in the meadow grass before they stowed the rest of their reunion's passion for later, she wouldn't have to remind any of them again.

All in the Garden

A construct had no soul. An avatar of the Archives could not dream, wish, or feel anything outside of its allotted purpose. When the Speaker came to him in a fractal shard of the All's essence, it filled the empty shell Goddess had Created.

That Bettina had enhanced. *Claimed.*

This she had done, but Magisend left her alone in the garden of prophecy because The Speaker walked their shared vessel away from her on a new path. The sound of her weeping behind him shouldn't have lingered in his ears, but it did. She was a tool just like he was…but a human one.

The All did not think of them with such distinction. That was him. Magisend.

"Archivist." The shadows of the garden melted into roiling yet eternally tranquil midnight as The Speaker stretched Magisend's arms out to fall into it. As he did, they melted apart to join the ether from whence they had been pulled out thread by thread.

He answered, hurt all over but numb to that pain. "I am here."

A prismatic effect flickered in the dark. There was nothing physical here; nothing to stand on, cling to, breathe with, or look at. After suffering the indignity of Goddess's abomination he should have experienced relief to be one with the All again.

Knowledge sustained his energy, anchoring him in the tide of the All, but he was still separate. So was The Speaker, enveloped in a mirrored, lesser pillar of green hues like a memory of a tree. Of every tree at once, and none of them.

"Swan-of-gold will comply," he said because Magisend had forgotten to confirm that news. The All already knew, but formalities needed to be observed. "It will be possible to restore this world to order in good time."

"*It is well.*" Agreement ricocheted against the distant borders of the chaotic flow of molecules in the dark. "*But not with the Archivist.*"

What is this? Magisend tested the crawling, skittering sensation with his mind, then his threads as they emerged reborn from the mire of knowledge. *Discomfort? Dread?*

That was what filled Bettina much of the time. Other things distracted her, but those two sensations had pooled in her ichor like stagnant microbes. Like venom that had become toxic to Magisend from the moment she had offered him "life" in exchange for the knowledge she had sought.

As the primary—and sole—Grand Archivist made by Goddess, Magisend relied on his own honesty as much as anyone else. He reminded himself this had all begun before destiny had inscribed Bettina's homecoming in Aebbenary. The moment Marzanna had chiseled him from the All, wrapped his chords around Her hands, and woven a shape of service for him from the matter She stole, it had all come to this.

"I am well."

"As much as he could be," The Speaker filled in the empty spaces Magisend had prudently arranged around the truth to obscure it. "As long as this separation must last, he will not be whole."

"*Is that so?*" The All prodded Magisend with the question and sent enquiring fingers of the surrounding energy to guarantee a satisfactory answer.

It was true enough. Magisend nodded, purposefully mute, and waited with his head strained of redundant confirmations of what The Speaker might already have guessed about him for the All to proceed.

"*How restrictive this world is.*" A complaint? From the embodiment of the universe? Bemusement troubled Magisend. "*Sacrifices and bindings. How archaic.*"

"Other worlds are older," he reminded the All, more by habit than anything else. "They don't rely on the same systems because they learned to exist without them. This one is in its youth—"

"Youth." An invective from The Speaker. "How they cling to it."

The Speaker was a warrior arm for the being they served: nothing more, nothing less. Magisend had been grateful to that splinter of the All for the kindness they had offered to Bettina, but he had not deluded himself further.

Though undoubtedly his sojourn would be brief, he had been allowed a return to his source—the only home he'd ever know—now he'd done his part convincing Bettina to make the sacrifice that would push this world back onto its destined journey. Magisend recalled the first perception he had ever experienced—pain at Goddess's will—and tried to be grateful.

Grateful? Something felt wrong about that. Wrong, terrible, indefensible. But what?

"You have taken a name."

Confusion reigned because the All wanted him to experience it. Magisend balanced this conversation in his mind like a delicate tome in his steady hands. Hands…as he thought of them, the merest suggestion of his abominable shape emerged from the ether. Bones, fingers, and skin vied for existence against the clysmic force of the All's plane.

"Swan-of-gold needed something to call me. In human terms, names signify—"

The Speaker interrupted. *"You* took a name. One we did not grant."

Something savoring of conceit inspired further separation in Magisend. Though it couldn't exist in quite the same fashion in this dimension, washed over and over with the flood of primordial energy, the rest of his body surfaced from the sludge.

I took something else, too. Her.

He'd had her. He had never possessed anything—had never wanted to—but Bettina had altered something fundamental about his entire self that no fragment of the All could deny.

She held these hands. Kissed this brutal shell, brought me inside, whispered in these strange ears…Magisend, Magisend.

Desire tightened his already tense muscles. Coiled in his borrowed blood like a fatal coagulant. The filaments that bound the comfortable cage of his body around his vitality lifted and burrowed again into his skin in undulation from his head to his feet. Flexing like his hands had against the plush curve of Bettina's hips.

"Earthly lust. How is this within you?" The Speaker could not be angered. It was curious…but not welcoming toward the new sensation. "Did she sow it?"

"No." Magisend knew that much. "Her intentions were pure. She only wanted an ally."

"*She Made far more than that.*" The All couldn't be amused, either, but he wondered if it might have been.

"She wanted me." He tilted his head back to look up, as high as his eyes could see with the facets shuttered, into the seething cobalt. The memory of the devastating force of his attraction to her when she had set her whole mind on seducing him made Magisend ache all over. She knew what she could do. The affect she had on anyone and everyone. And she had chosen him.

Surprise at his skill had led to her panting, gorgeous pleasure. They had shared a purpose—reaching the garden and unlocking its gates—but he knew as well as she did that they had forgotten it while in the throes of their passion.

I should not feel this. Magisend knew his responsibility. He had known his role from just before Goddess had peeled the sliver he became out of the All with Her divine urge tainted by calculating greed. *None of it. Not gratitude, not anger,* not.

"Walk with us." The Speaker intruded on Magisend's troubled musings. "Perhaps your deviance can be corrected if we humor your pretense of humanity for a time."

Mist became sky. Knowledge coiled into the shapes of clouds, trees, and all the other trappings of the primordial garden where they had led Bettina to the realization of Cristoval's doom. The Speaker stood in front of Magisend on the road, glorious in his mirror image and the armor he had donned for its symbolic purpose, and waited.

"We make the visions. We *are* visions. What could you possibly show me that I do not already know?" Magisend asked, hesitant to look down the stone path where truth waited for him. Dread and gratitude—both detestable—gave way to something more bitter.

Anger.

"Follow," the All commanded. Magisend obeyed.

The All knew of every creature great and small, and thus cared for the whole rather than the pieces that fit together with the rest. It and The Speaker had forgotten about the animals they had utilized to convince Bettina to obey destiny with their cruel fables. With only an Archivist—Grand or not—as audience the garden would not put on the same show twice.

The Speaker vanished as Magisend walked, becoming an entity of shadows serving as voice for the All in the murky dark around the garden path. The trees were frozen in motion and time as he walked, stricken by a heart that couldn't in any conceivable way belong to him, and waited for the vision to begin.

No fanfare announced its start; no dramatic redirection of light or pearls beaten into their road guided him on. Magisend was alone in the All in the façade of a garden…then she came.

Bettina mourned. Clad in ebony and sable, dragging the one wing she had kept behind her, she paced ahead of him on the path. If she heard his approach she gave no sign. Magisend realized he hadn't made a sound or even breathed since the garden had revealed her to him; he ran to join her, to move in front of her and reach with both hands to steady her trembling shoulders with both of his threaded hands.

All Bettina's attention rested on the wrapped corpse in her arms. Where her tears fell, they dyed the burial linen gold.

"My son. Have you seen him?" she asked.

"I'm here, Bett. I…" Magisend had nothing whatsoever to offer her. Even his presence had no value. Not in the face of this parental grief.

Bettina's face bore no expression; tears leaked from her eyes, but aside from the gold hue they resembled rain trickling over a statue rather than a manifestation of sorrow.

"I'm trying to reach him, you see. I want to go where he is. I want to lay in his grave and remain with him always. Have you seen him?"

Have you?"

"He's in your arms. Can't you feel the weight?" *What vile comfort is this?* Magisend marveled at his own talent for causing Bettina pain, even unintentionally. His tapered nails with their cobalt tendrils under their edges dug into her shoulders as his concern increased, but he forced them to loosen finger by finger before he bruised or needled her.

Bettina shook her head, over and over, still without expression. "No, he's gone. He's gone away from all of us. He is gone, and I have been left here. Have you seen my son?"

Her blue eyes flicked up for one solitary glance that convinced him this Bettina wasn't alive. This was her ghost: unquiet, overwhelmed by loss, and bereft of the warm heart he knew her to have.

The trees dripped rain from the sky that wasn't a sky above the garden. Cold water reminded Magisend this was a vision. This version of Bettina had yet to exist, if it ever would.

It will, he reminded himself, *because the boy needs to die. Nothing has changed…except for me.*

When Magisend let her go, the singular funeral procession carried on. Bettina left him alone on the path and carried the body she couldn't accept was Cristoval's down the road until she vanished into the nighttime mist.

"That soul has experienced an immense ordeal already, with more to come." The Speaker told him; Magisend wanted to snap his teeth in that direction to silence the serene, impassive reminder of what he already knew. "The boy should be her only concern. Yet you have shunted this matter aside in her heart to make room for yourself. How can you justify it?"

To save both of them an undignified squabble, Magisend locked himself in stasis on the path while his searching eyes followed the mist where Bettina had disappeared. As nothing more than a green nebula cloaking his shoulders, The Speaker waited patiently for an answer.

"It was necessary. We needed her trust."

"There is no one else she trusts. Not after Goddess." A test from The Speaker. Magisend mistrusted it, but truth was paramount here, and he could not suspect it for long.

"She…she needed me. To bring her to the garden—"

"Her devotion to you as an illusion of a man, Archivist, was not yours to claim."

"We may use it before the end of this event. But your indiscretion has been noted."

If only he could see her. Even entrapped in the continuous loop of her lament for Cristoval, Bettina was still Bettina. Magisend didn't look away from where she'd disappeared until the reverberating pressure of the All restructured his thoughts. It had surrounded them the entire time, peering through the layers of reality at its servants bickering near the basin of this doomed world.

"I am here to be useful. I know my role." Anger, dread, and anything else gave way to something somehow worse than anything: hopelessness. "I am to insure her compliance."

"You will see that she sacrifices the boy. Our mission is still of greater importance than anything else. Does that hold true for you?" The Speaker asked.

"No."

"No?" the All interceded. *"Your sentiments regarding this matter do not signify. Return to the woman, appease her affliction of grief, and ensure the sacrifice."*

Magisend rebelled. He did not even mean to: the emotion that flashed like a storm's rage charred his better judgment and pride at the realization that the All *had* had a hand in constructing whatever it was that bound him and Bettina together after her ichor had first wetted his tongue.

His will erupted with such power that it influenced The Speaker: when Magisend spoke, so did he, in synchronization rather than echo.

"I will obey what I must because the destiny of worlds is paramount over all. *I* will, because I *exist,* and because the choice belongs to me. You cannot order me to erase what I have become because you allowed Goddess to flay a new being from out of your fullness."

Prying energy targeted the root of Magisend's escalating independence. Even The Speaker cried out as the wretched sting of

Unmaking delved in the middle of their energies to extract them back into itself.

For the first time, Magisend resisted. Whole beings, let alone facets of one great entity, could not have fought back against the All, but he could not bring himself to accept the eradication of his identity. Not yet, not before the end.

Before Bettina passed through her deepest grief to find a new life full of freedom and possibilities in the aftermath.

"How is this here? How can this enigma reside in this shell?" the All marveled. Within the shade Magisend had dissolved back into when all his concentration had been occupied with resistance, he could scarcely believe his senses. The All *knew all.* What had sifted through the web of ostensible omniscience that filled that multifarious voice with fear and wonder?

"Do you not crave rest? Does any part here long for a return to your base state? Rest, Archivist, from your labors and your divine poison. It is inevitable."

The lure was perfectly matched to whatever heart or soul Magisend had grown. Mindless presence in the All had been everything he had longed for when Goddess had torn him from the whole. The meager pretense at a human-thing Her mortalborn brain could comprehend had been exhausting with every blink and shift since the beginning. Despite his insurrection, despite the determined claws Magisend sank into his memories of Bettina and his craving for her, the temptation to let everything go was as sweet as it was cowardly.

And futile.

"My Unmaking is inevitable…but not so near. Rest is not for me while I share this profound connection with her. I am not worthy."

"You were. When you were part of us." Another accusation.

"But I'm not anymore. I don't know if I will ever—"

For a while, spanning the birth and demise of many far worlds, the All considered him. It had no eyes to judge the expression Magisend arranged on the body he clutched around his vigor with desperation in his grip, but it looked.

"Go to her, then. We will wait."

"I am an architect of her misery. I will not worsen her final moments with her son for our cause. Not even for that."

"You attempt to broaden the boundaries of our understanding. You should not." The All swirled over, through, and around him in too many hues for even a prism to capture.

Magisend clenched his hands into fists so his own needles would jab into his skin. Some of the threads, working against his will, poked and plucked to peel it back so the unmaking of this shape would mold him back into the tide of knowledge that ruled all things. Part and parcel with destiny, the All had no place arranging anything but the grand order of the cosmos…and ending any threat that assailed the whole.

"Wait for me, then. I will return when it is over and our mission has been fulfilled." Despair that frothed with impotent, fruitless anger chased his declaration. While the All *looked,* gleaming violet and green in the aggressive dawn of a nearer world losing its timeline to a cosmic collision, Magisend tried to embrace what he felt so he would recognize it as long as he could. Soon, when the All swallowed his mistake of an existence, there would be nothing else to know.

Hunger, thirst, love, loathing, desire…these did not belong to him. Magisend gathered these emotions in a bouquet in the ichorous heart that beat in his chest and tried to tell them they had a home now.

Now, for now, for only an instant on the line of existence promised to no one, he thought as he left the garden behind, *I claim you.*

He would need to surrender them—sacrifice them almost as painfully as Bettina would need to sacrifice Cristoval—before long. But not before he showed Bettina which ones lived in her honor.

Rest. That was what he needed. He had been beaten, broken, and all but Unmade by everything…

Everything…

I am Magisend. His own name blazed in the cracked shell of self that remained, anchored by something even the All did not understand in the flood of dark.

Someone had flayed the dying vestige of whoever Magisend had been from where his husk had clung to its own existence. *How can it be?*

"You do not live, so you do not need to rest. Wake."

Magisend opened his eyes. The Speaker crouched over him, still a mirror of the person he had fooled himself he was, and frowned at the dull, dead expression he must have seen on Magisend's face.

"The All is uneasy about you. Can you comprehend why this is a travesty?"

Magisend could not answer, because he had no voice. The All had neglected to restore his, or restore it properly: the growl and whimper of an earthly carnivore punched out of his throat in a harsh wheeze. He shut his mouth again. The sharp nubs of his own teeth sliced his tongue.

Because I am separate. I should not be.

"You aren't meant to exist. I'm not either, not anymore. We served our role for the distinction of the All enfolding us back into itself. What have you done?"

Nothing. I am nothing, I was nothing, I will be nothing again…

"That is no longer true. You lingered in the bosom of knowledge as nothing but a memory and survived. How?"

I do not know. Leave me. I should not be…be…

The Speaker sighed. Beyond him, behind and all around, the All heaved an answering breath.

Life breathed into this nothing. False as it was, Magisend basked in it in his monstrous, temporary shape and waited for truth to find him.

She did. She came cloaked in the figure of someone he had loved. The first; the only; the penultimate reason he had adhered every scrap of shadow and thread to life as she could understand it.

Bettina knelt beside him—the body he occupied, impaired by the All's lack of consideration for the individual parts that constructed Magisend—and rested her cool hands on his shoulders.

"Where is defiance? Where is the rebellion you risked to comfort the woman in her hour of need?" asked the All.

I am here, Magisend replied. He struggled against the lethargy binding him to respond to her. He lay like a body on an altar, unable to breathe or move to give sign of consciousness. *Bettina, Bett, I am still here—*

The Speaker knelt on Magisend's other side, appearing thoroughly put out. "You are not what she is. You will outlast her by eons, in certain circumstances, and live in the dark of our absence until, perhaps, we remember you."

He laid a hand on Magisend's chest. The scene changed, influenced by the All's design. Abruptly human again—approximately—Magisend sat on a throne that wasn't his and watched with too many crystal clear eyes as Bettina danced for his enjoyment. Happy again…after everything.

After the basin. After Cristoval. After losing him, who she had somehow come to love.

The Speaker stood above Magisend's borrowed throne. His hands felt slick and without texture as they reached down to prevent Magisend from turning away. Where she twirled, leapt, and swayed, Bettina began to decay before his eyes. Not as flesh: as earth, as stone, petrifying into a suggestion of her former likeness.

"What worth is there in this? You could be more. You could be with *us.*"

Magisend watched without flinching as her limbs slowed, then froze in one final position that left her kneeling under the illusory sky with her arms stretched heavenward. Breath lingered in her body as all the water and ichor seeped down into the churlish earth that had enjoyed her happy presence for so long.

Something granted him power and independence once more. A will greater than The Speaker's: enough to bat his icy hands away like they were dandelion fluff and move his strange body on his own.

Magisend approached the haggard, wretched figure and stooped to tilt up its pocked chin. "There is paradise in those blue eyes. Solace in that fragile shape. That is not what calls me…not that alone."

"What does?" asked the All through the false Bettina's empty mouth.

"Even we do not know that. But I am hers…" He had nothing to speak of without the All. But Magisend knew much, more than thousands of other beings, and he would not let ignorance deny him what he desired. "…and she is mine. Eternity with her would not be enough, but I will claim it if that is your offer."

"We did not offer anything." The Speaker watched.

"You will. I am too tainted to stay and you do not want to destroy me, I think."

That was what had changed. What felt like a change in the wind, the ridges of a new rune on the Archival platform, or a new addition to the shape Goddess and Bettina had granted Magisend eons ago.

"We do not. We, who cannot change, have…"

Images siphoned from the tide rolled over and through Magisend. Maker and Unmaker, the All had encountered worlds without number and suffered more existences than any other could claim. Once such realm resided in the frozen heart of the knowledge entity.

Two figures standing in a land of snow and ice embraced and stared up, up, and further still with star-dazzled eyes to seek the All. Dark-haired, fair and pale but distinctly their own people, gifted with magic in a world rife with a prosperity of power shared among many, they waited beneath a veil of blue, violet, green, even red polar lights for knowledge to return to them. Someday…perhaps a time that might never come.

Except Magisend knew they would live as he longed to live before the All returned to welcome their souls into the whole.

"Other worlds." He had known of them, but knowing was not *seeing.* "You do not need me if you have them."

"You were part of us. Now you are yourself." The Speaker had seen too. Magisend wondered, generous now victory and freedom was in his reach, if the All would let him go in the future as well. "What does that mean for the future if even *we* are not meant to last eternally?"

Doubt reverberated through the empty space in the universe the All had carved out to sojourn with the remnants of Magisend.

"Not as you are. Even you must sometimes…*change.*"

Change as I have, Magisend continued in his mind. Thousands, near a million languages, had been granted to him in his first subsistence, but none of them spoke to the intimate heart of what he had learned. The All showed him what Bettina had done for him. The images she had stabbed into the prism that had represented the All for her world with her broken, stained rib in her hand. That was what it hadn't been able to fully comprehend: knowing everything, it couldn't quite grasp the nature of her devotion for Magisend.

Do not fear what you will become. This was all Magisend could offer. This, and the opening of the heart Bettina had helped him build to reveal how much her love meant to him, newly born. *Fear only remaining as you are.*

When the inspiration and scenes before him began to dissolve, he knew it was the last time he would see them. Everything, every sense and emotion, sharpened to a corrosive edge as the All mercifully cast Magisend out from its nucleus into the world he had left behind. The flow and ebb of untold knowledge leached from his consciousness in a final receding tide, leaving him intelligent beyond compare, but not burdened by it any longer. Filament by thread by tendril, his threads twisted and snapped as they withdrew with the knowledge; they left deep grooves in his restored shape.

Magisend thought only of Bettina, and reached for the illusion of the garden when it materialized from the void of the diminishing All to bring him back to her. It reached back to welcome him like a friend who had eagerly anticipated his return…and filled the spaces the threads had left with new life.

He saw her, walking with Cosima. So he entered the garden to meet them.

The Womb of Death

Lilias found him.

He remembered who he had been…vaguely. The veil that had torn asunder by his passing—he knew not what else to call it—had been stitched together shred by shred. The fibers reflected the ones he felt all over his body…melting already. Within minutes of his eyes fluttering open they were mostly dissolved.

As if no divide had ever taken place.

The child was called Lilias. But how could he know that? He, who was born, or reborn, and knew next to nothing besides the chill savor of sea salt on his palate and the skim of daylight before his eyes.

"I never talked much before," the child assured him. "That's why you don't remember my voice."

Someone had sculpted a shape for him from objects of power and the instrument of blood granted by this strange, fascinating child. They perched on his chest where he lay, splayed like a corpse and still until he tensed with restored life, and knocked their clawed fist against his forehead.

A journey across the sea; a life anticipating adventure replaced by a quest to a homeland that could only offer one lethal birthright. The waves had pitched around the vessel that had carried him home. Even then he had guessed he would not sail those waters again…

Anguish—physical, mental, and emotional.

"Who am I?" he asked. His voice was a rumble, coarse on his own ears, but that was better than the unease that vision brought him.

"You are!" The child said to him. They laughed.

"I…am?"

"Yes. And I am Lilias."

He nodded. Weight on his head he somehow knew was not familiar to him—his old self—made the movement more a downward jerk of his chin than a simple acknowledgment.

"I knew that. Remembered, I think."

"What do you *not* remember?"

"Not..." Thinking was so difficult. He craved his own name like hunger drove a man to consume foul or poisonous things in the name of survival.

"Cristoval."

She spoke. *She*. The woman who had...made him thus. In more ways than one, he felt.

Remarkable. Everything about her had been beyond comparison. Beyond any reproach. Destiny had brought them together for the purpose of tearing them apart, but that wasn't why he had loved her. Needed her. Worshipped her—

Cristoval was not his name. He merely existed—*now,* not a second before she woke him. He had yet to answer to any syllables or sounds that resonated with his soul.

He had closed his eyes to avoid this vision scorching them from their tender sockets. He opened his lids now; they peeled away from his eyes with gritty discomfort before moisture returned to them at the sight of the woman who had entered the room to examine him.

"You live." Her tone was flat; she didn't sound surprised, but there was an undercurrent of delayed shock that his discerning ears caught. "Can you tell me what you feel? If anything...if you're uncomfortable in any way?"

That splinter of Other knitted betwixt and beneath his bones as he looked upon her and felt her splendor smite him from crown to heel. Illumined by the hazy, silver aureole that surrounded her body, the woman's face was peerless in beauty and stark with contrasting elements. Pale skin, plum lips, eyes like a frosty plain unbroken by any breath or step of man defined by the shadows beneath. Silver-streaked dark hair damp from a fresh washing that hadn't quite banished some beads of dried ichor trailing from the jagged stump of a broken horn that had once mirrored its intact twin on the right.

The dead had energy the living could feel, but messages were all but a myth. Part of the man who had been Cristoval had left something in the unification of parts that made up this body and adhered to this fresh soul. That was all, and he didn't have to hearken to the memories beating like closed fists against a locked window…

…but he did. He couldn't help it.

Sovanna.

Space and time could not separate them. Death could not erase what had linked them together, heart and soul. The exquisite, brilliant, serrated edges that made Sovanna who she was—who Cristoval had known her to be—concealed the soft, bruised heart beneath the armor.

"I feel no pain," he answered. Swallowing hurt, but he managed. This time he tasted iron or copper along with the salt, but that was fading. "I lived. Part of this self walked the earth for a measure of years. I am new…but not all of me. Which parts aren't my own?"

Which are yours? He wanted to ask. Something she had given from her own divine shell throbbed with distinction but not clarity.

Lilias answered from where they hovered—floated by their wings— to the left of where he lay. On the altar, he supposed, where he had been born again into this existence.

"You have my blood. I was happy to give it to you."

"T-Thank you."

"Don't do that yet. Anyway…the Priest gave you a robe of flesh. We just helped you learn to wear it."

My skin isn't mine? It crawled like it belonged to him at the notion. The veins filled over again with blood that had never been tainted by mortality might have writhed like worms, once, but they had settled before he'd awoken.

"And my horn," Sovanna confessed. "You needed more than flesh and blood to make you become what I need. What *we* need."

Her admission was faint, but all he required. He guessed now why his head felt weighed down on his neck…though that feeling was fleeting, already almost gone. In her eyes, when she leaned over him to peer closer at the horns she'd given him—by intention or ominous accident she hadn't said—he saw an image of himself.

Crimson skin. An enclosure of bones and muscle beneath to

support a frame of menacing stature and strength. Wings half-crushed beneath his back, because even *he* guessed from the echoes of half-recalled dreams that these were a significant marker of defiance against the divine order that had ended Cristoval.

No longer a mortal man. He had become something between divinity, mortal, and the undeniable abomination called Lilias. Could he recognize anything, the old soul named Cristoval, who dwelled in its last gasp between his forged heart and lungs?

"One from many. You made me. Or...re-made him. Why?"

"I wasn't sure you'd remember," Sovanna began what sounded like a complicated answer. "You were Cristoval, once. Your mother's name is Bettina; you have a sister named Cosima. This island is ruled by Goddess—"

"She hurt them."

Sovanna frowned; the furrow between her brows sculpted her face into something better or worse than the artificial calm she had displayed so far. "Yes. She did, and She hurt you—him—too. That's why..."

Her voice faltered. Her attention hadn't flinched from his stare, but He sat up to save her the rest of the story.

To capture my mother, Goddess moved heaven and earth in audacious greed to bring all of existence to heel, Cristoval's bleak message echoed in his mind. *She cannot succeed. I could not save them...not in life.*

Moving more than his eyes and the air in his lungs solidified the reality of what he had become. Sovanna and Lilias both backed away as he swung his legs over the side of the altar where she had reconstructed him and accidentally flared his wings to their long, full span as he stretched.

The only pain that struck him was their alarm. Lilias didn't flee the dim cave outright, but they watched him anxiously from afar for any sign of insanity that would lead him to hurt them. For Sovanna's part, she didn't retreat again as she stared up at the spikes on the tips of his wings with an air of, if not joy, at least grim satisfaction that her experiment had become a success.

She was magnificent. He was monstrous, a hulking fiend with his leash in an angel's hand, and he feared only failing or hurting her.

"You made me to vanquish Her. I only hope I can."

"I've given you the best shape to help you with this task."

He wanted to touch her. Not in lust, though that was present because what man, even a monstrous one, could resist the siren lure of her intelligence and beauty? Not in love alone, though he felt Cristoval's memories of that changing him in secret beyond what even Sovanna could have predicted. She had fashioned him into a new god, a living weapon, a conqueror that even this world sieged by divinities had never seen the likes of before.

As a new soul, he could have resisted. He could defeat all compulsion to return, futile though it was, to a life that could never be his. To the life of the man he had been rather than the being he could become if he was strong enough. To him, though, something between those two options sounded preferable to losing the past or the uncertain future no one but destiny could predict.

He let the name of Cristoval settle in a mantle over this unification of sacrifices that he'd been born to and reached with a crimson, clawed hand to brush her hair behind her shoulders.

"Sovanna. I'm thirsty."

She stayed with him while Lilias flew by their sextet of wings to fetch fresh water for Cristoval.

Acknowledgements

This book took me very much by surprise! Bettina as a character really struck me as someone important when I introduced her in *Render to Silver*—I had to meet her again. Then the rest of the story unfolded, and I had an incredible journey writing it.

Daniel—you helped me work out almost every part of the plot I got stuck on simply by listening to me talk through the story over and over again. I have so much appreciation for your patience.

Therese—you outdid yourself with this cover. I think it's my favorite of all time. Thank you for working with me again.

To the friends who were genuine with me and waited so eagerly to read this super strange book I've written—thank you. I say it to you in person enough, I think, but I want it acknowledged here as well. Thank you for your friendship.

Next, for my readers, I thank you. Every one of you who gives my work a chance makes my day when I see the ways you experience and love my stories now and again. I will keep writing for you as well as myself.

May you always have another good book on the shelf.

Catherine Labadie

Don't miss Catherine's riveting Fate's Fall Duet!

LONG GROWS THE DARK

&

SLOW WANES THE NIGHT

A sorceress guards the crown and longs for the unattainable.

A gifted university student uncovers secrets from her casting book.

Bitter memories taint the present, and both new friends and old enemies fear the approach of the terrible dark.

Tales from Lyrassan

A Turn of the Wheel & A Song for the Road

Two romantic high fantasy standalones set in the same world.

In A Turn of the Wheel, *Aubria navigates around the life planned for her as one of many caretakers of an enchanted orchard. When a Potioner with a bad reputation moves into the neighboring village, she can't bring herself to stay away.*

In A Song for the Road, *unlucky, sickly Larkspur discovers an abandoned faerykind child and makes the choice to keep her. Even if that brings the call of dangerous adventure a little too close to home…*